THE STONE DOORS

Stoneborn Saga Book I

By Brendan E.J. Baker

*

This novel is a work of fiction.

❧ Dedicated to my grandparents ❧

May thou ne'er be led, where danger lurks, may harm not hinder thy will! At the doors I stood, on an earth-bound stone, while I sang these songs to thee.

Grógaldr, Olive Bray trans., 1908

❧ THE STONE DOORS ❧

Chapter 1

Iceland, 1013 AD

Orri lived in the stables at the Brauðavatn farm with his mother and several other horses. Like most Icelandic horses, he was short and stout, with a barrel-wide chest and a thick mane. The Brauðavatn horses were all five-gaited, and were particularly prized for the smoothness of their tölt. Even in difficult terrain or inclement weather they were sure-footed and fearless. It was said that a rider on a Brauðavatn horse could sip from a drinking horn, while riding hard across a field of lava rock, without spilling a drop.

The Brauðavatn family was Kveldulf Thorbjornsson, his boy Tryggvi, and a small, revolving cohort of farmhands and seasonal workers. Together they maintained a flock of sheep, fished the rivers bordering the land, and collected driftwood from the nearby shoreline for sale. Kveldulf was not wealthy, but the land and fine horses he inherited from his father allowed him to support his only son and the rest of the household in relative comfort.

Tryggvi Kveldulfsson had a particular affinity for horses, and had helped in the maintenance and running of the stables even from the time he was a small boy. Growing swiftly towards manhood, he was still a bit short, but strong and well-proportioned, much like the horses he looked after.

Orri was Tryggvi's own mount, and the boy would spend whole days riding him to and from the pasture, from the shore to the riverbed, then would brush and groom him in the stables until the call came for dinner and bed. Orri had been born the year Tryggvi's mother died, giving birth to a child who had not lived either.

1

Kveldulf had descended into months of overwhelming grief, and it had fallen on Tryggvi and the others to keep up the farmstead, full of living processes that did not stop for death or despair. When Orri was born, a healthy gray foal with a pitch-black mane and points, Tryggvi assisted with the birth and care of the young colt. He took to the task with all the attention he might have given to his baby sister, and boy and horse were like siblings from that time on.

The winter Tryggvi's mother died had been bitterly cold and unusually long. Kveldulf took to sitting alone in the marital chamber for days at a time, neglecting his duties. The household only survived because of the respect every member had for the grieving man.

As spring came again, and the sun started peeking above the horizon for more than an hour or two a day, Kveldulf finally began to pull himself together enough to resume management of his household and land. In short time he again became the hardworking freeholder whose horses were sought throughout the district, although the other farmers learned not to speak to him on the subject of taking another wife.

Tryggvi and Kveldulf also began to grow closer, the father recognizing the hardships his son had been through, and the strength he had shown. It was customary for children to be fostered out to other families for a time, in order to create enduring connections between the far-flung communities of the island. Without speaking on the matter, both Kveldulf and Tryggvi resolved that they would not be separated. Tryggvi began accompanying his father on business in the nearby districts and at the Althing, developing his own reputation as a fine judge of horses, while Orri attracted attention as a consummate example of the Brauðavatn stock.

During the Althing in Tryggvi's twelfth year, a lantern tipped over by a tent full of textiles, setting it ablaze. Tryggvi saw it happen, and managed to mount Orri in time to ride to the river, fill a pail with water, and return to the burning tent. Orri careened through the stalls with precision, carrying Tryggvi close enough to douse the fire from horseback.

The daring of this act, and the commotion it caused, helped mobilize other bucket-carriers. The blaze was quickly extinguished without causing serious injury to any of the sellers trapped within the tent, or even the bulk of their wares. There were many who said a man twice Tryggvi's age would not have acted so smartly, nor would it have mattered unless he had a horse as swift and fearless as Orri. The merchants gave Tryggvi many fine gifts, including a blanket for Orri and a cloak of midnight blue. Kveldulf bought his son his first spear, saying that a man should have a weapon.

Tryggvi returned home after that Althing in high spirits. He practiced with his spear every day, and often slept under his fine cloak of deepest blue. He had always assumed he would follow in his father's footsteps, someday running the farmstead and perhaps even becoming a goði in time. But now his young heart had had its first taste of adventure, however small. At night he would lie under his cloak and dream of brave feats he and Orri would accomplish, of the acclaim they would earn, the foes they would outwit, the marvelous sights they would see.

Orri, for his part, soon forgot the excitement of that day, and was simply content that Tryggvi began to brush out his mane more often and give him even more treats. Kveldulf would also come by the horse's stall from time to time, checking his hooves and giving him warm oatcakes.

In the year after the fire at the Althing, Tryggvi continued to grow into a confident youth on the threshold of manhood. He was fleetfooted, strong, and an accurate throw with his prized spear, even when astride Orri. The horse had become a powerful stallion, with an unusually eye-catching coat and tireless speed. Tryggvi braided bits of bone into the horse's mane, and these rattled together when he paced, giving him a fierce appearance. But Orri was truly gentle, hardworking, and devoted.

Orri was not the only fine horse on the Brauðavatn farm. He had inherited many of the qualities of his mother, Vaka, a pure white mare. Vaka was actually not an Icelandic horse, though she resembled them enough to deceive the untrained eye. Kveldulf had won her overseas in his youth, and given her to Tryggvi's mother as a wedding gift. After she died, Kveldulf dedicated the mare to Frigg, goddess of motherhood, and he made a grave oath that no one else would ride the horse again. He made sure she was always well-fed and groomed, and she was housed in the warmest section of the stable. Any foal from that mare would have fetched a fine price, but Kveldulf cared only that she lived in comfort, so Orri was her only progeny.

In the spring, the horses were put out to pasture, free to roam the hills around Brauðavatn. The first day out of the stables after the winter, they would frolic like a pack of pups, rolling in the grass, taking in the sun, celebrating the coming of spring in all the ways that horses do. They were so well-bred that often they would be left unattended. There was no danger to them here, and they always returned to the farm when it was time to be stabled for the night.

So it was that on the first spring day of Tryggvi's thirteenth year, the horses were alone in the pasture when two men approached them. Orri and Tryggvi were off practicing spear throws, and Kveldulf was mending fences at the farm, while the servants who had wintered with them opened up and swept out the turf house which made their home. No one was around to see the men approach.

Though the strangers made no overtly threatening movements or sounds, the horses scattered as they came near – all save one. Vaka, mother of Orri, stayed where she was. She calmly munched on a patch of early clover, even as the men began speaking to each other, becoming increasingly animated. They touched her, and she did not shy. Then one of the men grabbed Vaka's mane, and swung himself up onto her back.

Vaka seemed at first unresponsive even to this. The man on her back got settled, and began to address his companion. But just as he spoke, the horse broke into a sudden gallop, heading straight back to the Brauðavatn farm. Her rider, so assured a moment before, began to panic, pulling on her mane and digging his heels into her sides. But the horse did not stop, running faster and faster as the rider struggled to stay on her back.

4

Finally, when they were in sight of the Brauðavatn farmstead, Vaka gave a great leap. As she did, her rider jerked her head to one side by the mane. Her foreleg came down on a rock and went out from under her, and she tumbled, pinning her rider to the ground. Vaka was not badly injured, but as she struggled to stand, she fell again against her rider, whose own leg had been broken in the fall. Pained and frantic, the man managed to pull a small knife from within his clothes, and began stabbing the struggling horse around the head and neck. Vaka gave a great cry, just as Kveldulf stepped out of the stables to see what the commotion was. He looked out to see Vaka give one last gasp and collapse to the ground, her life's blood spurting over the prone rider, who was still under her, his knife lodged in her back.

Seeing his late wife's horse stabbed to death by this unfamiliar man, this stranger who had nullified Kveldulf's solemn vow that no one would ride the mare, caused Kveldulf to take leave of his senses. He sprinted from the farmhouse door to just outside the gate, and, hardly aware of what he was doing, brought his hand up in the air as he ran. Reaching the dying horse and the injured rider, he brought his arm down in a broad arc, and dealt the stranger a killing blow from the hammer clenched in his powerful fist.

The stranger's travel-mate crested the hill opposite the farm just in time to see Kveldulf put an end to his companion. The second stranger approached no further, but after a moment's shocked silence turned and fled. Kveldulf did not follow, barely took notice of the other man. He was too focused on the grisly scene at his feet, and the possible repercussions of what had just transpired. From the dead man's neck was hung a simple wooden cross.

⁂

Tryggvi and Orri returned that evening from tending to the sheep, and Kveldulf told them what had happened. Tryggvi said he had seen a man riding away from the farm in a hurry, but had not thought much of it. As no one on the farm recognized the dead stranger, there was little to do but bury him, and then to prepare for consequences. The stranger was laid down at the base of a hill facing away from the farm. Vaka was interred with great honor in the field, near the spot where Kveldulf had buried his wife and daughter.

Kveldulf sent riders out to the other homes in the district, letting them know that he would need their support. And he contacted as well his goði, Gunnar Ingolfsson, who was knowledgeable in the law.

Gunnar responded that he would represent Kveldulf's interests in court, should it come to that. But no further word of who the strangers were or what their intentions had been came to the farm.

Chapter 2

Kveldulf and Gunnar soon met to discuss Kveldulf's options, in case a suit was brought against him. They were somewhat hampered in this by the fact that no one had any idea who the interloper had been.

Kveldulf and Gunnar agreed, however, that Kveldulf was at a disadvantage in any legal suit that might arise. The man he had killed had been incapacitated under the fallen horse, and offered no immediate threat. The horse had fallen just within the bounds of the Brauðavatn property, and had been ridden in from far outside the property, so Kveldulf would have a hard time making a case that the stranger had been trying to steal the horse. Vaka had had no saddle, brand, or other mark of ownership. And because Kveldulf did not know who the dead man was, he could not approach the stranger's people in order to offer a blood-price before they sought suit against him, nor could he or his goði even guess what payment might be appropriate. All they could be sure of was that the man's companion had witnessed his death, and that the matter was likely far from over.

For his part, Tryggvi understood his father's actions. Vaka had been dear to him as well, and he was crushed to learn of her violent demise. He too felt the violation the stranger had unthinkingly perpetrated. Tryggvi had been a young boy, desperately missing his just-departed mother, when Kveldulf had taken Vaka out of her stall one evening, and led her into the field. There, under the stars, he cut his palm, smeared blood on the horse's head, and invoked solemn oaths to Frigg. He swore that no man would ride the mare again, so long as the goddess watched over the spirits of Kveldulf's dead wife and child. Vaka had not stirred throughout the entire ritual, not even shying at the smell of blood, but when Kveldulf finished the oath, suddenly she gave a whinny, reeled back on her hind legs, and pulled away from him.

She galloped once around the fence surrounding the farmstead, before returning to Kveldulf and nuzzling his hand.

Tryggvi did not have the same knowledge of the gods that his father did, but both of them felt that the horse's behavior was a sign from Frigg signaling her acceptance of the oath. Though it was still a long time coming, that night for Tryggvi marked the start of Kveldulf's return to something approaching his old self, and Vaka had been treated with reverence by the entire household since then. For her to have been killed, and Kveldulf's oath broken as well, was a great blow to all on the homestead, and none could escape some sense that it portended disaster.

However, no one could have predicted what darkness was to befall not just the Brauðavatn household, but the whole of the island. One late spring morning, a few weeks after Kveldulf killed the stranger, the entire household was awakened by sounds coming from the stables. The horses were giving a great cry, all as one. From up on the hillside overlooking the farm, the sheep started bleating, and the farm's two small, stout shepherd dogs started barking and whining miserably. At first no one could discern the cause of their distress. Then, just as suddenly as they had started, the animals all fell silent.

Kveldulf opened his mouth to speak, but as he did so, a great cracking noise reverberated across the valley, and the ground began to shake. Now it was the servants and bondsmen who started to yell. They came streaming from the house, with great clods of dirt from the turf roof in their hair, falling in their eyes. Tryggvi's legs went out from under him, and Kveldulf had to use the handle of his ax in order to steady his feet.

After an endless minute or two, the ground stopped moving, and a deathly silence settled in. But there were no more tremors, and on some silent signal, everyone began to stir again as one. As the stunned workers called to each other and picked themselves off the ground, it became apparent that no one had been seriously injured, although the roof of the house would need repairing.

It was Tryggvi who first noticed the column of smoke in the distance, rising steadily towards the sky. He did not know its meaning- at first he thought another farmstead must have caught fire, but it was too far distant for him to know what farms lay in that direction. Even Kveldulf, following his son's gaze, was at first perplexed. But Guðni, the old servant woman, who had lived at least eighty winters on the island's rocky face, knew at once what had happened. She knew that somewhere, far to the south, the ground had split asunder, and black ash was belching towards the sky like souls expelled from Hel itself.

Two weeks later came the time of the Althing. Normally this was a time of great excitement on the Brauðavatn farmstead, particularly for Tryggvi, for whom each new Althing was still an entirely fresh experience. He was usually crawling the walls with anticipation by the time the Althing finally came around, and his enthusiasm was liable to infect the whole household.

This year, however, a pallor hung over the Brauðavatn farm. Off to the south, a thin trickle of black smoke still wafted skywards. Sometimes when the wind blew over the farm, the air smelled of sulfur and ash. There had been no more earthquakes, but old Guðni had warned everyone that the danger had not passed, and a grim sense of anticipation hung over the farm that matched the murky air.

The issue of Kveldulf's killing of the stranger was no closer to being resolved, and everyone knew that if anything further were to come of it, it would likely happen at the Althing, where the yearly court convened to try legal cases from all over the island. This would be the best time for Kveldulf's accusers, if indeed he had any, to convene a suit against him. Kveldulf knew he had the support of his goði, Gunnar, but he could hardly help being anxious and irritable. As such, no one was in a particularly festive mood when the time came to leave for the Althing plain.

The ride to the Althing would take three days. Normally most of the household would go, along with several of the horses, but this year Kveldulf decided that only he, Tryggvi, and their own steeds would be going. They would travel lightly, stopping at Gunnar's house the first night, then riding on their own and sleeping rough for the next two days before arriving at Thingvellir.

It would cost Kveldulf to sell no horses and make fewer trades during the Althing than usual, but he thought it best to draw as little attention to himself as possible this year. Were he not obligated, as a free bóndi, he might not have gone at all. But he also knew that trying to ignore the situation was unlikely to improve the ultimate outcome.

So, after giving instructions to the thralls and farmhands, and making light packs with everything they would need, Kveldulf and Tryggvi rode to the west, away from Brauðavatn, and into the rocky, moss-covered plains of the surrounding district. They passed over rivers and hills, the gray sun at their backs, and cool wind in their faces. The sound of the horses' hooves kept a steady rhythm, and father and son each drifted into their own thoughts as they rode.

After a few hours they came in sight of Gunnar's homestead, and Kveldulf announced them just outside the gate. Gunnar came out to greet them, his wife and daughter by his side. He welcomed them to his home, and instructed one of his many farmhands to tend to their horses. Gunnar was fostering the son of another goði, who eagerly led the prize horses away to be groomed and fed.

Tryggvi and Kveldulf were led into the house, and given seats of honor by the hearth. Gunnar and Kveldulf soon fell to talk of various goings-on in the district, and of the affairs to be settled at the Althing. Both of them skirted the issue of the possible suit against Kveldulf. As the evening wore on, Tryggvi became bored, and excused himself to check on Orri. If anyone minded, they said nothing.

Tryggvi found his horse in the stable. A girl was tending to Orri, slowly brushing out his mane and whispering in his ear. Tryggvi was at first perturbed to see someone else acting so familiar with his friend. But after watching for a moment, he saw how at ease Orri was, and the obvious care that the girl was taking, and he relaxed.

"Are you going to stare at me all night, or do you have some other purpose here?" the girl asked without turning her head. Feeling heat in his cheeks, Tryggvi stepped forward into the horse's stall. "This is a fine horse," the girl said, before he could speak.

"His name is Orri. He has been my mount since I was a boy."

"And are you a boy no longer?"

Tryggvi knew when he was being baited, and simply placed his hand on Orri's mane, stroking the horse's freshly brushed hair. Orri nuzzled against him, but did not move so far that he could not continue to enjoy the girl's ministrations.

"Thank you for caring for my horse. I hope he hasn't given you any trouble." Tryggvi was eager to change the subject.

"He's beautiful, and quite friendly. He walked straight to his stall without any trouble, and he and the other horses have been nattering back and forth to each other like old friends," the girl said.

"Perhaps they are. Your father has bought some horses from mine. Brauðavatn horses are known far and wide for their quality," Tryggvi said proudly.

"It that why you wove these bones into his hair? To mark him as a Brauðavatn horse?"

"Brauðavatn horses need no mark, to the trained eye. Those bones are to show that Orri is a war horse, dedicated to Odin." Tryggvi kicked himself as he said it. As his father had reminded him more than enough times, it was unwise to openly speak of following the old gods.

But the girl seemed to take the comment in stride. "You have taken him to war, then?" she asked lightly.

"Well, no. But Orri is brave. Someday I will take him a-viking, and he will help me win riches and glory." Tryggvi did not know why he said this. True, he had dedicated Orri to Odin, in a sudden pique of adolescent faithfulness. But Odin was the god of poetry, and wisdom, and revelation, not merely the god of battle. Despite his boastful words, Tryggvi had no real intention of leaving the island to go on raids. He thought of it sometimes- all boys did- but truly he had riches enough at home. He hoped for excitement and adventure, but he hoped to find it here. He had started to develop a positive reputation for himself already, and did not wish to leave his father all alone for too long. The bones in Orri's mane were, more than anything, a stylistic affectation. Yet Tryggvi found himself wanting to impress this girl, Gunnar's daughter, who already seemed to have won over his horse, and who spoke to him directly in a way that the few young girls he had met before never had. He considered her round face, full lips, and long, curled red hair, and decided her looks were to his liking as well.

"And where will you go a-viking?" she asked him. "To Daneland? To the land of the Angles? Or perhaps you will go to the Green Isles. I hear there are great treasures to be found there...and slaves for the taking."

"Yes, perhaps I shall go to Ireland."

"And take gold there, and slaves?"

"I suppose." Too late, Tryggvi had the sense of a trap closing.

"My mother's mother was a slave from Ireland. She was taken when she was younger than I am now. When she came here, a young warrior was already growing within her."

Tryggvi did not know what to say to this. The girl stared at him as he opened and closed his mouth.

Then Orri gave a low whinny, and the girl laughed.

"Your travels will be an adventure indeed, if you are as easily shocked as that, Tryggvi Kveldulfsson." Tryggvi was taken aback for a moment that the girl had his name ready, and he still wasn't entirely certain whether she was trying to offend him or not. But she had shocked him, and he regretted again the boastful tone he had taken with her. His father had taught him not to brag, and that a man should never boast unless he planned on carrying through with his wild claims. To do otherwise displeased the gods.

Recovering himself, Tryggvi looked at the girl with an appraising eye. "You seem to know much of me already, but I know little of the girl who has taken such good care of my horse."

She smiled at him, then, and the tension in the room passed without complaint.

"Well, my father did introduce us, but as you have forgotten: I am called Njála. Njála Gunnarsdóttir."

ᚠ ᛉᛈᚳ ᛋᛉᚠ ᛩᚠᚳ ᛉᛈᚳ ᛋᛉᚠ ᛩᚠᚳ ᛉᛈᚳ ᛋᛉᚠ ᛩᚠᚳ ᛉᛈᚳ ᛋᛉᚠ ᚳ

THE STONE DOORS

When Tryggvi got back to the main house, his father and Gunnar were still deep in conversation, though the rest of the household had left the hearth. Tryggvi retired to one of the pallets just off of the main hall, and sank into a heavy sleep, thinking of distant shores, and poetry, and torchlight on red hair.

Chapter 3

Kveldulf and Tryggvi broke their fast the next morning with fine cheese, ham, sheeps' milk, and bread. Though they had brought sufficient supplies of their own, Gunnar insisted they take rations from his larder. He sent them off with their horses rested and fed, and both Tryggvi and Kveldulf were in higher spirits than when they had left Brauðavatn. Gunnar was also going to the Althing, but would follow in a day's time, as he had to corral a larger retinue and make sure his farm was prepared for his absence.

Njála came out to see them off, but not until Tryggvi and Kveldulf were already mounted. She and Tryggvi did not speak, but as they turned the horses to set off, she raised a hand in farewell. Tryggvi could not say he knew the girl well, but he had the sense that she could manage anything that might come up in Gunnar's absence. Riding once again over the flat, stony ground, he wondered when he would see her again.

Kveldulf and Tryggvi took a leisurely pace towards the Althing plain over the next two days. Occasionally they would pass a farmstead on the way. But mostly he and Tryggvi rode in companionable silence over an empty landscape, each occupied with his own thoughts.

For his part, Tryggvi always loved riding over the barren flats of the land. He loved seeing trickles of water come down from the glaciers and through the mountains on one side of the road, watching the sun sparkle off the sea when they came in sight of the coast. Though it was often overcast and rainy in the early summer, excellent weather had accompanied them on this journey, and Tryggvi was mostly able to dispel any sense of foreboding.

Not that it was all a pleasant ride. Having made the trip many times before, Tryggvi's least favorite part was always when the road wound through a particular gloomy valley. An abandoned building stood off to one side, partially covered by a rotting roof and looking as if it was slowly being expelled by the hill into which it had been built. The land there had a reputation for being haunted, and Tryggvi

14

sometimes felt a chill as they rode past. But in the day's sunny weather, and a year older than when he had last ridden through the valley, Tryggvi felt foolish for letting old wives' tales get the better of him.

Still, it was hard to deny that the final leg of the journey had a touch of the otherworldly to it. After exiting the valley with the decrepit shack, the road began to curve and wind erratically through a particularly featureless landscape. The careful steps of travelers over the year had worn a smooth, clear causeway, but because the land around the road was so bare, its sudden twists and turns seemed largely inexplicable. But here and there Tryggvi could make out small cairns, strange rock monuments which the road curved carefully around and away from.

While Tryggvi had never discussed it with his father, he knew that they were riding past markers of the huldufólk, the hidden people, those of the strange race that were said to hide in the mountains and lonely places of the island. They were neither friend nor foe to the human inhabitants of the country, and the civilized people of the land tried to give them a wide berth. But it was said that they might from time to time use their uncanny skills to help or harm their human neighbors, as fit their whims. Some people left saucers of milk or other small offerings for the huldufólk on the threshold of their homes, hoping to curry favor- or, at the least, avoid their anger.

Old Guðni swore that in her youth, long before she had been reduced to travelling from farm to farm seeking work, she had given bread and cheese to a beautiful girl who had appeared before her one winter evening as she was playing near her house. She said the girl had worn only a sheer shift of shimmery material, and had been barefoot, but had neither shivered nor did her breath mist in the air. Guðni said the strange girl has asked her for a gift of food, and that without thinking she handed her the crust of bread and hunk of hard cheese that she had been pretending to feed to one of her cloth dolls.

The barefoot girl took the food, but did not eat it. Instead she gave her thanks for the gift, and asked the child her name. Here, Guðni always mentioned that she had been warned never to give her

name to one of the hidden fólk, for names have power. Not wanting
to offend the stranger, however, she instead gave her the name of her
doll, thinking herself very clever for doing so. The barefoot girl had
thanked Guðni again, then turned and walked away from the farm,
the bread and cheese still clutched in her hand.

Guðni never saw the girl again, but that spring, all of the
pregnant animals on the farm gave birth to twins. Guðni also said
her doll had disappeared at some point during the winter. She always
slept with it in her arms, but one morning when she woke up it was
simply gone. "That," Guðni always ended the story, "is the essence
of the huldufólk. They never give without taking, or take without
giving, but the terms of the exchange do not conform to the logic of
man, and one can never say what they are truly after. For this reason
alone, the fólk are best avoided altogether- but should you happen to
meet one, never cause offense!"

Tryggvi had never seen one of the hidden people himself, and
he was not sure he believed the old woman's story, although as a
child he certainly had. But riding with his father along a winding
path, with dozens of strange stone markers on either side, he was
certain that many people did respect the hidden folk. And Tryggvi
knew better than to dismiss common wisdom when it came to
matters of survival in the bleak, harsh, beautiful land he called
home.

Finally, the ground began to turn green again, and the riders left
the rocky, misty landscape behind. They came to a shallow river,
and Tryggvi knew they were now only a short ride from Thingvellir.
Kveldulf said that they should water the horses, and both of them
dismounted their charges. Kveldulf's horse, a huge stallion named
Gauti, wandered to the water and drank, and Orri soon followed
him. While the horses refreshed themselves, Kveldulf pulled a hard
biscuit from his pack, broke it in half, and offered one part to his
son.

"We'll be there by nightfall," Kveldulf said.

Tryggvi nodded.

"I suppose we should talk about where things stand now, and
where they might be going." Tryggvi nodded again, and said

nothing, though he felt his stomach hitch for a moment. He had been doing too good a job of pushing everything from his mind during the ride.

Kveldulf continued. "We both know that the man I killed must have had people. So far, we haven't heard anything from them. Gunnar has discretely asked around, and so far as he knows, none of the other goðar have been approached about a suit against me. So it's possible that nothing will come of the whole mess." Tryggvi looked at his father hopefully.

"But we cannot count on it. If anyone is going to bring a suit, they will do it at the Althing. Gunnar will support me, but I don't know who the stranger's people might be, who they might have talked to, or who might support them. My case...is not strong." He sighed. "As Gunnar says, I killed a man outside of my property, who offered me no threat. If his friend saw most of what happened and can speak against me, it will be hard for me to present a strong defense."

Tryggvi had considered all of this as well, as best he could given what he knew of the law. He had to say his piece. "But Father, can't you tell them about your vow? No one was ever supposed to ride Vaka. And you found him stabbing her. For all anyone knows, that man was trying to kill her, or at least steal her. Were you supposed to do nothing about any of that?"

"What you say is true, and it will probably win me some sympathy. It is no small thing for a man to protect his property, nor to honor his oaths. But the law is still the law. I was not within my rights to kill that man. Because his companion rode off, I was not able to discover who he was, so that I could pay the blood-price and make amends. And while I did keep my vow- a man must never break an oath! things are not as they once were." He paused, pressed his lips together thoughtfully, and continued.

"We are meant to be a Christian people now, and have been since you were a child. There are many still who remember the old gods, who keep the ways of our ancestors. That is acceptable, so long as it remains in the home. But I let my respect for the old gods, and my anger, lead me to kill a man who presented no threat to me.

However righteous my actions in the eyes of gods or men, they were not lawful. Saying that I had to honor a vow to Frigg will provide me little defense before the law.

"Things are not what they once were, Tryggvi, even when I was your age. Things that were once known to be true are respected no longer, and new notions, even new gods, are spreading across the world. No place I know of is free from this change. Certainly our land is not. And all of us must be prepared." They sat in silence for a bit, chewing, before Kveldulf spoke again.

"Each man must make a choice for himself as to which gods, and which men, he wishes to give his allegiance. This is why I have told you the tales of the old gods, which my father told me, and his father told him. But I also agreed to have you baptized when you were a boy, and the priests started coming to the island. The people of this land have decided to follow the White Christ, and that this shall be a Christian land. Whether this will last, or if the people shall turn back to the gods of our fathers' fathers' fathers, no man can now say. But all of us will face a choice.

"I wanted you to be able to make whichever choice you decided would allow you to live as you wanted, to build a name and a reputation for yourself, and, not least of all, to survive. Men speak of honor; men speak of fame. But first, you have to live."

Tryggvi was not used to hearing his father speak at such length on any topic, and he grasped for a response. "I thought you had me baptized because my mother insisted on it."

Kveldulf smiled. "Well, yes. That as well. Survival often means knowing when to let a woman have her way."

Tryggvi couldn't help but laugh. He suspected his father had indulged his wife in all things. Tryggvi remembered her mostly as a warm, quick-witted presence, always knowing just what to do when the sheep were taken by sickness or someone was injured. When Tryggvi was very little he would sit at the hearth and watch his mother weave or cook, nodding along with the formless melody she hummed as she worked – though she wouldn't often let him sit for long without putting him to some task.

Both of them missed her terribly, and this unspoken acknowledgment passed between them, sobering their moment of levity. "What I mean to say is this, boy." Kveldulf gestured to the east and south, where the column of ash could still be seen trickling into the sky from the rent earth below. "Change has come to this land, and none will be untouched by it. Each of us must be prepared to do what is necessary. I do not know what this Althing will bring, but I know that there are trials ahead for us both. I can feel it in my bones. I can smell it in the air.

"You must promise me, Tryggvi, that when the time comes, you will do as I say. You are of an age where boys are disinclined to do as their fathers bid, and wish to be treated as the men they nearly are. This is natural, and believe me, I remember the feeling well." Tryggvi was embarrassed. His father continued. "But you must wait a while, son. I don't know what might be coming, and I need to be certain that, come what may, you can be trusted to do as I ask."

Tryggvi considered this. "I will do as you say, father."

Kveldulf pulled slowly at his beard. "You must swear it." Tryggvi furrowed his brow, but Kveldulf pressed on. "Yes. Swear it, by the blood of Odin, and the blood of Christ. Swear it on your spear. Then I will know you to be truly bound."

Tryggvi said nothing for a moment. He had not yet sorted out his feelings towards the gods, old or new. But an oath of any sort, regardless of what it was sworn on, was not something to be taken lightly. Tryggvi knew this, and he knew his father did too – to the point that he would kill in order to avoid becoming an oath-breaker, the most shameful creature in all the realms. In point of fact, Tryggvi himself had never sworn an oath before. He had been sorely tempted at times. As a child, when he wanted something desperately, like a new toy, or a real sword, or for his mother to rise again from a blood-soaked bed— then had he been tempted to swear an oath to whatever gods would listen that if his wish was granted, he would do their bidding and glorify their names throughout the land.

Yet Tryggvi had never entered such a bargain. He knew it was common enough, at least in the stories that people told of great men who had done great deeds in the past. But something stopped him.

Perhaps it was that he noticed how infrequently the gods actually interceded on anyone's behalf in the stories. He couldn't blame them; they had their own concerns, their own trials and tribulations, even their own dooms. Odin on his tree, or Christ on his cross; if the gods themselves were willing to suffer and die without complaint, how invested could they really be in what any individual person wants?

Tryggvi was neither priest nor skald, and he could not say. Mostly, he figured that if there were any good to come of begging the gods' intercession, then Iceland would be warm and dry and covered in forests, and his mother and sister would be there to enjoy it. This not being the case, Tryggvi assumed that the gods were too busy with their own affairs to spend much time helping man, and that man could best honor the gods by helping himself.

Now, it seemed, his father had decided he was young enough to be told what to do, yet old enough to be asked to swear an oath to do it. As Tryggvi considered it, this seemed at first like a violation of the easy understanding he and his father had come to over the years. Kveldulf did not often strike an authoritarian stance – at least not towards his son – and Tryggvi rarely gave him any reason to do so. He worked hard, he did his part, and he did not look for trouble in order to break up the frequent monotony of his daily life. He got along well with all the members of the household, and he did not waste food nor treat his possessions carelessly. He had maintained these habits even when his father taken to his bed for weeks in a state of grief that Tryggvi might have considered unmanly, had he not spent so much time hiding his own tears as well.

Kveldulf was still liable to disappear for a few days now and then, and could swing from jovial to morose in a heartbeat. Tryggvi sometimes struggled to keep up with these transitions, and he had become exquisitely attuned to subtleties in his father's demeanor. Yet despite this, he trusted his father, and most of all he wanted to please him. Tryggvi's biggest fear was that he should add to the core of pain that his father bore within him, that something Tryggvi did would finally break him for good.

So, after taking a few long moments to consider his father's request – appropriate consideration for an oath so serious, thought Kveldulf – Tryggvi nodded his assent. He retrieved his spear from its place at Orri's side.

"Say it, then."

Tryggvi took a deep breath. "I swear, by Odin's beard and the blood of the White Christ: I shall do at all times as you tell me." He paused, and watched his breath dissipate from the point of the spear. "Until such time as you should see fit to release me from this vow."

Kveldulf grasped Tryggvi's shoulder, and called to the horses, who were now standing side by side by the river. "Then let us ride to the Althing."

Chapter 4

It was early evening when Tryggvi and Kveldulf arrived at Thingvellir, the wide river plain where the Althing was held. The year's meeting would not be officially opened for another day, but already there were scores of people milling about the open plain. Temporary dwellings of turf and mud brick had been constructed for the visitors to stay in during the two weeks of the parliamentary conclave, and more were being constructed as Kveldulf and Tryggvi approached.

Although Tryggvi had been to several Althings, and Kveldulf over two dozen himself, both men still found themselves taken aback each year at the sheer number of people present. Other than the district things, which might have a few dozen people in attendance, most Icelanders did not see anyone other than their own household members for weeks at a time. There were no towns or cities on the island, and even a sizeable crowd was a rare sight to behold.

Yet every summer they gathered here from all over the island, forming for two weeks a sort of temporary but substantial city. By the end of the Althing, several thousand individuals would be living, working, and socializing together on the wide green plain. The interactions between these people – the friendships made, the deals brokered, the marriages arranged, the fights started – would carry repercussions to the far corners of the island, forming a loose web of social cohesion that would sustain the Icelandic sense of community for another year.

In addition to this social and economic activity, there was also the parliamentary meeting which was the nominal purpose of the Althing. The thirty-nine goðar who lead the various districts of the island would meet to discuss matters of national importance, make any necessary changes to the law, and resolve legal disputes. By law, all free men were obligated to attend the Althing, so that knowledge of the law could be transmitted and preserved throughout the island. As Tryggvi and Kveldulf entered the plain, they rode past the Lögrétta, the law rock, where each year the Law-speaker would recite one third of the total corpus of the law from memory, with the crowd gathered round and ready to correct him should he happen to skip or misstate anything.

Tryggvi and his father made their way through the throngs and stall, working towards a spot near the northwest corner of the plain. There they found a set of temporary turf-houses; they would stay in these until Gunnar and his household arrived, then take shelter with them. By arriving early, and without his goðar, Kveldulf hoped to discover whether anyone had spoken of a planned suit against him, and perhaps to determine the identity of the stranger he had killed. While Kveldulf was not unknown – hardly anyone was, truly – he hoped that coming with only his son, and housing on the edge of the Althing, would allow him a degree of anonymity.

Kveldulf paid the owner of the temporary houses, and he and Tryggvi approached their lodgings after securing the horses. It was a simple hut made of hardened mud and grass-covered turf, but it would keep them and their possessions warm and dry. The thick walls of the hut, and the heavy curtain over the opening, would also provide some cover from the sunlight, which at this time of year shone for all but a few hours each day, and could make it hard to sleep.

Tryggvi was tired from the long journey, but eager to explore the Althing. After getting their things settled, and promising his father that he would be careful about who he talked to, Tryggvi made his way towards the thick of the gathering. Orri and Gauti were with some of the other horses, munching contentedly on a pile of hay set off for them. Tryggvi stopped there first, both to make sure the horses were settling in and to check out some of the other mounts. There were many fine horses there already, and Tryggvi enjoyed seeing the different coat colors and patterns, as well as examining the musculature and even personality of the horses with a practiced glance. As always, Tryggvi decided that Orri was the equal of any animal there. He gave his horse an affectionate rub on the snout, and fed him a grain cake he had brought from the turf house, before turning and going to explore the rest of the gathering.

Although the Althing had not officially started, the plain was already organized into loose sections. There was the mercantile area, where vendors sold everything from cattle feed to saddles to fine cloth and clothes. There were even some valuable treasures brought from the mainland on raids and trading expeditions- weapons, armor, dishware inlaid with gold filigree, fur-lined cloaks, and other extravagances. Near this area were the food vendors, already selling bread and cheese, and servings of skyr in clay cups. Once the Althing was truly underway, there would be fresh and cured meats for sale, sweetened baked goods, and the meads, ales, and wines that were rather crucial to the air of easy conviviality that prevailed.

Past this area were the huts and tents of the goðar and some of the more powerful families of Iceland. In recent years even Tryggvi noticed that some of the richer folk's turf huts had been moved slightly away from the rest of the tents, and closer together. They were also growing larger, with fine cloth curtains and multiple rooms. These were all subtle indicators of the status of the hut's inhabitants- mostly goðar, but one or two wealthy bændr as well.

Past these buildings was another new addition to the parliamentary grounds. A church, with walls made of precious wood, had been erected just off and away from the tents and booth. From its top, a simple but large crucifix rose above the stalls, casting a shadow towards the booths in the light of the setting sun. It was said that plans were already in place to make the structure larger and more magnificent, but as it was it stood taller than any building Tryggvi had ever seen.

Tryggvi had never been in a church before, even during his dimly-recalled baptism, which had taken place by a stream. Nor had he much desire to do so. He liked some of the Christian stories he had heard. A traveler stopping by the farm had once told him of David and Goliath, and for a while he had imagined himself as the brave young man, striking down a great giant and saving his people. He had heard other stories at past Althings, where there was often a priest or a skald all too happy to entertain people with tales from the Christian book. But Tryggvi was still much more familiar with the old tales, of Thor and Loki and Baldur, and found that on the whole he liked these better.

For all that Tryggvi had heard about the new god, and his son, Christ – and Tryggvi was never sure which of the two Christians spoke of when they said "God", in any case – he never heard anything that he could relate to. In fact, the stories of this religion that he had heard all seemed to be about another sort of people, living in some other part of the world that he could not even imagine, trying to follow the rules of a god he did not understand.

Tryggvi just didn't quite grasp the point of it all, though he recognized that a steadily growing number of his countrymen did, to say nothing of those in the continental lands to the east. Tryggvi had heard that in England and Frankland and Daneland there were churches so large they could hold everyone who attended the Althing within them, all at once. He had no great interest in the simple church before him, but a sight like that was something he should like to see someday.

Now, though, the sun was starting its slow descent towards the horizon, where it would dip just out of sight before rising again in the night. Tryggvi was ready for sleep, and headed back to join his father at their booth.

ᚠ ᚱᚲ ᛟᚠ ᚫᚠ ᚱᚲ ᛟᚠ ᚫᚠ ᚱᚲ ᛟᚠ ᚫᚠ ᚱᚲ ᛟᚠ ᚫ

Tryggvi spent the next day with Kveldulf, walking around the Althing grounds, helping occasionally with setting up stalls and building huts. There were many others doing the same, and the communal air of the proceedings had begun to settle on the plain. It was not lost on Kveldulf that it might be good to help out and make or renew friendships with as many people as possible, and he was at his gregarious best, though careful not to draw too much attention. Tryggvi enjoyed being with his father, being introduced to other farmers his father knew, and also meeting youths his own age. He showed his horse to a group of boys just younger than him, who had heard about the Althing fire the previous year, and the brave boy who had saved the day by springing into action. They fawned over

Orri, who seemed to enjoy the attention, shaking his head and prancing about gallantly. Tryggvi felt a bit embarrassed that the boys seemed impressed by him as well, but he also felt a bit of a man, compared to these excitable youths scampering around him.

The following day marked the official opening of the Althing. The plain now held several thousand inhabitants: goðar and bændr, women, children, and thralls, along with a number of animals.

Gunnar and his household arrived in the early afternoon, their booths having been prepared already by thralls Gunnar had sent in advance. Tryggvi was pleased to see that Gunnar had brought his daughter with him. Sitting on a rock overlooking the plain, Tryggvi saw her riding a fine mare, a brown cloak draping her shoulders and fluttering in the wind as she rode to her father's cabin. He considered going to talk to her right away, but realized he had nothing in particular to say. As he and his father would be moving to Gunnar's quarters for the evening, Tryggvi decided instead to head back to their current camp and gather his possessions.

As Tryggvi approached the hut, he saw a young man standing near Orri, staring intently at the horse. Tryggvi veered towards them. As he did so, the other boy reached out to touch Orri, but the horse snorted and shied away from his hand.

"Do you need something?" Tryggvi asked, in a less friendly tone than he might have intended. The young man turned to face Tryggvi. He was tall, much taller than Tryggvi, with fair hair and blue eyes. He appeared to be trying to grow a beard, as his cheeks and chin were covered in wispy hairs. There was nothing particularly remarkable about his appearance, save that his nose was quite crooked from where it had obviously been broken at some point.

"And what is it to you?" the boy asked in a sneering tone, after regarding Tryggvi for a moment.

"That's my horse."

"And...?"

"And, well, I would ask you not to bother him."

"I did not think I was. We were just making friends, weren't we, you beast?"

As if on cue, Orri gave a derisive snort, and backed farther away from the young man. Tryggvi, not having anything to add to this, walked past the other boy, and went to comfort his horse. Orri nuzzled his snout into Tryggvi's hand, and turned his legs so that his back was to the other boy.

The blond boy gave a sharp laugh. "Finicky creature, isn't he? He must not be as brave as rumored, if a stranger can frighten him so." Tryggvi glared, feeling hot blood warm his cheeks.

"Insult my horse again, and find out what it is to be frightened," Tryggvi spat back.

"You should learn to control your anger, boy," the young man, who appeared barely older than Tryggvi, replied. He cocked his head, as if in consideration, before continuing. "Although, I suppose everyone knows how sensitive the Brauðavatn men are about their horses." And before Tryggvi could respond, the boy turned and stalked off.

"So what do we do?" Tryggvi asked his father, as they packed up their things.

"Well, first we talk to Gunnar. He knows the law, and has already assured me that he will speak for me before the other goðar, should it come to that. Also, now that we know there really might be a suit, the best thing we could do is find out who plans on accusing me before the court. We cannot effectively fight an enemy we cannot identify. Keep your eyes sharp and ears sharp. The sooner we know who is aligned against me, the better."

Kveldulf turned to his son. "We will fight this, Tryggvi. I did a rash thing – there is no denying it – but I have friends still, and a good reputation. Both will help us. And I did what I did to keep an oath. You are right, that is no small thing. Such is a man's highest duty. Though much has changed of late in this land, I believe that still counts for something, and not just among men. We are here."

Tryggvi looked up to see Gunnar's hut in front of them. Like most of the huts on the plain, it was made of turf and sod, but

Gunnar was able to afford a wooden door and reinforcements. The booth was also substantially larger than the one Gunnar and Tryggvi had just come from, and there was even a chimney opening set back into the far corner, so that a fire could be built inside.

Kveldulf rapped on the door, and Gunnar came out to greet them. He welcomed his friends warmly, but looked grim, and Tryggvi assumed that he too had already heard rumors of a suit.

However, this assumption was put aside once they entered the building. "I've just been to see some of the other goðar," Gunnar said. "This eruption looks to be bad news. There is an ash cloud moving over some of the eastern districts, and Thorsteinn Dvalinson says that some of his sheep died from drinking poisoned river water. Some of the other goðar say that the ground still shakes from time to time in their districts, and they're getting damned fearful. Hrafnkell says his cows are giving sour milk, and that some of his thralls went mad after eating a cheese that had somehow gone bad. Hogni Villarsson says his wife found three calves on the edge of their property, missing their hearts and heads. I doubt it's all related, but some of the more remote goðar say their districts are whipping themselves up into a frenzy, and not all of the goðar are immune from this hysteria themselves.

Damned superstitious fools!"

Gunnar absentmindedly fingered a pendant around his neck, a real silver cross with a single red gem set into its center. The cross had an unusually wide base as well, and as Tryggvi stared at it he became unsure whether it more resembled a cross, or a Thor's hammer pendant, like the ones some of the stubbornly devout still kept tucked under their shirts.

"If this madness gets any worse, it's going to be a long Althing, and a long winter. Anyway, come in, come in, my friends. Have some ale."

Over a drink, Kveldulf and Tryggvi told Gunnar of what they had heard so far at the Althing, only gradually working towards the topic of a possible suit, although Tryggvi found it difficult not to jump straight to the point. But he followed his father's lead, and neither of them wished to agitate their goði further.

"Well, I still haven't heard of any suit against you, friend," Gunnar said once they had worked their way around to the subject. "But it sounds like we must prepare, nonetheless. Tell me again everything you can remember about the incident."

Kveldulf did so, being sure to describe his victim, and the efforts he had made to determine the stranger's identity. Tryggvi then related his interaction with the young man bothering Orri.

"Well, blond with a broken nose doesn't exactly narrow it down. I don't know what his connection could be to the man you killed, Kveldulf, but I will ask around and see what I can find out. In the meantime, the two of you should probably lay low. Kveldulf, have you any business to conduct this year?"

"No, certainly not now."

"Then stay close to my booth, and make yourselves home here. I have good ale and cured lamb's meat, and my daughter will be around shortly. I'm sure she can keep you entertained." Gunnar glanced at Tryggvi then, an inscrutable look on his face, before continuing.

"In any case, relax, both of you. We will sort this all out. Assuming the whole island doesn't fall apart first." With this, Gunnar took his leave of them.

Looking around the large cabin, Kveldulf and Tryggvi found a hnefatafl set, and sat down to pass the time with it. Tryggvi had been playing since he was a child, and had consistently bested his father at the game for the past several years. But today he was distracted by his own thoughts, and a little tipsy from the ale they were both still drinking, and he kept making stupid mistakes. He was losing badly at the third game in a row when the door to the cabin opened again, and in walked Njála.

If she was at all surprised to see either of the men, she gave no indication, merely saying hello to them both politely. With her was her father's aunt, Guðrun, a toothless woman in a brown shawl like Njála's, with a wicked grin. She clapped delightedly at seeing the hnefatafl board, and challenged Kveldulf to a game. Tryggvi was relieved to resign, and let his father, rather bemusedly, set up the board again with the old woman.

This left Njála and Tryggvi with little to do but speak to each other.

"So," Tryggvi finally asked, "is this your first summer at the Althing? I have never seen you here before."

Njála tucked a long strand of red hair behind her ear. "I came a few times as a child, but then my mother decided to start staying home, and I decided to keep her company. So this is my first visit in some time."

Tryggvi suddenly remembered seeing Njála, with her mother, Finna, at one of the local things. It must have been when he was a child, and his own mother was still alive. Finna was a sturdy, vibrant woman, with hair of a deeper flaming red than her daughter's, and she and his mother had talked while their children hid shyly behind them. Tryggvi did not remember of what they had spoken- the memory was a sudden vision, slipping away from him even as he grasped for it- but he suddenly wished he had made friends with this girl, whose father was his father's friend and goði, and who had a loneliness within her that he recognized.

"Well, I am glad you are here now," he said, quietly.

For a moment Tryggvi thought Njála was going to mock him, but her face softened and she looked him in the eye. She seemed about to speak, but at that moment the wizened old auntie gave a sharp laugh, and Njála swayed back. Tryggvi caught a whiff of her breath as she did so, and he realized that they both had been drinking that day.

It seemed they also both suddenly realized that they had given the conversation nowhere else to go, and Tryggvi became self-conscious, as Njála turned as watched the board game intently. Mumbling to no one in particular, Tryggvi left the hut, and went to go tend to the horses.

Chapter 5

The next several days were a blur of activity. The Althing began in earnest, and the thousands assembled on the plain got down to the business of running the country. Wares were sold. Alliances were made, and broken. Romances kindled or fizzled. Children were betrothed to each other, and more children were made. The year's gossip spread through the tents and stalls, doubled back on itself, and propagated once again with the appropriate measure of embellishment, practiced delivery, and altered intentions. Ale flowed, food was abundant, there was even music. And there were oaths sworn- some to the old gods, still, but perhaps more to the new.

Despite all this, Tryggvi spent his days quietly, perusing the stable area, playing hnefatafl, feeding and grooming Orri, and, more often than not, either talking to Njála or waiting for her to return so that he could talk to her. The youths found that they had much in common, despite the difference in their sexes. Both were thoughtful, and had a tendency to listen to conversation rather than trying to direct attention to themselves, as so many other young people did.

Njála, however, was not about to miss out on the rare opportunity to socialize with other people her age, and she spent much time out in the thick of the stalls and crowds. In the evening, she would come back to the booth and relate all she had seen and heard to Tryggvi, who had no real interest in social intrigue but happily indulged her own. He in turn would tell her the few old stories he knew by heart, which she did not often hear on Gunnar's farm. When Tryggvi ran out of stories to share with her, he began inventing them, telling Njála of battles with giants and raids on Asgard, of quests for honor and treasure that he spun together during his long days sitting alone in the cabin. Sometimes, he would just talk about his life on the farm, especially about the small adventures he and Orri had together exploring the land around the homestead, or of funny things the farmhands had said and done.

31

Gunnar was often off on goði business during the day, but Kveldulf spent much of his time in the cabin as well, carving wood or drinking, so the youths were rarely entirely alone; it would have been a tad inappropriate for it to be otherwise. Still, old Guðrun could see that the youths were slowly forming a little world of their own, where two young people could find some respite from the pressures raging around and within them.

A week after arriving at the Althing, Tryggvi was in high spirits. He awoke one morning in Gunnar's cabin and resolved to purchase something for his host, as a token of gratitude. He was also eager to leave the confines of the living quarters and venture further into the mass of the Althing, if only for a little while. Tryggvi dressed and exited the hut, walked to where Orri was tied. The horse seemed to be in as high spirits as his boy, and shivered with delight when Tryggvi gave him a bit of honeyed oat, an extravagant indulgence.

Leaving Orri with a pat, Tryggvi made his way to the market stalls, hoping to find something worthy of his host, and, perhaps, to make a favorable impression on Gunnar's daughter as well. His own father had given him some baubles which he should be able to exchange for a gift.

Tryggvi was looking at a delicate bone brooch when he felt someone roughly bump into him from behind. Turning, he saw the sneering blond lad who had been bothering Orri several days prior.

"Watch yourself, boy! You don't want to break that piece of jewelry you're holding. It won't look nearly so pretty pinned to your dress then."

Tryggvi and the stall merchant next to him both gave a sharp intake of breath. The other boy had just leveled a grave insult at Tryggvi, and it demanded a response. The supercilious young man had just insinuated that Tryggvi was womanly, and several people had heard it- the boy's clear, loud voice had made sure of that. If Tryggvi did not address the insult, the charge would likely stick, and cause any number of problems for Tryggvi down the road. Calling a man womanly was no minor thing, nor was failing to defend one's own honor in the face of such an insult.

Tryggvi drew himself up to his full height – which still, he noted with chagrin, required him to peer up a bit at the other boy – and stared his adversary full in the face.

"I wouldn't know the first thing about womanly dressing, so I will have to take your word for it," Tryggvi said. He paused, for the briefest moment, nearly reconsidering, then barreled forward. "You will have to tell me all you learned of it from your father."

A few of the merchants nearby laughed, and the other boy flushed red, his skin suddenly showing in stark contrast to his light hair and blue eyes. He opened his mouth, closed it again. The boys were both skirting dangerous territory now. Everyone knew of serious feuds that sprang from a few insulting words.

Finally, the boy found his response. "My father," he spat, "is a goði, a mighty warrior, and sworn brother to the king of Norway."

And which king would that be? Tryggvi thought. The obvious petulance of the claim took him aback, made him suddenly see the other boy in a different light. He was taller than Tryggvi, but Tryggvi suddenly suspected that he was also younger, or at least less mature. It caused him to consider his possible responses differently, though he wasted no time in speaking.

"Then your father probably has better things to do than start fights at the Althing. It's a pity you don't seem to follow in his footsteps."

For a moment, Tryggvi thought that the boy was going to strike him. But Tryggvi's words actually seemed to sink in, and the boy collected himself. It was indeed extremely bad form to fight at the Althing. However, each year some petty personal disputes inevitably arose, and there were accepted ways of settling them.

The boy caught Tryggvi off guard by proposing one.

"And do you follow in your father's footsteps, Tryggvi Kveldulfsson? Do you love you precious horses more than a man should? You have a horse. Will you enter it in a fight against mine, or are you too *ergi*?"

With that, the boy pulled Tryggvi over the line they had both been dancing towards. A free man was within his rights to kill someone who flung such a charge at him, and if he didn't, then the charge was likely to stick.

The boy hadn't come right out and called Tryggvi ergi. But Tryggvi could not ignore the other boy's challenge. To do so would bring great shame not only on himself, but on his father as well. Tryggvi couldn't afford that, not when Kveldulf was likely to need all the support he could muster in fighting a lawsuit.

Tryggvi had no choice, and everyone within earshot of the conversation knew it.

"Alright, you... alright. We shall have a horse fight. Meet me at the ring at noon tomorrow."

Tryggvi abruptly turned and stalked away without saying another word. Later, he knew already, he would come up with all sorts of witty and cutting parting shots, but in the moment he was already too distracted, thinking of his horse. Orri would have to fight. There was no getting around it. It was, he realized, likely what the other boy had wanted in the first place. And Tryggvi had been forced into the situation. Yet even though he saw no way he could have avoided it, he could not help but feel sick with betrayal as he reached Gunnar's booth, and Orri popped his noble head up to look at him.

ᚠ ᚱᛚᚱ ᛒᚠ ᚨᚠ ᚱᛚᚱ ᛒᚠ ᚨᚠ ᚱᛚᚱ ᛒᚠ ᚨᚠ ᚱᛚᚱ ᛒᚠ ᚨ

Kveldulf was furious when he heard what had happened, although not at Tryggvi. "That shit-starting little...shit!" It was as animated as

Tryggvi or Gunnar had seen Kveldulf in months, perhaps longer. "Who is this boy? What's his game?"

"I don't know. He was over by Orri a few days ago, but since then I have been holed up in here."

Gunnar spoke. "But you say neither of you has had any dealings with him before?"

"No!" Kveldulf and Tryggvi said it together.

Njála had been chewing her lip throughout the conversation, but she spoke now.

"This boy... did he have a broken nose, and a personality that made you want to break it again?"

Kveldulf and Tryggvi both opened their eyes wide at this, and Tryggvi nodded.

Njála sighed. "I think I know that boy. His name is Haraldr Vigisson. He's been bothering me all week."

Kveldulf and Gunnar exchanged glances, while Tryggvi piped up,

"Why didn't you tell me?"

"I did not think it worth discussing. And it's not just me, a lot of the other girls are trying to avoid him. He's both annoying and persistent." She scrunched her face up as if she had smelled something foul.

Gunnar scratched his chin as he responded. "Hmm...That means his father is probably Vigi Haraldson. He's a goði. I don't know the family well. Vigi only just became goði a few years ago, and we have not interacted much. His district is not near ours."

"So why is he antagonizing my boy?"

"At first, it sounded to me like he knew something about what happened with you and the stranger this spring." Both Kveldulf and Tryggvi grimaced.

"But perhaps it is simpler than that." He looked at his daughter.

"I will find out everything I can about him. In the meantime, Kveldulf, you must prepare Tryggvi for the horse fight." Gunnar turned his kindly face to Tryggvi. "Have you or your horse ever fought before?"

"No. I have seen a few fights, of course, but I never even thought to enter Orri in one. I always, well, I always thought of him as meant for better things than that."

"And so he is. A horse fight can be a nasty business, and any horse without the fire in his belly will be in trouble. I don't know why Haraldr Vigisson is so eager for your horse to fight, but I can't imagine it is for love of competition. You say he made you no wager, but there is great honor just in owning a winning horse." He peered at Tryggvi. "Whatever Haraldr is up to, you must not lose to him. You don't know what could be riding on it."

"I understand," Tryggvi said, although he didn't, really. He was sick at the thought of Orri being injured, and it came down to the same point. "What can I do to help Orri win?"

At this, Kveldulf spoke. "My father's father's father brought horses to the island with him, horses he had taken on raids. He brought only the hardiest stock, and he made his name by fighting them, back when it was more common than now. Orri may be your companion, son, and he may be a gentle soul, but fighting is in his blood. Just as it is in yours. Orri will know what to do. It is your job to give him something to fight for. I will help you."

⨀ ⬡⬡ ⬡⬡ ⬡⬡ ⬡⬡ ⬡⬡ ⬡⬡ ⬡⬡ ⬡⬡ ⨀

The next day, Tryggvi, Gunnar, Kveldulf, and Njála all gathered with Orri at the horse-fighting ring. Word of the fight had somehow spread through the booths, and as it would be the first horse fight of the year, much of the Althing crowd was in attendance. Haraldr arrived with a sturdy, dun-colored steed of his own. The horse had long scars on his flanks and face, betokening him as an experienced fighter, though he was yet young and hale.

If Haraldr's father Vigi was there, he did not make himself known. But Haraldr had a small retinue of apparent supporters with him, a few cruel-looking men, and a couple women. Several of them has the same silver-blond hair as Haraldr himself, although this said little enough about their identities.

There was not much preamble to the fight. Each of the boys led his horse onto the fighting ground. The rules of horse fighting in this space were well understood. Each of the boys was to spur on his own horse, without help from a substitute or second as was sometimes the case. The fight would not end until one of them withdrew from the combat, or one of the horses was dead.

It was not necessary to speechify before a fight, but apparently Haraldr could not resist the opportunity. He turned to face the eager crowd, and spread his arms wide.

"I, Haraldr, son of Vigi, son of Haraldr, have challenged Tryggvi Kveldulfsson to prove his mettle by means of horse-fight. Some of you may have heard of the Brauðavatn horses. It is claimed that these horses are brave and strong, and reflect well on their...reclusive masters. Yet what good is a man's horse, I ask you, if it will not fight? What good is a man who calls himself a fine horse-master, but will not risk his beasts in battle? I will show you what a Brauðavatn horse is worth. I will show you what a Brauðavatn man is worth." With that, Haraldr stepped back to his horse, ready to begin the fight.

Tryggvi could not let the speech go unanswered. Clearing his throat, he too turned to the crowd, mindful of his father and Gunnar and Njála's eyes upon him, and especially of Orri, sturdy and warm at his back. He spoke.

"I do not know Haraldr Vigisson. Before this Althing I had never spoken with him. I do not know why he believes he has a quarrel with me or my father, when we keep to ourselves and quarrel with no one. But I do know this: those who start needless conflicts bring only shame to themselves. This is a lesson given to us by the old ways. And now I shall teach it to Haraldr Vigisson."

Tryggvi stepped back to Orri. The horses were on opposite sides of a large ring, marked with furrows in the ground. Each boy carried a stick. Tryggvi's was blunted, but Haraldr's was visibly sharpened on one end.

They glared at each other from across the ring. The crowd stilled. Then, with a harsh cry, Haraldr struck his horse's rump with the stick, and the beast charged forward. Tryggvi hesitated only a second, then shouted "Go!" to Orri, giving him a smack on the back with an open palm, as Kveldulf had taught him to do.

The horses ran at each other full-out, gaining what speed they could within the small space, and the crowd gave a cheer when they collided. Haraldr's horse caught Orri in the side of the neck with his head, and Orri spun around, his front hooves leaving the ground. The other horse reared up to kick him in the side, but Orri recovered himself and danced away at the last moment. The other horse's

37

massive hooves sliced through empty air, and pulverized the ground where Orri had just stood.

Haraldr was at his horse's right side, goading it on and striking at it with his stick. The horse reared again, and Orri backed away farther. Neither horse had been injured yet, but Orri was taking a defensive posture against the other horse's pressing attacks, and it was only a matter of time before one of the crushing blows connected.

Haraldr was whipping his horse into a frenzy, and it reared again on its hind legs while advancing on Orri. Tryggvi would not attack his own horse, but he had to do something to get Orri to respond aggressively, or the battle would end badly for them both. He carefully maneuvered himself around on Orri, approaching the other horse's plane of attack. Soon he was nearly between the two stallions. Haraldr's horse reached its head out and snapped at Tryggvi's face. Tryggvi jumped away from the bite, but lost his footing and fell. The horse, spurred on by a triumphant Haraldr, advanced on the prone boy.

Orri sprang into action. In two short bursts he was at the other horse's side, and he brought his hoof up into its flank. The hoof caught, and raked a long, shallow cut into the horse's skin. With a cry, the other horse turned away from Tryggvi, and the fight began in earnest.

There was a frenzy of flying earth and spittle as the two stout beasts bucked up to kick at each other again and again. Tryggvi rolled away and to his feet, leaping back to give them space. The crowd around them shouted and jeered, finally enjoying the sport before them.

The horses' blows were connecting. Orri caught a hoof in the shoulder, and thin trickles of blood streamed down his side. He shot his head forward, and bit the other horse on the ear, tearing it. Both horses were bloodied now, but there was no way to tell if either was winning.

Tryggvi, however, could bear no more. He had had to make Orri fight, but he could not stand to see him injured. If that made him a coward, he thought, then that was a mantle he would have to bear.

Tryggvi was just about to wade into the fight, to try to stop it, when Haraldr made the effort moot. He had been whipping and jabbing his horse into a frenzy, keeping it angry, confused, and frightened enough to attack Orri again and again. Experienced horse fighters sometimes controlled their horses in this way, but there was an art to it. Haraldr was not an experienced horse fighter, and his own aggression got the better of him. Haraldr's horse finally realized that the true source of its distress came from somewhere behind it, not from the stallion in front of it. The horse lashed out with a back leg, catching Haraldr near the shoulder as he raised his arm to thwack it yet again. The blow did not fully connect, but it was sufficient to knock Haraldr off his feet.

At the same time. Orri dealt the horse a huge blow on the head. Stunned, the horse sank to its knees. Orri did not press his attack further, and seeing his opportunity, Tryggvi called to him softly from the edge of the ring. Orri's heaving flanks began to settle, and he turned and trotted over to his boy.

Haraldr slowly sat up, a look of utter surprise on his face. But, seeing his horse on the ground, his features twisted. "Kill him!" he shouted at the beast. No one moved. The crowd had fallen silent, and was most of them were simply starting at the boy, although a few watched Tryggvi tending to Orri.

"Kill him!" Haraldr yelled again, louder this time, evidently addressing his stallion. The horse still lay semi-erect on the ground, tongue lolling out of its mouth. Blood poured down its flank where it had been struck, and as many of the wounds had been dealt by Haraldr as by Orri. The horse's breathing was rapid and shallow, and its eyes rolled in its head. It was soon obvious to all that real damage had been done to the creature.

Finally, one of the blond-haired men in Haraldr's party pulled a sword from his side, breaking the peace-band that had been tied around it in order to show that it would not be used for violence at the Althing. He walked over to Haraldr, handed him the sword, and returned to the crowd. With the fight clearly over, many of the spectators had already lost interest, and were discussing other, better horse fights they had seen, or beginning to wander off. But some still stood to observe the new drama unfolding before them, and none of Haraldr or Tryggvi's supporters had left.

With a wheeze, Haraldr drew up to his feet, sword in hand. He shambled over to where his horse lay gasping. Taking the sword in both hands, he raised it over his head, then brought it point-down on the horse's neck. It was badly done, and the horse screamed as it died.

Tryggvi watched in horror. He had not wanted the horse to die. He had wanted none of this. But it was undeniable that Orri had won the horse fight. Kveldulf, Gunnar, and Njála stormed into the ring to clap Tryggvi on the back, and a small cheer went up from the remaining crowd. Tryggvi and Kveldulf tended to Orri, bruised and bleeding, but already munching on a path of grass nonetheless. Meanwhile, a small cluster of Haraldr's people surrounded him, dragging the horse and the boy away from the field.

Gunnar watched them go. "You haven't heard the last from that one, boy," he said to Tryggvi. "He's an odd lad, and the rage is in him." He turned back. "But well done. Let us back to the booth. Ale and meat for all, and barley cake for this one," he said, patting Orri fondly on the snout. Kveldulf put his arm around Tryggvi's shoulder as they walked back.

Everyone at Gunnar's booth knew that Kveldulf's problems were likely far from resolved, and now it seemed Tryggvi had some enmity of his own to contend with. But a deed well done was a deed well done, and the horse fight had brought some measure of honor to Kveldulf's household, so that evening had a festive air. After making sure that Orri's wounds were not serious, and dressing them carefully, Tryggvi joined the others for a meal of smoked lamb, hard cheese, skyr, and copious rounds of ale. Tryggvi had been drinking ale since he was a child, but Gunnar kept placing round after round in his hand, and before long Tryggvi felt his head start to swim. Still, he wasn't about to refuse his host's generosity, especially not with Njála present, and herself matching him drink for drink.

Gunnar excused himself for a moment, and returned shortly with a tall, thin man unfamiliar to Tryggvi. The man took his place by the fire, gratefully accepted a full horn of ale, and pulled from his belt a large leather bag. From it he produced two long bones, and a hoop of wood with a calf's skin stretched over it.

"A skald!" Tryggvi thought. He had only heard one a handful of times before, and then only in large performances at a thing meetingnever in such an intimate setting. From his father and the farmhands, Tryggvi knew many of the old tales, but only as storiesnever told the way they were meant to be, in sung verse, accompanied by music. Despite the stress of the day, and the fog waiting to settle over his mind, Tryggvi felt himself alert and riveted, unbearably excited to hear the skald perform. The others in the room- Gunnar, Kveldulf, Njála, several of Gunnar's servants, even old aunt Guðrun, were similarly engaged.

Welcoming the attention, the skald cleared his throat, and waited for the room to settle into silence, until the only sounds that could be heard were the crackling of the small fire and the steady breathing of the booth's inhabitants.

Then, picking up one of the bones in his hand, and holding the drum in the other, the skald began a low, steady humming, which resonated from deep in his chest. Eyes wide, he began to sing the first lines of the evening's saga.

As the skald spoke, his voice lilted and pitched, somewhere between speech and song. He began to keep time with the drum, tapping out a persistent yet subtle rhythm with the bone on the calfskin.

On the poet went. When the narrative got pitched or the action picked up, he might raise his voice, spitting the words out with force. With the bone and the drum, he could simulate the sound of horses' hooves on turf, or the strikes and thrums of battle, or the slowing pulse of a dying heart.

The skald finished one song, and began another. Sometimes he placed the drum aside, and knocked the two bones against one another gently to keep time. Sometimes he raised his voice into true song, singing a melody, encouraging the audience in the cabin to

41

join in the rounds of bawdy chorus. He told of the gods and heroes of legend, of their adventures, their passions, their foibles. He spoke of animals- the bird on wing, the seal at swim, the ponderous, dangerous whale. He sang of lost love, and memory. He presented the listeners with clever riddles, and encouraged them to guess the answers; Njála was particularly adept at this game. Some of the skald's songs sang the praises of his host, and Gunnar toasted him in good cheer.

Then, as the bit of sky showing through the chimney-hole finally turned to midnight blue, and the listeners swilled the last dregs of their ale, and the shadows and smoke in the room swirled and coalesced into shapes and forms before Tryggvi's heavy-lidded eyes, the skald began his final poem of the evening. His drum and bones were set aside, and when he spoke his voice was low and rolling, waves lapping at the shore, thunder heard from a great distance.

Far þú nú æva, þar er forað þykkir, ok standi-t þér mein fyr munum; á jarðföstum steini stóð ek innan dura, meðan ek þér galdra gól.

The skald was still speaking when Tryggvi, despite himself, finally   drifted   off   to   sleep.

Chapter 6

Tryggvi awoke to his father shaking him. "Up, boy. Up." "What is it?" Tryggvi blearily asked.

"The Lögrétta has sent for me. It is time, son. It's happening.

Tryggvi bolted up, and immediately regretted the speed of the action.

"What do you mean?" he managed to ask.

"Gunnar is there now, and I have been summoned. That is all I know, but I can only assume why. Now come, get dressed. I want you to be there."

Tryggvi realized it must be much later than he usually awoke. He hopped out of his cot, and a wave of nausea shot through him. He had picked a poor day to have his first hangover.

Pulling on his tunic and boots, Tryggvi stumbled outside. Kveldulf was waiting there, Njála by his side. Her face was impassive, but she kept glancing from father to son, and Tryggvi could sense her worry.

She caught his eye, and spoke.

"Tryggvi, I'm so sor-"

"Save it, lass. We can't start that yet," Kveldulf cut in.

The three of them walked across the Althing plain. The merchants were already in their stalls. By the river, women washed clothes, children darting about their legs. The sky was cloudless, and a gentle breeze blew. It was a beautiful summer day, the kind that only came once or twice a season, and most everyone was intent on enjoying it. Yet Tryggvi was sure he felt eyes upon the small group as they made their way toward the Lögrétta, and the small circle nearby where the Althing council already sat. His stomach was raw from the worry gnawing its way through his guts.

As they approached the council, grim-faced Gunnar strode out to meet them. The heads of the other 38 council members turned to follow him.

43

"So you received the message. Good, good. With me, Kveldulf. You two, you may wait over there." Gunnar gestured to one side, where worried-looking wives and children sat on a long, low bench.

Gunnar led Kveldulf into the council circle, while Tryggvi and Njála made their way to the observation area. There were three rings of people arranged around a raised wooden platform. Each of Iceland's thirty-nine goðar occupied the middle ring. In front and behind each of them sat one of their bændr, acting as advisors, so all told there were over a hundred men facing towards the center, stern and serious. These were the leaders of Iceland, the men who oversaw each of the regional districts, and who, together, made the decisions that determined in broad form the shape and the course of the island's society.

Some of the men had been present thirteen years before, when the Althing had confronted the issue of conversion, and resolved to adopt Christianity. Others were younger, newer goðar, having come to fame or inherited positions in recent years. Many of them were wealthy, and a few were noted warriors. Some were simple farmers, the most prominent men in poor or underpopulated districts. Whatever their background and lineage, all of them had supporters, men who freely chose to follow their leadership over that of any other.

Yet for all their prominence, these men were only firsts among equals, and Kveldulf entered the council circle with his head held high and a proud look upon his face. He ascended the platform, and Gunnar came to his side.

"This is Kveldulf Thorbjornsson, of Brauðavatn farm in my district. I have brought him here, that he might face his accusers."

At this, a tall, rather rotund man stood up from the middle ring of benches, and stepped into the center circle. He had dirty blond hair, plaited in two braids that ran down either side of his shoulders to the small of his back. On his arms were many rings of silver, gold, and brass, denoting him as a man of wealth and accomplishment, though they sat rather loosely on his limbs. He stopped before the platform and looked around the entire circle before settling his eyes on Kveldulf and Gunnar in front of him.

"I am Vigi Haraldsson, goði, and here in this Althing court, before man and almighty God, I formally accuse Kveldulf Thorbjornsson of the murder of Adalbert, a free man, a man of God. I contend that early this spring, Kveldulf did willfully and unlawfully deal Adalbert a blow upon the head, which caused Adalbert to bleed, and to die. For this crime, I demand – the law demands – that Kveldulf be sentenced to full outlawry, and stripped of his land and possessions."

Before Vigi could go on, or Kveldulf could respond, Gunnar raised his hand and spoke. "Friend Vigi, I am Kveldulf's goði. Why was this matter not brought to me before, if, as you say, this incident happened in my district nearly a season past? Why did you wait until we were assembled today at the Althing council to raise this claim? You have not followed proper procedure for bringing suit against a free bóndi." Several of the men around the council circle nodded in agreement.

Vigi replied. "The identity of Adalbert's killer was not known to me until the Althing. I did not even know where to bring a suit. I did not hear of his death until days after it happened, when his companion arrived at my farm and begged my help. He was still very shaken by the murder of his fellow priest, and could barely tell me where it had happened or how he had made his way back. I took him in, and agreed to help him seek justice, but we both thought Adalbert's death might go unavenged. Yet, by chance, he happened to see Kveldulf at this Althing, and recognized him as the killer."

One of the other goðar stood and spoke. "But Vigi, have you anything actually connecting this man to the crime?"

"I have the testimony of this man of God." At this, Vigi signaled towards a group of men standing on the outside of the ring. One of them stepped forward, and entered the circle at Vigi's beckoning. He wore a black robe, and had a large silver cross around his neck.

"This is the man who was with Adalbert. He will tell you that he saw this man, Kveldulf, unlawfully murder his companion." "And what of the body?" the same goði asked.

"I know not what happened to it. This man was unarmed, and forced to flee when he saw his friend attacked."

"So you have no proof even that he is dead?"

"I have my word, and the word of this good priest here. We will swear, bound by oath, to what we know to have happened. Will Kveldulf do the same? What say you, Kveldulf?"

Gunnar spoke before Kveldulf could. "He says nothing. This is highly improper. You cannot just walk into this council and start throwing accusations of murder at free men, not without following the procedures we have all agreed to uphold." More nodding from around the circle.

"I seek only justice. Those men were sent on their mission here by the king of Norway – am I to tell him that this is how we treat his priests in this land?"

"There are no kings here, Vigi-goði. Only laws."

"And the law says you are responsible for managing your district. Are you really claiming to know nothing of this? Do you wish it to be known that murders there are of no concern to you?"

Kveldulf had no choice. "I will take an oath," he interjected. The others fell silent.

Gunnar turned to Kveldulf, raising a hand to show that he needed a moment to counsel his bóndi privately.

"I don't know what this Vigi's game is, Kveldulf, but he is trapping you. He hasn't followed proper procedure, and we should prevail on this basis alone. And something else just seems off about this to me."

"I know why I did what I did," Kveldulf replied, voice low, "And I know equally well that my actions will not be looked upon favorably by these men." He gestured at the goðar, a bit more dismissively than might have been prudent. "Many in this land have forgotten the old ways. I have had my crises and questions, like anyone else. But I did what I did because I had sworn to do it, and I could not break this oath. I must trust that keeping to it was the right decision." Kveldulf turned to the goðar.

"I understand from my goði, Gunnar, that proper procedure has not been followed in this case. This is unfortunate, as we must respect the law above all things. However, even the law cannot change the nature of man. Vigi has asked if I will take an oath. I will not have any of you say that I fear him, or the truth, or nature's judgment. I will take an oath. I swear, by whatever gods you might wish me to swear, that I have acted justly in all matters. Submit me to the turf ordeal, and you will see my innocence proven."

Vigi bellowed. "The turf ordeal? Pagan claptrap! Admit it, Kveldulf, you killed a priest in cold blood! Submit yourself to the judgment of the court!"

Kveldulf and Gunnar both began to answer him, but a figure stepped forward from the ring of goði. He was stooped with age, but his hair remained thick and brown, and his bearing exuded wisdom and authority. The others in the Lögrétta fell silent as he ambled towards the wooden platform. This was Thorgeir, son of Thorkel, and he required no introduction to the proceedings. It was he who had been Law-speaker in the year that tensions between the heathens and the Christians at the Althing finally came to a head, forcing the Althing to consider the possibility of conversion. Thorgeir had led the heathen faction, but was so respected that ultimately a vote was taken to place the decision of whether to convert the country solely on his shoulders. He took a day to consider the matter in private, reportedly laying under a sheet in his tent. Then he surprised everyone by announcing that the people should embrace Christianity, arguing that the old ways had not served them as well as the new ones might. Already, some of the more ardent converts had taken to calling him Thorgeir Ljósvetningagoði, the goði who brought the light.

He spoke. "The death of a man is a serious matter, and not to be squabbled over. This is no less the case when an accusation of murder has been made, and when the victim was an honored outlander and priest." He looked to man near Vigi, who had been standing silent throughout the confrontation. "I met Adalbert at last year's Althing, and I am sorry to hear of his death." The other priest, looking rather old and anxious, only nodded.

Thorgeir turned to the assembled goðar. "I would have you all remember that this is not a yet a trial, and none of this testimony is conclusive evidence. With that being said, Kveldulf, what do you have to say to this?"

"I have said what I will."

Thorgeir nodded. "It is true, as Gunnar says, that proper procedure has not been followed here. By rights, Kveldulf can be convicted of no crime in this case, not like this." At this, Vigi, the priest, and even several of the goðar began to speak at once.

Thorgeir held up his hand once again. "However – the murder of a priest on a mission in our land is a grave matter, and having been brought to our attention, this body must respond to it.

"I propose that we take Kveldulf up on his offer to undergo the turf ordeal. No, no, listen to me. If it is God's will that Kveldulf pay for the murder of the priest, then surely He can show it by means of the turf ordeal. If Kveldulf fails, the sentence should be lesser outlawry. We cannot condemn a man to full outlawry when we cannot even bring a legal case against him. Should Kveldulf pass the ordeal, then we must consider that by God's will, the matter has been properly settled, and any who disagree must take the issue up with Him." At this, Thorgeir returned to his seat.

There was logic to the old man's words, as there usually was. Another of the goðar called a vote, and it passed.

The ordeal would take place immediately. Two of the goðars' advisors cut a large strip of turf from the ground, and raised it into an arch. Kveldulf stood before this, and the current Law-speaker came to his side.

"Kveldulf Thorbjornsson, you have agreed to submit to fate and the will of God in determining your guilt or innocence in the murder of Adalbert, a priest. Do you vow to respect the outcome of this ordeal?"

"I so vow."

"Vigi Haraldsson, you have brought a claim against Kveldulf Thorbjornsson. Do you vow to respect the outcome of the turf ordeal?"

"I so vow," Vigi said, grudgingly.

"Then let the ordeal commence. Kveldulf, you will step through the arch three times. If the arch remains standing, then your innocence is proven. Should the arch fall, you will be judged guilty. Begin."

Kveldulf stepped forward. Behind him, Tryggvi, Gunnar, and Njála all held their breath. The turf ordeal was surprisingly unpredictable, and all had seen or heard stories of obviously guilty men who went free, and innocent men who were condemned. For this reason, it had fallen largely out of favor in recent years. None of them had expected Kveldulf to call for it. That each of them knew Kveldulf had actually committed the act for which he had been accused, whatever his justifications, made the ordeal all the more fraught with tension.

Kveldulf stepped through the arch. Some detritus fell from the sides, nearly stopping Tryggvi's heart. But the arch stood as Kveldulf passed to the other side.

Wasting no time, he turned and quickly stepped through the arch again. Again, the arch held. Kveldulf turned for his last pass. It was only two steps through the arch. He placed one foot through, ducked his head, then the other foot. He passed through the arch.

Tryggvi couldn't help himself. A cheer rose in his throat.

It died there as the ground shook, violently. Tryggvi, Gunnar, Njála, and anyone else standing was thrown from their feet.

Screams rose from the booth and stalls. Tents collapsed. Tryggvi heard the horses squealing, and looked up from the ground to see birds flocking frantically overhead, careening past each other, chaotically out of formation.

The rumbling stopped as abruptly as it had begun, though no one moved for a minute.

As Tryggvi finally stood, he saw, off to the east, a massive plume of smoke billowing into the sky, and within in flashes of lightning.

Drawing his gaze in closer, he saw his father. Kveldulf had fallen backwards, towards the arch. It lay over him now, collapsed. He was unharmed – it was only a bit of dirt, after all – but his eye caught Tryggvi's, and understanding passed between them. Tryggvi

49

felt his whole world shift beneath him, as surely as if the earth had moved   again.

Chapter 7

Gunnar's protests, and even those of some of the other men present, were of no avail. Those goðar inclined to see a procedural defect in Kveldulf's ordeal were convinced by the improbability of what had transpired. Many of those who had taken no issue with the procedure were now fervent in their belief that some supernatural force, God or gods, had intervened in the ordeal. Even those who did not think the earthquake had much to do with Kveldulf were nonetheless disinclined to argue about its effect on his ordeal. This disinclination was helped considerably by Vigi, who pointed to the plume of ash and lightning in the distance and proclaimed it God's judgment on Kveldulf, and on all other known heathens, and, he implied, on Iceland in general, for permitting such paganism in the first place.

It was obvious to Tryggvi, Gunnar, and doubtless many of the other clear-headed spectators that Vigi's hatred of Kveldulf extended far beyond what would be anticipated given his apparently tenuous relation to Adalbert, Kveldulf's victim. Yet it hardly mattered. Kveldulf had submitted to the ordeal, and his gambit had failed. Once the panic from the earthquake subsided, the Lögrétta reconvened to sentence Kveldulf. Vigi's rhetoric had been all too effective, and the goðar went beyond the original terms proposed by Thorgeir Ljósvetningagoði. They sentenced Kveldulf to full outlawry, effective once the Althing ended.

Watching the proceedings, Tryggvi saw his proud father deflate. For himself, he could barely process what was happening. He had thought he might lose his father for three years, and that was disaster enough. Now it seemed they were to be ripped apart, and Kveldulf was to lose everything he had worked so hard for, everything that had brought him back into the world whenever he had taken to bed to stew in his melancholy.

Together, Tryggvi, Kveldulf, Gunnar, Njála, and some of Gunnar's other bændr walked back to their booths in silence.

51

Kveldulf went straight to the hearth, and stared into the fire, speaking to no one as he gulped down a mug of ale.

It fell to Gunnar to take Tryggvi aside.

"Do you know what happens now, Tryggvi?"

"No. Not really. Must we leave Iceland?"

"Well, your father must leave. He can stay until the feransdomr, when Vigi comes to claim your father's property. But after that he must attempt to take the first available boat off the island. And he may not be safe even until then. I don't know what this Vigi is up to, but something does not fit. I think there is more to it than we have yet seen." He stared at the fire himself now, ruminating, before remembering his task of the moment and returning his attention to Tryggvi.

"Will we lose the farm?" the boy asked.

"Not if I have anything to say in it. Technically it is subject to confiscation, since you are not yet of majority. But you are close enough. If I can get the terms structured correctly at the feransdomr, perhaps I can hold the land for you until you reach an age to inherit. Until then, I will see that you and your household are cared for, I promise it. And we will have to make some provision for your father, the law be damned." Gunnar looked over at the man glaring into the hearth, then at the chimney-opening of the hut, then the ground beneath them.

"You must be prepared, boy. There are hard times ahead." With that, he clapped Tryggvi on the shoulder, and left to go speak to his men.

Still Kveldulf sat looking into the fire. Tryggvi wanted to speak to his father, wanted some reassurance from him. But he had learned over the hard years not to intrude upon Kveldulf when he was ruminating. Tryggvi stared at his father's back for a moment, then left to see to Orri.

The horse looked at him expectantly as he walked up. More than anything Tryggvi wanted to ride, but Orri's healing wounds would not permit it. Tryggvi checked these, relieved to see that they were healing well, beginning to mend themselves nicely after only a day.

Then Tryggvi lay his head against his companion's warm shoulder, and began to cry.

After some time, he heard a noise behind him. Njála was standing there, lit by the amber light of the evening sun.

"Forgive me, I did not mean to sneak up on you." she said, turning when she saw his face. Tryggvi quickly dried his tears.

"It is alright. I am glad of the company." Orri nattered in agreement.

"This grieves me, Tryggvi. Anything I can do to help, I will, and I know my father feels the same way."

"I thank you for that. You have given us so much already. I know we will get through this, somehow, but... it is difficult." He let out a deep sigh. "And I am angry. I do not know why my father offered to take the ordeal, when it sounded like there was no case against him. And I cannot believe our terrible luck, that the ground would shake just when it did."

"Many believe luck played no part in today's events." Njála had meant it to be conciliatory, but realized how it sounded a second after she stopped speaking. Tryggvi simply looked at her however, considering her words.

"And you, Njála? What do you believe?"

She brought her arms up, hugging herself for a moment against a sudden chill in the air, then spoke. "I supposed I believe that however a situation appears in the moment, it may seem different when we reflect upon it later." He just looked at her, so she continued. "I believe that we are often tested, and it is our duty to respond to those tests with courage." She had meant to comfort him when she saw him leaning there against his horse, looking so alone, but she felt she was making a bad job of it already. Yet Tryggvi had stopped crying, and was turning over what she had said, holding it up to the fading light to examine it.

"But what of gods?" he asked her. "What role do you believe about who makes things happen in the world?"

"Well, I believe that each of us-"

"The old gods, or the new? Who do you worship?" Tryggvi insisted,

Njála looked down, then looked Tryggvi straight in the eye. "I believe in the one God, Jesus Christ. As my parents do." Tryggvi returned her look, almost challenging, yet not harsh.

"Then pray to him, if it please you. On behalf of my father." He turned then, and strode away. But Njála had seen the bright glint of tears returning to his eyes as he did so, and she did not begrudge him his abruptness.

Tryggvi walked to a high spot overlooking the Althing plain. From there he could observe the daily ritual of the other attendees as they closed their stalls, fed their animals, fetched water from the river, and settled in for the evening. The end of the Althing was still several days away, but some of the convivial atmosphere had already dissipated. The last night would be full of rousting and drinking, but this evening was still and quiet. There were a few men sitting and talking around outdoor fires, but even they turned in as the sun finally dipped below the horizon, where it would tarry for only a few hours before rising again. Tryggvi sat and watched as the sky turned from orange to purple to a deep, rich blue, turning the forms on the plain below it to featureless, jumbled shapes.

Tryggvi remained there even as the last lingering activity died down, as the fires were extinguished, and a chill wind nipped through the air. Off in the distance, the occasional flash of lightning illuminated the plume of ash rising from the ground, but no thunder reached his ears. Tryggvi thought of how, when he was small and still scared by the crash of thunder, his father would tell him that it was the mighty Thor who sent the lightning to earth, while fighting great battles in the clouds above on behalf of Asgard and Midgard. Tryggvi wondered suddenly how the Christians explained lightning, if they did not believe it came from Thor. He pulled his cloak around himself, and wondered what he would tell his own children, if he ever had any.

He sat there until the darkest part of the summer night came on, when there was still just enough light for Tryggvi's eye to catch movement down near the booths below. There was a figure creeping across the plain. He watched it skulk from one side of the camps to the other. Tryggvi had not seen where the figure had come from, did not even know how long it had been lurking about below him. But as he looked closer, he swore he caught a shock of platinum hair in the moonlight, and guessed as to its identity.

Tryggvi could not imagine what Haraldr might be up to, and he did not particularly care. The important thing was that Tryggvi might not get another chance to confront the unpleasant boy who had insulted him and caused his horse to be injured, and whose father had gotten Tryggvi's outlawed.

Sneaking down from his place on the high rock, Tryggvi circled around the camp grounds to approach Haraldr from behind. He found the boy pressed against a booth, apparently attempting to hear inside. Tryggvi did not recognize the booth, but he could only imagine that Haraldr was up to no good.

Moving quietly to the other side of the hut, Tryggvi pressed his own ear against the earthen wall. Inside he could hear a low murmur of a man's voice. He could not make out distinct words, but something about the man's speech made his blood run cold. Within seconds, Tryggvi was certain he did not wish to know what was happening within the booth, or to hear any more of the strange, low chanting. He turned to leave, wishing only to get back to his own booth and the warmth of its fire as quickly as possible.

As he turned, Tryggvi saw a flash of starlight, and felt a tug at his upper arm. Confused, he looked up to see Haraldr standing in front of him. The boy had a wild grin on his face, and clutched a small dagger in front of him. No sooner had Tryggvi seen it than he felt a searing pain in his arm, and felt the blood begin to soak into his tunic where the blade had sliced him.

Haraldr raised the knife to strike again. Not pausing to think, Tryggvi leapt backwards, and Haraldr's swinging strike swept past where Tryggvi's head had been. Instinctively, Tryggvi bolted forward, driving his shoulder into Haraldr's torso. The momentum of the tackle carried them both into the side of the booth, denting the wall with their bodies. As they rebounded and fell to the ground, Tryggvi could hear confused shouts from within.

He landed on top of Haraldr, knocking the wind out of both of them. Haraldr's grip remained on the dagger however, and he brought it down hard at Tryggvi's back. Tryggvi sensed the movement, and turned himself slightly, managing to block Haraldr's descending forearm with his shoulder. The knife still dealt a shallow wound across Tryggvi's shoulder blade, and he gasped in pain. He reared up, gripping his thighs around Haraldr's waist, knocking the boy's arms open. Tryggvi gripped Haraldr under the chin, pushing up on his jaw, steadying himself, and with his other hand managed to grasp Haraldr's flailing arm at the wrist.

The wounds in Tryggvi's arm and shoulder throbbed with pain, and his hand was already sticky with blood. Haraldr still gripped the knife in the hand that Tryggvi grasped, and was able to bend his wrist just enough to jab the point of the blade into the meat of Tryggvi's hand between thumb and index finger. Tryggvi's hand spasmed reflexively, and loosened at Haraldr's wrist enough for the boy to pull his arm free and draw it back to strike again.

Panicking, Tryggvi shoved himself away from Haraldr as hard as he could. His only leverage was the hand still wrapped around the other boy's neck. He felt something give beneath his grasp, and the dagger fell from its arc towards Tryggvi's face. Haraldr's hands flew to his neck, clawing at Tryggvi's hand even as he retracted it.

Tryggvi watched helplessly as Haraldr struggled to breathe. Then strong arms gripped him from behind, flung him off of Haraldr and to the ground. Tryggvi looked up to see a man standing over him. His black garments and the large silver cross around his neck identified him as a priest. After a moment of both of them staring at each other mutely, Tryggvi realized he recognized the man.

Tryggvi rolled, and looked over to see the priest bent over Haraldr, evidently trying to help him. "His throat..." Tryggvi tried to explain, but the words would not come. It was as if he were watching the scene from behind himself, as if he could see himself on the ground, spattered in his own blood, watching Haraldr gasp in front of him, the priest bent over him like a great black raven.

In a rush of images, Tryggvi saw what would happen. He would be called before the Althing, and he would explain what had happened, that Haraldr had attacked him, that it had all been a terrible accident. They would believe him, but there would still be consequences, of course. He would be outlawed, like his father, though only for a term of three years, a lesser outlaw. He and Kveldulf would be forced to leave Iceland. They would travel to the continent together, have great adventures, and find some way to restore their honor and good fortune. Perhaps they would even remain abroad, make some new land their home. It would be alright. But first he had to find his father, and Gunnar. They would know what to do.

These thoughts flew through Tryggvi's head as he stood and turned towards Gunnar's booth. He could still hear the priest whispering furiously behind him, but he paid no attention to this. He had to get back, back to the warm hearth, back to his father. He would know what to do. He would know what to do.

Tryggvi had made it seven strides when he felt arms around him yet again. Again, a flash of reflected light, and Tryggvi felt a great thump upon his chest, like he had been kicked there by a skittish horse. He looked down to see a fist set upon his breast. It grasped a hilt of dark burnished wood. As he watched, the hand pulled away from him, and Tryggvi felt an odd tugging sensation as the blade slipped out of his ribcage.

An icewater cold spread through his torso, even as hot blood pumped down his chest and stomach, soaking his tunic. His slayer still held him close, and whispered something in his ear, but Tryggvi could not understand what he was saying. Then the man released him, and Tryggvi collapsed to the soft turf of the Althing plain.

As his heart's blood seeped into the ground, Tryggvi's thoughts were filled not with pain or terror, but with confusion, even indignation. This was not how things were supposed to go, not for him. He had seen it otherwise, just a moment before. No, this was not right at all. And who would take care of Orri, if not him? It was wrong, all wrong.

The night grew winter-dark. Then there was nothing at all.

Chapter 8

Kveldulf woke with a ringing in his head. Groggy from drink, it took several moments for the sounds outside the booth to intrude into his consciousness. He was yawning when he finally heard the urgency of the shouts coming from outside. Bolting up, he saw movement in the corners of the booth as the others awoke, and he saw Gunnar and Njála stirring.

Kveldulf stumbled to the door, then out of the booth. The low sun on the horizon told him it was still very early in the morning, but the brightness of the light still hurt his eyes. Gunner and Njála were fast on his heels, and they all squinted against the glow, watching others emerge from their booths. The shouting was coming from the eastern edge of the camp area, and everyone started heading that way.

One by one, they stopped short when they came upon the scene. Vigi Haraldsson was stomping across the Althing, grasping a bloody garment in each hand. "My son has been attacked!" he cried. "Vengeance! Vengeance!"

Impossibly, horribly, it was only then that Kveldulf realized Tryggvi had not exited the booth with them. He turned and ran back to Gunnar's hut. His son was not there, and his pallet did not look slept in. But his pack was still there, still filled with supplies for the trip back home. Kveldulf grabbed it unthinkingly, and swung it onto his shoulder.

He must be with Orri. Kveldulf ran to the post where the horses were tied for the night. There was Gauti, proud and strong, staring at him expectantly.

Orri was nowhere to be found.

Without stopping to consider the decision, Kveldulf untied Gauti from the post and swung himself onto his bare back. He rode hard around the Althing plain once, looking for any sign of his boy or his horse. Then, finding nothing, he did the only other thing he could think to do, and turned northwest, to follow the route they had taken from Brauðavatn, a few days and an age ago.

Kveldulf found Orri several hours later, wandering in an open field. As soon as he saw the horse, he knew his son was dead. Tryggvi's deep blue cloak had been secured to the horse's back, clasped around his neck, and it was stiff with dried blood. Tryggvi's or Haraldr's, Kveldulf could not say, and it did not matter. To see the horse and the cloak without their owner present could only mean one thing, could only confirm what Kveldulf had felt in his heart from the moment he realized Tryggvi was not in the booth.

Despite himself, despite knowing that Tryggvi would not have fled the Althing, even if he had somehow killed Haraldr, Kveldulf had allowed himself to hope. This hope left him now, flowed out of him like blood from a severed limb. He fell off his horse, fell to the ground, beat his hands against the earth until his fists were scratched and bloody. When he could take this no longer, he let out a great cry, which echoed across the open space.

Orri bolted again. Kveldulf watched him run, then pulled himself up, and back onto Gauti. He rode after his son's horse, wind whipping the tears from his eyes to dash on the rocky ground.

The Althing plain verged on chaos. Within minutes of Kveldulf's departure, word had spread through the entire encampment that a goði's son had been brutally attacked. True, the boy was clinging to life, drawing air through a wounded throat, but it seemed only a matter of time.

Back at his booth, Gunnar spoke with his bændr and thingmenn. "We must find Kveldulf and Tryggvi, if we can. A meeting of the goðar has been called for this afternoon, and surely suspicion will fall upon the Brauðavatn men then, if it somehow has not already. I do not know what will happen then, but I want us to find them before anyone else does. I would go myself, but I must represent at the council.

Thorkel, Thorsteinn, search for them. And Gisli, you will escort my daughter and Guðrun back to our farmstead."

Njála, who had been watching this all in pained silence, spoke up then. "Father, no! I must know what happens, what will happen to Tryggvi and Kveldulf."

"Trouble has come to the Althing, Njála, and more is brewing, I would not have you here when it strikes."

Njála opened her mouth, defiant, but Gunnar cut her off.

"And I need someone to make sure everything is well back at the farm. There is a damned mountain exploding to the east, maybe more than one, and I am concerned for your mother, for the others there, and the animals. I know you can manage seeing to them yourself in my stead.

Njála's mouth snapped shut. Even if it was also a pretext to get rid of her, this was still no small thing, her father trusting her to watch the farm, and she knew he was sincere in his trust in her.

"I will go, then. But you must send word or return yourself as soon as you know more."

"I promise. Now, without further delay, grab your things and prepare to ride. I will see you as soon as this mess is straightened out and I can get away." He considered. "You can wait at the booth until I return later in the day, if you'd like, but after that you must go with Gisli."

He turned from her. "Now, men- we must confer."

ᚠ ᚱᛚ ᚢᚠ ᚤᚠ ᚱᛚ ᚢᚠ ᚤᚠ ᚱᛚ ᚢᚠ ᚤᚠ ᚱᛚ ᚢᚠ ᚨ

Kveldulf followed Orri across the rocky plains and down into the last valley along the Althing path. Orri finally stopped here, near the dilapidated cabin at the darkest part of the valley, away from the path. Kveldulf dismounted from Gauti, and approached Orri slowly. His heart ached to see the horse without its rider, but he knew that ache would be even worse if Orri was not returned safely to Brauðavatn. It was all he could permit himself to focus on, lest his grief and his growing thirst for vengeance overwhelm him. Making soothing noises, he got within arm's reach of the horse, reached out to touch its mane, and though the horse shied away from him once, twice, he was finally able to calm it enough to hold onto it. Taking the rope that had tied Gauti to his post, Kveldulf secured Orri to an old hitch next to the abandoned farmhouse. He could not bring himself to touch the cloak on Orri's back, not yet. Instead he retrieved Gauti, walked him back to the other horse. No sooner had he done so than the storm which had been threatening for hours finally broke. Fat drops hit the earth, and a wind rose up that drove them sideways. Lightning crackled across the sky then, and the first peal of booming thunder made the horses neigh in distress.

Kveldulf tried to get the horses into the relative shelter of the abandoned building, but they would not enter no matter how he cajoled. With no other option, Kveldulf coaxed them as close to the adjoining hillside as he could, tied them to a beam of the house there, and entered the remains of the home himself. The thunder was getting closer, and Kveldulf could only hope the horses would be alright, out in the elements.

The interior of the farmhouse was surprisingly dry, and despite the grass growing along the floor and through the slats of the walls, part of the roof remained intact. The remains of a bench lay against one wall, broken in half, with mushrooms growing out of the rotted wood. Nothing else remained in the house to indicate who had owned it, or why it had been abandoned. It was unusual to find completely abandoned property, at least in this area of the country. But the valley was not ideal for settlement, and Kveldulf supposed the entire area had long been deserted. It was odd not to know the story, but Kveldulf assumed someone who lived nearby could tell him. It occurred to him that he had never asked, never really even wondered, despite riding past the farm at least once a year for most of his life.

On the heels of that realization came another. He could not approach the people in this region, or any other, to ask the story of the lonely farm. He was an outlaw now, a vargulf, a man outside the bonds of society. Anyone he approached would be obligated to kill him on sight, should they know or ascertain his identity. And when Kveldulf was finally killed, as he almost certainly would be, there would be no one to carry on his name or his memory, for his only progeny was dead.

He had nothing left in him, even to cry. Kveldulf numbly pulled a horse hair blanket from Tryggvi's pack, and spread it on the ground. He curled up on it, wrapped it tight around him. Long ago, when he was another man, he might have prayed. But here in this hovel, a fissure opening in his chest, Kveldulf had little faith that any god would listen to him, honor any request he might make. So Kveldulf did not pray. He listened to the wind howling through the valley outside the hut, to the rain and thunder as they passed over. Finally, in time, he slept. And, in time, he dreamt.

Chapter 9

The city was crowned in gold. It gleamed from the rooftops and parapets, dazzling the eye and stirring the soul. It glinted on the hair and bodies of the people in the streets, mingling with other colors, azure, crimson, jade, making the streets and bridges glimmer like shifting rainbows.

Kveldulf hadn't even stepped off the ship yet, and he never wanted to leave this place. Beside him, his friend Hrolf gave a low whistle. The docks alone held more riches than either man had seen in his life. Had either of them realized the value of the spices and crates of preserved fruits being unloaded in front of them, they might have grabbed all they could carry and made a run for it right there.

Perhaps this was why Hrolf's uncle met them at the boat's landing, or perhaps it was because Einar knew the dangers the city held between the docks and the gates of the Imperial palace. Or perhaps he merely wanted to see the looks on the faces of his young nephew and his friend as they gazed upon Constantinople for the first time.

Within a month the city began to lose its luster for them, as Einar had known it would. The gold faded into the background as the grime and the smells of the city became oppressive the boys, who before had known only the pristine waters and clear air of home. Kveldulf and Hrolf both took ill for a time, writhing in misery, their senses assaulted by the unfamiliar food, the constant din, the press of humanity all around them.

Before this, though, there had been another exciting experience for the boys, as they were introduced to the Varangian Guard, Einar's cohorts. This host of men- Rus, Swedes, the odd Frank or Saxon- were warriors of renown, sworn to personally protect the Emperor. And Kveldulf and Hrolf were here to join their ranks.

By the end of the first year, Kveldulf's skill at arms had grown such that he was the equal of any man in the Guard. Hrolf was not as good with weapons, but he was large and imposing, and this counted for much. Both men, fed on rich Mediterranean fare and far from the frigid winters that kept their countrymen inside for half of the year, had grown muscular and formidable in a way not often seen at home on the island. And they had earned the trust of their companions. Under Einar's watchful eye, they behaved honorably, avoiding the whoring and drunken brawling that occasionally brought shame or sickness to others of the Guard, and more than enough young men their age. They had shown their mettle in battle, for the Guard was often engaged in military strikes and missions at the Emperor's bequest. Yet the boys had also proven to be fair-minded and adept at persuading others to their point of view, without resorting to violence. Surely this was because Kveldulf and Hrolf, kinsmen now as much as companions, counseled each other well and kept a united front.

On an excursion in Thrace, Kveldulf witnessed a drunken guardsman attempt to ravage a woman. Before Kveldulf could intervene, she managed to wrest herself from the soldier's embrace, grab the spear he had set nearby, and run him through with it. The commotion attracted other guards, including Hrolf and Einar. Kveldulf quickly explained what had transpired, as the woman stood staring at the men defiantly, spear still in hand, awaiting her doom with a sneer.

Yet Kveldulf praised her skill with the spear. She had finally shown Hjorgur how to use his weapon properly, he said. After a shocked moment, Hrolf had laughed, and then others laughed as well. Einar reminded them all that it was forbidden to attack women in such a way, and that Hjorgur- never the most popular or respected of guardsmen- had brought his fate upon himself. Rather than kill or capture the Thracian woman, they decided to give her Hjorgur's arms and finery, and sent her on her way, with an apology. Perhaps some of the men thought it the Christian thing to do, but Kveldulf and Hrolf and some of the others silently bid the woman go with Frigg's blessing, thinking of their own strong mothers and sisters.

This story, retold throughout the Guard with no small assistance and some light emendation by Einar, brought both Kveldulf and Hrolf unexpected acclaim. Any man could kill, but to refrain from killing, to recognize higher principals, was a characteristic not often accredited to the Varangian Guard.

Perhaps this is why both Kveldulf and Hrolf were selected in their second year of service to accompany some of the Emperor's advisors on a mission to Kiev, far to the north. The Guard had been sent there before, years earlier, to assist the Kievan Rus in quelling some internal violence, and to bring the pagan city fully into the light of Christianity.

It was a story often told amongst the Guard. Vladimir, the prince of Kiev, wished to leave the ways of his pagan ancestors behind. He searched for a new religion to establish in Kiev, one which would unite the people of the land.

In his search, Vladimir consulted first with Muslim emissaries to his lands. They spoke of the grace of Allah, the eternal light shone by his prophet Mohammed, the struggle all men must face within themselves and the world without in order to attain the joys of heaven. Vladimir was intrigued, but after investigating further, he proclaimed that any religion requiring abstention from alcohol was not suitable for the people of Kiev, for drinking was a great joy of the Rus, and they were not inclined to go without.

Next, Vladimir met with Jewish envoys. Reluctantly, they spoke of wisdom from ancient times and ways of survival, of the coming of a great savior who would heal the world. Vladimir recognized the potential in much of what he heard, but he questioned the wisdom of following such a capricious god, who would allow his holy city to fall into the hands of foreigners, his people to be scattered. And although Vladimir had great confidence in his authority and powers of rhetoric, he suspected that convincing the men of the region to circumcise themselves in devotion to any god, Jewish, Muslim, or otherwise, was beyond the scope of his abilities; he wasn't exactly keen on the idea himself.

Vladimir met with his boyars then, and after consulting with them
he decided to send envoys to study the religions of the neighboring lands, to bring back news of the ways of worship there. He sent men to visit the Bulgars of the Volga. They returned to report that there

was no joy among these people, only sorrow and, they claimed, a great stench. He sent men west, to visit the great Christian churches in the Frankish lands. They returned to tell him that the churches were gloomy, that there was no beauty there. He sent men far to the north, to see the ways of the mysterious peoples who lived beyond the boundaries of any named kingdom. These men did not return at all.

But one man returned from the lands to the south, from Constantinople, the city straddling the narrow pass between two seas. There, he said, he and his companions had viewed the high holy rituals in a church of such surpassing beauty that they could not say whether they were in heaven or on earth, and he struggled for the words to describe it. He also affirmed that the rituals had incorporated wine, and that, to his knowledge anyway, the men of that faith were permitted to retain their foreskins.

Thus did Vladimir decide to reach out to the Emperor of Byzantium, to see what might be done about establishing the religion of the Byzantine Empire within the far realm of Kiev. As it happened, the Emperor was dealing with some troubles of his own, and in desperate need of friends like the prince of Kiev. The two powerful men negotiated an exchange: Vladimir would send six thousand warriors to the south to form the Emperor's personal guard, and in return the Emperor would provide the resources needed to help convert the people of Kiev to the Christian faith. Thus were relations between Kiev and Constantinople realized, and the Varangian Guard created.

The Varangians had assisted their powerful masters in maintaining order and spreading the word of Christ for several years, including missions to Kiev to assist the Emperor's long-time ally. Now, Kveldulf and Hrolf learned, they were called for yet again. Despite Vladimir's sincere efforts, a current of pagan worship continued to flow through the princely city, like ground water slowly seeping into the foundations of a home.

So Kveldulf and Hrolf traveled with a contingent of men to the northern capitol, to shore up the foundations of Christianity there. It was, as always, a somewhat ironic endeavor for the Varangians to take on so explicitly, as opposed to their primary duty of guarding the person of the Emperor. All of the men had been baptized upon entry to the Guard, and some had taken to the faith with surprising passion. The old gods were not often known to answer prayers, and some men felt the Christian god made a better offer. Most of the men, however, kept the gods of their homelands close to their hearts. They fought in a foreign land with foreign customs, but these men were warriors, and the White Christ did not impress many of them as a god for warriors. Kveldulf and Hrolf had barely paid attention to the words and promises of their baptism, knowing from Einar and the others that these were merely gestures to appease their new employer, that hardly anyone cared if they took them seriously so long as they fought well and truly.

The journey to Kiev took the cohort through unfamiliar lands with strange peoples, and most were glad to reach the city walls. They were escorted to the palace of the prince, and welcomed by Vladimir personally as "true brothers in Christ." They were given strong drink and roasted boar, and then Vladimir explained the details of their mission.

In his misguided youth, the prince, God forgive him, had sought to reintroduce the old ways of his people to the land, had encouraged his subjects to worship as their forefathers had. He had even built an altar to the father of their gods, a great graven image carved into a wide tree trunk and set on a hill overlooking the city, surrounded by effigies of the lesser gods. For several years, the visage of mighty Perun the Thunderer had looked out over the towers and wooden streets of Kiev. Vladimir had hoped by these means to unite his people, much as he had heard Earl Haakon of Norway had done. And for a time, it had worked. Under the aegis of the god of their father's father's fathers, the people of Kiev had found common ground and common purpose, and their prosperity had grown. True, his studies of the old religion had uncovered some rather unsavory practices, and Vladimir had been careful to exclude these from the reconstituted religion. But even so, it seemed that Kiev enjoyed some measure of divine favor.

Then the disappearances started. It began with the occasional pauper petitioning the court, claiming that a young child or elderly relative had gone missing. Such incidents were not entirely unusual in a city the size of Kiev, but at some point the prince and his boyars began to notice an increase in their frequency. Then the children of a well-known merchant all disappeared from their beds one night. Next it was the maiden daughter of a nobleman. It became difficult to deny that there was something sinister at work in the city. Finally, one of Vladimir's own young cousins, a ward of the court, had gone to use the facilities one night and never returned. The pain in Vladimir's voice as he related this part of the story was obvious to even the most obtuse of the Varangians.

At first, Vladimir explained, no one was quite sure of what to do. No struggle seemed to have occurred in any of the cases, and no notes had been left or messages of ransom received. The people had simply disappeared. Homes were searched, questions were asked, but the best minds of the court and its home guard were utterly perplexed.

Finally, the daughter of a minor court retainer was lying in her bed one night, by chance just falling to sleep in the wee hours, when she thought she heard someone slip into her room. She heard soft footsteps approach her bed, and sat up suddenly to see if someone was there. As she did so, a cudgel thumped into her pillow, just where her head had been. The girl screamed, and thrust out with the sharp dagger she had been sleeping with for protection, catching the shadowed figure in the stomach.

The girl's brothers and father rushed into the room, and there they found, bleeding on the floor, a man they all recognized: Czernai, self-proclaimed first priest of Perun. He had come from the east some years before, with his sons, begging entrance to the city where, he had heard, they were trying to reestablish worship of Czernai's own god. He had somehow managed to talk his way into an audience with the prince, and impressed Vladimir with his erudition, his passionate rhetoric, and his knowledge of the elder gods. He had become a fixture of the court for a time, advising

Vladimir on the finer points of Perun worship, and personal spiritual matters.

Czernai's eccentricities and religious demands soon began to grate on Vladimir however, especially when the old wanderer started darkly suggesting that more should be done to appease Perun. Vladimir began to distance himself from Czernai, and eventually stopped calling him to the palace altogether. There had been no dramatic split, and Czernai's knowledge of the old ways was undeniable, so when it was clear he had lost Vladimir's ear he and his sons were still able to make a living selling relics and charms to the more devout or superstitious residents of Kiev. For the most part they kept a low profile, which had been a relief to the prince.

Now it seemed, however, that Czernai had simply chosen to serve his god as he pleased, with or without royal endorsement. The royal guard searched Czernai's house, and made a grisly discovery behind the family hearth-altar. There, in a hidden alcove, they found a number of skulls, the marks of hammer blows showing clearly on bone that had been boiled clean.

The guard apprehended two of Czernai's strapping young sons, not without some struggle. They brought them before Vladimir, along with Czernai, bleeding but not yet dead. The priest freely admitted to taking all of the missing persons, at times assisted by his sons, bashing their heads in with a hammer, then separating the heads from the bodies. The heads he kept in his altar, and the corpses he said he dumped in the Dnieper, to drift away from Kiev. Thus did he and his family worship Perun, the Hammer-Lord, the Thunderer in the Stone Sky.

Vladimir ordered the three men beheaded immediately. Each of them met his fate without speaking a word of repentance or begging for mercy, and their final looks of pure hatred lingered in Vladimir's mind. He might have dismissed Czernai as violently misguided in his interpretation of the god's wishes, might have continued the popular forms of worship. But Vladimir had been unnerved by the true devotion Czernai and his sons had shown, had sensed the ancient truths in their words and ways. Perun was a bloodthirsty god. And as much as Vladimir wished to blame Czernai for all of the disappearances, his men had found only a half-dozen skulls within the hidden altar. Another dozen individuals had gone missing, at least. Vladimir could not discount the possibility that Czernai had convinced others to take up his ways. So too was he was keenly aware that Czernai's youngest son had not been found and captured. Before the situation developed further, he would have to do something drastic. So Vladimir's men tore down the monument to Perun on the hill overlooking the city. The prince denounced Perun as a false god, and swore he would find another deity, a more appropriate protector for the people of Kiev.

Thus did Vladimir begin the spiritual search which lead to his great alliance with Byzantium. And, he explained to the Varangians now in his court, he knew this alliance had served both of their peoples well, and shown the greater glory of God. Yet, he admitted, not everyone in Kiev had been willing to give up the worship of their ancestral gods so easily. Perun had been popular, and most people knew nothing of the dark worship which had occurred within the city. Vladimir did not want to popularize Czernai's beliefs, nor make a martyr of the man, so the sudden official shift away from Perun had taken many of his subjects by surprise. Despite himself, Vladimir had decided to tolerate the occasional slipped oath or concealed icon, in the name of facilitating unity and preventing discord. And so, for many years, all had been well.

However, in the past year, unusual disappearances had begun in Kiev once again. Czernai and his sons had been dead for nearly a decade, and his surviving progeny had not been seen within the city since then, so Vladimir was unsure of what to think. He tasked some of his most trusted men with discretely investigating these disappearances, and what little they had discovered was troublesome, but not particularly useful. No bodies or evidence of foul play had yet been found. However, discrete and random searches of homes in the city had uncovered a number of items and icons-- stylized hammers, carved figurines, and the like-- suggesting that the baptism of Kiev had not suppressed the worship of Perun as effectively as Vladimir had hoped. There was nothing connecting any of these objects, or their owners, directly to the disappearances.

Nor was possession of the objects a crime in itself, although it was certainly frowned upon. But the presence of such items had been much more widespread than Vladimir had anticipated.

Vladimir found himself in a delicate position. The disappearances were causing social unrest, and a pallor of fear was once again falling over the city. There was reason to suspect that Perun-worshippers might be to blame once again, but no solid leads had presented themselves. Vladimir had no reason to think that anyone possessing Perun iconography was involved, but he could not rule out the possibility that some of them were. In this case, he said darkly, he did not know who he could trust.

So he had asked Emperor Basil to send a contingent from Constantinople. Ostensibly they were there to further secure ties between the two principalities. Yet they also provided Vladimir with a cohort of warriors he could trust, lest any of his own people prove to be traitors in the name of Perun. He left this last part unspoken, but it was well understood by those present.

The 30-odd visiting members of the Varangian Guard took this information in impassively. There were used to missions with tricky political undertones, and occasional secrecy, and for the most part were not particularly interested in these aspects of their work. Men joined the Guard for prestige, adventures, and plunder, and so long as these were supplied they were generally not concerned with the bureaucratic details.

Kveldulf and Hrolf, however, were still less experienced than most of the other men in this select group, and so had stronger reactions to the details of their assignment. Hrolf was visibly disappointed that their mission was so open-ended, with little opportunity, it would seem, to gain further riches or renown. As the cohort retired for the evening, he grumbled to Kveldulf, wondering how long they would be expected to stay in Kiev, waiting for the king to control his own subjects.

Kveldulf, for his part, was more intrigued than his companion. He rarely followed the myriad courtly intrigues of Constantinople, but this mystery had some blood in it. Kveldulf had come across many different strange faiths in his time with the Guard, starting with the faith he had been obliged to ostensibly adopt upon joining up, though it held little sway upon his northern heart. Yet he had never before heard of this Perun, and wondered what sort of god he was. The talk of thunder and hammers made him think of Thor.

Kveldulf was also much more interested than Hrolf or his other fellows in exploring Kiev. He had heard, before they left Constantinople, that this land had been settled by Northmen, in the time of his father's fathers, and this intrigued him. The day after the Guard arrived, when it became clear that at present there was little for them to actually do, the guardsmen spread through the city in small groups, getting a feel for the lay of the land and allowing the locals to become accustomed to their presence. Kveldulf found it was different sort of place from either the Mediterranean cities or the Icelandic settlements with which he was most familiar, the difference marked most clearly by the wide streets of the city, paved in wood, of all things. There was in general a great deal of wood, from the streets to the homes to the churches, nearly as dazzling to one from tree-scarce Iceland as the great stone buildings of Miklagard. Hrolf did not warm to the place, spending most of the day sulking about how boring it all was, but Kveldulf felt a sense of curiosity that was not shared by any of his brothers in arms.

That evening the groups of guardsmen returned to the royal keep, where they were well fed and entertained, though the king himself did not make another appearance. The next day was spent in much the same way as the first, as was the day after that, and so the days stretched on into weeks. Sometimes Vladimir would dine with them in the evenings, perhaps suggesting an area of the city they might visit, people they might talk to, things they should look for. But Kiev was not so great a city that it took the guardsmen long to canvass it in whole, and soon Hrolf's was not the only voice that could be heard complaining about the drudgery and monotony of their current mission. Kveldulf resisted the urge, out of some contrarian impulse as much as anything else, but the allure of newness was wearing thin even for him. Vladimir, for his part, seemed happy that the Guard's presence appeared to have put a halt to the disappearances, and he did at least keep them well fed. But after two months, even the most stoic of the Guard began to openly question how long they would have to stay there, with so little to do.

Then, in the ninth week of the Guard's stay in the city, one of the men did not return to the palace for the evening meal. The Varangians had grown lax over the long, eventless weeks, and had stopped travelling in groups at all times, so no one had seen the man since he had left the palace that morning.

At first there was not particular cause for alarm, but when the man still had not returned by late the next morning, the Guardsmen began to wonder if something was amiss. The daily patrols uncovered no sign of him, though careful questioning of the townspeople indicated that he had last been seen, it seemed, leaving a tavern he had stepped into for an early ale.

When the man still failed to return to the keep that evening, the notion of his desertion was discussed, and just as quickly discarded. After discussing the matter with Vladimir, the senior members of the Guard informed the others that they would have to consider their comrade's disappearance related to the string of disappearances that had brought the Guard to the city in the first place.

Thus was the Guard finally inspired to get to the root of the mystery. With the prince's permission, the Guard began to actively search homes. Vladimir and his boyars taught the men to recognize Perunic totems, and where these were discovered, the inhabitants of the home were interrogated. Most of them were quite compliant, explaining that they had kept the objects out of habit or forgetfulness, but that they were good Christians at heart, and anyway knew nothing about the missing Varangian or any of the other disappearances. The majority of those brought for questioning were old and frail, and there was little reason to doubt their excuses. Still, the figures and relics of the god were confiscated wherever they were found, and burned in a pyre a safe distance from the wooden structures each night.

Kveldulf personally helped gather and burn some of these objects. He was struck each time by the odd familiarity they held to the relics of his own home, his own people. The small statues they found of Perun, bolts of lightning in one hand and a hammer in the other, would not have looked out of place in a Norse home dedicated to Thor, save that the symbols carved into them were unrecognizable. If others felt this similarity to their own people's native god, they were wise enough not to mention it, and Kveldulf did not even ask Hrolf about it. Hrolf, for his part, seemed relieved to have something to do, and he took to rounding up and burning the Perun relics with enthusiasm.

Still, after several days of upsetting elderly Kievans, the Guard was no closer to finding their missing man, or getting to the bottom of the disappearances. Vladimir called all of the families affected by the disappearances into the palace, and had them recount once again the story of their family member's apparent abduction. The only common factor in each case was that no one had seen or heard anything suspicious or useful. The families told of mothers who had gone to market and never returned, of children left at home for a moment who were not there when their parents came to check on them, of grown men who had wandered off for a piss in the night and hadn't been seen since. In one or two cases, a person had simply seemed to vanish from their own home in the dark, the family members sleeping nearby left undisturbed. None of the families could think of any reason why their son or daughter, father or mother had been taken. There appeared to be no common thread between them.

Finally it occurred to one of the Guard captains that while they had found Perun relics in a small portion of the homes in Kiev, they had no information on whether any of the families affected by the disappearances included Perun worshippers. When asked, the families had all denied any association with the cult, but so had all of the people whose homes had yielded up altars and relics.

The next day, the Guardsmen searched the homes of all the families with missing members. None of these searches turned up any statues or relics, which seemed to indicate something, but there was still too little information to say what, exactly. Perhaps whoever took the missing persons had avoided taking secret Perun worshippers, or perhaps it was just chance.

This latest action had made no one happy, and in the following days Kveldulf sensed that the attitude of the Kievans had soured considerably towards the Guardsmen. For their part, the Varangians were growing incredibly tired of this strange city, where they had little to do and had already lost one of their own. After a week with no fresh leads, the missing man was presumed to have met whatever fate befell the other victims of the mysterious scourge.

Despite their thirst for vengeance, or perhaps in deference to it, the Guardsmen were nearly ready to leave the city to its fate. The Varangians were anything but cowards, but this wasn't even a fight they were engaged in, and to a man none of them thought his particular set of skills well-suited unravelling the mystery of the disappearances.

They began to feel something deeply sinister about this place, and even their host. Hadn't Vladimir said that he too once followed this cryptic eastern god? Why could he not offer them more assistance, or even control his own people? Was this why none of the guardsmen on this mission were of the Rus, even though they comprised the bulk of the Guard? Hadn't Vladimir said that he had asked the Guard here because he didn't know whom to trust? Well, who could the remaining Varangians trust?

Hrolf and Kveldulf spent their days discussing the situation, as they patrolled rather aimlessly around the city. They were amongst the youngest of the Guardsmen, and consequently less jaded, less ready to declare it all a wash. But Hrolf made clear that he was with the bulk of the Guard in thinking that their presence served little purpose but to rile up the citizenry. Kveldulf, alone among the Varangians, remained intrigued by the mystery of what was happening in Kiev. He had not known the missing Guardsman terribly well, but his impression of the man had indicated competence and experience. Late at night as he lay on his pallet in the palace hall, Kveldulf considered what none of the other Varangians were willing to admit, at least not aloud: if whoever or whatever was at work in Kiev could make a victim of strong Storun, then perhaps none of them were safe. Since their man's disappearance, Kveldulf had noticed that the men of the Guard never went anywhere in the city without a companion, although there had been no specific orders given to this effect. The men might not be scared, exactly, but they were clearly unsettled.

As was Kveldulf, of course. He had seen many unpleasant things in his time with the Guard, and heard of worse, but this was something different. Whatever was happening in the city made Kveldulf think less of the crimes of passion and opportunistic murders that occasionally occurred in Constantinople, and more of old stories he had not thought of since he was a child, sitting in the hearth at Brauðavatn, listening to his grandfather tell tales of trolls and alvar, of nix and draugar, of the huldufólk who would sometimes creep through the window of a farm at night and kidnap a sleeping inhabitant, replacing him with one of their own. Kveldulf had not believed most of those stories, especially since he had left home and his world had expanded, but this city and its troubles had a touch of the unnatural about them.

Kveldulf replayed in his head everything he knew about the mystery of Kiev. The disappearances had started less than a year ago, as far as anyone could tell, when a young girl had gone to use the outhouse at night and never come back in. Since then, 11 other people had disappeared, including the missing Guardsman. There was no common factor between them that anyone could identify. The missing were young and old, male and female, strong and weak. Some disappeared at night, others in the middle of the day. No one seemed to have seen anything suspicious before any of the victims disappeared, and if any of the missing were known to have enemies, it certainly seemed unlikely that they all would have the same enemy.

Of course, there was the fact that none of the missing people seemed to be Perun worshippers. The search of their homes had yielded no evidence of such, and each of their families had professed to genuine worship of Christ. Perhaps, then, the victims were enemies of the followers of Perun. But this existence of any such actual, organized group was still pure speculation, and based on the owners of the Perunic objects they had recovered and burned, such a conspiracy would consist primarily of the elderly. Kveldulf had seen a man try to beat his elderly mother when a Perun idol had been uncovered among her possessions, and her cowering stance before the Guard pulled him away did not evince a character of preternatural cruelty and cunning.

Really, other than the fact that the city had seen such disappearances before, and that these had been linked to Czernai, priest of Perun, there was little as far as Kveldulf could see to connect the two events. The victims appeared random in both cases, but there were differences. In the prior situation, the disappearances had started with the poor and disenfranchised on the outskirts of town, only gradually moving up in social rank, as if Perun demanded ever more impressive sacrifices. In the present, the first known victim had been from a family of some social standing, and since then the disappearances had largely cut across class lines from person to person.

Also, in the earlier case, many of the bodies had eventually washed up on the shores of the Dnieper downriver from the city- the last of them finally appearing shortly after Czernai and his sons were captured. In the present case, not one body had been recovered.

That, thought Kveldulf, was an interesting distinction. What could have happened to all those people? Whether they were dead or alive, they had to be somewhere. If they had all been dumped in the river, or buried even, surely something would have been found by now. So why had nothing turned up?

And why had no one else been asking this question?

As Kveldulf finally drifted off to sleep one evening, he resolved to bring his queries to the attention of the other men tomorrow.

When he awoke the next morning, Hrolf was gone.

***

The men of the Guard were livid, and Vladimir had an ashen countenance when they confronted him. Another Varangian had gone missing, and this time the disappearance had occurred under Vladimir's own roof. Vladimir had failed to protect guests in his home, and the already tenuous trust between the Varangians and the court of Kiev was now stretched to the breaking point. It was difficult for anyone to understand how a man could be stolen away from the royal household without anyone noticing, unless someone within was complicit. Even then- Hrolf was a young warrior, and strong, and he had last been seen sleeping amongst his comrades. How could he have been taken even with the complicity of the king and all his court, without waking anyone else? Only this question kept the Varangians from making an all-out accusation.

For his part, Vladimir agreed that this event implicated the royal court, and reminded the Guardsmen that it was the suspicions Vladimir harbored against his own closest retainers that had caused him to send for the Guard in the first place. Yet he could not say who he suspected of involvement. He would not submit any of his people to torture to extract confessions, without something to go on beyond insinuations. He promised to have everyone who had been in the hall that evening to swear an oath to Christ that they were not involved in Hrolf's disappearance. It was obvious to all, of course, that such an oath would hardly be binding on a secret Perun-worshipper.

Kveldulf seethed with rage and concern for Hrolf, and had to be restrained from attacking the house guard, then burning the homes of every soul in Kiev until his friend was returned. It was not until late in the afternoon that he calmed down sufficient to remember the question that had been on his mind as he drifted off to sleep the evening before, Hrolf already beginning to snore just a few paces away from him: why had no bodies been found yet?

After discussing the question with the one of the senior Guardsmen, they both requested a private audience with Vladimir. The King was accommodating, and agreed to help them in any way he might be able. He confirmed that in the first round if disappearances, bodies had started appearing on the banks of the river shortly after people began to go missing. Not all of the missing had been discovered, but those that were had the same characteristic blows to the skull, proving they had been murdered. After Czernai had been captured and confessed, it became clear that he or one of his sons had based each of the victim's heads in with a hammer, as a sacrifice to Perun, then dropped the bodies into the Dnieper.

In this case, however, no bodies had been found whatsoever. As respectfully as he was able, Kveldulf asked Vladimir directly whether that struck him as odd.

And so the prince of Kiev, a captain of the Varangian Guard, and Kveldulf the unseasoned warrior spent the better part of an afternoon trying to intuit where a dozen bodies (some of them living, Kveldulf fervently hoped) could have gone without anyone finding them. Many suggestions were raised- could they have been buried somewhere within the city? Perhaps they had been fed to animals? Was there any chance they had indeed been deposited into the river, but not appeared on the shores? Every possibility was seriously considered.

It was Vladimir who finally mentioned the caves. As soon as he did, all present knew that this was where they must look. Later, Kveldulf would wonder how it could have taken Vladimir so long to mention them. Just outside of the city- so close as to practically be a part of it- it seemed there was a series of caverns. These, Vladimir explained, were regarded with fear and superstition by the Kievans, and they were universally avoided. Yet there could be no better place to carry out clandestine business, and perhaps even to conceal bodies.

It was decided then. So, not wishing to waste any more time, the entire cohort of Varangians prepared to go investigate the caves. The day was waning as they trudged out of the city walls towards the low hills surrounding it. Several of the men carried torches. According to Vladimir, no one had willingly entered the caves in generations, and they had no idea what to expect.

So they came to the mouth of the cave, a single hole in the side of a hill, wide enough to allow two men to enter together. The cavern beyond faded quickly into darkness.

Kveldulf insisted on entering first, and the captain, Bruni, entered behind him. Both of them carried torches, with swords unsheathed in the other hand. They stepped into the gloom, and behind them followed the others.

The air of the cave was musty and dank. The torches lit the way enough to walk, but before the men it was as if a curtain of darkness had fallen, and they could merely press against it. The ceiling of the cave narrowed away from the entrance, passing just above the head of the tallest man. The ground was of loose pebbles, and it was impossible to tell whether anyone had recently passed through.

On the men walked, the passage narrowing even further, until they had to stoop. Finally the passage closed so much that they could no longer walk side by side. The captain ordered Kveldulf to walk behind him, and over Kveldulf's protests he took point position. They gingerly made their way forward. Deeper they pushed, one after the other, into the cave. Any light from outside had long since ceased to penetrate the darkness, and if not for the weak light of the torches, the men would have found themselves in a hopelessly black oblivion.

Then, finally, Kveldulf felt a weak waft of air in front of them, and sensed the passage beginning to open up. Tight behind the captain, he made a sharp turn, then stepped out into an open cavern. The torch light flickered on the cave walls, but after a second Kveldulf realized the light came not only from their own torches. There was too much of it. Looking around he saw a pair of iron sconces set into the surprisingly smooth walls, and in each of them, a burning torch.

They were in a circular chamber. Looking around, Kveldulf saw that the ceiling of the chamber had some sort of complex symbol carved into it. It seemed to move in the shifting shadows cast by the torches and the men's bodies. At the far side of the chamber were two additional openings. Wordlessly, almost unconsciously, Kveldulf gravitated towards the opening on the right. Bruni stopped him, and stepped in front. Kveldulf followed, aware of the men behind him. Down they went, and the air grew cool.

Then, ahead, the terminus. The path ended. And Kveldulf stepped forward, through the threshold. In front of him he saw-

Chapter 10

Kveldulf started, suddenly awake in the darkness of the cabin. His heart was racing, but he could not move. He tried to call out – to scream, really – but he could not draw the air to make a sound. A great weight pressed down upon his chest, and his limbs were frozen. He could not even turn his head, could not look away from where his eyes already stared.

There was little light in the cabin, but in the corner opposite Kveldulf, the darkness itself seemed blacker somehow. And it seemed to be moving. Kveldulf, not normally one for panic, was gripped with a terror as deep as any he had known. What was in the corner? He could hear nothing but the light patter of rain on what remained of the cabin roof. Yet the shadow in the corner appeared to be growing, seeming almost to flow upwards from the ground. Kveldulf struggled still to draw breath, and managed finally the tiniest gasp, but the air that hit his mouth and nose was acrid.

Lightning flashed, and for an instant Kveldulf thought he saw a pair of eyes, red-rimmed, glaring, almost glowing with unspeakable fury, there in the corner of the room. He felt a presence, malevolent, powerful, and focusing all of its attention directly on him. Then he was blind.

In that moment, Kveldulf heard movement, and knew he was about to die.

An unearthly scream ripped through the cabin, and the walls shook. There was a great pounding, tearing sound, and suddenly Kveldulf could move his torso. He shot up in the bed, feeling his doom rushing toward him.

But it did not come when anticipated. He squinted his bleary eyes, and saw the head of a great beast thrusting over the cabin threshold. Orri had battered down the ancient door, and was now squeezing himself through the remains of the frame. Foam dripped from his lips, and the wet threads of this thick mane whipped the air as he shook his head, eyes rolling. Then he was in the room.

The horse bit and kicked- Kveldulf could hear his teeth clacking together- but Orri's body obscured Kveldulf's view so that he could not clearly see what it was fighting. Orri was bellowing, and along with his cries Kveldulf thought he could hear another, stranger noise, something between a rasp, a laugh, and a scream.

Kveldulf realized he could move his lower limbs again. He began to pull his legs under him, preparing to stand. As he did so, Orri reared up at something, kicking the air, then turned, and with a great crash, battered through the side of the cabin. After a stunned heartbeat, Kveldulf leapt from his resting place, and ran after the horse.

In the gray light of the night-rising sun, he could see the horse galloping away through sheets of rain, bucking his head as he tried to dismount the formless shape that seemed to grip his back and flanks. There was another flash of lightning then, farther away than the last, and for a moment Kveldulf seemed to perceive a dark form upon the horse. Then Orri left the valley, turning a corner, and Kveldulf could see him no more.

Kveldulf saw Gauti. The horse was wide-eyed with terror. Yellow bile spilled from his mouth, and he was jerking his head erratically from side to side. As Kveldulf watched, the creature blew the air out of its lungs, shuddered, and fell dead to the ground.

Kveldulf approached and knelt by the horse's side. Gauti had been Kveldulf's favorite mount, with him since before his wife had died. At another time, yesterday, when he was a different man, he would have been shattered by Gauti's death, for a while at least. He would have retreated to his bed, pulled the covers over his face, and slept until his body ached and he could sleep no more. But that man was dead, as surely as his son and his wife and his daughter and his horse were dead. That man had been used up, and only the shell of his body remained. Kveldulf Thorbjornsson, father, husband, and free man once, but no more, stood over a dead horse in a dark valley, and filled up with hatred. For the gods, for the world, for the men who had done this to him and his own; but most of all, above all this, for himself.

In the cabin, Kveldulf found Tryggvi's cloak, torn from Orri's shoulders and washed clean by the rain. He wrapped it around himself, and retrieved his remaining supplies. Then Kveldulf turned away from the cabin, and began a mindless trek to the east.

Njála did not know where her father was. He had been called to the council with the other goðar at the Althing, but Njála had seen most of them return to their buðir some time ago. She considered going to look for him, but did not want to risk his returning to the booth and finding her gone, with her things still there. With both Tryggvi and Kveldulf missing, she did not want to cause him any more alarm. She would leave a message with Gisli, who stood sullenly at guard outside, but she didn't think he was likely to take well to her wandering either.

For her part, Njála wasn't sure what she felt. She believed Tryggvi had been angry enough to want Vigi or Haraldr dead, but not that he was foolish or impulsive enough to actually commit murder, especially not in such a dishonorable way, like an assassin in the night. Granted, on balance she could not say she knew the boy that well, really. But she was a pretty, wealthy young woman of marriageable age, in a land full of men who were used to getting what they wanted. She had long ago learned the importance of being a good judge of character, and the actions Tryggvi was accused of did not conform with her judgment of him.

Vigi, on the other hand, gave her a distinctly unpleasant feeling, even at a distance. There was something profoundly distasteful about him, something that had shown through even his obvious and understandable concern over his gravely injured son. She would have to discuss this with her father when he returned- there had been no chance before the meeting, when both of them were still in shock.

And what of Kveldulf? Of the three men- Tryggvi, Vigi, and Kveldulf- it was him she knew best. He had often stayed at her father's farm, and she knew that her father had always trusted Kveldulf, always spoken highly of him. He had been kind to her when she was a girl, and respectful towards her as she became a woman. In the past summer she had noticed the way some of the men gazed at her a little too long, had occasionally sensed an undercurrent when they spoke to her even if she did not always grasp its meaning. But ever since coming to stay in Gunnar's booth at this Althing, Kveldulf had been kind to Njála without her sensing a hint of prurient interest. She knew he had faced great hardship- not that this set him very much apart from any number of other people she knew- yet he did not seem one to lay his burdens on others. More than once Njála had considered that if Tryggvi were to be the sort of man his father was, he would make a fine husband indeed- not to say she was in any rush to be married, to him or anyone else. For the moment, she was happy enough with her life as it was.

And now she felt some shame, for she knew she was avoiding having to consider what had happened to Tryggvi and Kveldulf over the last two days. For all that she tried to be level-headed, to think and act with maturity, Njála could only admit that she did not fully understand the import of what was happening, and it frightened her. Two good men she knew were in considerable trouble, and another boy was dying, and none of it was likely to turn out well for anyone. And beyond that, there was something fell in the air. The volcano, the earthquakes, and now this debacle, at the Althing of all places – somehow Njála felt certain that there was more heartache to come, and that Tryggvi and Kveldulf would not be the last to be tested.

The thought had barely crossed her mind when Gunnar returned to the booth. His fine face looked grimmer than Njála had ever seen it before, and he seemed even to have aged since last she saw him.

"The council took a vote. Tryggvi has been declared a full outlaw, in absentia. Never have I seen such a travesty of justice. Vigi offered no proof that Tryggvi attacked Haraldr, no witnesses. And Tryggvi, not being there, had no opportunity to speak for himself. Moreover, however it looks like things are going, Haraldr is not even dead. There has been no murder yet, only a case of battery. By our laws, this sentence should not have happened, not like this, not so quickly. But Vigi – Vigi brought his son's bloody clothes, and passed them in front of each man, asking who would deny him justice. He brought his priest with him, and went on about how God would punish us all if we allowed such a crime to stand. And then the worst of it – he swore he would seek no blood-vengeance against Tryggvi for what he claims the boy did – that he would forgive him, even. But he argued that Tryggvi's disrespect for the laws of the land and the Althing itself meant the boy must be outlawed nonetheless. The man is a snake."

Njála did not know nearly as much of the law as her father, but she immediately understood what Vigi had done. He had skillfully played on the values and sympathies of all those on the counsel, no matter what their private beliefs or inclinations, by building an argument that would be compelling to any of them, whether they approached the matter from a Christian or a more traditional perspective. He had spoken the language of vengeance, of lawfulness, and of forgiveness, and done it in such a way that even those who realized the arguments did not hold up would be hard-pressed to speak against them.

None of that mattered. "What do we do now?" she asked.

"What can we do? We do not know where Tryggvi or Kveldulf is."

"So you propose we do nothing, Father?"

"Of course not, my dear. But we must tread carefully. This situation would be precarious at any time, but I sense that there is more yet to come. I do not think we know the full story, yet."

"I feel the same way. And... I'm afraid. Not just for our friend, or even for us. But...for everyone."

"We must have faith, Njála. And keep our wits about us."

She surprised herself then. "Will you pray with me?"

The briefest pause. "Of course."

They clasped hands, but they did not kneel.

"Our Father, Who art in Heaven..."

Orri rode over wind-blasted flats, and hell rode upon him. The thing on his back was incredibly heavy, and his legs threatened to give at any moment, but the horse would not stop. He did not understand what was happening, of course- only that he had sensed something foul inside the cabin in the valley, and been compelled to attack it. He had chewed through the post rope, and broken through the wall to confront whatever was coming for his master- one of his masters, for he had not seen his boy since the night before, when he had smelled blood and felt the lash and been forced to run.

An observer who happened to see the horse gallop by might have seen nothing unusual at all, especially if he looked right at him. But if he were tired, or sensitive, or just luckless in some important way, perhaps he would perceive a shape upon the horse's back. Perhaps it would appear as a plume of blackest smoke, or an unnaturally large cat, arched spine, spitting. Or perhaps he would see the bloated form of a man, corpselike, yet animate, gripping the horse's mane with a grimace on its decaying face.

And then he would turn and run, for even the most steel-willed and rational mind is desperate to flee from the sight of the draugr.

The cabin in the valley was left empty for a reason. A man had lived there long ago, and then he had died, as men die. But some part of him, driven by vengeance or fury or simple greed for life, had refused to relinquish the flesh. It had stayed set in the body, growing more crazed and cruel with each passing year, confined forever to the shade of the valley. Until finally, in his own mindless grief and haste to take shelter from the storm, Kveldulf had entered the draugr's home and disturbed it. If not for Orri's intervention, the spirit-corpse would have fallen upon Kveldulf, rending him to shreds with clawed fingers, or throttling him, or poisoning him with its foul breath, for its only joy was bringing misery and death to the living. This draugr had been so long without a victim that no one even remembered why travelers to the Althing hurried through the valley where the moss-covered hut still stood, why they never left the road as they passed by.

Something had broken its bonds now, and the draugr was free. As it tormented the horse in his flight, the draugr reached out with its dire power and shifted the air, so that all around the two of them was rain and dark. It shifted through its forms, attempting to crush the horse, to punish him for attacking it just as it was about to sate its rage on a human victim.

Yet try as the draugr might, it could not kill the horse, nor could it leap from his back. It was as if some power, greater still than the draugr's own, kept it in place, and all it could do was rage against the horse it rode upon. The draugr's fury radiated outwards in cascading waves, spoiling the milk at every farmhouse within a day's ride, and causing two ewes to birth lambs prematurely. But for its purposes, the fiend was impotent.

This mattered little to Orri. That the horse's heart did not give out from fear and exhaustion was a testament to its impeccable pedigree and the care with which he had been raised. When attempting to buck the draugr from his back proved ineffective, Orri began to course northward as fast as he could. He was still recovering from his fight of only days before, and suffering from the fresh wounds his assailant had managed to inflict. Yet some core of strength and purpose in the horse spurred him forward, and kept his heart from bursting with the exertion.

The landscape was gray and barren as the miles of Orri's flight stretched out. Soon the only hints of color were splashes of bright green lichen growing on the faces of rocks and boulders, and the shrieks of the draugr rent the air unimpeded.

There were few signs of travel through these parts, and none of habitation, save that here and there the landscape was dotted with small stacks of stones. Here three flat rocks were placed one upon the other; there a dozen were arranged in a column as high as a man's waist. Neither horse not rider took notice of these- it would be difficult to say what really went through either of their minds in that mad flight- but a glancing blow from Orri's hoof sent one stack tumbling over, scattering stones that had stood unmoved for untold years.

Orri traveled forward in a straight line, until finally his way was impeded by a great boulder, jutting incongruously out of the empty horizon. As the horse and dark rider approached, the rain and gloom that had accompanied their journey suddenly abated, and the cries of the draugr fell silent, though its mouth remained open in a grotesque yawn.

A young girl stepped out from behind the boulder. She wore a simple shift, and her feet were bare, despite the sharp rocks that lay all around. On each arm was a wide woven bracelet, and her hair, black as coal, sparkled here and there with tiny crystal beads. The skin from her shoulders to her wrists was tattooed, covered in intersecting lines of purple ink that formed chaotic patterns. In Uppsala or Daneland, she might have been taken for a shield-maiden in training, for her limbs were well-muscled and her countenance was grimly determined. Yet she could not be entirely mistaken for such a woman, for her eyes were black, like the eyes of a mouse, or a shark.

The girl turned and stood facing the speeding horse and its unnatural rider. When they had come within a spear's throw of the boulder, the girl raised her hand, fingers splayed forward, and closed her eyes in concentration.

The purple lines on her arms flowed towards her wrist, like a river draining into the ocean. The girl opened her eyes as the purple reached her hand, still held out in front of her. The ink began to bleed out from her fingertips, pooling in her palm before diffusing into the air. Then, the ink suddenly shot forward in jagged lines and steep spirals, rushing forward from the girl's hand until they met with the oncoming creatures.

Orri rode right into this flow, and it washed over his brow, splashing over him without leaving a trace on his skin or mane. Yet wherever the ink hit the draugr, it stuck. In the blink of an eye, it flowed across its rotting skin, up its face, into its eyes, nose, and mouth. For a moment the revenant was frozen on Orri's back, a study in violet.

Then the ink began to flow back towards the girl, a painting composed in reverse, and as it flowed backwards it left nothing behind. The dark mass atop Orri swiftly lost all shape, and then there was only a galloping horse with an odd purple cloud hovering in front of him.

The girl made a low humming sound from deep in her throat, and the cloud of ink flowed back to her at the speed of thought, entering her fingertips and flowing back up her arms, coalescing into a new pattern.

Then she raised her other hand, palm up, and pointed it again at the horse, who had not slowed down in the least. But the girl spoke a quick word, and Orri finally slowed. He came to a stop just in front of where the girl stood, unflinching. She stepped forward and stroked his head, looked at his wounds, whispered in his ear.

She turned, and with one hand gently entangled in Orri's mane, walked him back towards the giant boulder. Still whispering reassuringly to the horse, she led him around to the other side of the rock. She stepped forward and pressed a hand against the stone. Then it was as if no one had ever been there at all.

Chapter 11

Sinmara drifted through the rock with purpose, barely taking notice of the slight tingling sensation in her core as she passed through trace deposits of iron ore. She had to hurry, if she were to reach the chamber before the meeting disbanded.

She was in luck. She stepped from the stone portico marking the entrance to the chamber just as the elders stood to leave. Four pairs of eyes turned to her. Before anyone spoke, Sinmara could sense the disagreement lingering in the air, and knew that whatever the elders had been discussing, the meeting had not gone well.

"Sinmara, what is the meaning of this disruption?" asked the woman seated directly to her right, at the closest of the low benches where the elders sat to discuss matters.

"I am sorry to interrupt, Mother...elders."

"It is fine, Sinmara. We were just finishing." This from Calkron, seated at the bench across from the entrance. "Speak your mind, if you would."

"Well, I- I was making my normal rounds along the Farger vein when I sensed a disturbance to one of the cairns above. I went up to investigate, and encountered an unsleeping spirit, riding on horseback straight toward the Killicut gate."

The others in the chamber looked at each other grimly with their black eyes, but did not speak. Sinmara glanced at her mother, who urged her to continue with a nod.

"Well, I absolved it, as I have learned to do. There was such rage in it, and it was attacking the horse- I couldn't wait to deal with it until I could summon one of you. But I didn't know what to do with the horse. It was no spirit-creature, and it seemed the unsleeping one had attacked it."

"Not out of character for one such as that, Sinmara," said wizened old Eltappa, who already had a touch of grey to her hair.

"Yet, but it is unusual for an animal to withstand such an attack, is it not? You know the Farger vein- the horse must have ridden for

91

miles with the unspirit on its back. And then when I approached it..." Sinmara paused, considering her words.

"Yes, Guardian Sinmara?" Fafnon spoke this time. If the others were surprised by his use of the title, they made no indication of it.

"The horse, he- it was as if he asked me for help. I cannot explain it, but as soon as I saw him, I knew I needed to protect him, and to help him."

"Perhaps the unspirit on his back had something to do with that assessment," said Eltappa, not unkindly.

"I am not explaining myself well. I am not certain I can. I just felt that- this horse was special, somehow. Like it was no accident that I found him. It just felt right, especially after I absolved the unspirit. I've never done that before and...it was so easy. So," Sinmara took a breath, "I brought the horse under with me."

"Sinmara! You do not have the right to bring animals, especially human animals, into the warren! You know better than that!" This from her mother.

"Yes, I know, but it felt like...exigent circumstances. And I have left the horse at the outer chambers. I came to ask your leave to take the him further inside. If you would permit me to place him in our stables, I will tend to all his needs. I will make sure he does not stray or cause trouble."

"But, why? Why keep the animal here? What purpose does it serve? You do not lack for companionship, Sinmara." Calkron seemed genuinely perplexed.

"I cannot explain it any better than I already have, and I know how unsatisfactory that must be. But I ask for your dispensation all the same," she looked to Fafnon, as she said this, "to let me look after the animal. I spend more time near the surface than the rest of you, and I see more of the world above." This was bold, perhaps, but largely true. "In my time as a guardian, no one, man or beast, has approached the Killikut gate. Yet the horse and the unspirit were headed right for it. There must be a reason for this, and all I can think to do is keep the horse here, and hope that reason reveals itself. With everything else going on...it just seems important."

The four other fólk in the chamber looked to each other again. Long years of familiarity permitted them to confer with little more than a glance, a turn of the head, a furrowing of the brow.

Fafnon turned to Sinmara. "Very well, guardian. You may keep the horse, for now. Be wary lest it roam, and remember it will need light and food. Do not let its upkeep interfere with your other duties. Now, please leave us." Sinmara nodded respectfully at each of them in turn, ending with her mother, and melted back into the stone portal through which she had come.

As soon as she was gone, Eltappa turned to Sinmara's mother. "It seems it is as we suspected then, Ailuwa." The other elders gathered around Sinmara's mother as she hung her head in quiet grief.

⟡ ⟣⟢ ⟤⟥ ⟣⟢ ⟤⟥ ⟤⟥ ⟣⟢ ⟤⟥ ⟤⟥ ⟣⟢ ⟤⟥ ⟡

Making her way to the corridor where she had left the horse, Sinmara tried to explain to herself what she had been unable to articulate to the elders. Yet even in her own mind, the words failed her. She had not hesitated to destroy the unsleeping spirit- they were vile beings, and she had never before had an opportunity to really use her defensive knacks- but she had also felt drawn to the horse. Perhaps its resilience had moved her. But there was more to it than that. Sinmara had spoken truly- she felt a connection to the beast, and it had calmed immediately in her presence.

Plus, there was the fact that she was able to bring it through the gate with her in the first place. Only after they were through had she realized that the horse should have been unable to enter with her. He had not been raised among her people, nor yet eaten of their food. Yet he had gone right through the rock face as if rockwalking came naturally to him. And inside the warren, he was smaller than above, better able to fit through the passages and portals inside. Sinmara supposed the explanation could reside solely with her, somehow. She had been feeling odd fits and spurts of energy lately, and her encounter with the unspirit had given her a charge. But she had never heard of such a thing. Not that anyone talked too frequently about the practice of bringing creatures into the warren. Perhaps it was not as difficult as she had understood it to be.

Sinmara stepped through the antechamber portal to see the horse licking at some moss on a rock by the edge of the chamber. He seemed thoroughly undisturbed by his present surroundings and the ordeal he had just endured. Sinmara reached a hand out towards the horse, and he nuzzled into it, seemingly expecting her approach. She inspected the wounds on his sides. None looked life-threatening, so far as she understood how horses worked, but they must be painful. "Come horse, let's get you patched up." She laced her fingers through his mane and led him from the antechamber, through the portal, and further into the warren.

They emerged in an oblate cavern with smooth walls, broken by the arch of several portals, and a gently rolling floor. Sinmara continued to find it surprisingly easy to take the horse through the portals; she needed only place a hand on him as she slipped into the mineral state, and the horse would enter rockwalk as well.

The room had a dim glow that bounced off the sheer surfaces of the walls and floor, green light emanating from luminescent mossy patches on the ceiling, blue light shining from bright veins in the walls. Sinmara could recognize that it was not nearly so bright as the full light of day, which she saw more often than most fólk. It was still more than enough light for her to see comfortably, and she hoped the horse could as well. She led him to the far end of the chamber, where there was a small shallow pool, bounded by the wall, and fed from an underground spring. Beside the pool were several thick pads of soft fibrous matter, growing upon the rock in clumps. Sinmara pulled one of these off, and dipped it into the water. She used it to gently clean the horse's flanks, paying special attention to his shallow wounds. The horse was calm as ever throughout these ministrations. He did not shy away at all until Sinmara reached into a small pouch tied at her waist, and pulled out a handful of fine powder, which she applied to his wounds. Then the horse whinnied in dismay, but only for a moment. The healing powder began its work, and with Sinmara's voice in his ear, he soon calmed again.

The treatment ended, Sinmara led the horse through another portal, and into the main chamber of the sprawling huldufólk warren in which she had lived all her life. The fólk were not a numerous people, and their dwellings were of modest scale in some senses, but their abilities permitted them to spread each of their communities over a great subterranean area.

This main chamber consisted of a wide thoroughfare. The walls were hewn smooth from the rock, and arched overhead to form a curved ceiling. Crystalline structures jutted from the curve of the ceiling in regular patterns, fractal forms that glowed with a soft inner light, gently illuminating the floor below.

On either side were rows of portals, demarcated by stylized arches of various sizes etched into the rock, thin bands filled with symbols that started at the floor, spanned upwards, then returned the floor again, enclosing an area of rock within them. There were also open entryways, marking passages that visibly lead to and away from the main chamber.

Sinmara did not really know how any of it worked- rockwalking, the cavern lights, her own knacks, or any of a dozen dozen other features of the world. As she grew and observed, she recognized that the others focused on their own particular talents, favored dream states, how they might tangibly contribute to the warren. Take the elder council: there was Fafnon, who dreamed into insects and spent most of his wake-time ensuring that the structures of the warren remained stable, including the relationships between all the fólk. Eltappa, who dreamed into plants and helped keep the warren fed and clothed. Or her own mother, Ailuwa, who dreamed into birds, and could use her far-sight to keep the warren informed of distant events.

Sinmara was young still, too young to dream into anything as complex as the elders did. But despite her hunger for answers, she found she did not care for dreaming into the minds appropriate for her experience, the various mineral or unicellular consciences and patterns that most of the other fólk dreamed into. And the others did not seem to understand this, did not understand her when she said she preferred the company of her own thoughts within the sleeping bier. She did not wake each day and emerge from her bier excited to apply all she had learned in her sleep. Yet she still was driven to contribute, somehow.

Thus had Sinmara become a guardian. The idea had been Fafnon's. Most of the fólk spent their lives wholly within the warren, where there was no risk of coming into direct contact with anyone or anything not of their people. As a rule, the fólk avoided all interaction with the humans who lived in the surrounding lands. Still, it was considered best for someone to know if any humans wandered into fólkish territory.

The position did not appeal to most fólk, but it did to Sinmara. As a guardian- the only current guardian of her warren, as it so happenedshe would spend her time patrolling the broad borders of the warren's land. She would be the first to know of any human encroachment on their territory, and was responsible for informing the others, so that they might decide what to do about it. And she had been taught by the elders, who knew most of what there was to know amongst the fólk, how to deal with any pressing threats that might arise. Many of the fólk had knack-marks set into their skin to help them perform various tasks, but only Sinmara had been taught to use hers defensively. It pleased her, to know things that the others did not.

However, opportunities to use her skills were extremely few and far between. In fact, there had been no real threats to the warren in living memory. Before today, the most excitement she had encountered in her task was seeing a rider in the far distance while she stood surveying the land around the Killicut gate. Sometimes a ghost or wight would drift by, but never creatures of the dangerous sort like she had seen today. She had heard talk of times when fólk the world over had been under constant threat, but those days were in the dim past, when it had been fólk who walked the face of the land, while men hid in their caves.

In Sinmara's time the role of the guardian was more ceremonial than anything else, especially in a warren such as hers which was fairly distant from human settlements. If the post was occupied at all, it was generally by a fólk who enjoyed the feel of the sun on her face, the wind in her hair, as Sinmara did. The seclusion gave her space to think, to ponder, and she always returned to the warren happier after she had been above.

Walking across the central chamber, she considered whether her feelings towards her position would change, now that she had encountered a real menace. As she entered the open hallway that led to her den, she felt a sudden surge of anxiety. She realized now she had been operating from pure instinct when she confronted the unsleeping spirit. If her knacks or her nerve had failed her, she might have been destroyed by the foul thing, and it would have had no trouble entering the warren. Yet Sinmara, it seemed, had been prepared.

She finally reached her own den, at the far end of a long, downwardsloping hallway, on the left side of the corridor just opposite her mother's. Stepping through the portal into the room, the girl and the horse entered another large chamber, the floor a wide oval, the walls sloping gently inward then flattening into a low ceiling. The floor was covered in a thick mat of clean moss, soothing and familiar under Sinmara's feet. At the top of the room, opposite the portal, was the low mound of earth and grass on which Sinmara made her bed. She was suddenly desperate to get into it, but she turned to the horse first. His smell already filled the chamber, but mixed pleasantly with the fresh green scent of the room, and did not bother her.

She stroked his mane. "You will stay with me for now, friend. We may be a little cramped, but at the moment this is the best place for you. In the morning we shall see about finding you a space of your own. And we shall have to give you a name."

With that the girl turned and fell onto her bed, where she immediately closed her eyes and sank into sleep.

Orri munched experimentally on a bit of the moss carpet, then drifted off into slumber himself.

Sinmara awoke some time later to find her mother standing over her.

"Daughter. We must talk." Ailuwa motioned for Sinmara to sit up and make room on the sleeping mound, then sat down and folded her hands into her lap. Sinmara's mother had long hair which trailed to her waist, framing a slim face only just beginning to show the lines of age and experience. Ailuwa's arms were bare in the simple tunic she wore, and ropy muscles flexed under the skin. She was the youngest of the elders in the warren, and for the first time in her life, Sinmara wondered suddenly exactly how old her mother was. Not all fólk aged in the same way or at a constant rate, which made it nigh-impossible to ascertain anyone's age. Everyone had a general sense of who was older or younger than themselves, though, especially as most fólkish gifts came only with time and experience. Her mother's gifts required much experience indeed.

Sinmara pondered this as Ailuwa let out a sigh, and began to speak again. "As you may have surmised, there is much happening in the land right now."

"I know, mother. The earth shakes. I have seen the smoke in the east. And an unspirit at our door...it is a strange time."

"Yes, well...there is even more to it that you can know." Ailuwa paused, and her daughter looked at her expectantly.

"But I am afraid I cannot tell you everything. Not yet."

Sinmara was used to her mother withholding information. Though she had never doubted that Ailuwa cared for her, theirs was not a close relationship. Her mother was always engaged in business of one sort or another with the other elders, and frequently left the warren for long stretches. The warren was far too small for Sinmara to have had a truly solitary upbringing, and she enjoyed her bonds with the other fólk. But this did not entirely lessen the pain of the distance she felt between herself and Ailuwa.

For some reason, this particular obfuscation made something within Sinmara break, and she released a torrent of palpable frustration that surprised her as much as her mother.

"What do you mean, you can't tell me? What are you even doing here? We have barely spoken for weeks, and now you awaken me only to tell me that you have a secret you cannot share? I am your daughter, and I am a guardian! What is it that cannot be shared with me?"

Sinmara expected her mother to snap back, to speak in anger, and for a moment it seemed she would. But Ailuwa's face remained maddeningly impassive.

"You will know everything I know, when the time is right. But the information is not mine to share." Finally, her face softened. "Although I wish I could.

"I have awakened you because you must come with me, immediately. We must travel to Ásbyrgi, straight away."

A rush of conflicting emotions spread across Sinmara's chest.

"But... I have never travelled that far! And... and I have this horse to watch!" She gestured to Orri, sitting sleepily at the edge of the room; truthfully, Sinmara had almost forgotten her was there, so quiet had he been.

"The horse will come with us. You will need a mount. We will be travelling overground."

"What? But...that is not our way!" Sinmara enjoyed being aboveground, but she had never been more than a few steps away from the gate before. She was not afraid, exactly, but...it was highly unusual.

"And what if we are seen?" The fólk were normally shielded from the eyes of men, but it was well known that this was due as much to inattention as it was to differences in being and perception between the two tribes, and could not always be relied upon. It was even said there were those among men who could always see the fólk, whether they wished to or not.

"We are unlikely to encounter anyone else on our travels. There is little to be done for it in any case. That is the route we must take. And we must leave now."

Ailuwa turned to leave the den. Sinmara opened her mouth to protest, but she recognized the implacable tone in her mother's voice and knew there was no swaying her. Besides, she realized as she regarded her few small possessions, she should be excited. Life in the warren was comfortable, but it could be dull. No one else seemed to feel this way, and Sinmara thought it prudent to keep to herself. But a trip to the capital- a trip aboveground, no less- would surely bring some new experiences. And she still didn't know the purpose of the journey.

Into a woven sack went three of her nicest shifts, a bone comb, several flats of dried mushroom. She walked over to Orri, and with a hand   on   his   back,   led   him   through   the   portal.

Chapter 12

Sinmara met her mother just inside the Killicut gate. Ailuwa was astride a large white ram, twice as large as any reared by the farmers of Iceland. Her platinum hair was wound in tight plaits around her head, to keep it from blowing in the wind. She wore a long robe, kohl dark, and carried a sack filled with food and other supplies. Sinmara knew her mother often traveled, but she had not seen her depart before, and was taken aback at how different she now looked- wiser, somehow. More powerful.

Ailuwa spoke. "It will only take us a day and then some to get to Ásbyrgi. I do not expect it to be a difficult journey. But you must stay on your guard. Do exactly as I tell you, when I tell you, without question. You handled the unspirit remarkably well, but things are different aboveground, and your talents may not come to you as easily the further we get from the warren. And if we see any men- which I don't expect we shall- just ignore them, and it is likely they will not notice you. Do you understand?"

Sinmara nodded. She still had many questions, but there would be time enough for those later. For now, her trepidation had turned to curiosity. She was going to see more of the world in the next few days than she had in all her life thus far.

"Good. Then we are off." She turned her ram towards the gate, and stepped through. Sinmara followed.

The sun shone brilliant on the rocky flats beyond the gate, peeking through pendulous clouds pregnant with rain. Ten paces from the door and Sinmara was in a foreign land. For a moment she was almost painfully overwhelmed by sensation. The sparkle off a smooth surface of stone, the fleeing line of the horizon, the movement of wind through her clothes and against her face, all of these were conspiring to knock her from the horse and leave her curled in a tight ball on the ground.

But the moment passed, and soon Sinmara sat taller. Her mother rode slightly ahead of her, turning her head from side to side to scan the landscape in front of them. Before this day, it had been long since the two of them were alone together. When Sinmara was a child, she had clung to her mother, told her secrets, asked her every question that came to her mind, and Ailuwa had always made time for her. Yet as the girl grew, they had slowly drifted apart. Ailuwa's increasing responsibilities took up much of her time, and Sinmara had grown less playful, less curious even, especially as she had focused on mastering the subtle, complicated knacks that came with her chosen role.

That had been a small point of contention between them. Ailuwa was an adept far-seer, but Sinmara had shown no talent for that path. Ailuwa had then expressed hope that her daughter might become an artisan, and it was true that she was quite good at weaving and at shaping rock. But without the will to master the proper dream states, there was only so much she could do, and both Sinmara and Ailuwa had often ended up frustrated. For Sinmara it had been a relief, and then a revelation when Fafnon had suggested she take up the role of guardian for the warren. It was not the most esteemed vocation, but there was a sense of purpose in it that finally appealed to Sinmara. She liked the notion that it was her responsibility to keep her clan safe in its warren, and she enjoyed practicing the means to do so.

She had spent months gathering the materials required to make her arm-marks, then grinding and mixing the inks in exactly the proper combinations. She had learned to clear her mind so that she might access her talents, and finally had applied the inks to her arms and performed the mental practices required to pull them into her skin and bind them to herself. Then there were further weeks of activating her knacks, of allowing the power to spill from and then return to herself. It all might have gone faster if she had had a mentor, another guardian to show her the ways, but as it was she could only rely on what guidance the elders could give her. It spoke to how well suited Sinmara was for her role, that she had been able to achieve as much as she had, for she had relied largely on instinct and faith in herself. Her experience with the unspirit showed that this faith and practice had paid off, and that her role was less perfunctory than the others might think. Sinmara was still deciding how she felt about this, and she presumed her mother was as well.

Sinmara's horse seemed to be enjoying the opportunity to run free, tossing his head gaily as they passed from the stony land around the warren and onto grassier terrain. Sinmara realized that she still had not named him; she would have to do so before they reached their destination. He was a beautiful animal, and he did not seem to mind being ridden at all. His wounds from the unspirit had already healed, and little sign of them remained save for faint lines running through the hair of his flanks. Sinmara wondered where he came from- he bore no saddle, but was far too well-groomed to be wild, and the little beads braided into his mane removed all doubt. She still questioned whether it was the will of the unspirit or the horse that had brought them to the Killicut gate. Perhaps Ailuwa would have some insight on the matter. Her vision was unpredictable, but she could usually produce useful information when called upon to do so.

The two rode on in silence for several miles. Eventually the clouds burst, and warm summer rain fell in gleaming sheets, still lit by sunlight. Sinmara knew what rain was, of course, and had heard its patter on the stones above the warren. She had even experienced it on occasion, stepping outside the gate to investigate a disturbance she had sensed there, invariably caused by a lost bird or, once, a fox. Yet never had Sinmara imagined the feeling of warm rain on her face, the prismatic fractioning of the light. She had no context for such a thing. She was surprised too that the sun did not bother her. It had nearly always been overcast or after sundown when she had ventured aboveground before, and the light now was far brighter than any she had ever seen. But her eyes had adjusted quickly, and now Sinmara wondered how she had lived without ever experiencing this joyful brightness. She grinned, and spurred the horse ahead so that she could look back at her mother. But Ailuwa had pulled a hood over her head, so that her eyes were shaded and unreadable.

They stopped twice in the afternoon to let the animals drink and rest. The first time, Sinmara's leading questions regarding the purpose of their journey were gently rebuffed, Ailuwa assuring her that this would be clear soon enough. The second time they stopped, as the animals munched on grass, and the women split a large mushroom cap, Sinmara tried another inroad.

"Why do you think the unsleeping spirit I defeated was attacking this horse?"

Ailuwa set down her food, and considered her words for a moment. "Unspirits are malicious creatures. In fact, they are less creatures than an embodiment of malice itself. They hate all life, and in particular animal life, for beasts are incapable of the hatred that feeds the unspirit. It is possible that the horse simply wandered too near to the unspirit's resting place, and it struck."

"But aren't animals able to avoid the unspirit's area of influence?" Sinmara wasn't certain how she knew this, but it seemed to make sense.

"Generally, but every rule has its exception."

"Well, I think that something else- someone else- disturbed the unspirit I encountered. This horse is well taken care of, I do not think it was wandering alone."

Ailuwa's face was expressionless. "Perhaps."

"And why do you think the horse and the unspirit came to our gate? Nothing larger than a lost tern has come that close in the entire time I have been a guardian."

"Which is not a terribly long time, after all," Ailuwa said, a small smile finally appearing on her face.

"True...but the horse was riding directly towards the gate, like it meant to smash itself and the unspirit against it. Was the unspirit steering it there?"

"Such a being is probably not capable of the kind of thinking that effectively managing a horse requires."

"Then it was the horse's intention to approach the gate."

Ailuwa seemed to ponder that for a moment. "I doubt that as well. In all likelihood, the horse was crazed with fear, and it was simply a coincidence that he happened to run towards our door."

"But that raises another question. The horse and unspirit could not have come from anywhere near the gate. How did the horse survive the attack for as long as it did? In all that I have heard of the unspiritsand, I admit, this is not so much," Sinmara said, as her mother opened her mouth to comment, "but in all such reports, unspirits have no difficulty at all slaying animals, or men for that matter. So how did this horse survive? I saw the unspirit attacking him viciously, but the wounds it inflicted were superficial."

Ailuwa was silent for a beat before responding, and Sinmara sensed her hesitation.

"This horse," Ailuwa began, "...this particular horse might be...special, in some way. It is probably just very lucky. But...even this is a quality not often noticed in a beast. In short, I cannot answer your question, Sinmara. But I agree with you that the circumstances seem unusual."

Sinmara looked over at the horse, bent over companionably beside the ram, sharing a drink of cool stream water.

"Well, in any case, if we are to continue to spend time together, I must come up with a name for him."

Ailuwa looked at her daughter, then walked over to the horse. She reached out a hand to him, and he shied away from her touch. This surprised Sinmara somewhat, since the horse had been uncannily placid and friendly towards her. But the horse did not flee, and with soothing words Ailuwa was eventually permitted to place her hands upon him. She moved in front of the horse, and stared deep into its chestnut eyes. The horse held her gaze. Then Ailuwa closed her eyes for a moment, removed her hands, and returned to where Sinmara was sitting.

"He is called Orri," she said. "It is a name for a black bird, in the tongue of men."

Sinmara never had reason to doubt her mother's perception, and in this instance she was immediately certain that Ailuwa was correct. The name felt right somehow, almost as if it was the one Sinmara had already chosen for the horse, without consciously knowing it.

"Orri..." She repeated the name after her mother. "Yes, that fits, although he doesn't look at all like a bird." She thought for a moment, staring at the horse, who was now grazing on the bank of the stream. "I wonder who gave him that name. Surely someone is wondering where he is, assuming the unspirit did not get them." Ailuwa said nothing.

ᛒ ᛟᛦ ᛋᛟ ᚦᛚ ᛟᛦ ᛋᛟ ᚦᛚ ᛟᛦ ᛋᛟ ᚦᛚ ᛟᛦ ᛋᛟ ᚦ

They reached their first destination that evening, and prepared to make camp. A large boulder stood alone in a field. Ailuwa explained that it was a waystone, a resting area for the any fólk who passed by on travels. Sinmara slipped into rockwalk and entered the stone, coming into a simple, plain chamber. It was larger on the inside than it looked to be without, but there was not enough room inside for both animals to fit comfortably, so Ailuwa tied a thin rope around each of their necks, and carried the ends into the rock with her. If any men were to pass by, she explained, they would certainly notice the two animals, one of them a great ram nearly as large as the young horse next to it, both of them with leads around their necks passing up and into solid rock. Ailuwa assured Sinmara however that men avoided this area, precisely because the sensed it to be frequented by things not of their own world.

"You mean us? Or are there dangers here?"

"There is danger everywhere, dear heart. But worry not, the animals will be fine." Sinmara would have pressed the question, but she could not remember the last time her mother had called her 'dear heart', and was taken aback.

There were no sleeping biers in the chamber, so Sinmara and her mother each unrolled a thick mat of woven moss from their packs, and laid these on the floor. Ailuwa also produced two blocks of pressed root vegetables, sweetened with precious sap. This was a particular favorite of Sinmara, one she used to beg for as a child, before she understood that the sweeting sap was one commodity always in short supply in the warren, to be used sparingly and on special occasions.

Noting her surprise, Ailuwa said, "Your first trip overland. I thought we should mark the occasion with something special."

Sinmara bit into the nutritious treat. It was particularly good, perfectly textured, and tasting lightly of delicious spices she could not identify. "I have picked up a few things here and there," Ailuwa said as she saw Sinmara trying to work out the taste.

"It's very good."

"So, you have now spent an entire day aboveground. What do you think so far?"

"It is warmer than I expected."

Ailuwa actually laughed at that. "You might not feel the same way had we come at another time of year. What else?"

"It...it changes so much. There is sun, then the sky turns gray, sometimes there are clouds, sometimes there are not. It rains, then it stops, then it rains again. And the land- it is bleak and rocky, then brown and muddy, then there is green. The green is what I notice the most. Never did I know there could be so much green. I thought I knew what it was like up here, from standing outside the gate. But I knew nothing."

Ailuwa nodded. "Yes, I remember feeling that way as well, when first I started traveling. At home, we have everything we need. But we have only the tiniest fraction of what there is. And we are happy for it, and fortunate, for we do not struggle, the way men do. But their world is bigger than ours. It is bigger even than they know."

"What do they know about us?"

"It is difficult to say. They know of us, surely, though some may choose not to believe. There was a time, as you have heard, when we enjoyed...warmer relations with each other than we do now. Some even say there was a time when we were one people, but if that is true it must have been a very long time ago indeed. What is certain now is that most of them cannot see us, unless we wish them to or are very incautious around them. They do not have the knacks to do many of the things we can do. They see themselves as separate from the world around them, and this keeps them from being in the world the way that we are."

"Yet they live everywhere, on the face of the earth, while we are few, and live belowground. Why is this?" Sinmara asked.

"Living the way we do, we have everything we need. We do not hunger. We do not freeze in winter, or burn in summer. We lead longer lives, much longer, and more peaceful. We live knowing the purpose of our talents, the order that they bring. We are more fortunate than men, in many ways.

"But they do have abilities which we do not. One of these, the most important one, is that they can see things as they are not. We see things as they are. We may be mistaken, particularly where the thoughts and motives of others are concerned. And each of us gains differences in understanding from our experience, and especially our time in whatever dream states we choose. But for the most part, all fólk perceive the nature of the world the same way.

"Men, however, perceive very little of the world as it truly is. Yet they are no less intelligent than us. They see much of what we see. They just comprehend it differently- from us, and from each other. Yet all men, or almost all of them, believe that the world truly is as they perceive it to be. They believe it so fully that this, each man's individual perspective, becomes a kind of truth unto itself. This means that there is much disagreement among men, for the truths of any two men may be fundamentally irreconcilable. So they suffer hatred amongst each other, and violence.

"Yet, for all the harm it brings them, there is also a great power in the ability of men to create their own truths. Fólk are much the same, wherever we are found, no matter how different we might appear to the men of our lands. Yet men have rich and varied cultures, organized around the few truths a given group of them might hold in common. Nature loves diversity as well as order, and because of this, men have been able to spread into many different corners of the world, and to thrive there after their own fashion."

"And could we not do so?" Sinmara asked, trying to take it all in.

"We already have. When men come into new lands, we are already there. And there are places still where we live, and men do not."

"But there are still more of them than us, are there not? And we still do not live above the ground."

"There is no reason for us to. It would bring us nothing we do not already possess, nothing we need.

"But, in point of fact, we would also find it very difficult to do so." She paused, while Sinmara considered silently that her people did not have the sun, the wind, the rain. Then Ailuwa spoke again, her voice lower.

"Some say the time is coming when it will be impossible for our kind to lay claim to any more of the world than we already inhabit. For, while our connection to nature is strong, so too is humanity's, and they are spreading swiftly. Once we covered the world; now they do, and in numbers far beyond what we were at our greatest. You must understand that nature loves them no less than us.

"Nature has granted our kind harmony. We are all able to do things men cannot do, such as travel through the living rock, control certain forms of energy and substance at will, dream into other states of consciousness, know things outside of our direct experience. All this because we perceive things as they are, and respond accordingly and harmoniously.

"Man's gift is not harmony. The gift of men is dominion. Men see the world as other than it is, but by first seeing the world in such a way, they are sometimes able to make it so.

"Men can make things that never were, things we fólk may understand upon encountering them, but which no fólk could or would have created. Doing so would first require an ability and a will to conceptualize the world as being different than it is."

Sinmara was getting lost, but her mother barreled on.

"Of more direct impact to us, there are things that a great number of men perceive to be true, simultaneously. In any society of men, there are a certain few things that most of them, from children to the elderly, will effortlessly, neutrally, and unquestioningly believe to be true.

"These groups unconsciously exert great willpower upon their environment. When we approach such places, even with our clear and true vision, we sometimes find that our own perceptions are affected. An individual fólk, meeting an individual man, might be able to do and show that man any number of things which would profoundly change him, opening his mind or even breaking it entirely. The false perception of an individual man is generally no match for the true perception of one of the fólk.

"But a group of men, believing enough of the same things... this would present a challenge to an individual fólk. The effect men assert upon the world, by perceiving it in the way they do, has the power to drastically alter the way an individual fólk can relate to the world as well. In such an instance, it could be that the poor fólk would be unable to effectively assert her will, or go insane, or even, and most horribly, lose her connection to the understanding of the fólk altogether.

"And should one of the fólk enter among men and prove able to resist the effects of their vision, she would likely find herself the target of man's rage. For if there is one thing their kind cannot tolerate, it is having their perceptions suddenly and fundamentally challenged. This is not their fault; as I said, it can be dangerous for them, whether they might wish it to be differently or not. But the responding consequences can be disastrous for our kind. Any fólk who finds herself in the company of men is in grave danger. There is little we can do to defend ourselves against the focused force of men's rage, for they are physically dangerous in a way we are not, and would not seek to be.

"And so we live as we do. Away from men, in our rocks and warrens, where we are safe, and powerful, and happy. Why would we do otherwise? We can leave them to their fate. We have our own.
"

Sinmara was not sure her mother had made her point, but it was clear she was finished speaking. As she pulled the moss cover around her and waited for sleep to come that night, Sinmara wondered just what the fates Ailuwa spoke of might be, and how the mysterious mission they were undertaking could fit into them.

ᚦ ᚱᛚᚷ ᚴᚠ ᚨᚠ ᚱᛚᚷ ᚴᚠ ᚨᚠ ᚱᛚᚷ ᚴᚠ ᚨᚠ ᚱᛚᚷ ᚴᚠ ᚨ

In the morning they loaded up the animals, mounted, and set off again. Sinmara found Ailuwa had returned to reticence, clearly preoccupied by her own thoughts, so the two of them rode out in relative silence.

By mid-morning they had reached a plain, wide and flat, covered in green grass, with a river flowing along one side through several small pools. There were a few ramshackle structures standing on the plain, and clear signs of recent human presence. At one corner of the plain stood a simple wooden building, its roof narrowing to a point. Sinmara had never seen anything like it, and guessed this was a human home. Ailuwa denied this, but would not, or could not explain the structure's purpose. Despite the obvious recent presence of people, the plain was currently uninhabited, except for a small flock of geese who did not deign to acknowledge the women's presence.

Sinmara could not hold her tongue indefinitely. "Why are we in a human area? Didn't you just tell me that such places were to be avoided?"

Ailuwa looked approving. "They are, and you are right to ask. We are here because, despite the occasional presence of humans, this is the best and safest way to reach our destination." She led Sinmara to one edge of the field, where a large rock stood in front of a sheer rock face, bounding in one side of the plain. She turned to face her daughter.

"This rock is a farestone. It was created long ago, before men came to these lands. Through it we shall travel to Ásbyrgi."

Sinmara nodded. She had wondered how they would get from the warren all the way to Ásbyrgi, which she had gathered to be somewhere far to the north, certainly farther than a day's ride away. She had never traveled by farestone before- there had never been a need, and as far as she knew there were none near the warren anyway. But she was familiar with the general concept- and, suddenly, a bit nervous.

"The resonance of this particular farestone is such that it will only transport those who have a stonekey." Ailuwa pulled a necklace out from within the collar of her shift. It had several stones on it of different sizes and shapes. Despite no two stones being the same, Sinmara thought it looked rather beautiful.

"I have the key for this farestone. You will enter first, bringing the animals with you. When I enter, we will all be transferred to Ásbyrgi. It is much like rockwalking, but not everyone experiences the journey exactly the same way. Just remember, no matter how long it seems to take, the transfer is actually almost instantaneous. The experience may be disorienting, but remain calm and everything will be fine. Do you understand?"

Sinmara nodded again, although somewhat less eagerly this time. Her mother's expression softened. "My first time through, I was advised to try mentally listing all of the different kinds of sandstone, if the trip started to feel long or uncomfortable. And it turned out I did not need to."

A strategy in place, Sinmara felt surprisingly reassured. "But what about the animals?" she asked.

"They will be fine. You will need to take them into rockwalk with you, of course, in order to enter the farestone, but they never seem to have any trouble with the journey.

"Now, are we ready? Let us be off." Ailuwa gestured to the massive rock.

With Orri and Brekka in hand on either side of her, Sinmara took a deep breath, then focused on the rock in front of her until she could feel herself resonating along with its frequency – and, through her, the animals as well. Then she entered the rock face. To her perception, the interior of the rock was entirely without features, other than a dim glow that allowed her to hazily sense its interior contours, and see the heads of the horse and ram raised in front of her. Then she sensed her mother entering behind them.

As soon as Ailuwa entered the rock, the dim light ramped up in intensity, until it was as blindingly white as the spark of metal hitting stone. Sinmara could see nothing but burning brightness, and could feel nothing at all. She had no sensation of a physical body, but she somehow had an awareness of the two animals and her mother near her.

After a moment, though Sinmara could not truly say how long it had been, she began to perceive patters in the whiteness, shifting specters of form that were somehow both amorphous and geometric, which fled from her sight whenever she attempted to focus her attention and resolve them. It was, Sinmara considered, much like when she had been a child, and would amuse herself by pressing her palms to her eyes until a sort of lightshow appeared behind her lids.

As she made this connection, the spectral forms began taking aspects of color, multihued and resplendent, although not colors that Sinmara could describe. The predominant perception was still of searing white.

In the lower corner of her vision, a black spot suddenly appeared amongst the wheeling forms of white-green-purple and white-orangeblue light. This attracted Sinmara's attention, and she found she was able to focus upon it. As she watched with her mind's eye, the spot slowly grew, until it occupied a full quarter of her vision. Small tendrils of blackness began to branch out from it.

Suddenly, a streak of utter darkness shot across Sinmara's field of view, as if her vision itself had cracked. Another crack appeared to bisect the first, and Sinmara perceived that both black fissures originated in the dark spot at the edge of her awareness.

Then Sinmara was engulfed. It was as if every fiber of her being was attempting to scream at once. There was no pain, no sound. Simply crushing, all-encompassing, primal horror. Then her vision seemed to shatter again, and there was only darkness.

Chapter 13

Sinmara opened her eyes just as the scream died on her lips. She did not know where she was — it took her a moment to remember even who she was, and longer still to orient herself in space. Hazy forms around her resolved into legs and faces. She was lying on her back, looking up at a half-dozen concerned strangers. Only the face of her mother was familiar, stricken and creased as Ailuwa knelt beside her.

"What...what's happening?" Sinmara managed to stutter.

"By the Light! She will be alright." Ailuwa clasped her daughter roughly to her breast.

"I don't understand..." Sinmara's tongue felt heavy in her mouth, and her limbs tingled as feeling slowly returned to them.

"I do not either." This from a woman standing at her mother's side, whose tightly-curled black hair framed a dark oval of a face.

"Ailuwa, what happened?"

Ailuwa took a moment to collect herself, still clutching Sinmara tightly, before replying.

"I cannot explain it. We entered the farestone over the Seam, and everything was fine. The next thing I knew, I was standing outside the farestone here, with the most awful feeling. And Sinmara was not with me. I turned just in time to see her fall out of the stone, and hit the floor. She wasn't breathing. I tried to rouse her, but she was unresponsive."

A young male spoke up. "That is what I saw as well. The girl finally took a great breath and started screaming, and she didn't stop or open her eyes until you all arrived."

"Most unusual," said the short-haired woman. "And you have no idea what could have happened?"

"No, but...we had two animals with us. A horse, and my ram Brekka.

I... I don't know what happened to them. They entered the farestone with Sinmara, but..." Ailuwa looked around helplessly.

The others looked at each other, but said nothing, until Ailuwa again broke the silence.

"That shouldn't be possible. Whatever goes into the farestone has to come out the other side. Otherwise...where did they go?"

The short-haired woman reached down, and placed a hand upon Ailuwa's shoulder. "I cannot say. But you and your daughter are here, and you need food, and rest. Tindar and Gamlu will help both of you to your usual quarters." She gestured to the young male who had spoken before, and to another, taller one. "I will join you shortly, to make sure you are alright and have everything you need."

The males helped Ailuwa up, as the others in the room backed away, then supported Sinmara as they raised her to her feet. Looking around she saw she was in an oblong room lit by crystal lamps. A bench was carved from the stone along the walls, except for the area covered by a portal arch. To her left, opposite the portal, was a thick slab of standing stone, taller than it was wide, and standing on its own in the floor, away from the walls. This was the exit point of the farestone they had traveled through.

As they moved towards the portal, Sinmara was stricken with a pang of despair as she realized the animals she had brought into the stone with her were likely lost forever. She did not remember releasing them from her grip at any point on the journey, but neither had she had any physical sense of them being with her, once her mother activated the stone. Whatever had happened to them in transit, without a fólk with them there was no way for them to rockwalk back into the world. And they had been her responsibility. Brekka, who had been her mother's mount since Sinmara was a girl. And Orri, whose name she had known for less than a day. She had saved his life, only to lead him to what was likely a far worse fate. Hot tears of shame stung her cheeks.

They reached the portal out of the room, and two of the group with them, a male and a woman, passed through. Next were Ailuwa and the short-haired woman. Before passing through the portal, Ailuwa looked back as if to reassure herself that her daughter really was alright. As she did so, she gasped, and stared past Sinmara's head.

With difficulty, Sinmara twisted in her assistants' arms to follow her mother's gaze. She turned her head just in time to see Orri's hindquarters exit the stone slab. The horse stumbled forward, the line of his body having exited the slab lower than necessary for him to stand. For a moment it looked like he would fall, but he managed to right himself. His flanks were heaving, his eyes were rolling, and foam began to drip from his mouth as if he had been ridden too hard for hours. But he was there before them, terrified but apparently whole.

"Impossible..." the woman with Ailuwa exclaimed.

Sinmara tore herself from Tindar and Gamlu's grasp, and rushed towards Orri on her own unsteady feet. She threw her arms around his neck, and though the horse reared momentarily, he stopped rolling his eyes, and his breathing began to normalize. The others in the chamber just stared at them, speechless, until finally Sinmara turned back towards the portal.

"Water. He needs water."

ᚠ ᚱᚲ ᛋᚠ ᚫᚠ ᚱᚲ ᛋᚠ ᚫᚠ ᚱᚲ ᛋᚠ ᚫᚠ ᚱᚲ ᛋᚠ ᚫ

Sinmara was surprised to find that the portal out of the chamber led not into the heart of the capital, or even to another underground cavern, but instead directly outside. Still leading Orri by the mane, she found herself at the bottom of a wide, open canyon. On either side of her the steep walls curved away gently. They were dotted here and there with openings, some of which showed the dim glow of crystal lamps from their recesses, faint in the murky light of the morning.

The group- Sinmara, Orri, Tindar, Gamlu, the short-haired woman, and another male, made their way across the basin of the canyon. Directly in front of them stood a towering stand of rock, set into the space between the canyon walls like an island in a pond. This, Sinmara presumed, was their destination, and the true heart of the capital.

Ailuwa was not with them. Sinmara turned her head and saw her mother exit the portal several paces back, a grim and defeated

116

look on her face. Ailuwa saw her daughter's searching look, and shook her head sadly. Howsoever Orri had made it through the stone, it was apparent that Brekka had not managed the same feat. Ailuwa made no effort to catch up with the rest of the group, and Sinmara understood that she needed a moment alone, now that it was clear her daughter was safe. Brekka had been family to her as well.

Soon they came to a stream wending its way through the canyon, and Orri was persuaded to stop and drink. Sinmara also bent, cupping her hands to bring the cold, clear water to her lips. Her throat was raw from screaming, and the water soothed it. Already the memory of her experience through the farestone was receding, and she was not at all certain she wished to hold onto it. She could tell that no one was clear on what had actually happened though, so she struggled to retain anything useful.

Once she and Orri had finished drinking, and some of the others had filled their skeins with water, the group continued towards the rock formation in front of them. It loomed above them as they approached, as high as the cliff walls to their sides and back. For a moment, Sinmara felt she could see the canyon as from above, and saw that the valley cutting through the cliffs and around the rock formed a shape like a cup cut in half, or the imprint left by a horse's hoof in the dirt.

Finally reaching the rock face, they came to another portal. The outline of the portal was quite faint, and Sinmara might not have seen it had she not been led directly to it, and known what to look for. The edges of the portal were as far apart as five adults standing with arms stretched finger to finger, and it was half again as tall. The entire group was able to pass through it all at once, rather than in ones and twos as was necessary with every other portal Sinmara had ever seen.

The passage through the portal took longer than Sinmara had anticipated, and it was obvious that they were passing quite far into the towering island of rock. Sinmara would have appreciated a warning; as the energy within the portal pushed her towards the corresponding entryway within the rock, she felt a momentary sensation of panic as she was reminded of her ordeal of just a short while before. Still, other than the similar physical sensations she perceived the experiences quite differently. Where before there had been searing white, now she saw only a boundless field of black, and she had a stronger sense of her physical self, feeling her hand upon Orri's back. This calmed her, and within seconds they had reached the inner chambers of the fólkish capital.

Once inside, Sinmara was somewhat surprised to see how closely the capital resembled her own warren, simply at a grander scale. She stood at the end of a long hallway, much like the one her warren was based around. As at home, portals on either side of the hallway marked passages through the surrounding rock. The light from the crystal lamps was brighter than at home however, and the stone floor had been entirely covered in a carpeting of thick lichen, which pressed back pleasantly against Sinmara's bare feet.

Opposite the entry portal, the other end of the hallway was open, and Sinmara could see fólk moving beyond. With the others, each of whom seemed to be lost in his or her own thoughts, Sinmara and Orri walked down the hallway. As they reached the exit, Sinmara could see that the hall was connected to a much larger chamber. It was as if the warren at home had been connected to another structure. Exiting the hallway, Sinmara found herself in a huge domed cavern. The floor formed a large circle, and other hallways spiked out from the edges of the chamber, like legs from a spider.

Under the high domed roof of the chamber were more fólk than Sinmara had ever seen at once. At least fifty fólk were milling about, chatting quietly with each other, or trading food and wares. There were even animals- a number of goats and sheep milled about in a pen at one side of the hall, munching on hay.

As she looked around, Sinmara could sense the others in the chamber similarly taking notice of her groups' entrance, but if they were at all surprised to see a stranger, or a horse, no one gave any indication. A couple fólk raised their chins to acknowledge one of the group- Gamlu, or the woman- but everyone continued whatever business they had been engaged in when the group entered.

Sinmara walked with the others across the open space. On one side of the chamber was a large semicircular dais, which jutted out of the wall. Hallways receded into the rock on either side of the dais. They walked past it, and into the hallway on the left.

The short-haired woman – Sinmara still did not know her name –turned to the others.

"I will take them from here. Tindar, Ferrok – go find Neref. I shall want to speak to him later. Gamlu, tell the stables to prepare for our guest. And tell Ailuwa that I will meet her in her usual quarters. I would speak with this one first," she said, gesturing at Sinmara. The others nodded, and turned to do her bidding.

She led Orri and Sinmara down the hallway, past seven or eight portals on either side of the wall, but they did not enter any of them. When they reached the end of the hallway, Sinmara looked up and realized there was another portal here, not on either side, but carved directly into the back wall bounding the hallway. The other woman stepped towards this door, and indicated that the girl and her horse should follow.

Sinmara walked through the portal and into a room unlike any she had seen before. Most chambers in her warren followed the same general pattern- more or less circular, with either a flat or a domed ceiling. Sharp angles and straight lines were not common features of fólkish architecture. This room, however, was nothing but angles and lines. The floor was a perfect square. From each side the walls extended upwards and inward, narrowing as they rose until the four walls reached a single point far above Sinmara's head. It was unusually dim, and the single lamp set into each wall glowed with an amber-pink light unlike the shades Sinmara had seen elsewhere in the capital. Along the far wall, cubby holes were carved directly into the rock, and various items had been placed into these, although Sinmara could not make out what they were. There was a sleeping bier directly in front of the far wall, as well as a thick circular mat of moss in the center of the stone floor.

The woman walked to the edge of the mat, and turned to face Sinmara and Orri.

"Do you know who I am, child?" Sinmara shook her head.

119

"I don't suppose you would. The Killicut warren has no inseer, and I gather Ailuwa has not told you much." This the woman said more to herself, before raising her head and looking Sinmara directly in the eye.

"I am Ruharra. I have known your mother since she was a girl, and her mother before that. You may not know me, Sinmara, but I know much about you."

Ruharra beckoned for Sinmara to join her on the mat. She reached out for Sinmara's hands, and clasped them in her warm, strong grip. "It gives me great pleasure to meet you. Your mother always speaks of you so fondly, and I hear you are developing into a most capable guardian." Sinmara was somewhat surprised to hear that her mother had sung her praises- Ailuwa was not the effusive sort.

Ruharra continued. "I know you have just had a terrible fright, and need your rest, as does Orri. I will not keep you long. But I must know more about what just happened, while the impression is still fresh in both of your minds. I am sorry to ask this of you, and I assure you I would not if the matter were not of utmost importance. Do you understand?"

Sinmara absentmindedly brought her hand to her throat, as if to still the echoes of her screams. "I understand. When we entered the farestone, at first there was nothing. Then-" Ruharra raised a finger to cut her off.

"Thank you, but you need not tell me what you experienced. I would not ask you to rehash it- I suspect you will be asked to do that enough in the next few days- and there is a better way."

Ruharra walked to the other end of the room, where the cubby holes were cut into the wall. She reached into one and removed a small stone bowl. Moving to another cubby, she withdrew a leather pouch, and a long, thin sliver of metal. She carried these items back to the moss mat, sat down, and arranged the items in front of her. She gestured for Sinmara to sit.

As Sinmara situated herself on the soft mat, Ruharra took the lid off of the bowl and set it to one side. She reached into the pouch, rooted around with her hand, removed something, and set it into the bowl. Then she picked up the shiny sliver of metal, which was just longer than her own hand. Sinmara looked at it suspiciously.

Confirming her suspicions, Ruharra looked up at her over the rim of the bowl. "I am afraid I must beg a few drops of your blood, Sinmara. I assure you I only ask because it is necessary."

Sinmara leaned back. "What do you need it for?" While she was not familiar with whatever ritual Ruharra appeared to be preparing, she knew well enough that there was power in blood. She was not distrustful by nature- she had never been given any reason to be- but this was an unusual request.

"With your blood, I can see what you saw, in clearer detail than your words could ever provide. In this way, I may be able to learn what happened when you passed through the farestone. But only if you consent. It will not work otherwise."

Sinmara considered this for a moment. She almost wanted to wait until she could consult her mother. Ailuwa clearly knew more of the capital than Sinmara had guessed. But Ailuwa was not here, and Sinmara was an adult. It was her decision, and in any case, she wanted as much as anyone to learn about what had happened.

"I consent." She held her arm out.

"Just a moment dear, we are not there yet. First, you must think back to the moment you entered the stone. Hold it in your mind. Picture it in as much detail as you possibly can- the sound, the smells. Close your eyes if you need to. When you have it fixed in your memory, then extend your hand. I will draw your blood then, as gently as I can."

Sinmara pulled her hand back, and set it in her laps. After a moment, she closed her eyes. She took a breath, and pictured the second she had entered the rock, Orri on one side of her, Brekka the other, her hand on their necks, her fingers curling in their coats. The twist of breathlessness as the prepared to walkrock, the sensation like tripping in place, then the awareness of the rock face in front of her, calling to her almost, pulling her into it. Moving forward, meeting the rock, its coldness, its age, its mineral wisdom reaching to embrace her, then darkness, utter darkness as she entered it. Then the soft glow, and she was aware of the rock's boundaries, the dual perception of standing within the rock, clutching two beasts, and of being part of the rock, of form without definition, of sizelessness and weightlessness and being-in-unbeing. Had it really been like this? She held out her arm.

A sharp shock of frost in the meat of her palm. Her eyes flew open.

Ruharra held the silver sliver gently between two fingers. A drop of bright golden blood beaded on the blade. Sinmara watched as it fell into the waiting bowl below. Quickly, Ruharra placed the lid on the bowl. She looked at Sinmara.

"Are you alright?"

Sinmara nodded. Ruharra handed her a small, clean cloth. "Press this to the wound. It will close in a moment." Sinmara's palm pulsed as she put pressure on the puncture.

Ruharra turned her attention back to the bowl in front of her. She placed her hand on the lid, and said a few words Sinmara could not understand. She removed the lid from the bowl again.

Sinmara leaned forward to peer into the dish. At the bottom, something small and pale moved slowly. Sinmara did not recognize it, but its jointed legs and translucent body reminded her of an insect, though unlike any she had seen before in the nooks and crannies of the warren. It was repellant and beautiful all at once.

Ruharra regarded the creature, then with one quick motion grabbed it up in her hand, and popped it into her mouth. She bit down once, and swallowed. She let out a sigh, and closed her eyes. She sat, motionless, in front of Sinmara, breathing slowly and evenly. Then her brow furrowed. Her breath quickened. Her fingers clenched where they rested against her knees. She let out a shuddering sigh, and Sinmara could see the muscles flexing in her neck.

Ruharra's eyes fluttered open. Her pupils were dilated, and it took a moment for her to focus on Sinmara's face. She held Sinmara's gaze for a long moment, looked down at her lap, then raised her eyes again.

"It is just as I feared, then. And worse."

"What? What is it?" Sinmara hated the edge of panic she heard in her voice, but it had been a long, frightening day, and the past few minutes had allowed everything to begin to seep into her feelings.

Ruharra cracked her knuckles as she spoke. "Even I cannot explain exactly how the farestones work, but I know that traveling through them is safe and instantaneous. When you enter one, it is as though you do not exist, until you exit the stone on the other end. It is only in rare cases that a traveler even senses the passage of time.

"Obviously, you experienced one of these rare cases. Perhaps there is something about you that permitted you to experience the journey in this way. I had hoped that by tasting your memories, I could determine whether it was something about you, something you had done somehow, that caused the connection between the farestones to fail, and the ram to be lost. Not that I have heard of such a thing happening," she said in response to the look of guilty horror on Sinmara's face, "and no one could think that what happened was your fault. But that was the explanation I had hoped for.

"Your memories showed me something different, however. I do not know how it is possible, but something reached out for you while you were traveling through the farestone. Even in your jumbled memories, I sensed another will suddenly intruding on your transit."

"But- my mother traveled with us. She had the key. Perhaps it was her you sensed. Or one of the animals?" Sinmara said hopefully.

"I will have to taste your mother's memories, and the horse's, although specific animal memories are not transferred as easily as ours. But the presence I sensed- it did not feel fólkish, or animal. It felt like nothing I have a name for. But it was powerful. Powerful enough to reach out and affect your passage through the farestone. And given how that turned out, I do not believe the source of that power is any friend to us."

Once Sinmara had left, Ruharra placed the bowl and the sliver of metal back on their shelves. She peered into the leather pouch-there were still four or five of the amphipods in there, their desiccated forms rustling against each other as she turned the sack. It should be enough for her purposes.

She placed the sack on its shelf, then reached further back on the same shelf until she felt the back wall of the ledge. Running her fingers down it, she found the edges of another recess, carved into the back of the cubby hole. Carefully, she removed a small wooden box from the hidden compartment.

Returning to the moss mat with the box, she sat down and set it on the floor in front of her. The box was simple and unadorned. Holes had been bored into the top. Ruharra opened it slowly.

The chitinous form in the box was not desiccated like the ones in the pouch. It moved slightly, extending segmented legs to grasp weakly at the air. Black eyes rotated on filamental stalks. In the dim light of the chamber, the creature seemed almost to glow from the crimson blood filling its veins, engorging its tiny body.

Ruharra regarded the creature until she was satisfied that it remained healthy. She sensed that it would soon be needed, which meant she would not have to keep it alive much longer. Doing so was difficult. She silently thanked the creature for its sacrifice, and hoped it would not be in vain. She hoped that none of their sacrifices would be.

ᚠᚱᛚᚾᛋᛏᚨᚠᛏᚱᛚᚾᛋᛏᚠᚱᛚᚾᛋᛏᚠᛏᚱᛚᚾᛋᛏᚾ

Sinmara left Ruharra's chamber feeling even more disoriented than she had been when she first entered the capital, but this sensation was soon displaced by simple, overwhelming exhaustion.

Following Ruharra's parting instructions, Sinmara dragged herself to the portal leading to her mother's guest quarters, and passed through, not quite knowing what to expect.

The chamber into which Sinmara stepped was not nearly as unusual as Ruharra's. It followed the familiar plan- roughly circular, with a domed ceiling. However, it was filled with far more knickknacks and objects of various sizes than Sinmara could have anticipated. There were decorative tapestries hanging from the wall, in styles Sinmara had never seen, each different from the other. All around the wall were cubby holes filled with geodes, small carvings of animals and people, even some bronzeware, a substance Sinmara could identify only by inference. The room also had its own cistern of water, carved from the rock into the wall itself. Sinmara could dimly sense the flow of water into the basin, from a tapped spring further underground.

Ailuwa was nowhere to be seen, although her pack had been placed in one of the cubbies. Sinmara wondered where her mother was as she moved into the room, but within moments she had laid herself out on one of the fine low sleeping biers lining the floor, and slipped into unconsciousness.

She awoke at some point to sense her mother standing over her, her presence unmistakable. Yet when Sinmara turned to greet her, there was no one there, and she passed back into sleep after a moment's   confusion.

Chapter 14

When Sinmara woke for the day she was alone, but looking around the room she saw her mother's pack missing. So Ailuwa must have been there at some point. Used to her mother's abrupt comings and goings, Sinmara did not think much of it. Yet as she pulled her shift over her head, and pulled back her hair, Sinmara realized she did not actually know what to do with her day. Ailuwa had remained maddeningly vague on the purpose of Sinmara's visit, and without her mother around she did not even know what she might do in this new, slightly strange place.

If she were at home, Sinmara would spend the day monitoring the lands around the Killicut gate, either by visual inspection or through sensing the cairn stones. Assuming all was well, after a few hours she might return to her room to practice her focus and her knacks. Then she would take her midday meal with some of the others of the warren, and listen to what they had to say of their days so far. If anyone expressed a need for assistance, Sinmara might spend some time helping to weave a moss net, or tending to the sheep, excusing herself periodically to check on the gate.

As the warren's only guardian, Sinmara took her duties seriously. She was well aware that many in the warren thought her chosen role rather perfunctory, especially given that the position had been vacant when she took it. No one ever disrespected her, but it was generally felt that the warren was quite secure, by virtue of its isolation and the general cluelessness of men. A guardian was welcome, but certainly not necessary. If the existing needs of the warren were not already being so capably met by others, and if Sinmara did not make such an effort to prove herself useful in other ways, she probably would have been more strongly encouraged to take on a different primary role, by more than just her mother.

As it was, no one particularly minded the warren having a guardian, and the attention Sinmara showed occasionally proved useful in unexpected ways, like when she sensed a buildup of ground water over one of the foodstores in time to divert the flow.

She noticed things others did not, and for this at least, Sinmara knew she was appreciated.

The appearance of the unsleeping spirit, however, had proved to Sinmara what she had always known somehow, even if the others of the warren could never admit it. There was a real need for a guardian, beyond her symbolic function or incidental usefulness. The tradition she had inherited when she took up the mantle, and the talents that came along with it, existed for a reason. She felt in her bones that the peace and abundance her people enjoyed could not be taken for granted.

Sinmara pondered this as she walked through the portal, down the hallway, and out into the large atrium forming the heart of the capital. The space bustled with activity. Fólk stood or sat in small groups, talking animatedly. Several of them were engaged in crafts of some sort, as they had been when Sinmara had first wandered through the previous day. She saw a group of boys shaping small sculptures out of stone, three women hand-weaving a garment, a set of young men and women making stylish drinking vessels of some sort. Fólk were entering and exiting the hallways radiating from the atrium, often carrying food or home goods in their arms. Here and there children chased each other around, giggling and shrieking. This was the life of Ásbyrgi in full swing.

Sinmara pressed her back against the smooth stone wall of the atrium, trying to take it all in. Her entire life, it had been rare for her to see an unfamiliar face. Here there were dozens, and of all ages to boot. Sinmara may have finally reached maturity, but she was still one of the youngest members of her warren, and there was no one close to her in age. Here there were several youths who might have been born around the same time as her, and even more disconcerting, there were children. In the warren, the appearance of a child was a rare event, and with so many adults around, childhood did not last long- Sinmara's certainly had not. But here there were children at play, something Sinmara had never truly seen before.

Even as she noticed their numbers, the children were taking notice of her. One of them turned from his companions and ran up to her, heedless of her attempts to blend into the wall.

"Who are you?" he shouted at her from less than a pace away.

"I am Sinmara. From the Killicut warren."

"Where's that? Are there giants there? Do you want to play a game with me? I'm Hanso!" This patter was delivered at such a rapid pace that Sinmara almost couldn't follow. But looking at the boy's eager, guileless face, Sinmara couldn't help but feel a bit lifted out of the morose mood that had been hovering around her all morning. She smiled at him.

"My home is to the south of here. It is like this, but smaller. And we don't have as many little boys there." Inspiration hit her then. "The giants must have gobbled them all up!" She roared and lurched towards Hanso, her arm outstretched and her jaws agape as if she meant to snatch him up and toss him down her gullet.

The child shrieked with delight, and ran back to his companions. Soon Sinmara was surrounded by a gaggle of giggling younglings, all of them chasing each other around, trying to make the most terrible growls and yaps. Several of the adults looked on fondly, but as the sounds of the children at play began to reach a crescendo, their parents began to materialize to lead them off to their chores. Hanso left with a well-built young man- his father, or perhaps an older brother- and waved timidly to Sinmara as he left, suddenly shy.

Sinmara watched them all go, feeling oddly wistful. There had never been so many children in the warren, and when she was still small her play had often been solitary. How nice it must be to have so many companions to choose from! It was strange, that there were so many here compared to home.

In truth, she reflected, she probably was not that much older than some of the children, by reckoning of cycles. She remembered her mother's confusion when she had first asked how old various members of their warren were, and Ailuwa's attempts to explain to her that everyone was exactly as old as they appeared to be, yet not by the reckoning of cycles or seasons. With some difficulty Sinmara finally came to understand that an individual's appearance was not always a clue as to how long they had been in the warren, especially if the fólk in question was one who spent much time in the mineral dream. As a guardian, Sinmara paid more attention to the passage of days than her brethren seemed to, and while everyone she knew ate and slept at regular intervals, only Sinmara seemed inclined to count these cycles. She had also noticed that sometimes when she came back in from standing outside the gate, more or less time would appear to have passed within the warren than she had expected.

All of which was to say, she had no guess as to when the children of Ásbyrgi might have appeared, or how long after her own birth this would have been. Perhaps had she been raised in the capital, she too would be playing with the very same younglings, laughing and shrieking as her mother looked on indulgently.

But, she reminded herself, whatever might have been had little bearing on her current responsibilities. She was a guardian, and it fell to her to keep the warren safe. She could not do this well if she did not understand her own circumstances. She had been brought to the capital for a reason, and it was past time she had some answers as to what that reason was.

The gloom once again threatening to spread over her mood, Sinmara trekked off to find her mother.

ᛕ ᚱᛚ ᛘᚱ ᚬᛕ ᚱᛚ ᛘᚱ ᚬᛕ ᚱᛚ ᛘᚱ ᚬᛕ ᚱᛚ ᛘᚱ ᚭ

Ailuwa exited the arch just as Sinmara passed the open end of the hallway. Seeing her, Sinmara scowled and started to stalk towards her with purpose. She stopped short when she saw that Ailuwa was not alone. Behind her, a fólkish man exited through the portal as well. He was short- shorter than Ailuwa, at any rate- and his skin was dark brown. He was bald above his sloping brow, but he had a great bushy gray beard, which shaped his face around a weak chin.

Sinmara did not know much of life outside the warren, but her home was still part of the greater fólkish world. She realized at a glance that the man with her mother was in all likelihood one of the firstborn. She knew there were a few in this land, and in fact had met a couple of them before, when she was a child, and they had visited her warren. She had been too young then to be anything but shy around the visitors, as they were amongst the first unfamiliar fólk she ever encountered. But she had noticed their features. The two dozen members of her warren all looked completely unique to her, and she had never assumed that other fólk would look like any of them. But the firstborn were shorter and darker than any adults in her warren, with small eyes and large noses, and a strange gait.

Several other fólk exited from the portal as Sinmara watched, stepping out one by one and nodding their farewells to each other before passing to other rooms in the hall, or heading toward Sinmara and the atrium behind her.

Realizing that so many adult fólk were around, Sinmara struggled to contain her frustration before she spoke to her mother, lest she appear petulant. She was finding more and more that her temper could flare up at inconvenient times, often without sufficient basis or provocation. Calming herself before she risked causing offense or embarrassment had begun to require an unfortunate amount of energy. She knew it was not uncommon for young fólk to struggle with powerful emotions, although she wasn't really sure just how she knew this. Still, she hated the constant reminder that she had only just reached maturity, and did not want to announce her emotional state to anyone else- least of all a firstborn. So she took a deep breath and let it out slowly, waiting for her mother to notice her.

The firstborn man saw her first. He looked up and his face broke into a grin as they made eye contact. His eyes were kind and welcoming, deepest black like those of other fólk, but the lines surrounding them showing the work of ages of easy smiles. He was far older looking than any fólk she had seen before, older even than the elders of her warren with their smattering of gray hair and gently creased brows. Despite herself Sinmara found she could not look away from him, so fascinated was she with the unfamiliar indicia of age. But he moved as lightly and spryly as any of them, balancing almost on the balls of his feet. He broke eye contact first, turning back towards Ailuwa as she herself turned and saw her daughter.

Now, for the first time, Sinmara could recognize the slow creeping of age into her mother's countenance. She saw the hair-thin lines at Ailuwa's mouth and eyes that would someday turn to deep wrinkles; the slightest softening of her shoulders into a rounded curve; even her hair seemed to have lost some of its luster. Perhaps the loss of Brekka had hit Ailuwa even harder than Sinmara had realized, or perhaps she was just seeing her mother anew. In any case, these realizations cooled the embers of Sinmara's frustration, and she stepped forward seeking to comfort her mother rather than to confront her.

The firstborn man spoke before she could.

"Greetings, Sinmara, child of Ailuwa! I had hoped I might meet you today. When last I saw you, you were no higher than my knee, and look at you now!"

So this was one of the firstborn she had seen before. Sinmara smiled at him graciously, uncertain of what to do otherwise. All respected the firstborn for their great age and their wisdom, but then fólk mostly respected each other anyway. Sinmara felt she should somehow acknowledge that she understood what sort of fólk this was before her, but had no intuition of how to do so. And, she realized, she was gawking. So she simply said, "I am pleased to meet you. Or...to see you again."

The man crossed one hand over his chest, and bent at the waist- a genuflection completely foreign to Sinmara.

"The pleasure is mine," he said. "It gives me great pleasure to meet a guardian among our kind, especially one who takes her duties as seriously as I am told you do. Keep us safe, Sinmara." With that, the strange little man turned on his heel, walked down the hall, and entered a portal on the far end.

Ailuwa watched him go, then turned to her daughter.

"Ananz has an odd way about him, does he not? Yet he is wise beyond measure. I often wonder if all the really old ones are like him. I am not sure whether I wish that to be so or not."

Sinmara collected herself, and opened her mouth to speak, but before she could her mother raised a hand.

"I am certain you have much you would like to say to me, and many questions as well. I will tell you what I can. But not here." She gestured for Sinmara to follow her, then walked back to the central atrium. The two of them crossed the mossy floor. Sinmara noted the children were back at play, though she did not see little Hanso. She followed her mother into yet another hallway. This one sloped downward gently, and was much longer than the others Sinmara had entered. Unlike the other hallways she had seen, there were no portals lining the sides of this path. The lamps were regularly spaced, but they dimmed slightly as the floor descended. Sinmara felt the air warming around her as well, and was surprised to find herself becoming almost drowsy. She had been anxious and confused, even angry just moments before, but now she felt only a subtle curiosity. Where was her mother leading her?

Finally, when they had travelled far and deep enough that Sinmara could no longer see the hallway entry behind her, they reached the terminus of the hall. The two women stood in front of what Sinmara at first took to be a portal. However, rather than rockwalk through the portal arch, Ailuwa simply pressed against the heavy stone with her hand. After a moment's resistance, the doorway split down the middle and opened. A blast of wet, warm air dampened Sinmara's hair as it rushed past her. The air carried an odd scent with it, loamy yet sharp, strong, yet not unpleasant, and strangely familiar. Yet even as she sought to place the scent, she was taken aback by the strange beauty of the scene before her.

She stood in a chamber not much larger than her own room back in the warren, but far more interesting. Dozens of stalactites descended from the roof of the chamber, all of different lengths and dimensions. They were each threaded through with glistening mineral deposits, like veins which sparkled in the pearlescent light.

Directly below these descending spires was a pool, occupying most of the center of the circular room. The light in the chamber seemed to come from the depths of this pool. The water itself was murky and clouded, and it was impossible to tell how deep it might be. But from somewhere in the depths of the pool there glowed a golden light, which filtered through the water and diffracted from its surface, casting shadows on the walls that undulated hypnotically. As Sinmara watched, a single droplet of mineral-laden water dripped from one of the spires into the waiting waters below, sending ripples across the pool's surface and scattering the light along the walls.

After a moment of silence, Ailuwa turned to her daughter.

"Do you know what this place is, Sinmara?"

Sinmara simply shook her head, feeling like she should not disturb the serenity of this place any further by speaking.

Ailuwa watched her daughter stare into the waters, then spoke again.

"This," she began, then paused. "This...is where we all came from.

This is where we were born."

"I don't understand."

"Have you never wondered how we come into this world?"

Sinmara was embarrassed suddenly, and felt much younger than she cared for. "Well...I know what you told me. That children come from the capital. And later, I... I simply thought it happened much like it does amongst the sheep."

Ailuwa smiled, but shook her head,

"You are clever. I was curious why you had never asked. But, in this case, your cleverness has led you astray. And, truth to be told, I should have explained it all to you sooner." She sighed. "There is great beauty in the ways that other creatures create their young. But our way is different from all others."

As she spoke, another drop fell into the pool. Ailuwa turned and gestured towards the rippling waters.

"Fólk come not from a womb, or an egg. We come from this place, and places like it elsewhere."

Sinmara's confusion showed plain on her face. Ailuwa continued.

"It is like this. When one of the fólk, or a fólkish couple, is ready to raise a child, a dream will come to them. Perhaps they will dream into a plant just as it bears fruit, or even an animal mother as she gives birth; sometimes it is nothing like this. The dream is different for everyone, but all wake with the same understanding, even if they have never been told the ways of our people. The dream will lead them to the chamber, and they will reach into the waters of the pool, and they will draw forth a child."

Sinmara stared at the pool in wonder, but said nothing. She could think of nothing to say. Her mother continued.

"This is the usual way of things. Sometimes, however, a child will simply appear from the waters by herself. Fólk check the pool regularly, and once in a rare while, someone will arrive to find a babe already here, sleeping on the edge of the waters. Such a child will be taken in by some fólk who has not yet had the dream, or perhaps a couple with another child already."

Sinmara looked at her mother questioningly, but Ailuwa was not yet finished.

"And sometimes, though even more rarely, a full-grown fólk will emerge from the pool. I have never seen this myself, but it is known to happen. I have heard that some of these fólk may even have lived once before, and emerge from the pool to return to us."

Sinmara had to speak now. "How is this possible? How...how have I not known any of this?"

"It is my fault. I...I was not prepared to have this conversation with you before. The others encouraged me to do so. It is normal for fólk to explain this to children when they are much younger than you are. Probably, you would have at least heard it from another child by now, but there have been so few of them in the warren since...lately."

Sinmara was reeling with this rush of information, while also wondering how it was possible that the million questions racing through her mind now had never occurred to her before. She felt offbalance, almost afraid.

"Are you alright?"

She struggled to control her emotions. "I am fine, mother. Please. Please continue."

Ailuwa bit her lip, searching her daughter's face. When she spoke again, her voice was slower. "Fólk may go into the pool as well. When one of us becomes very aged, and feels that the time is right, we may return to this place, and enter the waters from which we emerged. Some of those who enter the waters may return again, someday, perhaps when all who knew them before have similarly passed. Perhaps they emerge elsewhere, in other lands. Or they may pass from the world entirely. None can say when a fólk will go into the water, or what will become of them afterwards."

A thought had occurred to Sinmara, and she could restrain herself no longer.

"So which was I? How was I born? Did you dream me? Did I appear beside the waters? Or...have I lived before? I know I have been in this place," and she did, she felt it in her flesh, "but I cannot remember!" She looked around herself then, and seeing nowhere to recline, sat suddenly on the damp stone floor.

Ailuwa knelt beside her, and clasped her around the shoulders. She drew her into her arms, and Sinmara buried her face in her mother's hair. Her own strong emotions had taken her by surprise, but the equal surprise of her mother's embrace helped her compose herself somewhat. It had been some time since her mother had held her, since anyone had.

She relaxed in Ailuwa's arms, then with a quick squeeze, the older woman pulled away. They stared into each other's black eyes, each seeing herself reflected in the other's gaze, before Ailuwa spoke.

"There is more I must tell you. I am so sorry, so deeply sorry, to lay this all on you at once. But you must know. Are you prepared?" Sinmara swallowed.

"Please. Go on."

Ailuwa took a deep breath. "I did dream you. And you have been here before. But...it was not my dream alone that preceded your birth.

And you were not born out of these waters."

"Then...I came from somewhere else? A different pool?"

"This is the only pool on the island, the only pool anyone here was born from. You were born in this land, my child. But you were not born in the usual way of our people. You... You were born of a woman."

Sinmara did not understand. "So you did give birth to me, the way I thought before?"

"Not I, child. I dreamed you. I found you. I raised you. By the ways of our people, by the bonds between us, I am your mother.

"But I did not bring you forth into this world. You were born of another. A woman. An unfólkish woman. You were born among the men of this land, my daughter."

Sinmara pulled away from Ailuwa then. Her stomach hurt, and unbidden tears squeezed from her eyes. She wanted to stand and leave, to push this from her mind and forget it ever happened. But her legs were weak beneath her, and she felt dizzy. Nothing made sense. She heard the truth in her mother's words, and felt for a moment that she was trapped, here beneath the stone, within the earth, trapped and might never get out. She turned her back on her mother, and stared through blurred eyes into the deep waters of the golden-blue pool.

She had never suspected. She thought herself observant, intuitive. She had known that much about the world was a mystery to her, but she had thought she could count on a few things as certain. Never had she thought she was different from the people she had known her whole life. She had always felt before that she was in her proper place, even if she did enjoy visiting the surface more than some, even if she was the only person her own age in the warren, even if she didn't understand everything she saw and heard around her. And now...

"If...if I am really born of men, then why am I able to move as fólk do, through rock and stone? Why can I harness the knacks? Or are these powers not unique to the fólk? Can men do these things as well?"

Her mother looked relieved to have been given a question she could answer, then suddenly pensive as she considered her response. "No. They cannot. And I cannot tell you why, exactly, these things are possible for you. But I can tell you that when you were very young, when you first came to me, before I took you to our warren, I brought you here. I bathed you in these waters. And as you grew, you were able to move through the rock unassisted, once you learned the way, like any other fólkish child."

"But how did you know to do that? Am I the only human-born among our kind, or are there others? And why did you take me? Where did I come from?" Sinmara could not control her emotions any longer. As she sobbed, tears fell from her eyes into the waters below. Ailuwa approached and put her arms around her, pulling Sinmara in for another embrace. They stood pressed together until Sinmara's tears began to subside. As they did, however, her anger rose again, and she pushed her mother away one more.

"Answer my questions, Ailuwa. The story of my life is not what I thought it was. I deserve answers. Now!" she said, as she saw hesitation in her mother's face.

Ailuwa held up a hand, and composed herself before speaking.

"I brought you here to give you answers, and I will. But first you must understand some things. All of us, fólk and man, must live with some mysteries. Greatest among these is the mystery of our origins. We, the fólk, know that we are born of the earth, born of stone and water. We may return to the stone when we are ready, sinking deeper and deeper into the earth, or we may return to the waters from which we came. But we do not know how, or why, this came to be. It simply is, and we accept this. Accepting this, accepting that there are certain things we do not know, and may never know, allows us to see things clearly and truly. It is fundamental to our way of life."

Ailuwa stopped, sighed in resignation, and spoke again.

"You are here," she began, "because I brought you here. You are not the first man-child to live among our kind as one of our own. It does not happen often, but it does happen. Perhaps it was more common in the past. Apart from the differences in our births, our lives, our perceptions and our abilities, our two peoples are much the same, and we share many of the same lands. From time to time, a human child will come among us, and become one of our own. It can only happen with children, for only they can be brought to see the world as we do, to truly live among us as fólk. You must know this. You must know this is part of our way, and you are not alone in this regard.

"How it came to pass in your case, however, was unusual. I have told you how, sometimes, a fólkish couple will dream of a child. So it was with me and Shoka. We had been together for many years, and talked sometimes of children, but none came to us. We both became absorbed in our duties, here in the capital. She was learning to dream into plants, and I was honing my skills in farseeing and counsel.

"Then, one night, I had the child-dream. I saw myself holding a baby, nursing her from my own breast. But I was not in the capital, or underground at all. I had not yet been to see the birth pool, but I knew I was not there. I was aboveground, standing in a great field between two hills. All around me there was snow falling, driving against me and the child. I held the baby closer to me, for warmth, and as I did so I heard a great cry, rising above the sound of the wind, carried along by it.

"Then I woke, disoriented, with Shoka still asleep beside me. At first, I thought it had been a normal dream, but as I turned to sleep again, I felt that my breasts were tender, and cold. They were already beginning to swell with milk. I knew then that my vision had been no night-time fantasy, but a true child dream. Still I did not understand it, and as I pondered what to do, I slipped back into sleep.

When I awoke, Shoka was already up, and quite agitated. Before I could tell her of my child dream, she said she had had a strange dream herself. She could not tell me much of it- she either could not recall or could not describe the details- but she said we had to go immediately to the birthing pool. I told her then of my dream. We were both confused, but overjoyed as we ran down the hallway leading to this very chamber. Yet when we got here, and peered into the waters, we saw no babe waiting to be plucked out and into our arms. I was terribly disappointed, but Shoka seemed to have an understanding that I did not, and bade me wait while she returned to our quarters. Shortly she returned, carrying something clutched between her thumb and forefinger. She held it before her, and I saw that it was a single seed. As I watched, she reached her hand out over the pool, and held the seed under one of the spires you see descending from the ceiling, until a drop of liquid finally fell upon it.

Then she said we must visit her garden, and plant the seed. She could not explain why, but she assured me that doing so was instrumental to the birth of our child. Shoka had always shown herself to be reliable, and both of us knew to respect the power of child dreams, so we did as she thought we should. We planted the seed on the edge of her garden, one of those providing for the capital.

Then, we waited. We did not have to wait long. The next day, a green shoot sprouted from the ground where we had planted the seed. By the following day, leaves had appeared. On the third day, a bud formed at the top of the shoot. And on the fourth day, the bud opened and revealed a great flower, pink with spots of red, smelling of rainwater and iron. Shoka grabbed the flower at its base, and pulled it out down to the roots. There was a shape tangled up in the tendrils, and as Shoka brushed the dirt off of it, I could see it was the form of a tiny babe.

I was frightened, at first, when I saw it. I had never heard of such a thing. But Shoka told me there was nothing to fear, that she was practicing a knack known to the growers of our people, though one rarely used.

She pulled the tiny form from amongst the roots of the plant, and then handed it to me. It was a mottled gray-brown color, and cold to the touch. When I looked at it closely, it looked less like a fólkish baby than I had thought at first. There was only an impression of eyes, sunk into its vegetal features, a small lump where a nose would be, root-like protuberances suggesting arms and legs. And it was much smaller than a newly risen baby would be. Yet it was also heavier than it looked.

As I held the strange root baby, Shoka stripped the leaves and petals from the plant. She placed them in a bowl, then filled it with a bit of water from the garden spring. With a pestle she mashed the bits of flower into a thick paste. Then she insisted we return to our chamber.

Once there, Shoka ate a small dab of the flower paste, and sat on the floor. After some time, she reached out to me, indicating she wanted the root-child. I handed it to her, and she held it to her stomach, and closed her eyes.

Almost immediately they flew open again. Clutching the odd bit of root to her chest, Shoka looked up at me, and said we needed to prepare for an overland journey, immediately.

I tried to argue with her, but she was insistent. We quickly packed bags and food enough to travel for several days. We wrapped the root child in oil cloth to keep it from drying out. Then we set out on our journey.

First we took a waystone to the south. We had more of them at that time, and it was easier to travel long distances using them. We exited from a stone set into the cliffs by the sea. As soon as we stepped forth onto the beach, great whipping winds set against us, and I was chilled as never before. Shoka and I both adjusted as quickly as we could, but it was so cold that doing so greatly sapped our energy, and forced us to move slowly. We trudged forth against the battering wind. Every so often, Shoka would dip into the flower paste she had made, close her eyes for a moment, and then adjust our course.

I still was not certain what we were doing, although I had my suspicions. Shoka was so wrapped up in concentration that there was little opportunity for us to talk, and I was mentally occupied as well, using my farsight to scan the land around us, making sure we were safe and unobserved. So we moved forward, slowly and silently, the bundle on my back feeling heavier with every step.

Finally, we came to a long valley nestled between two low hills. Standing at the crest of one of them, looking down, I could see a human home nestled into the earth of the hill opposite. It was then that I knew what Shoka intended to do, and I finally balked. I said, "I want a child as badly as you, dear heart. But not like this. I cannot do this."

"Shoka looked at me from her spot just below me on the hill. The sun was setting at my back, and her eyes shimmered strangely in the light, perhaps from her hours of eating the substance she had made. When she spoke, her voice was rough and thick. I had never heard her sound like that before.

"You have had the child dream, the same as I have, Ailuwa. Both of us. You know what that means. We must do this."

"I know what I saw," I said. "But I cannot do this. Perhaps we should have waited longer for the pool to bring forth a child for us. This cannot be the way."

"But this is part of our ways as well. Why do think I know how to do what I did?" She gestured to the pack still on my back. "That is proof alone that we are doing the right thing."

"I pulled the pack from behind me, and unwrapped it. The bundle within looked grotesque to me now, with its rudimentary, bulbous hints of a face and limbs. I handed it to Shoka, as I felt the tears begin to fill my eyes.

"I know. I know that this is what we are meant to do. But I cannot." That is what I told her, and I feel shame for it still.

Shoka took the bundle from me, and held it gently in her arms. She gave me one long, searching glance. Then she turned, and descended into the valley.

I watched her approach the farmstead. It was surrounded by a low fence, enclosing a long, low building set against the hillside, and another smaller building set into the earth of the hill itself. It was towards this building that Shoka made her way. I watched her creep to the side of the building, and then she was hidden from my view.

I sat on the hilltop and waited a while. The sun set behind me and the sky grew dark. It was a moonless, clear night, and after some time

I could see the lights begin to dance in the sky. For a while I got lost in watching them shimmer and warp, and I forgot my fear.

Then I heard a sound drift through the cold, clear air. At first I thought it was the keening of some animal. Then it came again, and I recognized it for a human scream.

My first instinct was to run to the house. I even took a few steps. But, I am ashamed to say, I was too afraid, even knowing that Shoka could be in danger, could need my assistance. I was frozen in place by the sounds I was hearing. I had never heard anything like them, and they rooted me to the spot. Yet I had to know if Shoka was safe, even as I feared learning the source of the terrible noises.

I cast my eye out over the valley. I had never attempted farsight in such close range to myself, and never so near to a human dwelling. Yet it was as it always was, when my farsight worked: I could see everything with utter clarity.

I saw Shoka, pressed low against the top of the human building, nearly buried in the grass that grew there, the strange bundle still in her arms. That was a great relief, for she seemed unharmed. Yet still the sounds reached my ears, penetrating my consciousness even though my physical body should have shut out all sensation while I cast my eye away from myself.

Again, almost without intending to, I allowed my vision to drift, downward from the roof where Shoka lay, down to the ground. My eye moved forward, passing through the surface of the human dwelling, and then I could see inside.

The home was dim inside, and it was difficult to see clear details. This surprised me, for I can usually see as clearly with my outer eye as with the eyes in my own head. But the home was lit only by a small fire, burning in the center of the dwelling, and by this light alone could I see the scene within.

My eye was drawn then towards the people inside the structure. I saw a woman. She was lying flat on her back. Her brow was covered in sweat. From her determined grimace and the tears streaming from her eyes, I could tell she was in great pain. Beside her then I saw another woman, gray-haired, her face creased with lines denoting her advanced age, looking older by far than even the most ancient Firstborn. She held the reclining woman's hand, and leaned over, whispered something in her ear. Slowly the younger woman seemed to calm down, and her breathing slowed. She nodded once, quickly.

Still gripping the younger woman's hand, the old woman helped her sit up awkwardly, struggling to get her legs under her. The covers slipped from her, and I could see she was wearing only a scrap of fabric, soaked through by her efforts.

The younger woman squatted down on the flat surface she had lain upon, and the older woman used her free hand to clear the discarded coverings away. The young woman set her face with determination, and began breathing rapidly again. Then she began to scream. I could not hear her in my vision, of course, but I had the sense that the echoes of her screams were leaving the house and reaching my body, far on the other side of the valley.

The women let go of each other's hands then, and the younger woman reached with both arms under her shift. She gave one more sharp yell, and there was a rush of fluid onto the surface below. The woman brought her arms back up, and in them, she held a tiny child.

The woman slumped back against the wall, and slid down. She turned the child to look in its face, and she saw what I had already seen, already known without knowing how I knew. There was something wrong with the child. Something covered the child's face, something that was not supposed to be there. I saw the new mother begin to panic then, but the older woman quickly reached over. With her hand on the back of the baby's head, she rubbed at its face until the substance covering it peeled away and fell off. Now there was the perfect face of a newborn child, a sight which I had beheld but once in my life before, and not of a child born from woman.

But then I could tell from the women's faces that something was still wrong. The child did not breathe. Its limbs moved, and it had one eye open, open and searching. But it drew no breath.

The old woman reached over then, and removed the child from its mother's arms. She turned it over so that it was chest down in her hand, and began gently tapping and massaging its back.

The younger woman looked frantic now. She seemed to realize suddenly that there was still a cord connecting her to the child, for she reached down and began to pull it out of herself, even as she continued talking at the other woman.

It was then that I saw the blood. It was seeping through the front of the young mother's shift, and as I watched it began to spread out and away from her across the pallet. The young mother blanched, and looked away from her baby to the great pool forming under her. She said a single word, and the other woman looked up from her ministrations upon the baby to see what was happening. For a moment, the briefest moment, both of them stopped doing anything, and just looked at each other. Then the young mother reached out for her baby. It had stopped squirming in the old woman's hands, but one of its hands still clenched and unclenched. The old woman turned the baby over, and both of its eyes were closed. She looked down at it for a moment, then handed it gently to the mother.

The mother took the child in her arms, and sank further down against the wall. She looked into the baby's face, and smiled at it, weakly, as the blood spread further out from her. Without taking her eyes off the child, she spoke a word. The old woman stood there, looking helpless. The young mother spoke again. Then again, her lips moving in the same way. Still the other woman did not move. Finally, the pale young woman looked away from the child in her arms, into the old woman's face, and with all the force she could muster she said the word again, her eyes searching her care tender's face beseechingly. Again she spoke. A name, perhaps.

Finally, the other woman stood tall, turned, and rushed across the dwelling with all the speed she could muster. I followed her with my sight, saw her reach the portal, open it, and exit the dwelling. Then I turned my eye back to the woman in the bed. She was looking at the baby again, cradling its naked form. I focused on the baby as well, then. It had stopped moving entirely.

Then Shoka was there. I did not see where she came from, but now she was at the woman's side. She reached out, and touched the young mother's shoulder.

The unfólkish woman looked up at Shoka, and I saw the confusion in her face. For a moment the two of them just stared at each other, not saying anything. Then something seemed to pass between them, and the woman on the bed nodded once, weakly.

Shoka produced the bundle she had carried from Ásbyrgi. She also pulled out the remains of the flower mash she had made. As the other woman watched, Shoka dabbed a finger into the paste, then gently spread it on the forehead of the silent baby in the woman's arms. She pressed some of the paste to the baby's lips, and into its mouth. And she spread a dab across the child's chest.

The she picked the bundle up from the side of the bed pallet, and slowly unwrapped it. She held up its contents so the other woman could see. The produced object looked just as it had when I had seen it last. It was brown and splotchy, but vaguely child-like in form. The other woman stared up at it, her eyes suddenly seeming to have trouble focusing. Gently, Shoka lowered it to the woman's chest, next to the newborn child.

She then took another dab of the flower paste, and pressed to the reclining mother's lips. I could see Shoka's own lips moving slightly. She seemed to be whispering to the woman, who now pressed her lips together, bringing the paste into her mouth. Then she looked down at the two figures in her arms, the still child and the child-like root.

Then, suddenly, the root looked different to me. The features that before had only approximated a face began to sharpen. The protuberances that suggested limbs began to lengthen. The flesh of the root lightened, until it was bright and pink. In a matter of moments, it seemed there was not one newborn child pressed against the woman's breast, but two. And they were, in every way I could see, identical.

The woman and Shoka both stared at the tiny figures for a moment. Then Shoka placed her hand upon the woman's brow, shut her eyes, and uttered a word. The woman closed her eyes as well, and for a blink of time, everything in the room was utterly still. Even without the ability to hear in my vision, I could see that all was silent.

Then Shoka and the other woman both opened their eyes together. The woman pointed her chin at the newborn baby in her arms. For the first time since she appeared in my vision, Shoka seemed to hesitate. The woman became more insistent, and tried to push the baby towards Shoka, while still holding onto the root child-not that one could tell them apart. Even as she did so, I saw her white skin blanch, and her eyes started to roll back in her head. She was losing consciousness.

Shoka reached down then, and carefully pried the baby from the woman's arms. She arranged the root child so that it rested in the crook of the mother's arm where the newborn had just been. Then she quickly wrapped the child in the swaddling she had brought with her. This done, she looked back down at the woman on the bed. The mother was grasping the child-like form in her arms tightly, and her eyes were closed. Shoka bent down, and pressed her lips to the woman's brow.

Suddenly I was looking through the eyes of my body again, out over the flat of the valley. Down where the human dwelling stood, I could make out two figures running towards the door of the building I had cast my eye into. I feared then for Shoka; what would happen when they found her in the home?

Then her hand was on my shoulder. I knew not how she got there so quickly. I knew not the meaning of all that I had seen. Nor, truly, did I care. I cared only that here was my beloved, safe and sound, and in her arms a child. A child that I now recognized. The child I had dreamed about. You."

Here Ailuwa stopped.

"I don't understand." This was all Sinmara could say. She struggled to control herself now, and Ailuwa looked away from her, back into the gently glowing waters of the pool.

Sinmara took a shuddering breath, and began again. "I don't understand. Any of it. How did Shoka know where to find...that place? Why would you take a human child away from her family? What happened to them? Why would you leave some sort of root-baby with them? And if I... if I am really human-born, why can I do fólkish things, things humans cannot? Or is that not true either? Can humans do all that fólk can? And, are there others like me? Have other children been stolen from their families?"

Sinmara could put no name to her feelings. She teetered between rage, confusion, sadness, and curiosity. From what she knew of mankind- which, she freely admitted, was not much- their lives were much harder than those of the fólk. They struggled to find and keep food, they had to make their own flimsy shelters, and were cut off from the friendship with the earth that allowed the fólk to travel through rock, to fashion dwellings within them, and to have any number of powerful knacks, and skills, and senses, as their individual dispositions allowed. Even as she felt a sense of betrayal at discovering her origins had been different than she had always believed, than she had been led to believe, she could not deny her gratitude at having brought up amongst the fólk.

But so much of what she thought she knew had just been called into question, not least of all the trust she had always had in Ailuwa. Ailuwa who had raised her from her earliest memory, and with whom she had always felt safe and loved, if occasionally held at a bit of a distance. Perhaps the reason for that distance had just been given to her.

"Am I even fólkish at all?" she whispered.

Ailuwa moved next to her daughter, took her into her arms, and held her. At first Sinmara wanted almost to push her away, but she realized she needed this assurance. And after a minute in her mother's arms, Sinmara remembered herself. Whatever she might have learned about herself, whatever else Ailuwa might have to tell her, she belonged where she was. She was as connected to her warren and her people as any other fólk she knew. And that thought strengthened her.

She looked up at Ailuwa. "Tell me the rest."

Ailuwa nodded, released Sinmara, and took her place opposite her once again. She took a deep breath, let it out slowly, and began again.

"When Shoka showed you to me, you were still not breathing. But you were warm to the touch, and now I could see your eyes moving behind their lids. Shoka said that the plant medicine she had given you would keep you alive, but that we had to hurry and get you back here as quickly as possible. Then we would know if you could be saved. You see, had we not found you, had we not been led to you by whatever force sent us our dreams and visions, you never would have lived to draw breath.

"With no time to spare, we rushed away from the human home. We both feared we did not have enough time, so we pushed ourselves without rest, shedding all of our supplies, everything except for you. We passed you back and forth, taking turns carrying you as we rushed across the land. I do not know how we did it- I remember very little of the journey, in fact, but we somehow got back to the farestone before the sun rose again. We both held you as we entered, neither of us even certain that we would be able to carry you with us. But we did, and we journeyed through the stone, back here. We rushed into the atrium, and down the hallway to this very room, meeting no one on the way.

By the time we got down here, you had begun to turn blue. I was certain we had taken too long, that it was too late to awaken you. Not that I had any idea how to do so in the first place. But Shoka took you from my arms, and carried you to the edge of the pool. She laid you gently against the surface of the water. Still you did not breathe. Shoka tried to submerge you, but the water was too shallow, here at the edge. Finally, she handed you back to me, quickly stripped off her clothes, and reached for you again.

I could not believe she was about to enter the pool, but she assured me it would be fine- she had been born from this very pool, after all, and would be sure not to disturb it, and this was the only way to save you. This, she said, was what she had seen most clearly in her own child-dream: herself, emerging from the water, with you in her arms, healthy and crying. I was exhausted- we both were- and knew not what else to do. I handed you to her.

Slowly, Shoka stepped into the edge of the pool. As you can see, the sides slope gently towards the center, then turn sharply, so she had to step carefully. At last, she had to sit down and ease herself over the lip inside the pool, so that the water lapped at her stomach. Then she lowered you in, until you were immersed in the waters.

For a breath of time, nothing happened. Then, from the depths of the pool, I saw a light, brighter than the glow of the surrounding waters, rising slowly. I watched it grow brighter, until it was nearly at the surface of the water. Then the light rushed towards you, and into you, and then you opened your eyes.

Shoka raised you from the water, dripping light like molten gold, and you opened you mouth, and took a great breath, and then you let out an earsplitting wail that echoed throughout the chamber. It was a beautiful noise. You were alive. We had done it. She had done it. Shoka turned to me, wet and spent, and she smiled as I had not seen her smile since the day we realized a child was to come into our life. She held you to her chest, kissed your forehead, and began wading gently back towards the shore, and me. You were still glowing gently, and still wailing.

Shoka reached the edge of the pool, the waters lapping around her ankles, and before she stepped from them she held you out to me. I took you in my arms. I leaned over and kissed Shoka, holding you close between us. Then I turned away, and went to retrieve swaddling cloth from my pack across the room, by the portal.

As I walked away from the pool, the light slowly faded from your skin, and the room grew dimmer. I dried you off and began to wrap you up, then turned my face back towards the pool to smile at Shoka.

Shoka was no longer standing at the edge of the waters. She was nowhere to be seen. The surface of the pool was still and flat, as if nothing had disturbed the surface for some time. Shoka's clothes lay by the side of the pool, just where she had left them. But Shoka was not there. Other than the clothes, it was as if she had never been there.

I called her name, for a while. I ran to the pool, and looked deep into it, seeing nothing but the usual soft and pleasant glow. I'm certain I began to scream at some point, upsetting you in my arms. I was just about to set you down and dive into the pool when the chamber doors opened, and through them came Ananz. I recognized him. I had met him a few times at that point, although I had not seen him in years. He crossed the chamber towards me. Without saying anything, he put his hand on my shoulder, then helped me up. He led me from the chamber, still holding you in my arms, leaving our packs and Shoka's discarded clothes behind. I tried to explain what had happened, but he stopped me. He did not seem to want to talk.

Ananz led me back up the hall, and into another section of the capitol. To my surprise, I was fighting unconsciousness at this point, despite being nearly mad with confusion and grief.

Ananz produced a beverage, and insisted I drink it. Then he reminded me that you would be hungry. You were still wailing, and I was later to find that you had woken many of the other fólk in these halls. Hardly knowing what I was doing, I held you to my breast, and you began to feed. Somehow, holding you, I was able to calm myself, and I fell asleep on a bier, with you in my arms.

Later, Ananz told me his side. He had awoken from strange dreams of his own, knowing only that he must get to the birthing pool as fast as possible, a voice still ringing in his ears. He had not known what he was going to find, he said, but he had somehow known what to do. He tells me he has experienced many strange things in his time, before and since, but never anything quite like this. While I slept, he met with the other elders, and explained what he had witnessed directly, and deduced. When I awoke again, I told him the story I have just told you, in as much detail as I could remember. No one knew quite what to make of it, and as far as I know, that has not changed.

It was known that, from time to time, the unfólkish have come amongst us by various means. The other growers did know of the knacks Shoka had used, to make a root form resembling a child. But still there was much that none of us understood.

But what had happened to Shoka; that was not as confusing as some of the other elements of the story I have just told you. The oldest among us present at that time- not Ananz, but his companion, Oyu- reminded us of what we had each known already, and what I had greatly feared. Sometimes a fólk may return to his or her place of birth, enter the waters, and go to rejoin whatever force sent us forth in the first place. Perhaps, she speculated, the light that infused you had to be replaced by the light in Shoka. Or perhaps this was not the case at all. There were no easy answers, but whatever the reason, Shoka was gone.

I hope that someday she might return. But although the waters have sent forth new fólk since then, I have never again dreamt of the pool. I fear Shoka may not return at all, at least not while I am here to greet her."

Ailuwa was staring into the waters now, and though her face was impassive, she had struck Sinmara to the core, filling her with wonder, with doubt, with a formless regret. So much pain had accompanied her arrival in this world. So much pain...

Then Ailuwa spoke again. "Yet if this is so, it is as it must be. I will tell you truly that I have struggled with this, daughter, and at times allowed my grief to drive me away from you. It is an uncommon event amongst our people, to lose those closest to us, and it almost never happens so suddenly and unexpectedly. I could not tell you of my grief, not while you were young, and few of my companions or even our wisest elders seemed to fully understand what I was going through. So I have often turned within myself, and in some ways become less than what I was."

Ailuwa turned her head to meet Sinmara's searching gaze then, and peered deep into her eyes. "But I have also become more. You have made me a mother, and that is a gift I am thankful for every single day. It has been my greatest joy to watch you grow, to watch you find your way in this world, to take up the role of a guardian and a protector for our people, even at so young an age. If I seem sad sometimes in your presence, it is only because I know Shoka would be as proud of you as

I am, and I regret that she is not here to experience that joy, to share it with you.

"And the woman who gave you to us, that you might live; the unfólkish woman: She would not understand much about our people or our lives. But I looked upon her face. She gave you to us willingly, and with hope for your future. I believe she would be glad if she could see you now, see who you have become and are becoming. Sinmara, you are the daughter of three mothers, loved more than you can know, and the world is immensely richer for having you in it."

Ailuwa had finished, and for a moment there was no sound in the chamber other than the occasional plunk of a drop of water falling into the pool. Sinmara's voice was thick with emotion, but steady enough when she finally spoke. "I would've understood if you had told me before. I would have understood. You didn't have to keep this from me. I didn't have to grow up thinking something other than what was true."

Ailuwa opened her mouth to speak, but Sinmara continued.

"I know I should say I understand. I want to say that I do. But everything I thought I knew... It's wrong. You didn't have to do that to me. Why did you do that to me? And... why tell me now? Why, after letting me believe something you knew to be wrong for my whole life? Why are you doing this to me?" Sinmara looked away from her mother as she struggled to put a name to her emotions. Almost unconsciously she clenched and released her left fist over and over, and wrapped her knuckles against the rock upon which she was sitting. She had no experience with rage, or betrayal. But, even as she tried to name and acknowledge her feelings, they began to pass, or at least change.

She had always felt that she belonged here, among the fólk, felt it so fiercely that she had even set out on the path of protecting her people, a concept few others seemed to comprehend. And she had protected them – just a few days ago, she had deterred the revenant from encroaching upon her home, vanquished him by removing his animating force and taking it into herself. Didn't this prove that her place among the fólk was justified?

And hadn't she learned from experience and teaching, time and again, that dreams and premonitions such as the ones that had led Ailuwa to find her as a newborn were meant to be followed? If Sinmara had such visions now, she knew she would follow them unquestioningly, even after all she had just been told. In finding her, and taking her in, Ailuwa, and, Shoka, and perhaps even the unfólkish woman who had actually birthed her – had only followed the will of the hidden will which seem to protect them all. Sinmara found her anger dissipating, almost in spite of herself. Yet the question remained, even without the anger behind it.

152

"Why did you decide to tell me this now?"

Ailuwa heard the acceptance and resignation behind this question, and perhaps that sense, as much as her desire to be truthful, allowed her say what needed to be said.

"Sinmara, something has changed. Our people have lived in harmony with this land for ages. When humans first began to arrive, we hid ourselves from them, but this did not greatly change our lives. For the most part we continue to live as we always have, in harmony with and contemplation of the land."

"But for some time now a few of us have noticed...differences. Nothing major at first– troubled dreams, knacks that went awry. Nothing that could be said to form a pattern, yet unsettling nonetheless.

"Recently it's gotten worse. I first noticed that my sight, my farsight, was showing me things that should not be. Strange figures moving across the land. Great rivers of fire bursting forth, then disappearing just as suddenly. And, worst of all: a noxious, choking cloud, spreading over the whole island, and growing, spreading, ceaseless, deadly. These visions would come to me, unbidden, flashes across my sight when I was viewing something mundane.

"At first I worried that it was just me, but I spoke to some of the other farseers, and they were experiencing the same thing.

"Then these tremors started in the earth. They pose no direct threat to us – not yet, anyway. But ever since the first big one of this year, there's been a kind of blank spot in my vision. I cannot see parts of our land. And these areas have spread in subsequent months. Once again, the other farseers have noticed the same thing. It is as if our vision simply... fails in these areas."

Sinmara considered this. "That is odd, but I'm still not certain what it has to do with me."

"Well, we first noticed these blind spots when we were attempting to find the source of the ash and smoke that is spreading from the earth. But after we noticed them, we – the other farseers – began to cast our eyes over the rest of the land. In no time at all, we found other blind spots, spots we had not noticed before.

Further investigation showed that most of these spots were around and over men's dwellings. We are not in the habit of observing men in their private affairs, so in most cases it is impossible for us to say how long the blind spots have been there. But some of them, we are certain, appeared fairly recently. The most recent one, it so happens, appeared just over the land where we entered the waystone that brought us here. Shortly after we entered, as far as anyone can tell."

Sinmara opened her mouth to speak but realize she had nothing to say. She and Ailuwa had not actually spoken yet about their experience traveling through the waystone.

Ailuwa anticipated the question Samara had seemed about to ask.

"I do not know whether his anything to do with us, or with what happened to poor Brekka. Whatever the cause, it is most worrisome. Not being able to farsee into an area is one thing – it is unusual, but no one except a farseer would even be likely to notice, especially given where the blank spots have been appearing. Yet what happened to us suggests a greater threat. The waystone we took has been compromised somehow, and that is not something that should be able to happen. Imagine if other waystones were cut off– there are not many, but we depend on swift travel through them in order to get goods and news from place to place. Worse yet, imagine if we were unable to rockwalk freely within our own homes. No one has been able to sync with the waystone since the blank spot appeared at the other end, and we have stopped trying for concern about opening a connection that leads to the capital. If this phenomenon came here, with the effect we fear it might have… fólk could find themselves trapped in the separate chambers of the warren, unable to leave for food or air or light. It would take a long time to die in such a situation, but die we would, one by one." Sinmara shuddered.

"And so we come to you, dear daughter. You are one of us, as fólkish as any fólk. But... that is not all you are. Unlike any other fólk of these parts, you were born among mankind. Your whole life I have tried to believe this mattered little. I have not wanted to burden you with the sense that you were different. Nor have I seen any indication that you were different. You have grown like fólk do. You have all the abilities and qualities of a young fólkish woman.

"But, for the first time, I've come to believe that you might have certain characteristics in addition to those shared by the fólk." Sinmara's eyes widened.

"First there was the matter of the unspirit you faced. You were the only one in the warren to sense its approach. True, you are our guardian, and it is understandable that you should be particularly attuned to the cairns near the gate. But someone else should have noticed as well. All of us are tied to those cairns, yet no one felt the disturbance but you.

"Then you defeated the draugr. Again, you are a guardian. This is your purpose. But these are not the times that were. You have not been trained by anyone who has faced a draugr, and you had never faced one before this attack. Unless I am mistaken?" Ailuwa sounded almost hopeful, but Sinmara shook her head. Ailuwa might be away from the warren often, but Sinmara would have found some chance to tell her mother if she had ever defeated a draugr before.

Ailuwa sighed. "Yes, I did not think so. It is not often that we encounter revenants- they tend to avoid our kind, just as we avoid them. They are a mannish sort of entity, and they can be difficult for fólk to deal with.

"Yet you defeated your first draugr with little difficulty. This is impressive. But, if I understand you, you also seem to have absorbed its essence, not just dispersed it. Did you know that this is not meant to be possible for the folk?"

Sinmara was not sure she cared for where this was headed.

"Well, maybe the lore is wrong. You said yourself that we do not often encounter these draugr. Perhaps they are more easily defeated than we have realized? Or maybe this one was different?"

"I have studied the path it seemed to come from, and consulted with the other elders. Indeed, that particular draugr was different. It has been in the land for a long time, and our people have encountered it before. It is no small thing that you defeated and observed any draugr, but that one particular has proved...

Problematic in the past. No, you were able to defeat it because doing so was in your power, not because any fólk could have.

"Well, perhaps Orri had something…"

"You mention the horse. Do you realize you should not have been able to bring him in to the warren with you? The animals here have been raised amongst our kind. They have eaten our food, drunk our water, and traveled through our means from birth. The horse you rescued was a human horse. He should not have been able to enter our dwelling. Yet you brought him through, with no trouble at all, as if you had raised him here yourself."

Sinmara was taken aback by this. She was beginning to wonder just how well she actually knew the world she thought she had been born into. Of course, her mother could have told her everything she needed to know much earlier. She could taste the bitterness of the thought.

"So let's say that your suspicions are correct, but there's something different about me. What are you getting at, exactly? What is this all about?"

Sinmara sensed her mother hesitating again, and finally snapped. "Tell me! Tell me now! I have a right to know!"

Ailuwa could stall no longer. "I have discussed these matters with some of the wisest among us. Together we have reached a consensus. We need you, daughter. Your people need you. There are strange things happening in the land, and they are beyond our power to understand. But you – you might have that power.

"The common thread here is man. Something seems to be happening in the world of men, and it is affecting us. And you, brilliant girl, daughter of my heart – you are one of us, but you have a connection to men as well, a connection none of us share. We need you to try to discover what is happening, to understand it, to figure out how it will affect us.

"I have always believed, and believe still, that you and I were brought together for some greater purpose. How can I think otherwise, given how Shoka and I found you, how we saved you? Now, perhaps, that purpose is revealed."

"You're still young, and I've sought to shelter you – maybe too much. I want to shelter you still. But now I fear that we are all in danger, and I cannot protect you. I must ask you to protect us."

Sinmara finally felt her mother's pain then. Ailuwa could've just asked for her help straight out, but Sinmara supposed she understood why she had not. She had caught a glimpse of the way Ailuwa must always feel, the struggle she held within herself for Sinmara's sake.

And Sinmara, for her part, had always felt called to protect her people. She was a guardian, wasn't she? Ailuwa might not have seemed to understand that choice, but now she was asking no more than Sinmara had already offered. Perhaps this desire to protect was something she had inherited from her mother.

There was much to say, much that could be said. "What must I do?"

Chapter 15

In his home, Vigi stared into the hearth fire. The feransdomr at Brauðavatn would take place in another week, and the priest had warned him it might not go smoothly. Not that Vigi needed to be told – he was a goði, and suspected he could more readily list all the dangers of a feransdomr than the foreign priest could. He felt the quickest flash of irritation, thinking of the way the priest spoke to him – not quite condescendingly, but always in a manner that presumed Vigi would do whatever was suggested. Vigi would, of course – the priest had more than proved the value of his insights, justifying the deference already due to him as an esteemed father of the church- but Vigi was an important man himself, and it rankled some part of him to have another presume to dictate his actions.

Yet the thought barely had time to form before it flitted from Vigi's mind. Though a foreigner, the priest had a goði's comprehension of the political landscape of the island, and Vigi was certain the priest only ever suggested the course of action that he, the powerful, ambitious goði, would have taken anyway. Well, perhaps not where Haraldr was concerned- but Vigi had understood the logic even there, though reluctantly. If they were ever to root out the heathenism from this land, to bring it into the light of Christ, sacrifices would have to be made by all of them. Their struggle would be rewarded.

And their goal was nearly in reach. Vigi could feel it, feel it in his bones. The people were crying out for a savior, even if they did not realize it. Once the unsalvageable heathens like Kveldulf and his ilk were rooted out, once their influence had been scrubbed away, they would turn their faces to the light of God. And, perhaps, they would turn their grateful hearts to Vigi as well, he who alone had had the foresight to protect them. Who had perhaps even been chosen by God to aid the people in their hour of need.

But first he must get through the Brauðavatn feransdomr. He did not anticipate much trouble from the people of the district. The taking was as lawful as could be, and Kveldulf, while respected, was apparently not popular enough to inspire anyone to do anything stupid. The remaining household itself was unlikely to offer much resistance; without their bændr, most of the thralls and farmhands had probably left already.

But there was still Kveldulf himself. His whereabouts were not known to Vigi, nor to the priest, whose connection with God sometimes offered him information not available to Vigi. Vigi did not seriously consider that the people of Brauðavatn could cause much trouble for his own men, but he knew better than to discount a former Varangian. How a warrior for the Church itself could fall so far from the light...it sickened Vigi.

Still, Father Pétur had explained so much to him about the true faith, so much he never could have imagined. Kveldulf was far from the only man to have it all wrong.

A moan from the corner of the room disturbed his thoughts. Haraldr rested fitfully on a pallet behind Vigi. Vigi's wife rose from her own pallet, and went to tend to the boy. Vigi had not known she was awake. Tensions had been high between the two of them since he had returned from the Althing. His wife was a godly Christian woman – early in the marriage it was she as much as anyone who had shown Vigi the way to the light. But she lacked the element of judgment that was required to follow her convictions to their natural conclusion, to see that the old ways had to be rooted out from the land, if they were ever to prosper. And she seemed to dislike the priest, even before he had returned from the Althing with their injured boy, and unsatisfactory explanations of what had happened. Vigi thought of rising and going to them both, but he could feel his lady's reprisal from across the room, and did not wish to engage it at this hour.

So he turned back to the fire, and stared into the flames.

ᛏ ᛉ ᛃ ᛏ ᛉ ᛃ ᛏ ᛉ ᛃ ᛏ ᛉ ᛃ ᛏ

Njála, to the south and west of Vigi, was preoccupied as well. She had sent most of the day washing the bedclothes, sweeping out the living quarters, churning milk for butter and cheese. Gunnar expected visitors soon, and Fulla insisted on showing them a clean and welcoming home when they arrived. The remainder of the Brauðavatn homestead, its people and its wares, was currently unguarded and unspoken for. No one had seen Kveldulf since the Althing, and his people were unsure of what to do. Gunnar himself had ridden over as soon as they returned from the Althing, to tell the people of Brauðavatn what had happened. Njála knew he had half hoped to find Kveldulf there, but the farmhands and servants swore he had not returned. They took the news of his banishment poorly. For all that he could be a mercurial presence, Kveldulf was much loved by his people, for he treated them kindly and well. They were dismayed to hear that Tryggvi was missing as well. The life the people of Brauðavatn had known was forever altered. Gunnar had invited some of them to visit his homestead to discuss what happened next, and they were due to arrive shortly.

Gunnar had also arranged for another goði to visit. There had been little time to discuss the strange events at this year's Althing before the end of the session was declared and the assembled farmers had to hurry back to care for their homesteads. Much about this situation was unprecedented, and it seemed Gunner felt he could waste no time marshaling support and deciding the best way to proceed. One of his bændr had been outlawed, he and his heir had both disappeared, and a valuable property stood unspoken for. This was an inherently unstable position, and resolving it could prove complicated. Gunnar knew Vigi himself would conduct the feransdomr, and just having his people in the neighborhood was likely to cause trouble.

Njála understood all this without having to be told, although Gunnar had explained why their house would be filled to capacity for the next several days, and she had overheard her mother and father talking about the best course of action.

Njála found that keeping busy with the work—sweep, wash, sweep, wash – helped her from becoming mired in her thoughts. At the Althing, despite the excitement, she had somehow expected that things would resolve themselves happily. Tryggvi would be found. Kveldulf would return. The banishment and the violence would be exposed as the result of a terrible misunderstanding of some sort, and everyone would be reconciled. Perhaps there would be some lingering hurt feelings or loss of status, but nothing would really change.

Yet now it had been over a week since the end of the Althing, and nothing had been resolved, certainly not for the better. Tryggvi was still missing. Kveldulf was still banished, and had fled into the wilderness. And her father's heart was broken.

Njála had never seen Gunnar like this. He was normally so jovial, joking with the farmhands, flirting with her mother, always taking time to play a game with Njála or share stories. Now, he was stern and focused. He seemed to have aged in just the past few days. He blamed himself for the disaster that had befallen Kveldulf, his friend and bóndi. Njála knew they were close, but had not appreciated just how much Kveldulf seemed to mean to her father. She had finally asked her mother about it.

"Your father and Kveldulf – they knew each other from boyhood," she said. "Your father is a bit younger than Kveldulf. So they were not especially close then. But Kveldulf was best friends with your father's older brother. Together the two of them journeyed abroad as youths, seeking their fortune and renown. Gunnar desperately wanted to go with them, but his father said he was still too young.

"Kveldulf returned from his travels; your father's brother did not. Though he had no obligation to do so, Kveldulf paid your grandfather compensation for the loss of his eldest son. He blamed himself for not being able to save poor Hrolf. I never heard the full story of what happened to him – no one liked to talk about it, but I understand it was unpleasant.

"Your grandfather accepted compensation from Kveldulf, and used it to foster your father out to the family of the Law-speaker, that he might come to know the laws of the land. From then on, Kveldulf was almost like another brother to Gunnar, taking the place of the one he had lost. Gunnar helped Kveldulf grow Brauðavatn, establish his herd and breeding reputation. Kveldulf comforted

Gunnar when his parents died, within months of each other, and was the first man to pledge to Gunnar as a goði in his own right.

"Kveldulf introduced Gunnar to me at Althing, and I in turn introduced Kveldulf to his wife, who was my own dear friend. We were all of us quite close, and expected that we would raise our families together.

"You and Tryggvi even played as tiny children, while the four of us visited and spoke of our hopes for you."

Here Fulla stopped, and turned away from Njála while she folded the bed clothes.

"Then Freyja died, along with her newborn baby. I do not know if you would remember this, you were still so young. We were all of us stricken with grief. Kveldulf and myself in particular. Your father and I tried to help Kveldulf as best as we could, even offered to foster Tryggvi. But Kveldulf turned within himself, and did not wish to be seen. We had a young child of our own, and your father's responsibilities were growing. There was only so much we could do. After a time, I think it just felt too painful for any of us to see much of each other. I regret that now – I regretted it at the time as well – but there was little I could do.

"It is only in the past few years that Kveldulf has begun to emerge. There were years he even missed the local things, which your father excused, but made no great impression on the other bændr. I think his boy helped him very much – despite the sadness I know he was raised in, he seemed so cheerful when I saw him, as cheerful as he had been as a baby.

"I know your father missed his close friendship with Kveldulf, and he was so happy that they were reestablishing deeper ties. Your father never felt he had done enough for Kveldulf after Freyja's death, as a friend or as his goði, though Lord knows he tried. He had plans to make it up to him.

"Then this business with Kveldulf killing a man happened, and Gunnar was truly given the opportunity to help his old friend. Yet what has happened now? Kveldulf is outlawed, and off to heaven knows where. His son, the boy Gunnar would have fostered and been a second father too, is also missing, and maybe worse."

Fulla appraised her daughter, who had stayed uncharacteristically silent while her mother spoke.

"We must face this, daughter. Your father will do everything he can for Kveldulf, and for Tryggvi, if he is not beyond our help. But you and I must prepare ourselves for the worst. We must be ready to see your father through it, if all this only comes to more grief."

"And what of you, mother? Who will see you through it?" Njála had never known her mother shared in Kveldulf's tragedy, or had such a personal connection to the family.

"I am a woman, Njála, as you will be soon. Grief is our lot, and weathering it shows our strength. Now, run along, I am certain you have something more important to do than to listen to me babble."

So Njála swept, and folded, and cooked, and thought about how she could help her father. She found this a welcome distraction from the dark thoughts which would otherwise occupy her mind. She knew, as well as anyone, that something terrible had happened to Tryggvi. She had seen the unmistakable ill will that Haraldr and his father bore towards the boy, had seen it even before the horse-fight and the trial. Her father spoke hopefully that he might be found safe and sound, perhaps having stopped at another farm, or even sleeping wild with his horse. But Njála knew Tryggvi better than they did, though she had not known him as long. She knew he would not have fled like a thief in the night, would not have left his father behind without a word, no matter the circumstances. And, she suspected he would not have left her either.

Njála had been taken aback by Tryggvi's kiss, and was not at all sure how she felt about it. She had enjoyed teasing him, and just the opportunity to spend time with someone her own age. Now that she had learned the history between her parents and Tryggvi's, she could only assume that a match between them had been discussed at some point. Njála was nearing the age where her father would be expected to find her a suitable partner, and the son of one of his bændr, a man prominent in his own right, would be a viable option.

Njála was not yet certain how she felt about the notion. Tryggvi was – she could not yet bring herself to say "had been" – a kind boy. In their long conversations together had shown himself to be thoughtful and intelligent as well. Even so, he was close to being the only boy her age she had spent any time with. There had to be more to making a match than choosing the first eligible person who showed an interest in you.

When she had been younger she could largely do as she pleased, following her mother or her father as she chose, running freely between family members and the farm workers. But in the past few seasons, as she had sprouted up and began to fill out, as she came into her womanhood, she could sense a subtle shift around her. It was only through careful planning that she had been able to convince her parents to allow her the free reign she had had at the Althing. Soon, she would be wed away, and could only hope her husband would prove to be kind and responsible.

Perhaps that fed into her sadness about Tryggvi. Njála knew very well that her best hope for happiness was in finding a man who would let her be. She enjoyed her work around the home, enjoyed the fact that each day she got a little better at making comfortable garments or preparing meals the way she and her parents liked them best. She suspected she would always like these things, so long as she was with someone who appreciated them. Someone who respected her efforts as much as she respected her own father's, and her mother's. Tryggvi had been such a boy, and seemed like he might become such a man. Njála chided herself for her selfishness, but she knew her own mind well enough to admit that she felt some personal sadness at seeing one possibility for a happy future closed to her.

But it was not in her nature to think of herself for long. Her thoughts returned to her father, and the struggle he faced in trying to obtain justice for his loyal bóndi and dearest friend. How could she help? The Brauðavatn cohort would arrive shortly, and would need to be shown immense hospitality. This would be no issue for her, but hardly seemed to address the root problem.

The feransdomr of Brauðavatn would take place soon, and no one was certain what would happen there. What would Vigi demand? Would Kveldulf make an appearance? Would there be violence? These were the questions that worried Gunnar, and Njála could think of no way to help him answer them, or to prepare. He knew the law as well as anyone. So there was no issue there. But this did not tell him what to expect.

If only he knew what Vigi intended. Which – well, what was driving Vigi's actions, anyway? In the immediate, he seemed to be seeking recompense, for the slaying of his retainer by Kveldulf, and for the injury Tryggvi seemingly caused his son at the Althing. These were certainly sufficient causes for Vigi's anger and desire for vengeance. And yet ... as she considered everything she knew about the situation, Njála sensed there had to be more to the story. When she and Tryggvi had first encountered Haraldr, the boy had seemed to have a personal grievance with Tryggvi. He could have been close with the priest, she supposed. But for that matter, who was this priest, exactly, that he would approach and ride another man's horse, and in a district in which he was a stranger, no less? Njála realized with a shock that she had never really thought about Kveldulf's victim at all, even after she found out he was a father of the church, which should have changed her feelings substantially.

There was more to this than had yet been revealed. And if her father was to protect himself, to protect all of them, he would need to know as much of the full story as he could, as soon as possible.

That idle thought brought with it the seed of an idea. Gunnar kept a Christian household – as did Vigi, apparently, a point which would bear further consideration. But the old ways were still around, still honored by many, with a polite but not terribly serious discretion. Njála knew something about ways other than her own and those of her people. The skalds and their stories made that much certain. So Njála knew that there were those who claimed to be able to see the future, to see what lay hidden in the mind. She knew that only a generation or two ago, when her father's father was still young, that a man in her father's current position might have sought assistance in learning the mind of his enemy, in hearing what fate held in store for him.

He would have gone to a small hut, somewhere in the district. And in that hut would be a woman – or, very rarely, even a man. For a price, she would throw bones, or enter a trance, or consult the entrails of an animal, and then she would tell the inquirer what he wished to know. Or rather – she would tell him something. Even the old tales were ambivalent as to the trustworthiness of a seer's advice, which often as not was likely to be misinterpreted by the recipient.

Those were just stories, Njála knew. They depended on misdirection, on coincidences, on fatal flaws that brought their heroes low and propelled them forward. That was what made them compelling. But that wasn't real life. Njála's Christian education – such as it was, in this half-converted backwater – had nevertheless been sufficient to cause her to cast a skeptical eye on the tales of her ancestors. She appreciated them – everyone did – but she knew that ultimately they were just stories.

Still, she believed they each had a grain of truth in them. And the seers – those she knew to be real. She had heard her father's own servants discussing one, in fact. When young Grette thought she had caught the eye of a boy of the neighboring farm, hadn't she gone to have the runes read for her? And afterward she had stayed away from the boy she fancied, who died by falling from his horse just two months later, leaving a girl on another farm pregnant and alone. Didn't that count for something?

Njála entertained the thought, but not for long. Perhaps her people had once been able to see the future, if only in fits and glimpses. Perhaps some of them could still do so now. But these were not Christian people, and that is what Njála was resolved to be. So she could only hope for the best, and sweep, and fold, and cook.

ᚠ ᚾᛚ ᛋᛏ ᚨᛁᚠ ᚾᛚ ᛋᛏ ᚨᛁᚠ ᚾᛚ ᛋᛏ ᚨᛁᚠ ᚾᛚ ᛋᛏ ᚨ

After a day's ride, Sinmara came to a small farm at the junction of two rivers. She arrived in the evening, when it was still quite bright out, and kept to the edges of the farm, wary of being seen. Her own sight was excellent, and she was able to keenly observe the farm's inhabitants finishing their tasks and preparing for the end of the day.

Sinmara was certain she was in the right place. She had left Ásbyrgi with three boons, given to her on the threshold of the ancient capital. First, her mother had laid her hand on Orri's head, and closed her eyes for a moment, until the horse did as well. Then they both opened their eyes at once.

"The horse now knows the way. Simply stay astride him, and he will take you where you need to go." Orri nattered in apparent agreement.

Ruharra came forward then, and handed Sinmara a small pouch.

"Be careful with this, and do not open it until the time is right. You will know when the time is right," she said, before Sinmara could ask.

Then came Ananz. Sinmara had been surprised to see him standing outside the gate, already there when she and her mother and Ruharra and Orri exited together. He smiled at them, but said nothing until after Ruharra and Ailuwa had finished their farewells. The strange little fólk stepped forward then, and presented Sinmara with his clasped fist. He opened his palm, and in his hand was a large crystalline shard, attached to a thin loop of rope. He plucked the shard from his palm with his other hand, then held it before his eye for a moment and tilted his head skyward. Seemingly satisfied, he brought the shard away from his face and held it out to Sinmara, all without breaking his upward gaze. She hesitated in confusion, then took the shard from him, and bent her head to place it around her neck. She looked back up to see Ananz talking to her mother and Ruharra.

"I will go now, then!" she said, and they all turned to look at her, but did not speak. She pulled herself onto Orri's back, and when she looked back at them, they were standing in a line clasping hands, Ailuwa in the middle and the others on either side. It seemed they were all at a loss for words, and Sinmara could only call out "I will not fail you!" as she turned the horse away from the sun and set forth.

When Orri brought her in sight of this farm, and then immediately stopped, she knew she was in the right place. But she saw nothing indicating why this region was hidden from the farseers' sight. She felt nothing odd or off about the place. Searching her mind, she felt she still had access to the places within herself that allowed her to rockwalk and to activate her knacks, even though Ailuwa had warned her she might not.

If anything about the place was unusual to Orri, he made no indication of the fact. He chewed placidly on the grass near Sinmara, seemingly happy to have a rest after several hour's hard riding. They had made excellent time, arriving well before Sinmara had been given to expect. The horse had seemed pleased to stretch his legs and run after days confined underground.

The enthusiasm he exuded – which Sinmara could sense quite keenly – helped keep her from feeling more uncomfortable and exposed than she otherwise might. Ailuwa had assured her time and again that she would be protected by men's strange blindness when it came to the fólk, their apparent tendency to look at everything around one of her kind without really seeing the person.

But she could not know for certain how Orri's presence might affect men's perception, so she still had to be quite cautious. So far as she understood it, even if any men did see her they would be unlikely to attack her on sight, especially if they only saw her from a distance, and she could be mistaken for one of their own. Nevertheless, it was strange and unnerving to be this close to humans. So much of fólkish society was built around secrecy and avoidance of their brutish counterparts. Man was not held in contempt amongst the fólk, and from time to time a sympathetic fólk might even help a human in need. But, like wildfire and large predators, humans were understood to be best avoided. Encounters with their kind was simply too unpredictable, even before this business with the blank spots.

After watching for some time however, there was little that Sinmara had noticed to distinguish men from fólk. The people she had watched had gone about their tasks in camaraderie and focused effort, then retired to their resting spaces, shoulders stooped with exhaustion but faces warm with contentment. Was this so different from how her own people spent their days? Granted, physical labor was less an element of fólkish life, but Sinmara recognized the unspoken bonds between these people, their way of life. They were a family, much like all the fólk were family.

Or so it seemed to her from her lonely observation, anyway. Sinmara reminded herself that she should not read too much into what little she had seen of these people. Was she looking with uncritical eyes because of the connections she had just learned between herself and men? Did she hope to find confirmation that her heritage from these people did not mark her as so different from other fólk after all? If so, she must excise these desires from her observation and assessment, lest they warp her perceptions.

Now the men were in their home, and there was little for her to see. Smoke billowed from an opening in the top of the human dwelling, indicating a fire burning within. This might have alarmed her, had she not been told that men harnessed fire to heat their homes and prepare their food. This was one major difference between their people then– the common use of fire and the regular consumption of flesh– and it helped Sinmara remember that whatever commonalities she may observe between men and her own people, there were like to be as many differences as well.

Still, nothing Sinmara had seen thus far had given her any insight as to why this area would be hidden from her mother's sight. Admittedly, she was not entirely sure what she was looking for, but she had seen nothing she had not been given to expect from the concentrated education Ruharra and Ailuwa had given her on everything they knew of humans in this land.

She would have to get closer. Sinmara instructed Orri to stay where he was, hoping he understood her well enough, then shortly made her way towards the human dwelling. It was still quite bright out. Sinmara stayed close to the ground and tried to make herself as small as possible as she crept forward. As she neared the fence around the dwelling, some of the animals in the yard looked up at her, and her heart froze. But they simply regarded her calmly for a moment, then want back to chewing grass or scratching for grubs.

She neared the outer wall of the dwelling. From here she could examine the human habitation in more detail. It was, from the outside at least, a simple structure of mud, wood, and iron bits, built directly into the side of the hill abutting one edge of the farm.

The roof of the dwelling was covered in a mat of grass, and there were small openings cut into the walls on the two exposed sides she could see. She was opposite the entryway the humans had used to access the dwelling. Sinmara could not see into the building. The few small windows were high, and draped against the light. But her fólkish ears could detect some of what happened inside. She could hear the crackle of the fire, a cough from one of the men, the burbling voices of the children. As she listened, someone began to speak.

Sinmara had never heard human language before. Ananz and her mother had explained to her that she would be able to understand the meaning of human speech, so long as she opened her mind to it. The man was speaking of the day's work, and the work that would need to be done tomorrow. Yet the tone of his voice, and the words he used, were so different from the speech Sinmara was used to hearing. It was disorienting being able to hear these strange words and to recognize them as strange, yet nevertheless understand their meaning.

Now a female voice.

"Birch, bring your father the knife to cut the meat." "Yes, mother" a higher voice, smaller. A child.

"Thor-stone, did you brush out the horse's manes before you came in?" A man again.

"I did." Another man, a new voice.

"Good. Tomorrow we will take Eagle and Raven-Kettle up to the knell, I think the sheep have been throwing their legs in some old post-holes up there that we should fill."

So the talk continued. Some of the word-sounds Sinmara heard did not make sense to her, but she quickly understood that she was hearing names: Birch she knew, and Eagle, but Raven-kettle and Thor-stone still confused her. Still, it was remarkable that she could understand so much. She wondered what the humans would hear, were she to speak to them.

No sooner had she thought this, however, then she suddenly realized she could no longer understand the words coming from within the home. She could still hear the voices. They were speaking in unison now, the two men, the woman, and the child each speaking the same words. Sinmara could hear these words, distinctly, but she could not grasp their meaning. Nor, she found, could she hold on to the sounds, that she might repeat them later.

Somehow, this surprised her even more than being able to understand human speech had. The fólk could communicate on at least some level with nearly every thing they encountered. The simple thoughts and intentions of animals were known to them, by sound, sight, and an understanding that would flash into the mind unbidden. The grasses and moss whispered gently beneath them, making a quiet music like the trickle of a stream. Even the rocks in which they made their homes, through which they traveled, had a kind of speech, dimly perceptible if one wished to pay attention to it. This was how the fólk sensed which rock they could pass through, and build their homes in; how they enticed light and water and air into their dwellings. The myriad voices of the world were never far from fólkish ears, if they chose to listen.

Yet Sinmara had no idea what was happening inside the hut, just a few paces away from her. She grasped suddenly how disconcerting it must have been for her mother, so gifted in the farsight, to be unable to see this place. Further examining her discomfort, Sinmara realized that not only was she unable to grasp a shred of meaning from what was being said in the home, but the sound also seemed to be blocking out much of the sensations she was used to receiving – the grass, the wind, the small crawling things beneath her feet.

Sinmara had experienced nothing like it, and it was terrifying. Yet she could not tear herself away. As disoriented as she was, there was also something somehow seductive about the sensations she was experiencing. She felt she could lose herself in this sensation, allow the strange emptiness she was experiencing to draw her in, to envelope her. She closed her eyes, and began to drift.

Then she abruptly snapped back into herself. She found herself pitched forward onto the ground, her face resting against the cool earth. From inside the house the voices come to her again, but now she found she could understand them.

171

"Birch, the meat. Give it here."

"And slow down, child, before you choke"

In a sudden rush, the sounds of the earth came roaring back to her.

As soon as she got her feet beneath her, she was rushing away from the farm, back towards Orri, back towards a world she understood.

⸎ ⟁⟟ ⟐⟟ ⟁⟟ ⟁⟟ ⟐⟟ ⟁⟟ ⟁⟟ ⟐⟟ ⟁⟟ ⟁⟟ ⟐⟟ ⸎

He removed the dripping cowl from his head, and set it next to the fire. This godforsaken place – it seemed he could not get comfortable for more than a minute without this land coming up with some fresh means of making him miserable. Some days he felt as though the land itself rose up against him, sought to divert him from his sacred purpose with all the physical discomforts it could levy on him. Well if that was the case, he considered, the effort was rather pathetic. No earthly power was like to dissuade him from his course- certainly not some inclement weather.

He removed his boots, set them to dry as well. As he did so, the idiot farmer came up beside him, silently proffering a bowl of ale and hank of bread. Pétur frowned slightly as he accepted it – this was woman's work, offering such hospitality. For all their blustering, the men of this land were far too accommodating of their women-folk.

He had heard even that here a woman might leave her husband, should she find him not to her liking. Such nonsense only underscored the need for him to put these fools in their place.

Pétur sighed inwardly as Vigi opened his mouth to speak.

"Did your trip go well, Father?"

"Yes, my son." He considered his words carefully. "The people of your district are most eager to hear the good news I bring, and the Lord has assured me that he will continue to guide and bless our hands, that they may perform his holy works."

Vigi let out a sigh of relief that he might have been holding in for days. "Bless his name. I confess, Father, it has not been easy to see the path lately. My wife... "

"It is not for you to see the path!" Pétur snapped, more harshly than he had meant to. He forced his voice to turn softer. "The Lord asks much of those to whom he would grant his greatest blessings, my son. Trust in his plan for you, even when the way seems dark, and his light will appear to guide you. I know – believe me, I know – that it is not always easy. That is why the Lord comes first to those with the strength to do his bidding. That is why he – and I – have chosen a man such as you, friend Vigi." Pétur restrained the sneer attempting to sneak into his words, and even chastened himself for it. Whatever Vigi's myriad faults, he had been chosen to this purpose for a reason, and Pétur would do well to remember that. Even when Vigi, a breath before so deflated, began to puff up his chest with unseemly pride. "I thank you, Father. I apologize for seeming to doubt."

"Think not on it. Now, what have you to tell me?"

"We are prepared to ride to Brauðavatn. Kveldulf, by all accounts, has yet to show his face again. His household has left, either to join with Gunnar or to seek employ elsewhere in the district. We will have to send notice to Gunnar of when the feransdomr is to occur. And he is unlikely to be happy – by all accounts he and Kveldulf were close. But there is little to suggest we are likely to encounter any problems."

"Of course," Vigi said, anticipating Pétur's interjection, "these things rarely go as smoothly as one might hope. I am bringing my strongest bændr, and they will be prepared to take the property by force, if need be."

Pétur nodded approvingly. For all that Vigi irritated the priest, he had a low cunning that had proven quite useful, to say nothing of his resources and knowledge of this land. Not for nothing had he been able to claw his way to this position, and despite Pétur's personal disdain, it was irrefutable that the two of them had been brought together for a greater purpose. Pétur would work to remember this, even as he exhorted Vigi to do so.

"And your boy" Pétur said, suddenly remembering. "How fares he?"

Vigi knitted his brow, "His injury still troubles him. He still can barely speak. But the healer was here yesterday, and says he will recover, given time. I ... I am not certain that it comforts him, or my wife."

"Your boy will be regarded greatly for what he has given, Vigi. You all will. The ways of the Lord are often mysterious, sometimes frightening, even to those of us who have felt him guide our very hands. Perhaps especially to us.

"But he rewards his faithful servants, in due time. Always. He rewards us beyond measure, beyond what we could imagine to receive in exchange for what he asks of us, even when he seems to ask too much. Please remember this, my son, and help your boy and your lady wife to understand."

Vigi kneaded his hands together, anxiety still plain on his face. "I will try. They are only in the other hut now, perhaps if you could speak to them–"

"It is you they need to hear from, now, Vigi. Remember well my words, and all will be well. Have faith." he admonished, with a gentleness that actually took him by surprise.

"Now," Pétur said, "I am weary, and there is much yet for me to ponder. Leave me now, and we will speak again later." The dismissal brooked no argument. Pétur might need Vigi to remember his mastery over his own household and district – this was crucial to Pétur's plans. Yet so too must Vigi remember that he was not his own master, not where the Lord was concerned.

After a moment – a moment perhaps a beat too long for Pétur's liking – Vigi lowered his head, and turned to shuffle from the booth and   across   the   farm   to   his   own   home.

Chapter 16

There were four men in the cave. For all Kveldulf knew, there might be more, tucked away in other furrows of the system. It was quite extensive. Tunnels branched off the main lines at steep inclines, occasionally gusting out hot breaths of air that would make the head spin for a moment, and must come from deep within the earth. But this little cave, not far from the entrance to this section of the cavern system, at least stayed dry, and the men within did not venture far.

Kveldulf could not hold the other men's names in his mind, save for the youngest. He had heard them many times, he was certain, but each time the sounds slipped from his grasp, and his arms were already too laden to snatch for them. He hardly cared to. So there was the big one, the bald one, and Thorgeir. He remembered this last only because it had been the name of his mother's brother, and the two even bore a superficial resemblance.

In any case, he did not speak to any of the men often enough for his lack of formal address to present a problem. For the most part, he kept to himself, and so did they. They talked amongst themselves of course – the three of them had arrived together – but even so the other big one, the bald one, and Thorgeir were just as uncommunicative as Kveldulf, most of the time.

Only the bald one seemed particularly inclined to speak, mostly to the big one. His rasping whisper rebounded through the cave, filling it with a low white noise which Kveldulf paid little conscious attention to, but was impossible to completely ignore.

The other men were also outlaws, that much was obvious. If their threadbare clothes and hollow cheeks did not make this clear, their presence here was confirmation enough. Only outlaws came to these caves. No free man in his right mind would, for they offered little beyond isolation, somehow accompanied by the constant sense that one was being watched. Even the protection they provided was barely worth it.

The upper caves were mostly damp, and the air blowing through them sounded a low moan that reminded Kveldulf of some great beast growling as it gorged on a kill. The inner chambers were likely warmer and drier, but even Kveldulf, not overly concerned with self-preservation, had been overcome with such a sense of foreboding when he ventured further into the caverns that he had been forced to turn back almost despite himself, and he had watched the other outlaws do the same.

So here they sat, each of them, even the bald one, mostly absorbed in his own thoughts. The others had appeared at the mouth of the cave perhaps a day ago, chatting amiably as they entered. Once they got over their evident surprise at seeing Kveldulf pressed against the cave wall, staring at them, they even offered him some of the food they had with them. They had not asked his leave to remain in the cave, but neither had Kveldulf sought to expel them, or to leave himself. They had mostly ignored him, and he them. In any case, within a few hours their companionable conversation amongst themselves had tapered off, and each man found his way to a section of the cavern wall to sit in his own thoughts. Something about this place discouraged conversation, and coaxed the mind to turn in upon itself.

So it had been for some time. Kveldulf was not concerned with keeping track, and the murkiness of the cave made it difficult in any case to determine just what part of day it even was. Kveldulf had no reason to venture outside, and other than passing further into the recess of the cavern in order to relieve himself, he barely had cause to move. His trek across the land to reach this cave had taken its toll on his legs and feet, and now the bare igneous rock was leeching his spirit.

His thoughts turned constantly to Tryggvi. The boy had been there with him one day, then gone forever the next. Just like his mother, and Hrolf, and so many others Kveldulf had lost. But his boy. His boy! How could they have taken his son from him? What cruel workings of fate would allow him to lose his home, his status, and his child, all within the span of days? Now that the initial shock had subsided somewhat, Kveldulf was slowly assembling the shattered pieces of his world, seeing what bits remained unbroken. There was not much left, not for him. Gunnar, he knew, would take care of his people. He was unlikely to expend too much effort looking for Kveldulf – Gunnar would understand that it was best if no one knew where Kveldulf was. Kveldulf would not foist his troubles upon Gunnar and his family by letting them shelter him in any case.

With a sharp pang, Kveldulf realized that Gunnar might nevertheless waste resources trying to find Tryggvi, or determine what had happened to him. It was a pointless endeavor. Kveldulf knew with crushing certainty that Tryggvi was dead and gone. He knew, as Gunner surely must, that Vigi held more answers than anyone. But it didn't matter. Knowing how and why Tryggvi had died would not bring him back, would do nothing to lessen Kveldulf's loss. Nor would it do anything to serve Brauðavatn or remove Kveldulf's sentence. Knowing more could only give detail and specificity to Kveldulf's pain. Not that anything could truly add to the infinite chasm of hopelessness that had opened within him. He could protect no one, so he had nothing left to protect. Perhaps those under his care did not deserve to be punished for his inadequacy, but he certainly did. If anything, his decrepitude proved that there really was justice in the world, at least as applied to Kveldulf Thorbjornsson. So he would take his punishment. He would stay here, in this cave, until there was nothing left of him but gray bones and a forgotten name.

ᛈ ᚱᛚ ᛋᛈ ᚨᛈ ᚱᛚ ᛋᛈ ᚨᛈ ᚱᛚ ᛋᛈ ᚨᛈ ᚱᛚ ᛋᛈ ᚨ

Orri flew over the glistening grass, glad to have his hooves on soft earth again after days of nothing but stone beneath him. He was accustomed to a heavier rider than his current companion, but nonetheless she had been riding him harder and for longer than he was used to. Following this thought, he wondered yet again where the other one was, the familiar one, who smelled of dirt and smoke and sweat, who spoke to him low and soft in a voice that teetered, who gave him treats and stroked his mane, his funny herd-mate. He felt a low whine start in his throat as the memories came unbidden, thought-scents of blood, a throbbing on his flank, foam in his mouth as he ran in terror until he could run no more. This was not the first time his thoughts had cantered along this path, nor the tenth, and as before he felt his heart grow heavy, his pace slowing. He stopped. But he did not turn back. Here, in this field, fresh grass beneath him, sun on his head, clear sight in all directions, he could find the strength to hold his thought-scent-sense to its course, rather than skittering away in discomfort. Where was his friend?

Then a hand on his back, a gentle voice. Was it him? No, it was the other, the new one, longhaired, water flowing over rock, strange and yet strangely familiar.

Sinmara could sense the sadness and want from the horse, the sudden, almost palpable loss and confusion radiating from his noble head and heart. She chided herself; in all the activity and emotional turmoil of the last several days, she had all but neglected Orri, taking him readily as her mount, yet giving little thought to his inner wellbeing.

He had been through much lately as well, and Sinmara could only speculate what he had endured before he appeared outside the warren, dark passenger upon his back. It spoke to his resilience that he had only now begun to express his trauma strongly enough that Sinmara could feel it, and it spoke to her thoughtlessness that she had not looked for it before. This was unlike her, and stroking his mane, she resolved to do better by the horse from now on. Even as she had the thought, the low keening in his throat began to subside, the voices of despair to dissipate.

They had ridden hard away from the human farm, Sinmara wishing only to put distance between herself and the strange sensations she had experienced within the area her mother described as a blank spot in her vision. She had gotten ahold of her emotions as soon as the farm was out of sight – or so she told herself– but she had kept riding hard nonetheless. Even away from the farm, it was as if a light fog had settled in her head, distracting her and making it difficult to focus her thoughts. She could only trust that Orri was still taking them in the right direction, and she made her camp only when they were both too tired to go further. She slept directly on the ground, pulling her moss blanket over her head and falling immediately into a dreamless sleep, while Orri laid beside her.

Yet now, in this field, bright of a morning, she was ready to consider what she had learned. Something the humans were doing was obscuring them from fólkish vision. It was not a natural phenomenon, that much seemed certain. Yet the purpose of their actions was unclear. It did not seem likely that they were intentionally casting the blank spots over the dwellings in order to deter the fólk, for as far as Sinmara knew or had ever been told, humans did not know the fólk could view them remotely in the first place.

Of course it was possible this knowledge had come to them somehow, but still Sinmara could not understand the point of them taking such an action. What good would it do them?

The more Sinmara considered it, the less certain she was of just what she had learned. Yet she could think of no means of discerning more, short of asking a human – which was not an option. Though the thought shamed her, she did not wish to experience again any of the sensations which were just now starting to fade from her head. She did not know just what she had learned, but she had enough to report back to her mother and the other elders, who would surely understand her experience better than she did.

But first, she had another errand to run. She had been to see a human dwelling, and hoped what she found would be useful. Now she must look into the unexpected disturbances that had been shaking the earth recently. Once again, Ailuwa and Ruharra had told her precious little, only that she should go where the horse took her, and make whatever decisions she saw fit upon her arrival.

When Sinmara was sure that Orri had finished eating, she swung herself up upon his back. "Come, friend. Just bear with me a little way further, and we can both rest." Orri whinnied appreciatively, and Sinmara leaned into his neck as he tölted away to the south.

Once again, she was surprised at the speed they made over land. If anything, the horse seemed to have gotten faster, and the miles stretched under them smoothly. In no time at all, Sinmara saw the crest of what could only be their next destination.

Mountains rose swiftly before them as they approached. Nestled between the peaks was a great expanse of gleaming white. A tongue of ice descended through a valley, touching the ground and forming a steep path onto the glacier.

Orri pressed forward, leaping from the ground to the tip of the ice without pause. His hooves chipped at the ice and found purchase, and they ascended the glacier almost as quickly as they had passed over the ground below.

Sinmara had no reason to doubt the horse's sure-footedness, but she felt herself growing uncertain as they climbed into the mountain pass. She had gotten used to the wide expanses of the open road, but even without looking behind her, she could sense the line of the horizon falling farther and farther away from her vantage point. At the same time, the peaks around them began to loom over her, and she felt oddly exposed, almost like she was being watched.

Then even the peaks began to fall away behind them, and they reached the wide, snowy plateau of the glacier's crown. The sun beat down on them relentlessly, and although Sinmara was not uncomfortable, the competing sensations of heat and cold upon her skin were most curious. But these were nothing compared to the light. Sinmara's unfólkish appreciation for sunlight had helped set the course of her life thus far, but never had she experienced its full brilliance as she did now. Her eyes worked hard to adjust to the unprecedented intensity, and as they did Sinmara could see the faint swirls and eddies of energy where snow from the skin of the glacier sublimated directly into the shifting wind.

It was beautiful, bordering on painful. But apart from the light and the snow, the top of the glacier was completely barren. As they pressed across it, Sinmara could see no sign of a destination in front of them. It was even difficult to tell how far or how fast they were travelling, with no reference point other than tiny snowcaps here and there.

Just as Sinmara was wondering whether they were meant to ride right over the entire glacier, Orri began to slow his pace to a trot.

Sinmara eagerly looked about her, but could see no indication as to why the horse had chosen this spot. Then he veered sharply to the left, and Sinmara had to grip his mane and sides to keep from sliding off.

Orri galloped in a wide circle, arcing to the left and then around and back towards where he had first turned. As they rounded the curve towards where they had begun, Sinmara could look back over the end of the long course they had just traveled. She could see the bottom of the circle Orri's hooves were drawing in the snow, a wide groove through the pack which stood out starkly where shadow bent the light to blue. But before the circle, and all the way off towards the edge of the glacier where Sinmara's line of sight terminated, there was nothing. No hoof prints marked their passage across the glacier to this point; it was as if they had been dropped from the sky onto the glacier, only to make this circular mark in the snow.

Orri returned to his starting point and perfectly closed the loop, then abruptly stopped, still facing the direction he had started. Sinmara waited for a bit, but nothing happened. The horse swished his tail and breathed mist into the air, but made no other movement in any direction.

Finally, after some consideration, Sinmara grabbed her pack, and hopped off of Orri, stepping down into the closed expanse of the wide circle they had just drawn. As soon as she had both of her feet on the ground and stepped away from him, Orri bent his legs and jumped out of the groove he had created in the snow, landing on the outside of the circle. He shook his head a bit and neighed, then regarded Sinmara with what she interpreted as an expectant look.

With a shrug, she turned away from him and walked towards the center of the circle. Reaching it, she turned and scanned the horizon in all directions, searching for any indication of her purpose here.

Completing her first turn, she felt a sense of insignificance, as if some deep part of her mind knew that the expanse it had just surveyed was too huge to hinge on such a tiny point as herself.

Her head spun, and she sat with a soft plop into the snowpack. Then she was not alone. Nothing changed in her sight, but she felt a presence all the same. Orri was in view off to her right, but he seemed unperturbed, licking experimentally at the tip of a snow cone. Nor was Sinmara disturbed, exactly. She knew she was not alone, but she was not distressed by this new presence- it was somehow as unthreatening as it was unfamiliar.

Sinmara could not even tell which of her senses this presence was registering on. She did not see anything, yet it almost seemed like there might be something there, on the edge of her vision, if she could just look at it fast enough. She could smell Orri, and herself, and all the scents of the ice around them, including odd, thin whiffs of the minerals absorbed by the glacier and churned up to the surface during its slow slump through the eons. She could not say whether the scent of some third party was mingled among them. And all she could hear was the wind, sometimes soft and low, then whip-quick, making the folds of her shift and the pack on her back snap together with the sound of wings.

But still, there was a presence. And Sinmara felt she was being asked something, felt it somewhere between her chest and her gut, felt it with a sensation that was not quite a push or a pull, but some strange response between the two- a question: Would she help? Would she help?

Silently, unthinkingly, she agreed. Then, she heard something. A sharp crack split the air, and Sinmara turned her head to see the ice opening up at the edge of the circle to her left. The surface of the glacier was crumbling inwards, and before Sinmara could react, the fissure shot directly towards her with another ear-splitting series of pops and cracks.

She pitched downwards with a yelp as the ice gave out beneath her. Her pack caught for a moment, and then she was sliding at a steep angle against a smooth surface, even as the ice continued to split around her.

The light turned dim and blue as she slid towards the bottom of the glacier, split now and then by a bright beam brought from above when the ice shifted to accommodate Sinmara's passage. But soon and Sinmara found herself slipping through a cobalt gloom with only the sounds of her own slide around her. She wondered if Orri was still standing at the edge of the circle above, or if she had run off when it started to collapse; then she worried that he might have fallen in and been injured, even as she continued sliding further and further towards the earth.

Then she felt the angle of her descent begin to change, and she slowed. The light around her shifted slightly brighter again, and suddenly she tumbled into empty air. She let out a sharp huff as she impacted the ground a split second later, loose gravel cushioning her fall.

Sinmara stood, and made sure she was uninjured. She looked about her, still a bit disoriented from her descent, and saw that some of her things had fallen from her pack- a spare shift, some food, and the pouch that Ruharra had given her. She gathered them back together, then turned to take in her surroundings.

She was at the bottom of a narrow crevasse, just wide enough for her to pass through comfortably. The ground beneath her was black stone. The passage shifted in front of her so that she could not see far ahead, but she could sense an open space some short ways up. She looked behind her, and saw a jagged hole in the ice at the back of the passage, marking the end of the chute she had come down. As she watched, water flowed down over the hole, and then the back of the passage was smooth and unmarked.

Sinmara walked towards what she only hoped was an exit. Sure enough, after a few short turns she stepped around a bend in the passage, and her destination came within view.

She walked into a vast cavern, formed entirely within the ice. Soaring, rippling shapes arced overhead, lit by the dimmest glow of sunlight coming through the ice and into the highest point of the cavern far above. Yet it was warm here, too warm, and Sinmara could see the water dripping and running along the ice in places.

The black gravel on which Sinmara stood formed the shore of a subglacial lake, a great body of water at the heart of the cavern, in the heart of the glacier. One finger of the lake was not far from where Sinmara stood. She walked down to it slowly, and peered into its still, black surface. Sulfurous vapors rose from the waters, dampening her hair. She could not help but think of the conversation she had had with her mother just a short time before, sitting beside the waters of a different pool.

The surface rippled. Sinmara straightened, and stepped back.

A wide plume of boiling water shot up with a blast, soaring high, melting the inside of the glacier wherever it sprayed. Sinmara leapt back in surprise, then kept retreating. She felt steam across her skin, but it cooled quickly.

As the mist dissipated, however, Sinmara saw she was no longer alone. But the figure in front of her could not be the presence she had sensed on the surface, could not be that which had drawn her here.

It sat coiled and black at edge of the pool. Thick scales and sharp bristles glistened in the dim light. Wicked claws clacked against the stone. Its long tail curled around it, serpentine tip raised to flick eagerly in the air. Every inch of it was dark as pitch, save the eyes. These were brilliant pinpoints of crimson, set deep in a wolfish head – and fixed on Sinmara.

It leapt at her, slicing through the air, and only instinct saved her. A smear of purple ink appeared in the vanishing space between them, and the black beast sailed right into it. It hung in the air, suspended in the force of Sinmara's power just long enough for her to dive out of its path. Then it crashed to the floor, rolled, and turned, tail whipping around and back to propel it on another strike. It was still awash in the purple ink of Sinmara's knacks, droplets of mineral energy dripping from its chin and floating freely for a moment before being drawn back into the flow.

The creature did not seem bothered in the least. Before her disbelieving eyes, the monster shook its shaggy head, and waves of heat radiated from it. With a sizzle, the ink on and around it boiled away to nothingness. Sinmara felt it go, her arms reddening and burning as her hard-earned power was taken from her, destroyed.

It struck again, charging her. Save for the scraping sound it made against the stone as it moved, it was eerily silent, and quicksilver fast. But Sinmara was fast too, and again she was able to evade the beast's sharp teeth and claws, dancing to one side so that it passed just to the left of where she had been.

Then the foul thing's tail curled, and looped around Sinmara's neck just as the beast slowed its charge and turned to regard its prey. It dug in with its talons, and lifted Sinmara's kicking body off the ground. She felt herself rotating, as the creature pulled her in, coiling more of its tail around her neck and upper body. She raked at its skin, gouging long furrows, but it was useless. Whatever substance the creature was made of collected under her nails, but it neither bled nor showed a wound.

It brought her around to face its slavering maw. Black liquid oozed from jaws packed with teeth like obsidian daggers. As it squeezed Sinmara and pulled her close, she felt some heat and pain, but beyond that was a great emptiness. With every inch the creature drew her nearer, Sinmara cared less what was about to happen to her. Her arms fell at her sides, and she stopped struggling, as she realized how little any of it mattered. Either she would be destroyed here, by this stygian fiend, or she would meet her doom later. But doom would come, surely, so why should she fight it? She did not even feel pain, now. What better could she ask for, than a death without pain?

Her head was almost inside the creature's waiting mouth when one tiny spark of emotion flared in the deepening fog of her mind. Not panic, or anger, or fear; nor hope, nor even will to live. It was simpler than that: she was confused. What had been her last thought? A death without pain? Where had that thought come from? She was not a plant, not an animal, not a man. Her kind did not fear pain, or death!

She felt something then, something in her chest. No, not in her chest – but on it, between her skin and her shift and the squeezing coils of her would-be devourer. The pendant Ananz had given her, the shard of spar, was digging into the top of her sternum. Weakly, not quite knowing why, she bent one hand towards it, the grasp of the beast's tail around her shoulders making it difficult to move her arms.

The tip of her finger made contact with the crystalline edge of the spar, just as black teeth descended towards the back of her head. Finally, the creature made a sound, a chthonic roar ripping from its throat as it lashed its tail and threw Sinmara, sending her skipping across the gravel towards the edge of the water.

She scrambled to her feet, expecting to be met by a rush of teeth and spines. But the creature still sat on its haunches where it had thrown her, silent again, but staring at her warily now.

She felt a tingle in her palm, and look down at her hand. It was entirely encased in a thin layer of liquid crystal. It flowed over and between her fingers as she bent and flexed them. The play of light through it was so unusual that Sinmara felt she could stare into it for hours, lost in prismatic reverie. Then she heard a soft scrape, and looked up to see the creature slinking towards her, head low, ears flattened back.

She did not wait. She ran forward to meet it. As she moved, the crystal around her arm shifted and coalesced, thinning, sharpening, until Sinmara held a gleaming crystal blade in her hand.

She slashed downward, to meet the creature's rising claw. The blade passed through its arm, meeting only the tiniest bit of resistance at the very center of the limb. An onyx paw smacked wetly to the floor, then dissolved, staining the ground and releasing a foul smell into the air. Again the creature roared, and just for a moment Sinmara felt another wave of utter futility. Then she twisted, and drove her crystal-sheathed arm into the beast's side.

It exploded with a malodorous pop, spraying Sinmara and everything around her with whatever noxious substance the thing was made of. On the very end of her weapon, pierced through by the diamond-sharp point, was a tiny black organ. It still pulsed somehow, and Sinmara could feel the oily liquid on her skin attracted to it, being called back to it.

With a thought, she pulled the organ into the blade, containing it, distending it, pulling it apart until only thin wisps of black showed through the clear crystal of her weapon. Finally, she felt the pull on her skin no longer, and the scattered remains of the beast vaporized just as its severed arm had.

She waited a bit, even walked towards the edge of the pool again and stared in, until she felt sure that no other strange creatures were about to appear from its depths. The air above the pool felt cooler now, and putrid steam no longer rose from its surface.

She bid the crystal around her arm return to its original shape. It shifted and flowed again, and she felt the leather strap being dragged from its place by her elbow back towards her palm. In a moment, she clasped the unassuming bit of spar in her hand. She held it up, to see that a thin, branching vein of black was still visible within it, encased like a twig in clearest amber. She placed it back around her neck.

Once more, she became aware that she was not alone. But she did not start; she recognized this presence. Gratitude rained down on her. And far across the lake, on the other side of the cave, she heard the ice begin to shift. A joyful, shattering clamor rushed towards her, as the walls of the glacier closed over the still lake, each side meeting the other with a clap of thunder.

She watched it coming, and did not budge as the great sheets of ice collided towards her. Then she was moving, being lifted, carried, as she heard the fading sounds of the glacier healing around her.

She was back on its surface, back in the wide circle, in the orange-pink haze of the evening sun. Just a few paces away stood Orri, looking at her with his usual expression of placid expectation. As she watched, the edge of the circle between them began to fill in, and continued to do so all the way around its circumference, until no sign of it remained. Sinmara felt one last sensation of thanks and relief drift through her, and the crystal on her neck seemed to warm for the briefest second. Then it was just her and the horse again.

"This has been an odd day, Orri," she said to him.

Chapter 17

In his weaker moments he thought of ending it all himself, of tearing at his veins until the heart's blood spouted out of him and he fell finally into Hel's cold embrace. Sometimes he convinced himself that his hesitance to do so was mere cowardice, that a stronger man would know when to end it, that his refusal to do so simply showed the flaws that had caused him to lose all those he was meant to protect. It was in these black moods that he would take his knife from his belt, point it at his heart, tell himself to run towards the cavern wall and drive it into his chest. He had not yet brought himself to follow through, but he would eventually, he knew. In the meantime, he would excoriate himself with his own thoughts, he would prolong his life only to prolong his richly deserved misery. This was his duty, and he was not ready to delegate it to Hel and her minions.

He hoped only that the other inhabitants of the cave would leave soon, and leave him to it. They had surprised him by coming upon him so suddenly, startling him out of his fugue.

He might have driven them off, or left himself, had they not offered him food. It was weak of him to accept, he knew, but he had paid the price in additional flagellation, knocking the back of his head against the cave wall as he ate. If the others noticed, they made no indication. Besides, had he tried to drive them off, they might have fought him, and, in his weakened state, perhaps even killed him. To die in combat like this would have been unacceptable; it was a far better death than one such as he deserved. He could not rightly take a place in Valhöl, could not face Odin and the Einherjar in his failure, or bear the disappointed gaze of Frigg. He had failed his gods as well as his family, and only the halls of Hel or oblivion would do for such as he.

Perhaps it would be different if he knew where Tryggvi had gone.

His wife, he was certain, was in whatever realm was opened to the most virtuous women who died in childbirth- Helgafjell, perhaps, feasting in the warmth and love of the Holy Mountain; or perhaps with the Lady and her warriors in Folkvángr. He longed to be reunited with her- had longed always for this- but even if he could be sure to send his soul to her realm, he could not face her ever again, not after failing to protect their only son.

Nor could he hope, though he fervently wished it, to ever be reunited with Tryggvi. Kveldulf did not know the circumstances of his son's death, and knew he never would. He knew he should hope that his boy had died bravely, had faced down his death like a man. But he couldn't know, and whenever he turned his thoughts to the question, a great yawning blackness opened within him. He did not know what gods Tryggvi worshipped in his heart, or what his heart had held when he had gone to meet them. He could be in Valhöl, or Fólkvangr, or Helgafjell, or with Hel, his spirit forever expressing itself accordingly – battle-ready, sun-dappled, hearth-warmed – or grave-damp and joy-starved.

He might be in another realm altogether, one Kveldulf could not begin to imagine: the realm of the eastern god, the White Christ, the god who claimed to be the only god, whose worshippers had so influenced the course of Kveldulf's life. The god who had never penetrated Kveldulf's heathen heart, nor even shown his works to him. To imagine his son with the White Christ was no comfort.

Or, worst of all, perhaps Tryggvi was simply ... gone. Perhaps there were no gods, no reward to be gained, nor punishment. Perhaps, there was only cruel Fate, setting the course of men's lives, then cutting them short- not as it pleased, but with supreme indifference. Kveldulf had wondered as much before. Little he had seen had convinced him it must be otherwise. His people, the Greeks, the Rus, the Jews, the Moors, even the blood-stained creatures under Kiev—all believed in their own gods with similar fervency. Most of them believed their god or gods to be the only force in the world, to have started the heavens in motion and formed the earth and all that moves on and within it.

Kveldulf was no scholar, and had never had much interest in other faiths, but he knew that much. He had seen men die with

Odin's name on their lips, and also Christ, and Allah, and Perun. The words may have been different, but the deaths were much the same.

What he had seen of the world – which was far more than most – had convinced him finally that it might all be no more than a cruel joke, or a meaningless folly. So, when he considered the final fate of his son, Kveldulf's thoughts turned inevitably to diabolism or idiot randomness, and the black maw opened further.

What thoughts filled the minds of the other men in the cave, Kveldulf did not know, did not consider. Only when the bald one's harsh voice intruded on his own contemplation did Kveldulf spare any thought towards them, now that they had shown they were there only to seek shelter. Who they were, why they had been outlawed – such natural questions were beyond Kveldulf's interest at this point.

He would not move at all, save that the demands of his body stubbornly required it. He would tip over to one side to sleep, often passing into sleep and then back into consciousness with the voice of the bald man still in his ears.

Now, though, he was awake, and the others were sleeping. Kveldulf was not eating or drinking much, and thus did not often leave to venture outside or further into the cavern to relieve himself, but he could not avoid the habit altogether, and nature called him now. Bracing himself against the wall - he was growing weak already - he pushed himself up, slowly, until his feet were beneath him. They held his weight, for now, but Kveldulf knew if he did not obtain regular sustenance, he would soon be stuck. The thought passed through his mind like a low ripple upon the water, which could not be held. Survival was not of any concern to him, now.

Pushing towards the back of the cavern, Kveldulf passed small openings, branching off from the cave he was in. Past there, the walls and ceiling narrowed, and he had to stoop down slightly to pass into another large chamber. To the left was an alcove where Kveldulf had been to doing his business. The chamber was beginning to reek of it and Kveldulf allowed this assault on his nostrils to feed into his self-hatred. He was living like an animal, and even this was better than he deserved.

His business completed, Kveldulf returned the way he had come. He made it through the stooped entrance and halfway back to the cavern when his legs went out from under him, and he fell to the ground. He felt hot tears begin to stream down his cheek, and a sob wrenched itself from his throat. He tried to stem the tide, but it was no use. He could only bunch up a section of tunic and clench it in his teeth, to keep his low keening from echoing through the chamber, as the dam within him finally broke and unleashed what he had been holding inside. Gone, gone, all gone. Those he had loved best and longest taken from him. Even the few still living – Gunnar, his farmhands, his noble horses – he had been ripped away from them as suddenly as if the veil of death lay between them. And, soon, it would. Kveldulf was as one already dead; his actual passing to the realms beyond was mere formality. He wondered only if he would still be able to weep for his own dead there.

So Kveldulf sat there, gnawed his clothes, and choked out sobs, until finally there was nothing left for him to give. How long he had been there he could not even say. But his breathing slowed, and he began to come back to himself. To his enormous surprise, he felt more himself in that moment than he had in days – not better, exactly, but less filled with hatred – his despair had taken on a different sheen. He remembered, in a flash, all the other moments he had felt drained of the will to live, yet had somehow managed to survive.

Yet, no sooner did this thought come then it was followed by a black hand, reminding him that in the past he had always had someone to live for, some reason he could not crawl forever into the pit and join oblivion. No such obligations bound him now. So what was the point of delaying the inevitable? Perhaps he need not punish himself anymore. But nothing more was left for him. Sighing, he wiped his face and rose.

Then he froze, before he even realized what he was doing.

Impossible, but he had seen it, from the corner of his eyes, just a flash in the near-dark, but it had been there, off to his right at the entrance to one of the side-passages. A face. A ... human face? Slowly he turned to the mouth of the passage. Peering into it, he could see nothing. Yet he could sense, he somehow knew with certainty, that he was not alone. He wondered how long this had been the case, how much of his pathetic display had been witnessed by this unexpected intruder. He leaned towards the passage, squinting his eyes, trying to pick out any detail in the darkness.

He should be terrified, he knew. There were stories of things that haunted caves, worse things even than whatever had come for him as he slept in the abandoned cabin, the night after his son had disappeared. Kveldulf had seen enough to believe there was likely some truth to these stories, and he was surprised he had not thought of them more often while making his shelter in this place. Yet whether because he had lost his fear of pain and death entirely, or for some other reason, Kveldulf was now only curious, not afraid. He merely wished to know what was happening, to confirm what he was certain his eyes had seen.

"Hello?" he gently whispered, suddenly mindful of the sleeping men, just around the bend in the larger passage. "Who is there? I mean you no harm." he strained his ears, hearing nothing. Yet still he sensed a presence. He took a small step towards the passage, then another. There! He heard something, he was sure of it. The barest rustle, cloth upon stone. Yet still he saw nothing. He took another step, intending to march down the passage.

Then he came back to himself. Whatever was back there, friend or fiend, clearly it did not wish to be seen. Whatever it was, if it meant him no harm, he had no reason to disturb it. And if it did mean to harm him, then it was welcome to. But he would not help it. He had mourning to attend to, and he would not bring it to a close by running after some cave-beast. So, after nodding his head deferentially in the general direction of the passage, Kveldulf turned and walked back towards the entrance.

"... kill you."

The sound stopped Kveldulf in his tracks. What was happening? A silence, then the sound came once again, urgently this time.

"They will kill you!"

Confusion still. He had heard the words perfectly, yet they had sounded strange somehow, and though he had discerned their meaning, they made no sense. They sounded like a warning, not a threat. He was turning back towards the passage, for what purpose he could not say, when an image popped into his mind, as if some internal eye had opened, then snapped shut just as quickly- the big man and the bald man, bent over their companion as he bled into the ground.

One part of his mind began to tell him that he had begun to go mad, was seeing things. Yet the image of the men's cruel faces, blood splattered, was still seared into his mind, like the shadow of the sun after one stared at it for too long.

Warily, he headed back to the main cavern. Rounding the bend, he was surprised, but relieved to find the cavern empty. Yet he saw the others had left their bags behind. They would not have gone far.

No sooner had he thought it than the bald one and the big one darkened the entrance to the cavern. Kveldulf started to step back into the shadows, but the bald one fixed him with his eye, and his face broke into a grin that did not reach up past his mouth.

"Hello, friend! We thought you had left us! Come, we have more food to share with you!" He beckoned, but Kveldulf kept his feet rooted to the ground, still wary, alone and confused. What exactly was happening?

Seeing Kveldulf make no motion, the bald one's smile died on his face. Without breaking eye contact, he spoke to the large man at his side. "Take him!"

The other man started forward. He was heavily muscled, perhaps ten years younger than Kveldulf, and while cheekbones showed through the skin of his face, he did not look half as weak as Kveldulf felt. He brought one hand up as he advanced, and in it was a knife, showing dark with blood in the pale light filtering into the cave.

"This is it, then," Kveldulf thought, as the man advanced on him. Kveldulf wondered, mainly, whether he would appear in Hel immediately, or have to journey there by some spirit path. The men were almost upon him.

Then there was a flash, not so much in Kveldulf's eyes as behind them, and in the next second a great crashing sound. A section of the cave ceiling had sheared away, smacking to the ground just to the left of the outlaw approaching Kveldulf. The man skittered to the side, surprised but injured.

Kveldulf did not even realize he had moved until he felt his hand on the man's wrist. His momentum carrying him forward, he wrenched the big one's arm away from his body, smacking the back of his hand against the cave wall. The other man's hand spasmed, and the bloody blade fell to the floor.

With his right foot, Kveldulf stepped to the man's left side, still holding his opponent's right wrist in his left hand. In one fluid motion, Kveldulf set his hip against the outside of the other man's leg, and drove his open palm up into the man's chin, snapping his head back and setting him off balance. The man toppled backwards, and Kveldulf drove the side of his skull into the wall. His head hit the rock with a wet smack, and his legs buckled out from underneath him. Kveldulf removed his hand and released his grip on the man's wrist, and the big one flopped bonelessly to the cold stone beneath them.

Kveldulf looked into the man's unseeing eyes, then glanced up to make eye contact with the bald one. The man at the cave opening had not moved, save that his mouth had dropped open. Looking at Kveldulf, he started forward, took two steps. Then he seemed to think better of it, and turned on his heel, showing Kveldulf his back.

In the time it took him to step forward and turn, Kveldulf reached down and picked up a heavy stone, part of the cave ceiling which had splintered to the floor. Snapping his arm forward, he released the stone, sending it straight at the bald one. It caught him where thigh met buttock, and with a cry he stumbled forward, flinging his arms out to brace himself for impact with the ground.

Before he had gotten off his skinned knees and palms, Kveldulf was on him with the knife. The man never got his feet under him again.

As the bald one bled out on the ground, Kveldulf returned to the back of the cave, and drew the knife across the big one's throat. A prayer came to him unbidden, and he spoke it into the stunned silence of the morning. "Cold-armed Hela, take into your hands these men, that they may serve as it please thee." Kveldulf had not spoken such words in nearly 20 years, and they felt odd on his tongue.

Wiping the blade on the big man's tunic, Kveldulf stepped out of the cave and into the light of the day. Even though the sun was still low on the horizon, for a moment he was blinded. As his vision adjusted, he was able to make out a crumpled figure on the ground, near the river flowing past the cave. Quelling the rage still burning in his heart, he approached the prone form.

Thorgeir lay face down in the thin dirt. Kveldulf turned him over, gently, to see that he had been stabbed, savagely, in the throat and chest. The cuts were ugly and inelegant, but he had died quickly. He had a Thor's hammer around his neck – rough and wooden, he had probably carved it himself. His hand was empty however; no sword or weapon had been clutched in his grasp as he had passed into the next world.

Kveldulf closed the boy's eyes and said another prayer, one more familiar to his lips, and far more painful, than the last. "Gods, you receive today a warrior's soul. Welcome him, and make him a champion, to fight for you in the end of days."

With a sigh, he stood, and walked back to the cave. Already it smelled of death. Kveldulf returned to his resting place, set his back against the wall, sat, closed his eyes. He felt his heart begin to slow its pace, felt the rush of sudden activity drain away from him, leaving exhaustion behind. He had not meant to defend himself, had not meant to protect his own worthless life. Add this to the great heap of his failings. He could not even die right.

Yet, he considered, as he drifted into divine unconsciousness, he had avenged the young one, who had been cruelly cut down by these men, probably through deceit. In this, perhaps he should not fault himself. The weight crushing his spirit lifted, ever so slightly, as he drifted into dream.

Captain Bruni shouted in front of him. Kveldulf came around the final course to see that the passage opened up into another chamber, wide and long, with a low, curved ceiling. And filled with people. There were at least twenty of them, staring at Kveldulf and his compatriots in naked shock and anger. They were each dressed in dark robes that covered their bodies, made them blend together in the flickering light. But though they were dressed alike, the people in the room were male and female, young and old. And few of them were unknown to Kveldulf. In an instant he recognized Yarka, the blacksmith; Stena, the butcher's wife; the tavern keepers, Curzen and his brother, Duran; and others besides, men and women he had met while traveling in the city, or those he had interviewed in connection with the disappearances.

Kveldulf looked to his right, and saw Bruni standing over Babke, the kindly old fisherman, who moaned on the floor as he clutched at a deep cut in his cheek, blood leaking out from between his fingers.

No one else moved or spoke. Kveldulf looked back at the queer assembly, then past them. At the far end of the chamber was a stone altar, carved directly from the rock. Behind it stood another robed figure, face obscured by the large hood pulled over its head, arms raised high. In these arms was a large dagger, pointing downward at the altar. And upon the altar, directly below the dagger, was a supine form.

Kveldulf rushed at the altar, and the spell was broken. The robed townspeople parted before him, for a moment. Then as a mass, they moved to meet Kveldulf, and the Varangians who followed behind him.

Kveldulf hacked about indiscriminately, sword flashing in the torchlight. The chamber filled with the cries of the wounded and dying. Kveldulf barely noticed the cacophony. He had eyes solely for the two figures at the far end of the cavern.

He was steps away, kicking unconsciously at a hand wrapped around his ankle, when he saw the flash of the dagger's fall. He brought his hand forward, releasing his throwing axe. The axe caught the robed figure high on the chest, the force of it knocking the dagger from its course. Kveldulf reached the altar as the body hit the damp ground.

Hrolf was spread-eagled upon the oblong surface of the altar stone, his arms and legs affixed with heavy chords threaded through openings in the top and bottom of the table. He did not turn his head to see Kveldulf as he approached, nor did he struggle against his bonds. Hrolf's face remained pointed towards the ceiling of the cavern, his eyes opened wide, showing the whites all around his unmoving irises.

Only the rapid, shallow rise and fall of Hrolf's chest showed that there was life yet within him. But he was alive! Kveldulf had saved him! He bent to release his friend him from his bonds. He bent, and froze. Some small part of his mind shouted a sudden warning. He snapped upright again, and looked down at Hrolf on the table.

A shadow moved there, between Hrolf's legs. As Kveldulf watched, it detached from Hrolf's thigh, raised itself slowly. For a moment Kveldulf was transfixed. Then he leapt backwards just as the triangular head shot forward, fangs slashing through open air where only a breath before Kveldulf had stood.

Off-balanced, it dropped to the floor in front of him, but the lower third of its body was still braced around Hrolf's leg, and it began to pull itself up and backwards, muscles bunching as it prepared to strike again.

Hardly aware of what he was doing, Kveldulf struck before the great serpent had a chance. With speed he did not know he possessed, he whipped his hand forward, grasping the snake just below the head as it struggled to rise. He attempted to pull it off of Hrolf, but it had surprising strength in its narrow form, and resisted his grasp. Kveldulf could not reach his dagger with his other hand, and although the snake could not turn its head to bite him, it was only a matter of time until it unfolded in his grasp enough to turn back on itself. Even now it was uncurling its form from Hrolf's leg, seeking to draw its body up and around Kveldulf's extended arm. With his free hand, Kveldulf grasped the serpent further down its body. Its tail was free now, and it lashed violently through the air, transferring its startling weight to Kveldulf's outstretched arms. He pulled his elbows in, dropped his head forward. He brought the body of the snake up, and into his open mouth. Its muscles rippled against his lips, scales on its belly rasped against his tongue. He bit down hard, grinding his teeth until he felt the small bones of the snake's vertebrae snap and separate from each other.

Abruptly the portion of the serpents' body leading out of his left hand went limp. Kveldulf removed the snake's body from his mouth, the terrible taste of reptilian skin and blood on his tongue. The body had stopped moving but still the arrow-shaped head squirmed in his fist, jaws opening and snapping shut, venom dripping from bared fangs onto the stone floor. Kveldulf threw the snake away from himself as hard as he could, using its limp weight to whip it against the wall nearest him. It hit with a dull thunk, and fell to the floor, where the jaw continued to work even as the body lay awkwardly twisted and motionless.

This struggle ended, Kveldulf turned back to Hrolf. His friend's face was still pointed straight upward; his eyes were still open. But the white around his irises no longer showed. His chest did not rise and fall.

Once they had killed everyone else in the room, it took four of Kveldulf's compatriots to pull him away from the stone altar, away from the dead form of his friend, away from the blood-reek and death rattles of the unholy chamber, back through the narrow passage, and into the rising light of the new morning.

A dozen men and women of Kiev met their end in the cave under the city. When the rest of the armed company entered the cave to search it and clear out any remaining cultists, men tramped down both passages away from the antechamber. The men who went to the left recovered Hrolf's body, then the bodies of the Kievans. Between them, the Varangians were able to identify each of the traitorous Perun worshippers. Yet one body was not recognized by any of them: a woman, perhaps thirty, an axe in her chest and a polished dagger still clenched in her hand.

The men who ventured down the right passage did not return empty-handed either. With them, pale and starved but apparently uninjured, came three of the missing persons. There had been more, these fortunate unfortunates explained when they found their voices again, but they had been carried off one by one. None of the prisoners could say why they had been spared while others were taken first. Their captors had been people they knew, and people they had seen in the market, even at church. Familiarity had spared no one.

Other living things were brought up from below. Cats, birds, two sheep, a piglet – all had been kept in cages or enclosures in the extensive tunnels leading away from the right-hand passage. There was a room filled with jewelry and coins, perhaps taken off the victims who were brought below to be sacrificed. It was decided that these treasure would be split amongst the men who had fought in the caves, per the standard arrangement of the Guard.

Strangest and most impressive of all was the final possession recovered from the tunnels. Two men returned from deep within the caverns, leading the finest filly any of them had ever seen. She was still young, and not large. But her coat was whiter than white, and strong muscles rippled under her flanks. As soon as the horse scented open air, for the first time in who could say how long, she began to nicker and snort, her relief to be back aboveground nearly palpable.

More than one man thought to himself that sacrificing such a creature to some dark god was a worse affront than others the cultists had committed. Each of them wanted the horse for himself, but the best of them prevailed. By unanimous vote they gifted the horse to Kveldulf, who had managed to pull himself together somewhat but was still visibly distraught. The others understood – all of them had lost a friend at one time or another, and knew that pain. To have one go as Hrolf had – alone, poisoned, helpless, in terror – was even worse. None could say where Hrolf's spirit might end up, having passed from this world without sword in hand or battle-song in heart, with none present to administer last rites. It was a tragedy, and Kveldulf was not alone in his grief except by degree. Hrolf had been well-liked.

Finally, as the sun began to climb back westwards towards its resting place, the men made their way back to the palace. A messenger had been sent ahead, and Vladimir was prepared for them. He seemed to have aged since the men saw him last, only a day before. But he welcomed them heartily, commended them on rooting out the evil in the city's midst, feted and fed them generously. The next day he sent them on their way, and all involved hoped desperately that the Varangian Guard would never set foot in Kiev again.

Chapter 18

When she reached the caves, Sinmara first searched for any evidence of fólkish presence – a waystone or portal, anything that could provide her with the reassuring sense of home. She was disappointed, but not surprised to find her efforts in vain. While it had become abundantly clear to her that she had much to learn about the fólk, about the world itself, so far as she knew there was no warren in these parts, no reason for traces of fólkish presence to be found in this land. She wondered why Orri had led her here, although after their last two stops she was not in any particular hurry to find out.

She wished she had some way to communicate with her mother. There was nothing to be done about it now, though. Sinmara could feel a bone-deep weariness spreading within. If she were home, she would settle into her sleeping bier and be refreshed in no time, if she so chose. But out here she would have to sleep rough, as she had the night before, and this would take time.

She had found a shallow cavern that would keep rain and light off her. There were numerous others, carved into a hillside. Hers overlooked a large swath of grass next to the river, a rare patch of bright green in this mostly rocky and barren landscape. She led Kveldulf to the patch to eat and drink, and left him there as she climbed back up to her shelter, after speaking his name and asking him not to stray too far. He had flickered his ears in a gesture that Sinmara took as a sign of consent, then turned back to his repast. It still surprised Sinmara somewhat that Orri was apparently able to understand her so easily.

Ailuwa had told her that all animals could be spoken to and made to understand, could even communicate back sometimes, but the effectiveness of such communication depended greatly on the willingness of both parties. Orri had proven a willing and cooperative companion, although he would not or could not give her any sense of where he had come from, or what his life had been before he had appeared with the draugr at the door of the warren.

Perhaps horses did not remember things that way, she speculated. But he rode where she asked, and when they stopped he would sometimes come and lean his head against her shoulder. She trusted him to take care of himself, and to stay with her.

Settled down to a smooth spot on the cave floor, Sinmara helped herself to some food from her pack. Then she placed it on the ground as a head rest, before pulling her cloak around her and lying back. Forgetting herself for a moment as she drifted towards unconsciousness, she slipped into rockwalk, as she would have on her sleeping bier at home. Nothing happened of course, but she did get a quick sense of the ground below and behind her, the extent of the cavern system, the way it reached deep into the earth. Sinmara was not a path forger, she had no training or talent or interest in joining the fólk that chose the best places for portals through the rock, who used their special knacks to connect one place to another. Her warren had already been fully developed anyway, and the population was nearly stable, so there was rarely need for such a skill. Still, most fólk could use any knack found amongst the people, even if age and experience was required to develop it to useful levels. As she returned quickly to trueform, Sinmara wondered faintly what it would be like to found a new warren, to pick and forge the portals and footpaths, to delve into the earth and make it fit for fólkish life.

She awoke sometime later with a start. She had no idea how long she had been asleep. The light coming into the cave seemed the same, but this did not tell her much. She gathered her things and walked to the mouth of the cave. She looked towards the river, expecting to see Orri down there. There was no sign of him.

Sinmara groaned. It appeared she had been foolish to think she could command the horse to stay in place. She hoped he had not gone far, perhaps just around the river bend in search of fresh grass. She descended from the cave entrance to look for him.

The river curved around the outcropping of the cave system, mouths of gaping stone pocking the hilly landscape. Sinmara stayed close to the caves as she followed the bend of the river, feeling exposed as she considered the possibility that Orri had left – or been driven off – and she was all alone in this unfamiliar landscape. She didn't wish to consider her options if the horse had abandoned her – none of them were likely to be pleasant.

She was relieved beyond measure when she came around the bend and saw Orri standing between the river and the sheer side of the hill, staring right at her. She began to walk towards him.

She stopped short suddenly, not even really knowing why. A moment later she realized they were not alone. She had been so focused on Orri that she had paid no attention to the cavern she was skirting. Just in front of her was the mouth of a cave entrance. Her eye had been called to it by movement. Sinmara froze as a figure emerged from the cave opening.

He stepped into the thin morning light, rubbing his eyes, then stretched, yawned. He had not seen her yet, but she couldn't risk drawing his attention by moving. Evidently he had not seen Orri either. Still stretching, the human made his way towards the stream. When he reached it he bent down, cupped his hands to draw water to his mouth.

This was Sinmara's chance. She could flee while the man was distracted. But she hesitated. Orri was just downriver from the man. If the horse didn't move, he would surely see it any moment, and Sinmara did not know what would happen then. Would Orri flee? Would he approach the man? Would the man try to harm him, or capture him? She couldn't just abandon Orri.

In her tortured inaction, Sinmara lost her opportunity to escape. While the man was still drinking from the river, there was more noise and movement at the mouth of the cave. Another man emerged, and another followed him. They also made their way toward the river, towards the first man, without looking over to see Orri. They did not stretch or yawn as they made their way forward.

They reached the river just as the first man was standing from his drink. Hearing them behind him, he turned, a smile on his face. Sinmara was pressed now against the rock behind her. She dared not move lest the sound of her feet on the loose gravel alert the men to her presence, so she crouched down slowly, trying to make herself as small and inconspicuous as possible.

It was not enough, for she could not look away. As the man at the river stepped forward to greet the other two men, his gaze swept along the rock walls in front of him. He looked right past Sinmara. Then he looked confused for a moment, and his eyes came back, and locked upon her own. His eyebrows rose, and Sinmara prepared to run.

The other two men reached the man by the river. With his attention focused on Sinmara, he did not see the big man's arm lash out. He broke eye contact with Sinmara as the other man's fist caught him just below the ribcage, doubling him over.

Before he could rise again, the other man, the bald one, was on him. His arm struck down into the first man's back.

The man facing Sinmara immediately pitched forward to the ground, with a spray of blood as the knife in the bald man's hand ripped loose from his flesh. Then he was on him again.

Panic such as she had never felt gripped Sinmara, worse even than when she was in the farestone. She was exposed. These men were killers, and in a moment they would see her. She was certain the first man had, that the supposed invisibility of her kind had not protected her. She needed to be underground. She needed to be away.

But she could not tear her eyes away from the scene in front of her. Then the big man moved, to better watch what the bald one was doing, and her view was blocked, breaking the sudden spell she had fallen into. One of them spoke, and just as she had at the farm, she realized she could understand the words: "What about the other one?"

She ran then, the wet thuds of knife on flesh masking the sound of her footfall. In a dozen steps she was inside the cave the three men had just come from. She had to get as far underground as she could, far from these men. So she ran, through corridors and passages, taking the splits in the path as instinct directed her. Finally, she could go no further. She hit a dead-end, and sank to the ground, straining with every sense for any indication that she had been followed.

Only when the enveloping darkness and the feel of stone upon her back had calmed her enough to think did she realize the mistake she had made in her rush to get underground. She had gone into the cave the men had just come from. If it had been without further passages, she would have been trapped, completely cornered when the men returned. Or there might have been more men within the cave, more killers. She had been extremely fortunate that neither had been the case. Even so, now she was at a dead end, and in order to get as far from the men as possible, she would have to double back, to take one of the other paths she had passed. It probably wouldn't lead her back to the surface. Eventually she would have to go back the way she had come.

Sinmara turned and headed back to the nearest branching path of the cavern. Just as she was about to step out, she stopped. She was not alone. Heart racing, Sinmara pressed herself back against the wall of the passage, hiding in shadow. She dare not move, could only hope she would not be seen. She saw the men in her mind's eye, saw them slaughtering the man on the ground.

With her keen eyes she could see a figure crouching in the main path, less than a dozen paces away. A man in a filthy tunic, a beard on his chin, his hair clumped and lanky. As she stared at him, he rose, and for the briefest of moments she swore their eyes caught.

This man she did not recognize. He was not one of the ones from before. So perhaps he was the other one. The one the killers spoke of, as she fled. Another intended victim? But this did not mean he was not a threat to her.

It was only a fraction of a moment, and the man turned away. Perhaps he hadn't really seen her, perhaps he only wanted her to think this. She shrunk back further, willing herself to be invisible.

"Hello?" The man spoke, peering into the darkness. He stepped towards her hiding place. "Who is there? I mean you no harm."

She should be terrified still, and preparing to defend herself. Yet Sinmara found her fear receding, even before the man turned, and continued to stumble through the cavern. Somehow she thought that this man would not have intended her harm, even if he had seen her. As the sound of his footsteps receded, Sinmara found herself hoping that this man had not been with the others she had seen, and that he would be safe.

She surprised herself when she spoke. "They mean to kill you!" Still he was moving away. "They mean to kill you!" She shouted it, hardly knowing why, then turned and ran.

She still had to exit the cave somehow, and she didn't know if that was possible without going out the way she had come in. She turned away from the entrance, walked further into the caverns. As she began to enter one room, a foul smell assailed her, and she turned away. She did not wish to follow that path. Yet she did not know where else she might go.

She was pondering this predicament when her foot went out from under her. She tumbled heavily to the stone floor, bruising an elbow on the way down. She tried to rise, but found she could not. It was as if a cord had been wrapped around her spine and was holding her to the earth. No, it was pulling her. She felt increasing pressure on her back, and struggled even to raise her head. Panic gripped her too – what was happening? Hardly knowing what she was doing, Sinmara reached out with her mind, frantically cycling through what knacks she knew. But her arm-marks were gone, and she could not move to grasp the spar around her neck. There was only the pulling sensation, intensifying, making her gasp.

Finally, she lost the battle, and slipped into rockwalk. For the briefest fraction of a beat, she could sense the minerals around her. These tunnels were mostly lava rock, relatively new, and not the sort which fólk could manipulate. But in a blink, Sinmara could feel tiny pockets of usable mineral in the igneous forms around her, and she grasped at these somehow, clung to them with her mind. For a heartbeat, the pressure on her back lessened, she felt herself stabilized by the familiar ores around her.

Then a great ripping, as she was pulled through the floor of the cavern. She felt the rock anchors attempt to follow her, shearing away from the stone that held them, careening towards the spot she had been, crashing into the rocky ground of the cave. She was being pulled through the earth, faster than she had ever travelled through a portal. It was like traveling through the farestone, except she could feel the movement somehow. She thought of that black moment in the farestone, when everything split from white to dark. Perhaps this, she thought, was what Brekka had experienced.

ᛒ ᛥᛚ ᛟᚠ ᚨᛈ ᛥᛚ ᛟᚠ ᚨᛈ ᛥᛚ ᛟᚠ ᚨᛈ ᛥᛚ ᛟᚠ ᚨ

Kveldulf woke slowly, the smell of ocean lingering in his nostrils. He had been dreaming of his journey from Miklagard back to Iceland, of comforting Vaka as the ship rolled on the gentle waves, of whispering soothingly in the horses' ear. How she had danced when they reached land! Her joy to be back on solid ground had proved infectious, and Kveldulf had laughed to see the horse prancing about, tossing her mane. He had laughed for the first time in the months since Hrolf had died. Kveldulf's life began again in that moment, and he rose now with a smile on his face.

It took several moments for him to realize where he was, to remember what had precipitated his exhausted collapse into dream. He smelled now not the salt-scent of sea water, but the tang of drying blood. He saw the still form on the opposite side of the cave, then turned to see the other one in the cave mouth. Anger flared in his chest, bringing him further into wakefulness, but it burned out quickly, doused by hunger. He needed to eat.

Bracing himself against the wall, Kveldulf made his way upright. The dead men's packs were set against another wall of the cave. He crossed, avoiding the sticky spots where blood had pooled. There was a feast within the first pack – salted lamb's meat, a hard cheese wrapped in cloth, even a hardened half loaf of bread that needed only to be soaked in water. Kveldulf had no desire to speculate as to how the men had acquired their food. He set in to fill his empty gullet, remembering barely to chew slowly, to swallow small bites, to allow his body time to adjust to food after days of feeding off little more than self-contempt.

Even after Kveldulf had had his fill, there was still enough food left to last a single man days, provided he were careful. And there was another pack besides. He reached out and opened it.

This pack held no food that Kveldulf could see. It seemed to be stuffed with clutter. Yet there was something heavy in it, set against the bottom. Kveldulf reached in, and pulled out a large bundle, wrapped tightly in cloth. He began to unwrap it.

The smell hit him as he uncovered the first wisps of hair. Despite himself, Kveldulf dropped the bundle, and struggled for a moment not to lose his repast. He did not, however, and soon regained control. He crouched down, and gingerly wrapped the bundle again in the cloth he had just stripped from it. He did not need to see more to know what it was.

There were no jails in Iceland, no strongholds to keep prisoners in, no sheriffs or soldiers or king's men to hunt down law breakers and bring them to justice. There was only one way to punish those who had lost their right to remain in society – outlawry and banishment. The outlaw lost all claim to the rights of freemen. He was ordered to leave the island, and given time to do so. He was not to be helped, not to be sheltered. Once the term of his outlawry began – whether it was the three years of lesser outlawry, or the lifetime sentence of full outlawry – the outlaw was effectively an unperson. Anyone could kill him on sight, needing no excuse or justification whatsoever.

Yet that did not mean anyone would. It was no small thing to take another's life, even an outlaw's, in a community as small as the Icelanders'. No matter his standing, an outlaw still had kinsmen, usually had people who cared about him. Whatever the circumstances, these kinsmen might feel bound by blood and honor to avenge the outlaw, bound by rule and custom far older than any law of Iceland.

This was why there was no executioner, no capital punishment. Far better for everyone if the outlaw was simply forced to leave, to seek his fate outside the bounds of society. Some outlaws found new lives in other lands. Many more were brought down by hunger or nature or shame and loneliness. Outlaws were as those already dead, and in the case of full outlawry it was certainly meant to be a death sentence. But the punishment did not force anyone else to take on a blood-debt, to give anyone still within the bounds of society a cause to feud.

Of course, like any principle, this law had shortcomings in practice. A grudge against an individual might not be satisfied by outlawry alone, particularly when the convict was welcomed back to society after three years. This was usually enough time to allow passions to cool, but not in all cases, and from time to time old feuds were rekindled despite the dampening effects of the law.

Then there were the outlaws who refused to leave. Without any support or assistance, shunned by all, such men tended not to last long. But sometimes an outlaw might be sheltered by family, or even his goði. This could lead to problems, but it was a rare enough circumstance. Few people wished to impose such complications upon their kith and kin, and few households could tolerate them indefinitely.

On the occasion when such circumstances were indefinite, it was often because there was widespread ambivalence about the sentence as applied to that particular outlaw in the first place. From time to time, a harsh sentence might be necessary to preserve the rule of law, but still seem fundamentally unjust. In such cases, an outlaw's presence might be tolerated, especially if no one wished to take further vengeance.

Such circumstances were exceedingly rare however. As a rule, most everyone in Iceland knew the law, knew why it was as it was, and respected it. It had been developed by the Icelanders themselves after all, by those who had first come to the island, and not so long ago. It was not received law, imposed from on high by some so-called authority, as was the case in Norway and Denmark, in the places the settlers of Iceland had left behind. The people themselves were the law in Iceland – the free people, anyway. Listening to the Lawspeaker recite a third of the law each year was one of the most popular events at the Althing, and all the fun came in waiting to see if he would make a mistake. People knew the law and respected it, even when it went against them.

Of course, in any group of people there are some scofflaws and roustabouts. Young men were sometimes outlawed for youthful hotheadedness of one sort or another. They would leave the island, sow their wild oats, and come back ready to take on adult responsibility, to reintegrate into society – or not come back at all. It was common enough for a prominent man to have been outlawed for a time; in some circles an errant adolescence was practically a rite of passage.

But criminals, true and dedicated criminals – they could pose a threat. Outlaws might receive little help or aid from the good people of Iceland. But not all of them wished to leave for greener pastures, and not all of them were easy to kill on sight. Such men might be expelled from the sheltering boundary of the law, only to remain lurking on the edges, like predators just beyond the limits of the firelight, waiting to strike at those who wandered too far from its safety, who didn't look for the flashing of bright eyes in the dark.

From time to time, a sheep might disappear, or a girl, or a man traveling alone. "Trolls", said some. "Shape-changers. Ghosts." Yet often as not, thoughts would eventually turn to the bleak-eyed convict who had disappeared before he could be escorted to the boats the previous summer, or the farmhand who had run off with the silver just as the winter broke. There were plenty of places to hide on the island, lonely holes that could shelter man or monster.

A lone outlaw, gone rogue and feral, ready to prey upon those who had banished him, could prove problematic enough. It was dangerous to create a man who had nothing left to lose. Even more worrisome was a group of such men. Some years might see several men sentenced to outlawry, even in the same district. It did not happen often, and was never likely, but such things were not unheard of.

Such situations could be easily imagined.

Sometimes outlaws might band up and leave together, seeking mutual aid and support in foreign lands. The Varangians had filled their ranks with just such men, nor were they the only mercenary force boasting a high share of outlaws seeking death or glory. It was a happy irony that these men inadvertently served the society that had expelled them, bolstering a fearsome reputation abroad for the very people who no longer claimed them.

But not everyone left. Some had no wish to see new lands. Some felt too old, some too proud. Some were just crazy. And such men, if they were not killed outright, might find their way to caves and gullies on the edge of the settlements. They might meet others like them there, might realize that company was company and that they could survive better together than alone. In time, like wolves, they might form packs. The threat was there. Such things had been known to happen, in other places with untamed wilderness and rich farms, where desperate men all too easily made enemies and outlaws of each other.

From the start, the people of Iceland were smart. They had to be, to succeed in such an inhospitable place. Their lives required foresight, planning, and an evaluation of all potentialities. And the founders of this land, up through the first several generations of settlers, included many who had been driven from ancestral homes by laws and customs largely lacking in foresight, planning, and consideration. When they considered how to protect their nascent society from wrongdoers, they did so with fresh eyes, and often from the perspective of those who had been banished themselves. Thus they developed procedures to help ensure that only those who really needed to be punished were punished. They understood the importance of leaving convicts with some measure of hope, if they chose to embrace it.

But they also knew the rage that could burn within the outlaw's heart. They knew the threat a mass of them could pose, the potential for all of it to come crashing down if ever a dedicated cohort, fueled by a thirst for blood and revenge, set its mind to sowing chaos.

So, the early settlers inserted an exit clause from the harshest sentence the law could impose. An outlaw could have his sentence of outlawry diminished or even extinguished, could be reinstated as a full and valued member of society with all the privileges such entailed. All he need do is announce himself when encountering a free man, and present the heads of three other outlaws. One or two heads would grant a reduced sentence, but a full outlaw who could prove he had killed three others was an outlaw no longer.

No man had yet succeeded in this task, which suggested that the law was effective. The unease and distrust it sewed into any meeting of outlaws had, thus far, prevented any bandit cohorts from forming and presenting a threat to the law-abiding populace.

Kveldulf considered what must have happened. Everyone knew that outlaws were rumored to haunt the caves – that had probably been why Kveldulf, in his near-mindlessness, had made his way there. The men he fought must have been waiting here to pick off any other outlaws. They had already encountered one such unlucky individual, killed him, and taken his head. Then they befriended the boy and Kveldulf, hoping to do the same to them. Or, he considered soberly, perhaps Thorgeir had been in on the first murder with the others, then they had turned on him. If so, the boy was stupider than he had seemed in the admittedly brief moments Kveldulf had been aware of him, and had chosen his companions unwisely. Or maybe he had had no choice. None of it mattered. The law stated that each outlaw must provide three bodies to have his sentence revoked, and whatever the relationship between the big one and the bald one, it was unlikely that both of them were to be long for this world, once Thorgeir and Kveldulf's heads had been collected.

He wondered what the dead men had been outlawed for. The law said that outlaws could not gain reprieve, even by killing other outlaws, when their conviction was for theft or a killing crime. Though it also said that the Lögrétta could grant special permission even in such cases.

And with that, Kveldulf realized that his fate had possibly changed once again. Whatever else might have happened, when it came right down to it, it seemed he was not yet ready to die. He did not know what he had to live for, yet he had fought to live. With time, perhaps he could answer why.

But he must hurry. He rose to recover the knife, then set to his grisly task.

When it was done, he ventured down to the river to clean himself. He had not set foot so far from the cave in days, had not expected to do so ever again. The sun was setting, beginning its shallow dip below the edge of the horizon, and the rosy light reflected off the water as Kveldulf bent to drink. The cold, clear water was at that very moment the most delicious thing Kveldulf had ever tasted, and he had to stop himself from drinking over much. The night air was gentle and warm, and on an impulse Kveldulf stripped off his filthy clothes and washed them as best he could. He wetted his hair, scrubbed his face, cleaned the grime from under his nails and clipped them short with his teeth. Slowly he emerged from his cocoon of filth and despair, and as he did so a queer feeling stirred within. God or gods, fate or chance, it seemed the world was not yet done with him. What could he do but laugh? He had wished only to die, had sought punishment and death, and in so doing had found his possible salvation.

It seemed it was his lot to live while others – friends, lovers, children – fell into the abyss. He could choose to jump in after them. He could join them in oblivion, or some afterlife where he would have to explain why he had thrown away the gift they each had clung to until it was ripped from them. Or, he could live. If not for himself, he could live to honor them. Death would find him in her own good time. He had no fear of that. His duty now was to see what else life might bring first.

So decided, he stretched out on the ground next to the cold glacial stream. He lay there for a while, until the sun had set, and the brightest stars began to appear in the long twilight of the summer night.

He did not stir again for hours, but neither did he sleep. He stared at the night sky, until it began to brighten once again. By then his body had relaxed into its own contours upon the ground, and he struggled for a moment to sit up and look around.

He was not alone at the edge of the river. Further upstream, forty or fifty paces away, a horse bent down at the water, drinking eagerly. Kveldulf twisted about to look for its owner, but saw no one. The horse was unsaddled, so perhaps it was wild. Yet that could not be the case. It took his eyes a moment to catch up with his heart, which had already started thumping in his chest. The horse drinking at the river was well known to him.

Chapter 19

The air was already beginning to cool, and the nights had been getting steadily darker. Summer was coming to an end, and Gunnar would be happy to see this particular disaster of a season go. All districts, all goðar, saw their share of rough days, years when the sheep fell sick, or a serious feud broke out, or too many men went out a-viking and didn't return. Compared to years like that, Gunnar had little to complain about presently. But there had been no year more wounding to his heart than this one. It was true that he and Kveldulf had not been as close of late as they once had been, that he had not been at Gunnar's side to help the district thrive. Fate had not permitted this, nor had Kveldulf, isolating himself for so long on his farm. Yet Gunnar had always hoped that one day his old friend would reappear, would find his way back through grief and weariness to rejoin society, and the friends still waiting for him. And his boy, Tryggvi, despite being kept from much of social life as well, showed great promise.

Now all that hope and promise were crushed. Today the destruction would be made complete. Gunnar watched from outside the fence of Brauðavatn as Vigi and his men approached. His heart seethed with rage, but he kept his face impassive. The law said Kveldulf's property was now Vigi's to do with as he pleased. Gunnar would respect that, though already he felt a piece of himself dying as it choked on the idea. The law must be followed, for without it there was only chaos. Gunnar would not be the one to bring that upon the land, though the conviction was bitter in his mouth.

Vigi pulled his horse up short in front of Gunnar's. "Hail, friend Gunnar-goði. A grim day for such business is it not?" He gestured to the grey sky, threatening rain at any moment. Gunnar was taken aback. From what he had seen of Vigi, he expected him to open with a taunt.

Yet the man seemed almost resigned. The light hair framing his face hung loose and limp, and the expression of Vigi's plain face showed no contempt.

Gunnar considered his words carefully, mindful of the strong looking men Vigi had brought with him.

"Greetings, Vigi-goði. A grim day indeed. Let us not tarry in the task it brings us." Vigi nodded, and both men dismounted.

Gunnar met Vigi just outside the Brauðavatn gate. Facing him, Gunnar spoke the formal lines to commence the feransdomr.

"Vigi Haraldsson, you have brought suit against Kveldulf Thorbjornsson. Kveldulf has been sentence to outlawry, and is as the dead." Gunnar paused, but only for a moment, and when he spoke again his voice was still just as stern and strong. "Kveldulf's property is forfeit to you. Take what you can from this place, and the matter is concluded." Gunnar opened the fence gate to him. With a nod to Gunnar, Vigi entered, and his men followed.

It was done, then. Kveldulf was outlawed, fully and irrevocably.

Gunnar had anticipated no other outcome, but still he sighed inwardly. He had hoped something would change somehow, some solution might be found. At the least he had hoped to assist Kveldulf in any way he could, even if to arrange the terms of his exile, to provide for him to be well situated until he began his banishment, perhaps with an ally in Norway, or back in Byzantium where he had spent time in his youth, along with Gunnar's late, much missed brother. He would have done something, anything he could, but Kveldulf's desertion had prevented any such possibility. He could have stayed with Gunnar, or even at Brauðavatn, up until the court of confiscation took place. But now it was done. Kveldulf was an outlaw, unperson, anathema, and any righteous man would be expected to kill him on sight.

Gunnar wouldn't do that, of course. He would still help his friend any way he could, the law be damned. The vehemence of this thought surprised him. He was goði, and the foster son of a law-speaker. He knew as well as anyone the importance of the law – "without law, the land shall be torn apart," he had heard so many times in his life. But as he watched Vigi's men burst into Brauðavatn, watched them ransack his friend's home in search of valuables, saw the fear in the prize horses' eyes as strangers grabbed their manes, he felt that the law was worth little indeed if it could not prevent such fates from befalling good men, if it in fact demanded them.

Kveldulf had acted rashly in killing the man he had slain, certainly. But there was a time when such an action would have been understood, even defended, by enough of the goðar that Kveldulf's harsh sentence would have been unlikely. Killing a man was a serious thing, no doubt about it. But he had found this man, his victim, astride one of Kveldulf's own horses, with no permission to be there. Worse, the stranger had injured the horse. Once, such offense would have been a killing crime itself, or Kveldulf's actions at least seen as excusable. But the man he'd killed had been an important Christian, the witness to the crime had been an important Christian, and no matter what the private feelings of the other goðar about Christianity, no one was in a rush to provoke religious conflict. The king of Norway, it was said, was a true believer, and was unlikely to take ignore Christian fathers being murdered with impunity in a land that Norway had some desire to claim. The goðar were nothing if not pragmatic, and there was little to be gained from letting Kveldulf off lightly. Not when a goði with ties to the church prosecuted a convincing case against him, and when the status of the conversion was still being settled. Even the traditional turf ordeal had suggested that Kveldulf, a man too sullen and solitary to evoke much fellow-feeling, should be punished to the fullest extent.

That was the worst thing. Gunnar understood it, even as he hated it. Had Kveldulf been a man from another district, and not so well known to himself, he likely would have felt as the bulk of the other goðar did. The realization troubled him. Gunnar had never been a pious man, and when the conversion was decided, he had been willing to give it a chance. Since then he had followed the new religion, and forsaken the old, as best he could, though he had not immediately erected a church upon his land and hired a residential priest, as a few of the goðar had done. Gunnar held little allegiance to the old ways simply because they were the old ways – if the old way were the best way of doing things, no one would ever have come to Iceland in the first place.

Yet the new ways, it seemed, were not without their drawbacks. They had led to one good man being lost, in any case – to say nothing of his son. What else might be lost under the ways of the new god? Where would this all lead? No man could say, but watching his friend's ancestral farm get looted gave Gunnar an uncharacteristically bleak feeling for the future.

Shouts broke the air. One of the horses was bucking under strange hands, and pulled loose from Vigi's men as Gunnar watched. It skittered away nimbly, then broke into a trot around the farmstead, keeping just ahead of its would-be captors. Kveldulf's horses were magnificent beasts, Gunnar thought as he watched the young mare lead two men on a chase from here to there, watched them fumble and tumble to the ground as the horse kept just ahead of them, slowing, then dancing away as they reached for her, almost as if she were playing with them. Under other circumstances, Gunnar might have chuckled. There had always been something special about the Brauðavatn horses, even the ones Kveldulf merely purchased and introduced to his stock. They were known for being strong willed, brave, and intelligent, to an unusual degree – all qualities much sought after in a good horse. Despite Kveldulf's social isolation, the reputation of his herd was well known, and not just in this district.

That was all over now, Gunnar thought soberly as he watched Vigi order his men about. Perhaps, he considered, and not for the first time, that was a factor in why this tragedy had occurred in the first place. Affable nature aside, Gunnar was a realist about men's minds and motivations. His position as goði gave him ample opportunity to see how petty disputes and jealousies could lead to more serious troubles if left unchecked.

This was something he liked about the new religion. He was not a theologian by any means, and had less knowledge of the White Christ than he probably should, given that his own father had voted in favor of conversion. Yet he felt he had a good grasp of the basics, and he knew that the new religion stressed forgiveness and repentance. If he struggled with these concepts, watching his friend's home violated, Gunnar could nonetheless admit that forgiveness and repentance might keep such scenes from happening as often as they otherwise would. Above all Gunnar wanted peace, wanted a society in which his bændr – and his daughter – would not be caught up in feuds and bloodshed. A Christian Iceland seemed the best bet for ensuring this.

Of course, Vigi was one of the more prominent Christian goðar, and here he was rifling through Kveldulf's life. Gunnar ran a hand through his short-cropped beard as he considered that there was still much about this entire debacle that did not add up, and he had difficulty letting go of it. He was sad, even horrified for Kveldulf, but when he tried to consider the situation objectively, he understood why Kveldulf's actions had led to this, why the other goðar had acted as they had. Yet no sooner did he make his peace with this than he would consider how the underlying circumstances made no sense – why would a priest wandering through the district mount another man's horse? How had the man even managed it? Evidence of these horses' stubbornness and pride was before Gunnar even now. Why had these priests come all the way from Vigi's district, alone and unannounced, only to mess about with a man's property?

Then there was everything that had happened after Kveldulf was outlawed, at the Althing. Gunnar did not doubt that Tryggvi might have confronted Vigi's boy – the enmity between them had sprung up hot and fast, and was clear to any who saw the ill-advised horse fight between the two.

But for Tryggvi to engage Haraldr, in the middle of the night no less, when both of them should have been in their buðir... Then to run off after injuring him, leaving Kveldulf behind ... this went against everything Gunnar knew of the boy, which admittedly was less than he would have liked. The situation had been suspect from the start, not least of all because of the inherent unreliability of the supposed witnesses, all in Vigi's camp.

Kveldulf had not helped things by running off after his son. Gunnar understood why he had, and further understood that his friend was probably not thinking rationally in any case. But as it happened it had helped neither of them. If he had stayed, perhaps the situation could have been resolved without Vigi being able to control the narrative.

Kveldulf running off just made him and Tryggvi look suspicious – and, worse than that, it seemed it had come to naught, as no one had seen either of them since the Althing. A part of Gunnar still hoped that Kveldulf had found the boy, and that there was still some resolution that didn't see both of their lives destroyed. But he couldn't convince himself this was very likely.

Soon it was over. Vigi's men had collected everything of value from Kveldulf's home – six fine horses, lambs, goats, sheep, a number of cloaks and furs, gold braces and baubles Kveldulf had won in his time abroad, various victuals and sundries. One of them had a mass of blue fabric slung over his shoulders, and Gunnar's heart broke a bit when he realized it was Freyja's finest dress, which Kveldulf had purchased from a Danish trader shortly after they were married. For Kveldulf to have kept it all this time, only for it to be taken now by his enemies – this, perhaps more than anything else, set a pain upon Gunnar's heart which he knew would be with him for the rest of his days.

Vigi approached Gunnar. "Well. It is done, then." Again, he was without the gloating, sneering aspect that Gunnar had come to expect from their dealings at the Althing.

"So it is. Did you find everything you were looking for?" Gunnar asked, gesturing at the man with the dress.

Vigi did not rise to the bait. "Indeed. The property is now yours, to do with as you please."

"Wonderful. Now get the hell out of my district." Gunnar was not usually so impolite, but something about Vigi's resigned demeanor irritated him even more than his brashness had before. Again, Vigi did not react. "Of course, Gunnar Thrainsson. I will see you at the Althing next year." If there was any threat intended by his words, his tone did not convey it.

Vigi turned, gestured to his men. They mounted their horses, tying the rest of Kveldulf's herd to three of the men's saddles. They began to ride away, Gunnar's eyes boring into Vigi's back. As if he could feel the other goðar's gaze upon him, Vigi turned back, and met Gunnar's eye. He seemed about to say something.

Then one of the men shouted. "It's him! He is coming!" Gunnar looked up to see a figure on the hill overlooking the farm, framed against the clouds by the mid-day sun. Though he was some way off, and Gunnar's eyesight not as strong as it had once been, the form, and the horse it sat upon, were unmistakable. It was Kveldulf. Kveldulf and his boy's horse. He pitched forward, and began to ride towards his home – his former home, came Gunnar's thought.

With a wild cry, one of Vigi's men spurred his horse forward. "Wait!" Gunnar shouted, but to no avail. The man already had his axe drawn, readied it as he galloped towards the island's newest official outlaw. After a moment, the others followed behind him, leaving only Vigi behind, his face drained of color. He was the only one, it seemed, not eager to increase his reputation by taking on the disgraced bóndi.

Kveldulf had his hands up and open in front of his body, showing that he was unarmed. Still, the men came. The lead man was almost upon him. Gunnar found himself urging Kveldulf to flee, knowing that he would not get far, that it was all but over for his friend.

Then, as Vigi's man came within striking distance, Kveldulf lowered his hands. He clutched Orri's mane, and in the last second, as the ax began to fall towards him, the horse jumped to the left suddenly, and Kveldulf leaned into the leap. The axe in the other man's hand whirled past him harmlessly, and the man was so unbalanced by the unanticipated miss that he tumbled from his horse, and pitched onto the ground.

The other men approaching saw it all, and raised an indignant holler. They spurred their horses on faster. They had axes and swords. One man wielded a long spear. On they came, each one feeling suddenly that the fight was personal. That they would show this man, whose home and valuables they had just raided, what it meant to be an outlaw, to be the unperson that he was.

Kveldulf could not hope to feint away from that many blows. They would aim for the horse now, cut Orri out from under him. Had it been him alone, he might have allowed it. But he would not let them hurt the horse. He jumped off suddenly, leaped nimbly to the ground, and ran over to the first man, who was just struggling to his feet. Without pausing, Kveldulf kicked him back down to the ground, knocking the wind out of him, then bent and rose with the man's ax in hand. He turned to face the oncoming attackers.

Gunnar had never seen a berserker in battle, but he knew of them – men who would enter a battle rage so powerful that they could take on scores of warriors, brush off wounds like fly-stings, fight with skill and strength surpassing all reason.

Kveldulf was no berserker. He was methodical in his brutality. He attacked weak points as they opened up, redirected blows that could have felled a man, pressed his attack when it would be most effective, retreated when it would not. Kveldulf was not the biggest or the strongest man in the fray, but he was the only one who had been bloodied in the Varangian guard, who had lived and fought alongside elite warriors from far reaches of the world – and against them as well.

When it was over, five men lay broken and bleeding on the ground, and one stood over them. Impossibly, none of them were dead, but neither were any of them going to be fighting again soon. Kveldulf had a large cut across his chest where he had taken a glancing hit from a sword, and a broken finger on his left hand from blocking a blow. But he was not the worst out of them.

Dripping blood, head erect, Kveldulf walked toward the gate of the farm that had been his life, once. When he was between the pile of men and his destination, he called for Orri, and the horse trotted over to him from where he had been standing with the other horses. They had gathered by Orri after Kveldulf had pulled or challenged their riders from them, one by one.

Gunnar and Vigi were both in a state of shock about what they had just seen. It had been so unlikely, yet somehow everything that had happened once the fighting started seemed almost inevitable. It defied reason. But here was Kveldulf, standing up before them.

"I tried," he said. "I tried to tell them not to fight me."

Vigi found his voice. "It is their duty to fight you! You are an outlaw! It is everyone's duty." Still, Vigi made no move to jump down from his perch atop his own horse, to fight Kveldulf.

Kveldulf ignored him, kept his focus on Gunnar. "I brought you something," he said. He removed a pack from Orri's side and walked over to Gunnar, still on his own horse. Vigi gripped the hilt of his own sword – an Ulfberht sword, finer than any for a hundred miles, and never used – but did nothing, as Kveldulf passed the bag up to his former goði. The sack was evidently heavier than it looked, as Gunnar's arm dropped when he took hold of it. But he pulled it into his lap. He opened his mouth, started to ask Kveldulf where he had been, but realized that there was nothing he wished to say to his friend with Vigi sitting next to him. Instead he fussed with the tightly tied strap of the pack in his lap, finally got it open, and peered inside.

No sooner had he done so, he began to wretch, and the pack fell to his side. Vigi followed it with his eyes, and saw it hit the ground, the items within shifting on impact. There was something sticking out of the mouth of the bag, a round, smooth object almost like a large egg. It wasn't until Vigi saw an ear attached to the egg that he realized what he was looking at.

"Careful with that," Kveldulf said, calmly. "That bag contains my freedom." He walked over to the sack, gathered it up and cinched it again. He handed it back to Gunnar, who held it at arm's length.

Then he turned to Vigi, and there was ice in his eyes. "And as for you ..." he strode forward, hand on the hilt of a sword he had taken from one of Vigi's men, and jammed into the belt around his tunic.

"Wait!" Vigi said. Kveldulf had expected him to turn his horse and attempt to ride away, was prepared to chase him down with Orri. Still he came forward.

"WAIT!" Vigi said, more forcefully this time, as he met Kveldulf's eye. "If you want to know what happened to your son, for the love of God, you will wait." This stopped Kveldulf short, despite himself. "Speak." He forced the words through gritted teeth.

Vigi looked around with nervous resignation. "Not here," he said. "And my men need attention." Kveldulf began to stalk forward again.

This time it was Gunnar who spoke, startling both men, who had nearly forgotten his presence in their intense focus on each other.

"Kveldulf. Friend! Stop." Kveldulf did not break gaze with Vigi, but arrested his approach. Gunnar continued.

"I can't imagine what you have been through," he began. "And I know that you want your vengeance. I want it for you," he said, taking a moment to glare at Vigi, though neither man noticed. "But I beg you, consider your next steps carefully. You didn't kill those men, and you could have. You are not mindless with rage. So listen to me now.

"I do not fully understand what is happening here, or what happened at the Althing. I do not think you do either. But I know this – if you have been wronged – and I believe you have, I feel in my bones that you have – then you deserve justice. I will do everything in my power to give you justice. But I ask that first you help me understand what is happening. I think that Vigi can tell us, but not if you kill him first."

Kveldulf said nothing, did not take his eyes from Vigi. But after a tense moment, he visibly relaxed his grip on the sword at his waist.

Encouraged, Gunnar spoke again. "You did not kill those men, and I think I understand what you have given me," he said, raising the bag. "I will help you in any way I can to get back what you have lost. But I must understand what is happening. And, above all, we must follow the law. It has been much abused of late."

Vigi piped up. "The law says this man is an outlaw!" Then Vigi lay on the ground, clutching a bloodied nose and groaning. Kveldulf stood over him, but his sword stayed in his belt, and he made no move to harm Vigi further. When it was clear he was done, for the moment, Gunnar spoke again.

"I offer you all my protection as goði. Vigi and I will lead his men onto the horses, and we will all go back to my farm. We will sort this out there."

Chapter 20

Fulla, Njála, and some of the thralls attended to Vigi's men, while Kveldulf, Vigi, and Gunnar settled in for a discussion.

"I offer you both the protection of my home. No violence will come to either of you here, on my oath," Gunnar said, looking both men in the eye.

Vigi glanced at Kveldulf nervously. "He is outlawed. No oath can bind him, yours, his, or any other." Kveldulf glared back, but said nothing.

"The saddle bag he gave me: it had the heads of three outlaws in it. He presented it to me, a goðar. And you, also a goðar, saw it as well, for that matter. Kveldulf's outlawry is revoked."

"That ... that cannot be so! How do you even know those men were outlaws? I do not. What does the law say of this?"

"The law says only that an outlaw can have his outlawry revoked if he kills three other outlaws. As you should know, goði. As you should also know, the law has never actually been invoked before. The process is not entirely clear. But we must strive to follow it nonetheless. We must assume that these men were outlaws. Later, you and I will both observe the heads, and try to remember them as best we can. Then I will pack them in salt, which hopefully will preserve them. Kveldulf will tell us all he knows of the men. The faces are not likely to stay recognizable for long, so this will have to be sufficient to determine their identities. At the next Althing, I will tell the court all I know of these men, and will call you as a witness as well. Then the court can make an official pronouncement reinstating Kveldulf as a free bóndi.

"But until that time, he must be considered provisionally un-outlawed. I will send messages to some of the nearest goðar, and perhaps they can assist further. For now, Kveldulf will stay with me. But know that, as far as I am concerned, Kveldulf is a free man."

He looked at Kveldulf significantly, and both men in that instant felt some of the weight lift from their shoulders and their hearts.

"And what of my own men? Kveldulf attacked and injured all of them. For this alone he could be outlawed. What of their rights?"

"Well," Gunnar began, "that is a trickier question, I grant you. Your men attacked Kveldulf first. If he were a free man, no one could fault him for defending himself. That would have been his right. But," he said, heading off Vigi's objection, "it is the right and the duty of men to attack outlaws when they see them. In this, your men were in the right." Vigi began to nod his assent.

"However, your men failed to kill Kveldulf, try as they might. Kveldulf did what comes natural to all men, and defended his life. No law can compel a man to lie down and die without a fight. No man could respect our laws, if they asked for such a thing. And now, the same law says that Kveldulf is no longer an outlaw. Your men cannot attack him unprovoked – no man can."

"But what of the injuries he caused?"

"If you or your men wish, you may bring suit against Kveldulf at the next Althing. But you will not take the law into your own hands. And, to save all of us some time, I will tell you this – at the time Kveldulf fought your men, he was an outlaw, a full outlaw. A full outlaw cannot be made more of an outlaw. There is no further punishment which can be meted out to him. He is as the dead, and under the law, your men killing him would have been the same as nothing happening at all – a legal non-event. Likewise, his killing or attacking your men would be a legal non-event. The law is silent on such things, because the law can say nothing to an outlaw. Any man has the right to kill an outlaw, no matter what that outlaw does or does not do. So an outlaw can do anything, and fare no further consequence under the law – he has already been punished with the greatest consequence."

"What is your point?" Vigi interjected.

"No suit against Kveldulf for attacking your men will stand. You cannot bring suit against a full outlaw, and Kveldulf was a full outlaw when he attacked your men."

"But he isn't now!" Vigi spat. "Or ... so you say."

"So says the law. But it also says that Kveldulf was an outlaw right up until he presented me with the heads of the other three outlaws. At that point, and only at that point, did Kveldulf exist again in the eyes of the law. What happened before, the law is blind to. If Kveldulf attacked your men now, you could certainly sue him for it, or they could themselves. What happened before – well, that's the risk of taking on outlaws. They have nothing to lose, and so make dangerous opponents. All things considered, your men were lucky that the outlaw they encountered did not kill them and make his escape when he could have." Try as he might, Gunnar could not keep a slight smile from creeping onto his face.

It was not lost on Vigi. "So my men get nothing for their injuries?" he cried. "Where is the justice in that?"

Kveldulf exploded. "Justice? Justice? What of my injuries? Tell me what happened to my son!" He shot up from his seat, and Vigi shrank back.

Gunnar clapped his hands together, and the sound was piercing in the small space of his cabin. Both men stopped, and looked at him. Gunnar was often smiling, gregarious, but he could be a commanding presence when need be – not for nothing was he a goði, the son of a goði, and the son of a son of a goði.

He addressed Kveldulf first. "Soon enough, my friend. I promise you." He turned to Vigi. "If you desire compensation for your men, you may give it to them yourself." He sighed. "They have no case against Kveldulf that can be prosecuted now. But that is only because the feransdomr had occurred, and Kveldulf was properly outlawed when your men attacked him. He is not an outlaw now. But neither does he have any claim to the fruits of the feransdomr. All that you took from Brauðavatn – the wares, the food, the clothes, the horses – that is still properly yours. You cannot claim you came out of this empty handed. If you wish that your men receive compensation, you are free to give them a portion of the take, or whatever else you might have as you judge appropriate. Currently, Kveldulf has nothing with which to compensate you anyway." Gunnar looked apologetically at his friend, but Kveldulf only pressed his lips together and nodded once, solemnly. He had expected as much, and more, he was past the point of caring about such things now.

Gunnar turned back to Vigi. "Now," he said, his voice grave and carrying malice that had not been there only a moment before, "Now you tell us what happened to Kveldulf's boy, Tryggvi."

Vigi looked from one to the other and knotted his hand in his lap. "You already know," he began. "He attacked and injured my son, then ran off when my men approached him." A disquieting sound filled the room, low yet reverberating. Kveldulf was growling at Vigi. Vigi looked to Gunnar for support, but the look on the other goði's face told him he would find none there, not over this.

"You are under my protection, Vigi. I have sworn that no harm will come to you in my district, and certainly not in my home. But," Gunnar said, as he cracked his knuckles, "things will go much better for you if you tell the truth now. Consider your next words carefully."

But before Vigi could speak, Kveldulf did. "I already know he's dead." The other two men looked at him in surprise. "I can feel it. I know he is gone. I just need to know how, and why. You had already taken everything from me. Why did you take my son?"

The anger that Kveldulf had filled the room with moments before suddenly disappeared, leaving behind a current of sadness that both of the other men felt sharply. They thought of their own children, saw their faces. Njála, quick witted and kind, sharp-tongued and softhearted, hair as the fire from the mountain and eyes like ice on the sea. Haraldr: Sullen, angry, especially these last few years. But the light in his mother's eye. And strong – a hard worker, a welcome hand on the farm, and pious, faithful, praying to Christ every night with a fervency unmatched in the rest of the household, though they were Christians all. Vigi saw him he was now – pale, fine hair plastered to his forehead, moaning with pain in his sleep.

Vigi made a decision. He spoke. "Fine. I will tell you everything.

But you must understand. I have to start at the beginning." "No! Tell me now! Where is my son?"

"I think you are right. I believe he is dead." This said quietly, though Kveldulf felt it like a crack of thunder. "And that he died at the Althing. But I didn't do it, nor did my boy, or any of my men. I swear to you."

"Then what happened?" Kveldulf managed the words.

"I wasn't there; I didn't see it. But Haraldr was. You will remember the priest who testified against you. Pétur, he is called. He showed up at my door this spring, desperate, begging our help as good Christians in protecting him and seeking justice for his companion. I took him in, as anyone would." He glanced at Kveldulf, then away.

"Haraldr was quite taken with Pétur from the start. He is a good boy, and seeks to be a good Christian, and I suppose he looked up to the priest. The evening after you were outlawed, Haraldr snuck away from the booths to listen in on the priest's evening prayers. I still do not exactly understand how or why, but your boy found him and confronted him there. They fought. Pétur heard them fighting, and...he protected my boy. He told me that he pushed your son off mine, and that your boy ran away while he was tending to Haraldr."

Kveldulf could not stop a low moan from starting in his throat, but he did not interrupt.

"I only learned all of this later, when Pétur brought Haraldr back to me. Haraldr was in rough shape, and while my wife and I were tending to him, Pétur explained what had happened with your boy. Haraldr could not- he could not speak. It is still difficult for him.

"You know what happened next. We tended to Haraldr, and then I came to confront you. I confess at this point I was still quite upset and angry. Haraldr was – is – quite injured, and I thought I might find his attacker with you. I did not expect Kveldulf to run off so suddenly," he explained, "and when you did, I wondered if you had sent your son to attack mine. And I wasn't the only one."

"And do you think that still?", Gunnar asked.

"No. Later – after we had packed up our booth and left to return home – I realized that it was unlikely your boy would have known beforehand that Haraldr would be away from his booth in the middle of the night. Even if you had ordered him to take vengeance, it had to be pure coincidence that your boy had encountered mine there."

"I ignored him." Kveldulf whispered it, then cleared his throat, spoke again, "I couldn't bear to speak to him after I was sentenced, so he left. That is why he wasn't in our booth that evening." He paused, silently flagellating himself. "He must have seen your boy, and gone to ... confront him."

"There was no love lost between those two," Gunnar said. "Especially not after Tryggvi humiliated your son at the horse fight," he reminded Vigi, not without some satisfaction.

"Yes. Haraldr seemed to take the feud between us," he gestured at himself and Kveldulf, "very personally. I wanted only justice for the priest – the man you killed. Haraldr though, he was quite furious, not just that a priest had been killed, but that a Christian man had been killed by a pagan. I'm not sure where he got such strong ..." Vigi stopped abruptly. The silence stretched, as each man considered his own thoughts.

Gunnar spoke first. "So this priest, who protected ... -" he caught Kveldulf's eye, changed tack, "... the one who you say found Tryggvi and Haraldr. You say he helped Haraldr, while Tryggvi ran off. The two of you told this story to the Althing, and got Tryggvi outlawed.

Are you telling us now that there is more to it?"

Vigi closed his eyes, considering. When he spoke, his voice was quiet. Unconsciously, Kveldulf and Gunnar both leaned forward to attend to his words.

"Pétur is his name. 'Pater Pétur,' he says he is called, in the language of the Church. He has been in Iceland over a year now, since last year's Althing. I met him there, in fact. There were a few priests there, as there have been the last several years. I was looking to build another church in my district, that my bændr and their families would have a bigger place to worship. We are good Christians in my district," he added pointedly, deflecting his comment at the last minute away from Kveldulf, and towards the world in general. "Anyway, I sought out the priests for advice, and met Pétur and Adalbert amongst them."

"He is not an Icelander though? Where is he from?" Gunnar demanded.

"I ... no, he is not from here. He said ... I know he came here from Norway, but he I don't think he is from there, either. I suppose I have not thought about it much." He frowned. "Priests often travel, you know. He has told us tales of his brothers in Christ, setting off for the most remote, unknown places of the world.

"This is what he was doing in your district. He and Adalbert were spreading the light of God. Then...afterwards, he made his way back to me somehow, and begged aid and shelter."

Gunnar tried to catch Kveldulf's eye, but the other man was still staring hard at Vigi.

"We were dismayed to hear his tale, but he was unable to tell us where exactly he and his companion had been traveling, so it seemed there was little we could do. I planned on asking around at the Althing, seeing if anyone could help."

Vigi took a deep breath, released it slowly, then straightened his back and looked Kveldulf in the eye.

"But almost as soon as we got there, Pétur saw you, and recognized you. I knew of you too, Kveldulf, before the Althing, before this summer, though only by reputation. It was said that you bred and sold fine horses, and that you had been a warrior in your youth. When your boy helped stop the fire at the Althing, people said we could expect great things from him as well. I will admit I was perhaps a little jealous of you. I am a goði, but I am not known for much, and my district is small. My son is a fine boy, a good boy, but ... if I were not goði, I sometimes wonder what he would make of himself.

"When I heard it was you who had killed the priest, I was dismayed and angry, as anyone would be. But I also saw the chance to make a name for myself, or at least to show that you were not so much better than the rest of us. But that was it.

"It was Pétur who asked me whether you were follower of the old gods. Pétur who said that my God would be angered by the death of a good Christian priest such as Adalbert at the hands of a pagan such as yourself. I respected Pétur, and I heard what he had to say. But I am also goði. I know the law. I know that there are others who keep the old ways. I pray they will turn away from them and truly embrace the White Christ, but that is not the law. Not yet. Pétur does not understand this. He was convinced I had to make a stand for us Christians against the likes of you, and Haraldr began to say the same thing as well.

"And I did. I followed the law, and the law said you must be outlawed. And I still believe that was right. You killed a man, a good man, for riding your horse."

"For killing my horse," Kveldulf interjected.

"Even so," Vigi said quietly. "The priest deserved justice, and justice was given.

"But I was satisfied when you were outlawed, even with how you were outlawed. I would have preferred you face the decision of the court, rather than demand an ordeal. But the way your ordeal ended – I was as convinced as anyone that God was showing His displeasure to you that day. And perhaps He was.

"I was satisfied. I had no wish to cause you further injury, and was reminded by my wife that evening of the Christian duty to forgive. I was ready to do so, in my heart. And I certainly held no ill will against your son.

"Haraldr still did, however. From the start, he had been perhaps the angriest about everything. He is an angry boy in general. Even though we got our way, and won out against you, Haraldr still held a grudge against your son for embarrassing him in the horse fight. And he had grown close to Pétur. I sympathized with him, but I was ready for the whole matter to be done with. I resolved to keep my boy away from yours until the Althing had ended.

"As you know, I failed in this. I still don't understand how they came to meet each other that evening. But they did, and they fought, hard. Your boy got the upper hand on mine, and injured him gravely." If this comment was meant to pacify Kveldulf, it had the opposite effect, though he managed to remain still and silent, needing to hear what Vigi said next.

"But Pétur stepped in. He told me that he pulled your boy off of mine, and that Tryggvi fled. But..."

"Speak!" commanded Gunnar.

He did, and for the first time, Gunnar and Kveldulf could both unmistakably hear fear in Vigi's voice. "Haraldr and I spoke just before I set out this way. He does not remember much of that night, and has been in great pain since. But ... he said something came back to him, something he could tell only me. He said ... He said that Tryggvi beat him, but it wasn't Tryggvi who cut him, made him bleed.

He...he thinks Pétur did it."

"I don't understand," Gunnar said.

"Nor did I, at first. I thought he must be confused. And with his injuries...it is difficult to understand what he says. I had no reason to doubt what Pétur told me. Yet ... the priest has been odd, since we came back. I assumed he was still upset over everything that happened. But ... there is something strange about him. Perhaps there always was, and I never had reason to notice."

"It ... when I tell it, it sounds silly. Pétur ... he is very well liked." Vigi said, to no one in particular. "And he is a man of God. He has been teaching us the ways of Christians in the east, and of course these new ways seem strange at first. But I had no reason to question any of them."

"But you are questioning now," Gunnar said.

Vigi looked at them both beseechingly. "You must understand what Pétur has done for us. He has become my closest counsellor, and he has brought me, my family, and my people closer to God. I have felt God in the last few months, felt his presence around and within me. Never did the old gods show themselves to me in this way. I have been nothing but grateful to this man for showing me the light. And my family loves him as well.

"But ... But I cannot ignore what my boy said. I know my boy. He is many things, but he is not a liar."

Vigi ran his hands through his thinning hair, and considered his words carefully. "I have seen this man fight." He gestured to Kveldulf. "I am in your power, as are my men. You are angry enough, without me making it worse for all of us by lying to you. And ..." he stopped suddenly.

"I have promised you safety," Gunnar said. He stared at Kveldulf until Kveldulf made eye contact with him, and nodded. "We both need to hear this," he told Vigi.

Vigi sighed. "My son... he said he remembered something else, as well. He said... he thinks he saw Pétur kill your boy."

Kveldulf smacked his fist into the wood of the bench, then buried his head in his hands. Gunnar felt his heart sink as well. Both of them sensed that something was very wrong, very out of place with Vigi's story. Gunnar was thinking implications, repercussions. Kveldulf on the other hand was struggling to control himself. He had known his son was dead, but to hear it confirmed ... nothing could prepare him for those words. His grief was like a candle that had burned down to the base – then set the table beneath on fire.

Yet somehow, even in his despair, Kveldulf also felt a glimmering of purpose, saw the path forward more clearly than he had in ages, perhaps since his wife had died.

"It sounds like it is past time for me to meet this priest," he said.

Chapter 21

Sinmara knew not for how long she fell, or even if she was truly falling. She knew only that after interminable darkness and the sensation of movement, there was suddenly light, and then, shortly after, rest. She was lying face up on soft grass. She could feel the individual blades bending under her back, supporting her gently, curling under her fingers, the skin of her outstretched arms.

For a moment she just lay there, utterly disoriented, not sure even if she was alive or whole. Yet, she was calm. Above her, far, far above her, there was a gentle mist hanging in the air, cloud-like yet somehow more diaphanous, dispersed, almost smoky. And through this mist shone the light of a great orb, directly above Sinmara, dimmer than the sun yet brighter than the moon, bathing all below it in a gentle glow that shimmered and shifted with the movement of the mists below. Sinmara had no idea where she was, but it was the most beautiful thing she had ever seen. A part of her wanted to lay there, feeling warm and rested, forgetting what troubles she had, the confusion she felt, until the grass grew up around her and she was gone.

Perhaps she would have. But as she lay there, she became slowly aware of yet another strange sensation within her body, a sort of humming buzz that she felt in her back teeth. For a terrible moment she was afraid she was going to fall again, through the grass, through the earth, fall until she landed who knew where, or perhaps fall forever. But she did not fall. The sensation resolved itself. It was a sound – or rather a medley of sounds. Sinmara had heard nothing like it before, could not imagine what could produce such sensations. They slid from a deep, thrumming tone that she felt resonate against her sternum, to a flitting, piercing series of pitches that seemed to dance across the membranes of her eardrums. As she began to focus on the sound, to tune into it, she recognized repeating patterns, sequences that seemed to fit together, and she felt her emotions respond in turn.

She sat up, looked around for the source of the sound. She found herself at the center of a large field. Forms circled her on all sides, and Sinmara recognized them as trees, though they were much larger and of a different sort than she had ever seen before. They stood close together, and beyond them, all around her, stretched a dark and dense wood. No breeze stirred the leaves of the trees, or bent the blades of grass about her. All was still, and the only sound was the strange music which seemed to be everywhere, yet come from nowhere.

Sinmara got her hands under herself, rose to her feet. She turned, scanning the entire periphery of the field. Everywhere her eyes met the dense bounds of the forest, the trees so close together that they appeared impassable. But wait – there, on the edge of the field just opposite, was a small parting in the sturdy line of tree cover, the barest gap suggesting the chance of a path through the wood. Sinmara took a step toward it, and as she did it seemed the sound she was hearing became just a little louder. She took another step, and the pace of the music quickened slightly – she might not have noticed were she not listening to it so intently, but she was certain that the sound had changed. Seeing no other option at present, Sinmara set across the open field, under the light of the not-sun-not-moon.

It took her some time to reach the edge of the field, and in that period the music had warped and changed perhaps a dozen times, yet somehow remained coherent, compelling. The dark trees towered as she approached, everywhere but directly in front of her, where she could see the narrow gap in the tree line extending straight back for some ways.

As she stepped off the field and into the path however, the sound abruptly dropped away, and all was silent. Sinmara could hear only the beating of her own heart in her ears, the crunch of the forest floor under her feet. Experimentally, she stepped back from the path back into the field. Still there was silence. Whatever was producing the music had stopped suddenly, just when she entered the wood. Still, Sinmara saw no reason not to continue down the path. She turned back, and entered under the leafy canopy.

Only a few steps into the wood, and the light swiftly dimmed, the dense leaves blocking nearly everything that came from above. Sinmara could see fine in little to no light, but she noticed the difference. The path itself was straight and quite narrow – too small for two fólk to walk abreast without running into the thick, mossy bark of the trees on either side. When she peered through the small gaps between the wide trees, Sinmara could only see trunks of more trees pressing close, and not any distance into the forest. She reflected that if she were to meet anyone on the path, or someone was to come up behind her, she would have no place to run, barely even room to turn. Yet for all this she did not feel any fear. She was wary, but she accepted that there was little to do save press forward, to see where the path might lead her.

So she walked, and walked. The light in the forest never changed, nor did the scenery, and Sinmara found it impossible to tell for how long she had been walking.

And then the path ended. After traveling so long in a straight, level line, Sinmara nearly walked face first into a tree trunk. For a moment she thought she could walk no further, that she would have to turn back and walk out of the woods the way she had come, back to the open field, without receiving any answers about where she was or how she had gotten here or how she might leave. She began to turn. But as she did so, she saw that the path didn't truly end, it just cut away sharply, to the left. With a shrug, she pressed on into this new section.

More walking, but where the previous path had been straight, this course turned endlessly. It was disorientating, and although the curve was gentle, its steady progression made Sinmara somewhat dizzy. Still she walked on.

Then, finally, a change. One moment Sinmara was still on the path; the next she found herself in another clearing. The path was cleared through the trees in such a way that the open space was not visible until she actually entered it. It was smaller than the field she had awakened in, and darker – far above, the thick, leafy boughs of the trees came together over the clearing.

Within the grove, towering gray stones stood in a circle. Their sharp edges and even faces showed precision that no human hand or tool could manage. Sinmara could see shapes carved into them, and as she stared, she felt a gentle thrumming behind her eyes, just as she had at the farestone. Had that really been only a few days prior?

She looked up, and there was enough space between the foliage at the very center of the canopy above to admit a glimpse of the sky. Instead of the single glowing orb, now Sinmara saw tiny lights like stars in a moonless expanse of midnight blue.

The music started up again. The sudden sound after so much silence startled her, and she leapt back onto the path. Then, embarrassed despite herself, she stepped forward once more. While the sound was similar, the rising and fluctuating tones already feeling familiar, she no longer felt it physically like she had before. It was just music, now. And it seemed to be coming from within the ring of standing stone.

Sinmara stepped forward, until her view inside the ring was unobstructed by any of the standing stones. Right in the center of the clearing was a circular slab of black stone, set into the grass like the pupil of an eye.

Then the music stopped. Suddenly there was a dark form within the ring, a shadow, monstrously large. Perhaps it had been there all along, and Sinmara had just not seen it.

Instinctively, she reached to the place within herself where her power rested, prepared to draw it forth in defense. Her arms stung sharply for a second, as she unthinkingly tried to activate the knackmarks she had lost.

But wait- This was no monstrous form. It was a person, and a rather small one at that, standing near the edge of the black slab. And she recognized this figure, even in the gloom, recognized the rounded shoulders, the burnished skin, the white beard. She stepped forward, and spoke his name.

"Ananz?"

He smiled, teeth shining.

"Sinmara. Well met. Come, come. Let me see you."

Sinmara stepped between two stones and fully into the circle. She felt a slight tingle in her limbs, but it disappeared once she stepped further onto the grass within.

Her tongue burned with questions, but somehow she restrained herself until she had reached the circular slab. Ananz sat there now, legs crossed, a warm and welcoming expression on his face. Yet he said nothing more as Sinmara approached, nor as she stood before the slab, regarding him. Finally, she could take it no longer, and her curiosity won out.

"Elder ... what are you doing here? What am I? Doing here? Where is this place? What is this place?"

Ananz tilted his head, then patted a space on the black stone just in front of him. "Sit with me here, and I will explain it all."

Eager for answers, she took the last few steps to the slab, and stepped onto its polished surface. The black stone was smooth under her feet, and pleasantly warm, as if it had been sitting in the sun for an afternoon. She smoothed her shift around her, and sat to face him.

She opened her mouth to prompt him, but he immediately began to speak, looking not at her, but at the palms of his hands, lying open in his lap.

"First, there was the void. A great emptiness, containing only itself. Silent. Dark.

"Then, in a flood, a dream washed through the emptiness, taking shape and substance, creating boundaries, time, change: existence. A dream calling itself reality, containing all that was, is, will be. But also all that never was, and never will be. And all that cannot be contained."

Sinmara had no idea what he was talking about, was confused as ever when Ananz stopped speaking.

"You have given me much to think about, Elder ..." she began, cautiously. "But I still don't understand why I am here, or what this place is. Was it you who brought me here?"

He nodded. "This place is mine, just as your chamber back in the Killicut warren is yours. It is rather larger than your room, but then I am much, much older and wiser than you."

"But how did you draw me here? What was that…sound, that I heard in the field, through the woods?"

Ananz simply smiled at her. "That, my child, you must figure out for yourself." He stood, and turned away.

Sinmara made to follow him. She stood, and stepped off from the warm stone surface. Yet she did not feel her feet hit the grass. She was still seated on the slab. She tried again. Again she stood, stepped off. A brief sensation of movement, and in a blink she was on the slab again. The stone beneath her hands was perhaps a little warmer than it seemed to have been a moment ago, yet otherwise it was as if she hadn't done anything at all.

Before she could try again, Ananz spoke from the edge of the clearing, his voice sympathetic. "I'm afraid you will find that you are quite stuck." She looked at him, confused. He held her gaze, his eyes liquid, frowning slightly.

"I do apologize," he said. "But important things are happening in the world, and we fólk must look after our own first. I must look after the fólk. And I simply cannot do that with you in the mix, child of man."

She was taken aback, but only for a moment. "I am not a child of man! I am of the fólk. I have known nothing but life among the fólk! What threat do you think – what threat could I possibly pose – to my own people?" She jumped to her feet, and pushed off from the stone with all her might. A second of weightlessness, and she felt the rock under her once again. She glared at Ananz, fury masking her fear.

"Release me!"

He looked back at her with maddening calm. "You say you are fólkish, like any other amongst us. But you know your origins now. You cannot truly believe you are the same as other fólk, any more than I do. And I have seen enough that marks you as different. Your calling to be a guardian, when we have not had one amongst us for longer than most can remember. Your encounter with an unsleeping spirit that our people have avoided since it first appeared in this land. The fact that you were the only one to even sense its approach. Perhaps it was drawn to you." Sinmara recoiled. Ananz pressed on.

"When you first passed through the waystone, something went wrong. Not even I, who has seen more of the world than any fólk alive, can say what happened, though I have my notions. But whatever happened should not have been possible. Nothing can touch fólk when they travel by waystone." Sinmara's mouth went dry, remembering the sudden terror of the experience, the pressing darkness she had felt around her, and then her mother's despair at learning her beloved ram was gone. Her mother...

"My mother will not allow this," she interjected, hating the pleading weakness she heard in her voice. She was experiencing – had experienced, in the last few days – so many emotions that were new to her, emotions she wasn't even certain she had the names for.

For the first time, Ananz looked away from her.

"Ailuwa was resistant at first, it is true. But she came to see that this was the best way of removing the threat."

Sinmara's eyes felt hot. "What are you saying?"

"We are not in the practice of sending young fólk by themselves away from the warren, away from home, and certainly not into the lands of men. But we had to see what you would do, what would happen. It took much persuasion, but your mother agreed to let you go. It would have been difficult to send you away otherwise."

"Of course she agreed to let me go. She's the one who told me to go! But I only went where Orri took me, where she told him to take me. She – she didn't send me here!" She was grasping, desperate.

"It is true that you were sent to examine the human dwellings. We needed to see what would happen when you approached them. To see if it was any different for you than for other fólk."

"Yes, I know! And I was to come back to Ásbyrgi and explain what

I saw! I haven't even done that yet. My mother will be expecting me!" Again the irritatingly sympathetic look.

"There is no need for you to return to report what you experienced. You were never completely alone in your journey." Sinmara's stomach dropped to her heels, anticipating what Ananz would say next.

"Your mother was watching the whole time, and reporting back to me. She is the best farseer among us now, and her relationship with you only strengthened her ability to see what you were up to. She saw you approach the first human dwelling you were sent to, and enter into the blind spot. She could even follow you in for a ways with her vision, although she says it became very hazy outside of your immediate vicinity. She saw you crouch by the edge of the human dwelling – closer and much farther into the blank spot than any other fólk has yet been able to pass."

Sinmara was already heartbroken, but she would try to reason her way out of this. "Then she also saw me lose all sense, and flee until I was as far from the humans as the horse would take me."

"She did. And from there, you set your own course. None of us knew where you would travel, once you left the human dwelling."

"But I only went where Orri took me, where my mother had already told him to take me!"

"So it may have seemed to you, but I assure that was not the case. And where did you go? To the dark caves. Caves no fólk would willingly enter. They leave a foul sensation on us. They are not a place for our kind. And what did you do there? You found humans once again! You are drawn to them – because they are your kind, too."

"That was just ... coincidence! And what-" She was about to ask him why he hadn't mentioned her second stop, atop the glacier, but he interrupted her.

"There is no such thing, my dear. My years have taught me nothing so well as that. Your mother told me what was happening, and I needed to hear no more. It was time to bring you to this place." He spread his arms wide, again encompassing everything under the strange nightlike sky.

"You are in a place few fólk have ever seen. It is a relic of a time that none today can remember, save myself. Your mother, for all her skill, could not say where you are now, could not even describe it.

That you could be drawn here was, in fact, the last test, and it confirms what I already knew. Whatever your provenance, Sinmara, you are not of the fólk, not truly. And that makes you unpredictable, and dangerous. I am sorry, my child, I truly am. But there is nothing to be done for it."

Sinmara could barely think. "Then what is to happen to me? What are you going to do to me?"

"I am going to do nothing to you! As for what will happen to you, however – that I cannot say. You are quite stuck on that stone. I suspect that in time, you will simply waste away, although time does not work in this place quite like it does in the land above. And, not knowing just what you are, I cannot say with certainty how you will fare down here. But you will be here, away from the fólk above, and that is for the best, I am certain."

Sinmara leaped back to her feet, and faced Ananz, defiant. "I don't care what you say. I have only ever wanted to protect our people, my people, even when no one thought it necessary. I have left my home to do so, put myself in danger, not even understanding why, only because you asked, because you said it would help."

"So you have. But this, I could not ask of you. It simply is as it must be."

"Says who?" she asked, but he had already turned his back.

"Goodbye, Sinmara," he called over his shoulder. "May your next life be better to you." He walked away from her, passing directly into one of the standing stones surrounding her prison, and was   gone.

Chapter 22

The long ride to Vigi's farm provided them with plenty of opportunity to talk. Only Gunnar seemed particularly inclined though, filling the spaces between any necessary communication with a stream of chatter – about the weather, about the health of his animals, the antics of his farmhands. He seemed to sense that any empty stretch of time could quickly fill up with unbearable and perhaps explosive tension, and was doing everything in his power to keep this from happening.

Kveldulf and Vigi, for their parts, did little to help Gunnar fill the space, nor were they inclined to pay much attention to his rambling. Both of them were lost in thoughts of their sons.

Vigi hoped his boy was healing well. He hadn't wanted to leave Haraldr in the first place, but unless he conducted the feransdomr, under the terms of the law Vigi himself could be banished. By the time the date had rolled around, he found his anger toward his rival had largely dissipated, his mind preoccupied with other thoughts.

It made Vigi feel weak and womanish to admit it, even to himself, but Pétur scared him. A part of him had been glad for the excuse to get away from his guest. But now, returning with Kveldulf in tow, he could think only of the fact that he had left his wife and boy behind with the man, and was returning now without his most loyal bændr.

If Kveldulf had known Vigi's thoughts, he would have scoffed. Vigi had more to fear from Kveldulf at present, more than he appreciated any way. Kveldulf believed that Vigi's judgment had been tainted by this mysterious foreigner, but he hardly cared to make excuses. Kveldulf thought only of the fact that his son was dead, dead and gone, and Kveldulf had nearly followed him out of this world without ever seeking justice. He burned with a cold fire now, his rage and despair tempered by an awareness that he must remain in control of himself if he was to honor his boy. And, though he would go to the halls of Hel herself to seek his vengeance if he must, he knew too that he would not throw his life away, not yet, not

243

if he didn't have to. His instincts back in the cave had showed him that he wanted to live.

What happened to Tryggvi happened because someone wanted Kveldulf dead, wanted him punished and dead, and he would not give satisfaction to one such as this. He would have his vengeance, and he would not give his enemies even a shred of consolation by dying in the taking of it. He would let Vigi live, for now, because he might be of use in helping Kveldulf destroy his child's murderer. Once that was done – well, Kveldulf had a greater thirst for vengeance than one man's blood was likely to slake. Gunnar had kept Tryggvi's spear, left behind in their booth at the Althing. It hung from Kveldulf's saddle now, and the heft of it by his leg calmed and reassured him.

Yet even as he marinated in these crimson thoughts, another voice, a calmer voice, spoke the wisdom of experience. Tryggvi deserved justice, it said – no one had ever deserved it more. Yet, it reminded Kveldulf, he had walked the path of vengeance before, had found it did not always lead where one wished it to. Kveldulf was trying to ignore this voice, but it was marshalling his own considerable intelligence against his baser instincts. Nothing will bring them back, it said. Once again, you have been given a second chance. Fate has been cruel to you, but so too has it been kind. Two days ago you were cold, alone, and ready to die. Now you are amongst friends, food in your belly and fire in your gut, an outlaw no more. You have been given a greater gift than the chance for revenge, a greater gift than revenge can offer.

Kveldulf heard these words, and was struggling to decide whether they were the voice of experience or cowardice. In his youth, before he left for Miklagard, Kveldulf would have disdained any thought of failure to seek vengeance, and the possibility of forgiveness would never have even occurred to him. He had prided himself on following the old ways, and, like many youth, sought to follow them with greater fervency than did his parents. The adults around him had spoken of

Odin Battle-cry and Thor the serpent slayer, of Tyr the mighty and just and Loki the cunning and tricky. But they lived as farmers and traders, lived lives with little adventure or battle or bravery or cunning. This disconnect – this hypocrisy, as a younger Kveldulf called it – had led him to leave his land behind, to seek what glory might come in the world beyond his hardscrabble home. How well he remembered standing aboard the ship that took him from family and familiarity, feeling the wind gradually warm against his face as they sailed south and east, imagining himself as Odin Wanderer, off to see strange lands and peoples that the folk back home could only dream of. Few had the courage to seek out such sights, he had thought.

Now he was older, and had seen more of life. Sometimes he felt he had seen more of it than he wished to. He had seen strange lands and people, had made his name in battle, had sought vengeance, had sung glory to the gods in word and deed. And so too had he come to see the ways in which life was the same everywhere, how all people simply lived their lives as best they could in their circumstances. He had come to know that courage and cowardice both resided in the hearts of most men, and women too. He knew that battle bravery was not the only form of courage, perhaps not even the greatest. The glory of battle lay in the telling, not in the doing. He had learned that vengeance was a deceptive dish, promising satisfaction but concealing poison within. And, finally, most painfully, he had learned that the gods cared not who sang their glory.

The fates could raise any man up, or lay him low, no matter what god he gave thanks to, or called upon in his direst need. Whosoever the true gods may be, they had not saved Kveldulf's son, nor his wife, nor their daughter. They had not saved the friends he had watched die, screaming and shitting themselves as they passed, nor had they saved his foes as he fell upon them. They would not save the priest, and they would not save Vigi if Kveldulf chose then to turn his vengeance upon him. Nor, finally, would they save Kveldulf from his fate, whatever it might be. So what good were they?

When he had returned from Miklagard, returned to the land from which he had fled to become a man, Kveldulf had been for some time angry with the gods. He had seen too many die in the gods' names, die calling the gods' names. He struggled to understand the purpose of any of it.

Then he had met Freyja, met the woman who would become his wife, and the world had seemed to make sense again. She saw within him things he thought he had lost, teased out joy and wonder and laughter that he thought he was forever done with. She told him of her faith – in the gods, but also in herself, and in him. For all that he had seen before, she showed him lands he had never known, lands within her, within himself, and, for a time, he was happy. He came to realize that if he had once been too quick to worship the gods, so too had he been hasty in his dismissal of them. For the gods were more than just Odin and Thor and Tyr. What of Frigg, motherly and loving? What of Iðunn of the golden apples, joy of youth and simple pleasures radiating from her? What of Baldur, beloved by all, bright-voiced and laughing, Baldur who had died but would someday return, whose resurrection had been promised? He had felt these gods near him when he looked at his wife, when she snuck up behind him and took him by the waist, when they would lay together in bed and talk through the night, when he watched her nurse his child. He felt their blessing upon him and his family, especially the blessing of the Lady, for most of all they had love, and so his wife was called as well, and surely the goddess could be no lovelier or loving than his wife- although she could also show the rage of Thor, the cunning of Loki, the wisdom of Odin, he recalled.

And so they had been happy, for a while. All the more so once they had a son, a small, bright boy, who grew into a quick and curious child. Kveldulf and Freyja each found they were meant to be parents, that raising a child of their own brought out aspects that neither knew they had. Tryggvi had made them a mother and a father, and Kveldulf felt he was born anew himself. They had been delighted, all of them, when Freyja became pregnant again, and no child had ever been conceived or carried with more love around it.

And then it had all been ripped away- mother and child in a day, and the son in but years and a day. All were gone now, and only the shade of the husband and father remained- though he hardly wished to. He did not know how he could yet live, when so much of him had already died – the husband, the father. He was these men no more.

Yet. Yet. He was also all that was left of the family that had been, the only living artifact of something that had been good and beautiful. And this, he realized finally, was something he had to protect. Freyja, Tryggvi, their daughter – some part of them would remain in the world, while Kveldulf did. And he could not destroy that, not willingly.

So he would face his enemy. Face the foe who sought to destroy Kveldulf, had already killed his boy and damaged him irreparably. He would face him, and he would defeat him– not just for vengeance, not only for justice, but so that the living memory of his family would not pass from the world entirely, not before its time. Kveldulf could not live while the priest did, so the priest must die. And then Kveldulf would see what else had to be done to honor and to preserve the memory of the departed beloved.

The sky opened, and they rode through the mid-summer rain for a while. Late in the afternoon of the second day, the party approached a spectacular waterfall. Here, Vigi informed them, had Thorgeir Ljosvetningagoði come, after deciding that all of Iceland should become Christian. Here he had taken his personal icons of the old gods, and cast them into the water, to tumble over the falls and into the deep, swirling pool below. So this place was called Goðafoss, the Waterfall of the Gods. Gunnar decided this was as good a spot as any to refresh their horses, and they made camp away from the rushing waters.

They slept on the open ground, Kveldulf always a bit apart from the others, especially Vigi. They spread out oiled cloth to lay on, to keep the groundwater from soaking into them in the night and chilling them in their sleep. They did not speak much before turning in, at least Kveldulf, Gunnar, and Vigi did not. If the other men spoke amongst themselves, Kveldulf paid no mind to it, and soon fell into a dreamless sleep.

He awoke suddenly in the black of night. A terrible smell filled his nostrils. He came to quickly, and sat up. He peered through the dark, but saw nothing. He heard only the sound of the falls.

Then a scream- terrified, anguished. It died away as quickly as it had come, but the echo seemed to linger in the air. Kveldulf's heart raced. He heard the other men, now, moving about him. Then the scream again, longer this time. It seemed to come from nowhere and everywhere, the dull static roar of the falls making the source of the sound difficult to place. Kveldulf sprang to his feet. He joined his call to the shouts of the other men.

"What's happening? Who is that?" Others called as well, but it was impossible to see who in the black of the night.

"Kveldulf! Kveldulf! Are you there?" This was Gunnar, Kveldulf was sure. "Here!" he shouted in response.

His goði stumbled up to him.

"Gods. Men! What's happening?"

"I have no idea."

The scream again, farther away now, higher pitched. Gunnar shuddered, ran his hands through his long hair. "That is the scream of a dying man," he said, though he needn't have. Kveldulf knew the sound well enough.

One of the Gunnar's men managed to strike a flint, and breathe the spark into a torch. They found each other, gathered there in the small circle of light holding back the impenetrable night.

Looking around at the pale, stricken faces in the torch light, Kveldulf immediately noticed one was missing.

"Vigi," he whispered, then cleared his throat, spoke again. "Where is Vigi?" The other men merely looked at him, at each other. As a group, they made their way to where Vigi had made his bed.

The bed was still there, but Vigi was not. The blanket he had pulled around himself was ripped to pieces, and the same foul smell that Kveldulf had awakened to emanated from it. He leaned closer, and saw that oiled cloth below was wet and stained. Tentatively he pressed a finger to one edge. It came back looking black in the dim torchlight, but there was no question but that it was blood. And there was more on the ground, glistening in the torchlight, leading away from the camp.

As a group, they followed it for some ways. The sound of the rushing waters grew louder with every step. Finally, however, the trail simply disappeared as if Vigi had vanished suddenly, or was lifted into the sky.

They had no choice but to follow the trail back to their camp. When they got there, they realized that the horses had not been disturbed at all, in fact were mostly still asleep. None knew what to make of this, or what could have carried off a grown man of Vigi's size. Foxes were the largest predators in this land. Each man had heard of other dangers in the night, of course, but none wished to speak of them now. They spent the rest of the night huddled back to back, facing outwards in a ring, each man with his weapon in hand, and no one slept until the face of the sun first peaked over the far horizon.

Once it was well and truly day, they followed the trail of blood again. In the daylight they could see that it led directly towards the water, though the trail stopped far from the edge. The surface of the water seemed odd to the sight as well- part of it was not whirling and churning under the constant disturbance of the falls above. Gingerly, the men pressed further, until they were at the edge.

The surface of water had been partially turned to ice. Although the night had been chill, was nowhere near cold enough for the water to freeze. Nor should the ice be so clear. It was clear enough to see that there was something trapped within, although it was impossible to make out from the shore.

It was Kveldulf, most of all, who needed to know. Without protest from the other men, even from Gunnar, he stepped gently out onto the ice. It held his weight. In fact, it seemed frozen to be solid all the way down to the bed, at least in this one place.

Two, three more steps onto the ice – not far – and in the bright light of the day he could see what it held within. What had at first seemed to be one object was in fact several, tied together by the dark threads between them. An arm here. A hand there. A leg. Scattered randomly, no apparent pattern. Except there, in the very middle of it all – a face. Vigi's face, turned to the sky, eyes wide and mouth open in a never-ending scream.

Sinmara spent an interminable period attempting to fling herself from the stone, until she was exhausted. Even her garments and accessories rebounded from the edge when she removed and threw them. It seemed nothing could penetrate the invisible barrier within which she found herself. She tested every spot along the entire circumference of the slab, even throwing her items as hard and as high as she could, to no avail.

When she finally accepted that she could not break through by sheer force, she attempted applying every fólkish skill she knew. She touched the spar around her neck, but it was as still and cold as it had been since she left the glacier. Slipping into rockwalk, she was even more confined than when she took solid form, for she found that she could not even move about on the stone in this state- she was rooted to the spot. Nor could she sink into the stone. She was, it seemed, well and truly stuck. Sinmara let out a wordless shout of rage, then sat down heavily, bruising her tailbone.

Something moved in the pack on her back. She froze, and the movement stopped. She wasn't even sure she had felt it. But there it was again, a sort of rustling sensation.

She removed the pack, and held it away from her as she set it on the stone. She stepped back and stared at it for a moment, but it made no overtly threatening movements.

Leaning over, she peered into the mouth of the pack, but saw nothing. She upended it in one quick motion. Her remaining rations landed with a soft puff, and the last item hit the ground noiselessly. Looking at the soft pouch Ruharra gave her, Sinmara could see the fabric moving ever-so-slightly.

She reached down and grabbed one edge of the pouch, then turned it out onto the stone as well. Out fell a wooden box, sliding lid partially removed. And something else, something curious. Tiny legs stretched in the air, above a bent, chitinous carapace. It appeared to be one of the strange creatures Ruharra used for her knacks- larger, perhaps, but of the same general form.

Sinmara stared at it for a long time, well past the point of making her decision. Ruharra had said she would know when to open the pack. There was little question as to what to do with its contents now.

Finally, Sinmara steeled herself, and gently lifted the creature in her hand. She whispered a quick word of thanks and apology, then popped it into her mouth. She bit down once, as she had seen Ruharra do. The taste was like nothing Sinmara had known before, somehow metallic, yet sweet, and the brittle texture of the creature's body felt strange as she choked it down. Not knowing what else to do, she focused her mind not on any of her knacks, but only on the hope that, somehow, there was a way out of this predicament, and an explanation for the pain and betrayals she had experienced.

She waited a moment, but nothing happened. No sensations, no visions. She wasn't certain what she was even waiting for, but she was certain she had done all that she could do.

"So it ends." A voice that carried the weight of years.

Sinmara whipped around to see Ananz standing on the bloodstone now, just across from her. He spoke again before she could react.

"I am sorry for the fear I have caused you, and the deceit. This will all be over soon."

Bright light filled the murky glen. It was as if the sun had suddenly manifested itself in the night sky. Indeed, where before Sinmara had seen something like stars above her, now she could again see the blazing orb that had been above her in the field.

Ananz was looking up at it too, and before their eyes the light shifted from bright yellow to auburn, then finally a glowing red, casting all below into stark monochrome.

"This is my fault." She looked back at him as he spoke.

"Please understand that. Mine, and mine alone. I am firstborn. I was here before any of you, and you were all my responsibility, before men came to this land, and after.

"I am firstborn, but I had never dreamed into men before they came here, before I had to. Just as we dream into minerals and stone,

251

into plants, into animals- so we must dream into men, some of us, if we are to remain in harmony with nature, while they live around us.

"For so long, it has been only me here, dreaming into the men of this land, but it has been enough. Enough to ensure that we could live here, without men's minds trapping us, changing us.

"Then, these blank spots began to appear. I noticed them first, not long before you were born. I had never seen anything like them. When men first came here, even before I learned to dream into them, I could sense their presence. I could sense the boundaries around their homes, their persons- the spheres of perception that all minds produce, to varying degrees. I could sense them, but I did not fear them. And once I did learn to dream into men... I could not explain the experience to you, but I knew immediately that I could always make a place for our kind here, even with them encroaching.

"Whatever is making the blank spots appear, it is different. You know that now, yourself. You know what they do to us. But there were so few, at first...they were more a curiosity than a concern. Only I could be expected to do anything about them, and I was certain I would, when the time was right.

"When you first came to us, when I dreamed of you in the birth pool, I thought- I hoped that perhaps you might have come to help. When your mother told me that you did not seem to care for the dream states a fólk of your experience would usually spend time in, I took this as further sign that there was something special about you, beyond the circumstances of your birth. I kept my eye on you, from afar.

"Then, in the past year few years, the blank spots began to spread faster, and to grow larger. Even though they were still few, and far from our homes, it was clear that they presented more of a problem than I had understood at first. And that is how I made my mistake."

Slowly, Sinmara became aware of an uncomfortable heat. She didn't have time to ponder the novelty of the sensation before it ramped up yet again, to the point of being nearly painful.

"Before, I was always so careful. I would dream into men only rarely, and briefly, just long enough to understand them as necessary to keep us in harmony. But with the spots spreading, I became less careful. I pushed myself. I sent my mind into more and more of their kind, and I stayed in the dreams longer, trying to find the solution, hoping it would present itself to my waking remembrance. Yet the spots only seemed to grow faster. And, finally, I dreamed into the wrong man."

The air was rent with a cacophony of cries and trills. The sky – Sinmara kept thinking of it as the sky, even though she knew it was not – filled with flapping, fluttering forms of all sorts. Birds, unseen and unheard by Sinmara during all the time she had spent in the woods, now took to frantic flight from the treetops. So too did forms Sinmara did not recognize. Thin, iridescent wings sparked in the red light, and great leathery forms soared above as well. Sinmara watched as birds, insects, and things she had no name for swooped and scattered, fleeing, attacking each other, falling to the ground.

Ananz's deep voice carried above the growing din.

"I knew right away that something was wrong, even before I woke. Every human mind I dreamed into was different, but this one... Even with men, when we dream into them, it is as if we ARE them. I know you never much cared for the dreams, but you know how it is all the same. We are not ourselves, in dreams. The dream ends, we wake and recall the experience, and this memory guides us, teaches us."

"Yet this man knew I was dreaming into him. He felt me. He...spoke to me, somehow. And as he spoke, I became aware of myself dreaming into him. I knew, even in the dream, that I was dreaming.

"It did not last long, I don't think. It did not seem so, when I woke back here in my home. But even after I woke, I could feel that something was different. I could feel that I was different."

The sky cracked. Far overhead, bright orange lines streaked across Sinmara's entire field of vision. They began to bleed, dripping onto the ground far below.

"And so I was. I have watched this land for ages, even by the reckoning of the fólk. I have moved through it, shaped it, maintaining harmony and order. Simply by observing, and desiring,

I have protected this land, and the other minds within it. I have kept us all from falling back into the abyss."

The air filled with smoke. The trees were burning. The roar of flame quickly drowned out the cries of the flying creatures overhead.

"I cannot any more. My vision fails. Doubt creeps in around the edges of my own mind. I know confusion. I know fear. I even know apathy. I am infected. And because of who I am, because I have been here for so long, I cannot protect the rest of the fólk from my own decline."

Great globules of molten rock splashed around the standing stones in the clearing, releasing blasts of hot air when they hit. Sinmara felt her skin on the edge of blistering. Such pain was so foreign to her, and had come on so suddenly, that she could almost ignore it.

Besides, she was entranced by the sight in front of her. Some of the molten globules had already cooled to black on the ground within the clearing, solidifying. Before her eyes, they began to move once again, flowing slowly towards the center of the ring within which she and Ananz still stood.

They changed shape. Long spines emerged from the formless masses, spindled joints, armored hides, burning eyes, open jaws.

Sinmara saw Ananz watching them as well, before he turned his mirror-dark eyes back towards her own.

The smoking black things penetrated the ring of standing stones behind Ananz, and rushed towards his back. Still, his eyes remained fixed on Sinmara.

The beasts reached the very edge of the black stone, crouched, leapt – and splashed to dripping smithereens across the invisible barrier that confined Sinmara, and now protected Ananz. The pitch-like substance of the things beaded and ran to the ground, where it flowed, reforming.

Again and again, the creatures dashed themselves against the solid air surrounding the stone. They roared, making unholy noises of rage or pain; Sinmara could not say. But the barrier appeared impenetrable.

As the woods burned, more creatures slouched into the clearing, or fell from above. As they smashed and spattered against the barrier, their bodies clotted and congealed. The tar-like mass of them began to block out the light from the burning forest, the orb overhead. They smoked and sizzled, yet Sinmara found she was not even as hot as she had been, either the barrier or her skin finally compensating for the temperature of the surrounding air.

"And so it ends, Sinmara: with just you and me." Ananz gestured at the fiendish forms now surrounding them, engulfing them in darkness and heat. "The land above will fall to chaos. But you and I will be safe here. Then, when it is all over, and all is quiet – then we can emerge, and start again. With my ancient wisdom and your new, unfólkish nature, perhaps we can shape a new land above, one that will never be threatened by the treacherous minds of men."

"But what of the other fólk? What of the other creatures of the land? What of men?"

"The land above is out of harmony. Chaos will reign until all the dreaming voices are silent. Only then will we be able to ascend, and start once again."

"So you are saying…"

"That we are the last. Even I cannot say how long or how far chaos will spread before we can return, but when we emerge, it will be into a dead land."

The sizzling, shifting substance of raging chaos-forms was slowly covering the sides of their protective enclosure, climbing towards the apogee, cocooning them. Through the dwindling circle of light, Sinmara could see the cracks in the roof of Ananz's realm splitting even wider, more magma pouring in. Idly, she wondered just how far below the surface they were, how far into the earth.

It didn't matter, really. Sinmara didn't understand half of what Ananz had just said, but she had grasped this much: Ananz's plan was to let the land above die, while saving himself, and her. And this was not what she wanted. She did not know what she did want, did not even know what she could hope for, at this point. But to sit here while above her everything she had ever known passed from the face of the earth- whatever she was, she was not going to passively let this happen.

There was only a tiny spot of light above them now. Sinmara looked at Ananz, but he had his eyes closed, and was sitting in the very center of the stone circle. She looked up just in time to see a hideous, predatory face appear between her and the last bit of sky. It shrieked out a piercing howl, then smashed itself into the barrier, and all within was profoundly dark.

In the lingering reverberations of the thing's cry, Sinmara felt a tug around her neck. Her hand flew up to grasp the pendant there, the crystal spar. Nothing happened; it felt no different. She pulled it from around her neck in one motion, held it close to her face. Still nothing; she could not see her hand in front of her nose, let alone the spar.

Then another bellowing, bawling sound penetrated the thickening dome of pitch around her, and the spar in her hand jerked, ever so slightly.

She had moved away from the edge of the stone once danger presented itself, but now she held her arm out in the darkness, feeling for it. She jammed her knuckles slightly when the tips of her fingers made contact, the inside of the dome as smooth and as hard as volcanic glass.

She pressed the pendant against it. Nothing. Harder she pressed, feeling the edges dig into her skin. Still nothing. It was quiet now, and all she could hear was Ananz, breathing deeply, somewhere in front of her.

Ananz had given her the spar. Why? And why had it behaved so wonderfully and surprisingly before, only to sit motionless and cold when she needed it now?

She held it before her in the darkness again. What was it Ananz had done when he gave it to her? He had held it up, looked through it.

Looked through it at the sun. Only there was no sun here, in this black cocoon, under the earth.

Or was there? What about the light that had been in the sky above the field, as she had journeyed through the wood? Sinmara held the spar in front of her eye, tilted her head back, searching, looking for any glimmer of the bright orb that had been visible above her just a short while ago. But still, there was nothing.

She tipped her head back down, and pulled the loop of rope wide to place it back around her neck. She bent to do so, and just as the pendant passed between her eyes and the ground, there was the tiniest glimmer. She would not have noticed it in anything less than total darkness. Yet there it was, again, just for a second, a flash through the dangling shard of crystal. She held it back up to her eye, this time looking down, searching.

There – not above her at all, but below. It was faint, so faint, but she could see it now. Somehow, with this little hunk of mineral, she could see the sun, see it even through the black cocoon, through the stone below her, through the body of the earth itself, wherever she was within it.

The crystal was flowing up her arm. It filled the space with light, suddenly, as it took shape, and she could see Ananz then, staring right at her, watching her as she raised her arm, cocked her shoulder, and then drove the point down, plunging it with an ear-splitting crack into the very stone she stood upon.

The cocoon blew away like ash in the breeze. Across from her, shuddering upon the splintered stone, lay Ananz. He made no sound Sinmara could hear, other than the occasional smack of his hands slapping against the rock. One of his eyes was closed. But a thin wisp of smoke or vapor rose from the other, rose from the ruins of his black eye in its socket.

Then he showed his teeth, and began to laugh. A bead of magma plunged down from above, enveloping him with a sizzle, and he was gone.

Sinmara felt a slight pull along her arm as the black filaments within her crystal weapon bled out through the point, infusing into the stone slab. Then she pitched forward to her knees as the crystal collapsed, condensing back into its pendant shape.

She looked up to see blazing, primordial forms, titanic, voracious, all around her, towering over her, leaning eagerly forward.

Another sharp cracking noise. A rush of liquid fire from above. A scream cut short, and then all Sinmara knew was burning.

Chapter 23

Ruharra floated above the ground in the center of her pyramidal chamber, eyes closed, legs crossed beneath her. Her mind wandered freely through the whole of her existence, remembering, reliving, associating.

Inevitably, it returned to the point she knew it would, the point she had hoped and dreaded it would.

She was young then, so young, still half-drunk with the joy of existence. How far she had ranged in those days, far from the desert sands of her home, through swamps and forests, even skirting the edge of the endless waters, taking it at all in through her nameless and numberless senses. Had they really been so free then?

Across the land, through it, she followed the voiceless call. She knew not what she sought, only that she was drawn to something. Something wonderful sang out in the night, rousing her, and she sped towards it with blissful assurance. She was too caught up in the enticing sensations to question what drew her near, to wonder what even could call her so sweetly, from so far away.

She floated upwards through the rock as her destination neared, and then she passed out of the stone, and stepped softly onto solid ground. The sound she followed came to a sudden crescendo, then fell to silence, and Ruharra looked about her with a start, as if she had woken suddenly on her sleeping bier just now, instead of many long miles ago.

She was near the surface, but still a bit underground, in a small cave. It was natural, but Ruharra could immediately sense the presence of stonework as well, could feel where the walls of the cave had been hewn and smoothed by hands.

Men's hands. Somehow, Ruharra had been called into a cave used by humans. Still, she did not panic. She had no reason to fear man, not when that kind occupied so little of the wide, wide world, and always fled so amusingly at the sight of her. She had even wondered, lately, whether she might be able to draw the blood forth from men, and use it to taste their experiences, the way she had found she could with the animals she was still too inexperienced to dream into. She felt a trill of pleasure at the idea.

But where had that beautiful voice come from?

Only then did Ruharra realize she was not alone in the cave. Once she noticed the body, a wave of alarm finally washed over her- how had she not seen it immediately?

It was a man's body, she could tell that much, though it was covered from head to toe in a tightly-wrapped shroud. And now she could smell the blood on it- not sense it the way she could the blood in the lizards and mice she found, but actually smell it.

She moved closer. The body was set on a slab carved from the cave's side, looking a bit like a half-formed version of Ruharra's own sleeping bier. As she leaned over, Ruharra could see spots where blood had soaked through the cloth. Staring at the unmoving body, staring at the drying blood, for just a moment Ruharra thought she caught a snippet of the magnificent sound that had called her to this place.

She could not resist. She pressed a long, dark finger into a damp spot on the side of the body, hard, and then touched it to the tip of her tongue.

Even now she could not say what happened next. Sometimes she felt as if she had fallen into someone else's dream, and was caught in it still, had been caught in it all these long years. There had been a sudden stilling, a pause, a moment that felt like a gasp. Then she was hurtling upwards, feeling the pull of the earth below her but, even stronger, the hold of some other force from above, drawing her up, up, through an infinite expanse of blinding white light.

Or perhaps she had just fallen backwards a little, landing hard on her tailbone against the earthen floor. But when she looked up, he was standing before her. The shroud had fallen from his face, and his damp hair was plastered against his forehead. He stared down at her in evident confusion, thick eyebrows scrunched together, one hand rubbing his side where she had pressed on it.

"That hurt," he said.

Then the cave was filled with light- not a harsh light, like that Ruharra swore she had seen a moment before, but warm, welcoming, the red-amber glow of the fires men slept around at night, the special light she liked to sit just outside the sphere of, sometimes, and watch.

She blinked, and saw that the light was coming from the man, shining from his pores, his eyes, like he held dancing flames within himself, though he did not burn. He was not looking at her any more, but over her head, chin forward, as if he were trying to see something important from a terrible distance.

She still sat where she had fallen. As she watched, the man lifted one shroud-covered arm. Liquid fire pooled in his palm. He tilted his hand, and the fire trickled out of it, incandescent drops landing with a splash against the ground.

A bit of dirt shifted nearby, and before her eyes a small, black shape poked up through the soil. As its heavy carapace caught the light, Ruharra could see it was a scarab beetle of some sort; there were many in the lands she called home, though none perhaps that looked quite like this. It scuttled across the cave floor towards the man's feet, where the earth still pulsed with the light of his blood.

With animal efficiency, the scarab loosened the soil around each of the glowing droplets, and one by one began to roll them together. Soon it pushed a sphere before it, black soil shot through with bright red veins. When the last of the blood was thus collected, the scarab dug in its limbs, spread its iridescent wings, and took to the air.

It hovered just in front of Ruharra, perfectly in place at first, but then bobbing up and down as it seemed to struggle with the weight of its radiant cargo. Finally, she lifted one hand- not the hand she had pressed onto the man's side- and the beetle dropped its burden into her waiting palm. She worried for a moment that it would burn her, but she felt only a moist ball of dirt, for all that its appearance belied its uncanniness.

Then she looked up, and the man was looking at her again. He smiled, but his eyes brimmed with tears, sparkling brightly where they scattered the light from within him.

Then Ruharra really had awoken, atop her own sleeping bier, far away, where the wondrous call had first come to her.

And so she opened her eyes now, in her chamber here at the top of the world. But this time, a thousand years later, she did not still clutch the smoldering orb in her hand. This time, she did not run to find the first creature she could that might keep the blood alive, to sustain the glow that was already fading from it when she woke. No longer would she have to race through the ages, transferring the blood from vessel to vessel, watching the light get dimmer and dimmer, always worried that it would dwindle away before the purpose of her peculiar vocation finally revealed itself.

Much she had learned on her journey; much she had seen. But only now, in this season, so unlike the southern summers she had known in her youth, only now did the purpose of her wanderings become clear. The others agreed; if there was a way forward, this was it. This must be it, for all other possibilities had been exhausted.

And so her journey came to a close; or, perhaps, a waypoint. Even now, with all she had seen, she could not say what she expected next. She could not guess why she had been chosen for this, why any of them had. But they knew that they had been chosen, now, each and every one of them, as they woke from their strange slumbers.

They filed down the long stone hallway in pairs. None spoke, and eyes were lowered. Each knew their destination, and there was nothing to say.

The doors were open at the end of the path, waiting. Two by two they passed through the entryway – couples, friends, parents grasping children's hands.

As they reached the shining waters, each paused for just a moment. What thoughts they had are their own; it was only the briefest moment. Then each pair entered the pool. A few steps into the water, ripples scattering blue-gold light. Then they slipped under the surface, and the waters stilled, just as the next two approached.

The line passed out of the chamber, up the long hallway, out into the high atrium. At its end, lagging a way behind the next pair, now came Ruharra and Ailuwa, and with them Ananz. Alone of all the fólk, they spoke, whispers too low to carry.

"The animals have been seen to?" Ruharra kept her eyes cast downward as she spoke, and Ananz and Ailuwa answered her together.

"Yes." They both paused, then Ananz continued. "She will do it. I can feel it, stronger than anything I have felt before. It's like that moment after you step into a portal, just before you exit. That anticipation.

"I cannot see her," Ailuwa said softly.

"I wouldn't expect that you could."

Ruharra interjected. "We have each done what we could, and now we do what we must. It is out of our hands. But then, what isn't?" They walked a bit further in silence.

"Ailuwa." Ananz stopped, and she tuned back slowly to look at him.

"It is like nothing you can imagine. For her, it will be like nothing I can imagine. And for all of us, perhaps, in time."

Ailuwa took a deep, shuddering breath, closed her eyes, and exhaled heavily. Then she smiled, and when she opened her eyes again both Ruharra and Ananz felt steadier in her gaze.

"I know." She took Ruharra's dark hand in her own, and turned towards the heart of the earth. Ananz watched them with his inscrutable black eyes, then walked out of the atrium, off to meet his own doom.

ぴ ℞ ℔ ぴ ℞ ℔ ぴ ℞ ℔ ぴ ℞ ℔ ぴ

Only Kveldulf and Gunnar suspected that Vigi's death had anything to do with the errand they were on – the half-dozen other men had been told simply that Kveldulf and Vigi had agreed to lay their enmity to rest, that Kveldulf would now confront his son's killer, and that they were there to provide Gunnar help should anything unexpected happen. Vigi's vicious and inexplicable death certainly qualified, but the men were surprisingly stoic. Gunnar had picked well for this task – none of his men was inclined to cowardice, and none wished to be the first to suggest they turn back. Besides, even with Vigi gone now, no one was enthusiastic about spending another night in the open when his farm could be reached before the sun set again. And, as Gunnar pointed out, they owed it to the people there to let them know what had happened. So, after swiftly packing up, the men set back on their original course.

Gunnar and Kveldulf rode close together, and although the speed of the ride prevented easy talk, they found time enough when they stopped for water and rest.

"What do you make of it?" Gunnar asked.

"I don't. It is a queer thing, but this is a queer land. And Vigi's is not a death I can mourn overmuch."

"But what we saw ... it's not possible. Or it shouldn't be. It's like something out of the tales old women tell to scare the children."

"Perhaps there is more truth to those tales than we often care to admit. This is not the first time either of us has seen something strange, Gunnar."

"Yes, but-"

"We have two options. We can leave, and hope that what happened to Vigi is just a coincidence, that it was the end of it. But we won't know, and will spend our nights wondering. Or, we can go ahead, find this priest, and see what he has to do with all this. If it's by his design, we kill him. If it's not, we kill him. Either way, we both rest easier."

"You think we could kill a man who can do this?"

"I think we have to try. Now more than ever. And now all of us know what we might be facing," he said, gesturing towards the other men, talking amongst themselves nearby.

Gunnar sighed. "You are right. Gods. I wish we had a seer or a völva, even a seiðrmann with us. This is more their area of expertise." Kveldulf said nothing, and soon they were on their way again.

They reached Vigi's farm in the late afternoon. The first thing any of them noticed was that it was eerily quiet. No dogs ran up to greet them, nor were there sheep in the pens. This time of day, on a farm like Vigi's, there should be someone about, but there was no movement to be seen. All was still.

Gunnar announced himself at the gate. His voice echoed back at him. No one replied. The men all looked at each other. It was not wise to enter within a man's gate uninvited. But, then again, the man of the farm was no threat to anyone, now. As a group, the men moved towards the large, turf covered building that Vigi had called home.

The door to Vigi's house creaked open. The threshold was black and empty for a moment. Then a white face appeared, seeming to float in the doorway until a dark form materialized below it, in robes blacker than the darkness within.

"Welcome, little warriors!" The priest stepped out into the light. His face was lined with deep wrinkles and his hair was shot through with gray; he was perhaps twenty years older than every man there, and he seemed to carry no weapon. Yet his back was straight, and he grinned as he stepped towards them on the lawn of Vigi's house.

"Where is the lady of the house?" Gunnar called to him.

"Oh, it's only me here, now," the man said, stopping before them in the afternoon sun.

"Are you the priest, Pétur?" Gunnar knew it must be, yet he could not place the man, could not find his face anywhere in the memory of Kveldulf's aborted trial.

"Yes, that is the name I have traveled under here, though it is not truly mine."

"What did you do to my son?" Kveldulf barked at Pétur, and the other men tightened their grips on their weapons.

Pétur just looked at him. "I had another name, long before I came to this land. So did Adalbert. We gave up our old names when we gave up our old lives, when we gave ourselves over to Christ. For years we travelled, spreading the Word. We were converts ourselves, so we excelled at converting others. In time our work brought us to the attention of a great king, a powerful man in the church. And he sent us here, to continue our mission.

"That is how our paths crossed again. Last year, at the Althing."

"What does that mean? Kveldulf, what is he talking about?"

"I have no idea. I don't remember meeting him, last year or any other time." Truthfully, Kveldulf could not even remember seeing him at the law council, although he knew he must have been there—hadn't Vigi called him forward? Why hadn't Kveldulf paid more attention to his actual accuser?

Pétur chuckled. "Quite right! We have never met! I never would have recognized you. But Adalbert did, somehow. I didn't believe him, not for a long time, but he was so insistent. He had seen you, down in the caves, had seen you with the other little warriors, when you came to kill my people.

"What is he talking about?" Gunnar addressed Kveldulf without taking his eyes of the priest.

"He knows," Pétur replied for Kveldulf. "He knows where I came from."

And Kveldulf did. "Kiev. You are from Kiev."

Again, that mirthless laugh. "Yes. Kiev, as you call it. My people have a different name for our land, the land that has been ours since long before your kind came, with your iron swords and your false

gods. Before you came and killed my family, my friends."

"Kveldulf…"

"He is talking about when I was with the Varangians. When… when your brother died."

Gunnar addressed Pétur directly now, his face already flaring to red. "Are you saying you had something to do with that?"

"When the little warriors came into my home, I was not yet in the temple. I was below, waiting for my spirit journey to begin. Adalbert had given me the sacred libation, and gone to participate in the ceremony. He came running back just as I slipped into trance. He grabbed me and dragged me up out of the caves, even as you were slaughtering the rest my flock. If not for him, I surely would have died with the rest."

"So that's what all this is? You swore your revenge, and came here to take it on me?"

"Not at all! I returned from my spirit journey, the strangest of my life, to find myself far from my home, in the woods, with a sobbing young boy as my only companion. He told me what happened, how he had escaped with me. And right then and there, the two of us gave ourselves over to Christ."

"You what?" One of the other men shouted this; Kveldulf started, having almost forgotten there was anyone there but him and the priest.

"Oh yes. What happened that night... it was the final proof I needed that my god was a dead god, that he could not protect my people. Your god was stronger. Your god killed my flock. But he spared me, spared me for some purpose. It had to be so. So Adalbert and I became new people. We helped others to become new people. And eventually we found ourselves here, where we hoped to continue our good work."

This time, Pétur's laughter seemed genuine. "What plans we had! Yet barely a month in this land, and Adalbert sees you." Now he pointed at Kveldulf.

"How proud you were of your boy that day, as the merchants thanked him at the Althing, gave him gifts. Adalbert and I saw the whole thing, saw him douse the fire. 'I wonder if he is a Christian,' Adalbert said. And then he saw you. He saw you, and here we are now.

"He said nothing about it for days, and when he finally did, I did not believe him. I thought he must be mistaken. We returned to our mission. For nearly a year we travelled the island, converting little warriors to Christ. But whenever the chance arose, Adalbert asked about you. And piece by piece, we put it all together, until it was clear to both of us that Adalbert had been right all along."

"So then you sought your revenge." This time, Gunnar stated the question.

"Wrong again. Once we were certain, we only resolved that we should meet you. We had a shared history, and thought perhaps God had brought us back together. We wanted to know what kind of man you were, to see if you had changed as much as we had since that terrible night. I had many feelings in my heart as Adalbert and I approached your farm, but a desire for revenge was not one of them.

"But when we saw the horse... I was overcome. We both were. We recognized her immediately, and she seemed to recognize us. In my previous life, that horse was meant to be my spirit mount, to bear me along the ghost roads and through the realms of the dead. And here she was, a world away, stooping her head in a field, inviting me onto her back.

"Yet Adalbert swung himself up on her before I could. I do not know what possessed him. He had cared for her too, had tended to her so long ago in the caves. But she was mine, she was always meant to be mine.

"And you know what happened next. You killed them both."

"I did not! I found him killing her, and I reacted. That horse was dear to me, and I made an oath to protect it!"

Pétur scoffed. "You know nothing about that horse. And now you never will. Because of you, she is dead. My family, my friends, dead. Once, even my faith was dead, killed by your hand just as surely as the others.

"But no more."

The black of darkest night descended on them. As one, they cried out in surprise. Each thought he had been stricken blind, and it was only after hearing the others similarly panicked that the realization spread that they were all in darkness, though the sun had been above the horizon only a moment ago.

Then the smell came. An overwhelming, gagging stench, rotted meat and putrescent vegetal matter.

To his left, Kveldulf heard a scream. He though immediately of what Gunnar had said the night before - "That is the cry of a dying man." The sound cut off abruptly.

Something huge was moving amongst them. Kveldulf could not see the others, but he could vaguely sense them around him. And he could feel the disturbance in the air, a faint tremor in the earth, where something else passed.

It pressed close, and he lashed out with his spear, realizing even as he did so that he was as likely to hurt one of his companions as he was whatever stalked them.

The head of the spear sank into a pliant surface with a palpable thunk. He felt it bite into flesh, rebound against bone. Then the shaft split apart, throwing him off balance.

He heard another scream, then a laugh.

A voice spoke in his ear, though he felt no one nearby.

"Not enough, little warrior."

Kveldulf whirled around, grasping, but felt nothing. Then the darkness lifted as suddenly as it had come. The terrible stench remained.

Strewn around Kveldulf were the bodies of the men who had accompanied them. He searched first for Gunnar, saw him still standing, his sword out and blood on his face, wild eyed, but alive. So too stood Thorkel, one of the other bændr. Everyone else was very dead, and few of the bodies remained intact.

The laughter came again. All three survivors turned, looking for its source.

The priest stood atop the turf roof of Vigi's home now, grinning, gray beard spilling down to his navel.

"I fled, when I saw you kill Adalbert, who had been like a son to me. When I saw you kill my spirit horse. When I saw you take everything from me, once again- I fled. I ran. And I prayed. I prayed to Christ. I called to God, in my despair, in my fear, again and again I called. But there was no answer. I heard nothing. I felt nothing.

"I found shelter. I curled up in it, shielded myself against the wind, and still I prayed, prayed into the night. When I could pray no longer, when my voice grew weak and my throat turned raw, I closed my eyes, and thought only of my losses.

"Until, finally, in the dark and the cold, I felt the presence of my god. Not the White Christ. Not the god who had taken so much from me, then ignored me when I called to him with all my heart. Not him. I was thinking of the night my flock and my faith died, died while I was off in a trance, waiting to hear the voice of the god we worshipped and sought to invoke. Not some foreign god, but a god of my people, a god worshipped from time beyond all memory."

"Perun." Kveldulf whispered the name, staring up at the priest in wonder, hardly scared, so hard was he struggling to understand.

Pétur chortled mirthlessly. "My father worshipped Perun, above all other gods, and it got him and my brothers killed, when the prince betrayed them. Perun has power, but he is not the god we worshipped that night, not the god I taught my flock to honor and strengthen with their deeds.

"We worshipped Veles! Veles, god of the underworld, god of the wet earth, god of serpents and magic, enemy of Perun! When Vladimir betrayed the people of my land, he tore the gods from their place on the hill atop the city, took them down to the waters, smashed them, floated the pieces down the river. All but Veles. Just as he resides in the lands below, away from the other gods, so his shrine was apart from the others, down in the marketplace. We were able to save it, when the others fell, save the figure of the god and take it with us, down into the caverns.

"Veles is who we worshipped that night. That is who we sacrificed your friend to. That was the name on my woman's lips as she died." Kveldulf saw suddenly the image of a lithe form falling backwards, an axe buried deep in its chest. Still Pétur spoke.

"And that is who I prayed to, finally, in the night, after I fled your farm. I prayed to Veles – and he answered me. In the dark, he showed me the way. He touched me with his power. With true power."

Thorkel startled them all by shouting and charging forward. He seemed set to run up the side of the hill where it met the house, in order to get to the robed priest on the roof. Yet he had not made it five steps, Kveldulf and Gunnar had not even had time to react, when he suddenly began to sink into the ground. Thorkel pitched backwards, crying out as he did so, and in a blink there was no trace of him.

"Now he knows true power as well." Pétur said. He gestured, and something shot up from the ground. Pieces of Thorkel rained around them.

"And so will you," Pétur said, and gestured past them, over Gunnar and Kveldulf's heads. They turned.

The ground just within Vigi's gate began to swell, then split. A form rose up from it, enormous and misshapen. Its skin was mottled black, and its limbs were swollen with fluid. It was twice the size of a man, but it was unmistakably mannish in form. No, more than that – Kveldulf looked hard at the distended face.

It was Tryggvi.

Kveldulf gave out a cry greater than any from the dying men, and fell to his knees. He retched, bringing up the thin gruel he had had to break his fast that morning. And when he looked up again, Tryggvi was still in front of him. Now he was his nearly normal size, the size he had been when his father saw him last, and as Kveldulf watched, Tryggvi's limbs returned to their proper form, his skin became clearer, his appearance less overtly monstrous- but even as the transformation occurred, the figure became almost more disturbing for its uncanny, partial semblance of life.

Kveldulf could not tear his eyes away.

"H ... how?" he gasped.

Behind him Pétur chuckled. "You people know so little. You worship a dead and resurrected god. You tell stories of creation and destruction. Yet you know nothing of true godhood. You know not where your stories come from. You are like children." he laughed, then cut it short.

"But you are nasty children. Children who bite. And you deserve to be punished."

The earth rumbled beneath them, and Kveldulf and Gunnar struggled to keep their footing.

"My god has given me power over death itself. I am going to use your boy to rip you apart, limb from limb, slowly. Then I am going to bring you back as my slave, and force you to kill your friend, while you still have sense enough to know what you are doing. And then I am going to use all of you to flush out the blight of false gods, and return Veles to his rightful place of power."

More forms burst from the ground, surrounding the two men still standing in Vigi's yard. Whatever Pétur had done to Tryggvi, it was apparent he had not stopped there.

The Tryggvi-draugr advanced on Kveldulf, and Kveldulf did nothing. He watched him come. He welcomed it. Gunnar, too, was frozen in his spot.

Then Tryggvi stopped, just steps before the kneeling form of his father. When the anticipated blow did not come, Kveldulf looked up. He saw the terrible face that was nearly his son's looking down, not at him, but at the ground in front of him, where the head of the spear he broke had fallen.

Kveldulf looked at the spear, then back at the draugr, before he understood. He shot to his feet in one fluid motion, snatching the weapon up as he did so. He thrust it before him, thrust it at his child and adversary.

"Yes!" he cried. "Yes, remember! You remember!"

The draugr remained motionless, and Gunnar looked at them in fear and confusion.

Pétur shouted again, and the Tryggvi-draugr began to swell once more, its grotesquely expanding form rising above Kveldulf's head. But it came no closer, and Kveldulf did not look away. He spoke to it, clearly and urgently.

"Remember, son. The oath you swore. The oath you swore over this weapon, Tryggvi, sealed by deed and word. Obey me. I have not released you from your duty." His voice caught then, looking up into the milky eyes above him. "Obey me."

Behind him, on the roof, Pétur screamed in fury. Kveldulf did not turn, did not react, eyes still fixed on his sons's. But Gunnar looked to Pétur then, saw him shaking his fists in explosive rage.

The other undead forms in Vigi's yard began to move again, making an ungodly noise as they moaned their murderous intent. They were nearly upon Gunnar, but he could not take his eyes off the old man on the roof.

He saw movement behind Pétur. The priest did not seem to notice, focused only on killing the men in front of him. Then suddenly he went tumbling, skidding across the green turf with a huff.

Now Orri stood on the rooftop, and Pétur was at his feet. The old man gestured frantically, screaming as Orri's hooves flashed in the air. They slammed down once – again – and then there was silence.

The undead creatures around them sank into the ground as suddenly as they had sprung up. Gunnar turned back towards Kveldulf. Tryggvi-draugr stood before him still, animate yet lifeless, swollen and disfigured.

Then he was contracting, receding, diminishing again onto a human scale. As he did, for one instant his eyes fixed on his father's.

Kveldulf rushed forward as Tryggvi fell backward. Kveldulf caught his son, and bore him gently to the ground. His body was light, impossibly light, yet solid. Kveldulf grasped him close. He pulled back, and looked him in the face.

"Live," Kveldulf whispered furiously. "Live! I command you!"

Tryggvi's lips moved. His jaw worked. His eyes rolled, then focused. He drew breath.

"Father?", he said.

Then, like mist on the water, he melted away in the afternoon sun.

Void and darkness. Utter stillness, the stillness of untold eternities. For a time beyond time, only the abyss: yawning, gaping, empty...

Then, something. Where once was nothing- where notions of "once" and "was" cannot even cohere- there appeared an IS. Some stray spark of phenomenon drifted into being, and soon the abyss was ignited, burning, resounding, matter engulfing the void in a great swell of noise and light. Then it was all contracting, condensing, falling, dying. Then it was gone, and the void resumed its state of restful inertia.

An unending eternity. Then another spark, another flame, another conflagration: here, and then gone. Another. Another. Always here and then gone. Each time, the same. Each time, completely different. Nothing. Something. Nothing. On and on, forever and ever. Pointless, yet profound. There was almost a pattern to it, a rhythm.

She laughed, once she understood. She laughed, and laughter bore her through space and ages. She was joy, and joy gathered about her. She was rising, and condensing. A blue-gold radiance enveloped her, waxing brighter as she drank it in, drank until she had her fill, and burst.

Triumphant, she vivified. Sudden limbs stretched and grew, shot high and dug deep, drawing nourishment from the air and the earth.

One spinning instant, and she was incarnate with it all. She was the wind that stirs the boughs. She was light and leaf, and the line of their communion. She was the mineral that moves from dirt to root, that feeds the bud, that grows into the fruit, that falls back to the soil and the hungry roots again. She was the breath of the world, the tension in the sinews of creation.

And then she was herself again. Again she was Sinmara: daughter of three mothers, a guardian on the threshold, the hope of her people, and their sacrifice. It fell to her now to repair, to restore, to remember. She had returned to hold back the void, to feed the flame in the dark, here, in this place, for a while. And so she would.

She stepped down from her tree then, and onto the land. She stepped down from her tree, newly sprouted in an empty field, bright branches beckoning down the heavens, black roots gripping the cold bones of a good woman and her pale mare.

ᛈ ᛊᛚ ᛋᛟ ᚨᛈ ᛊᛚ ᛋᛟ ᚨᛈ ᛊᛚ ᛋᛟ ᚨᛈ ᛊᛚ ᛋᛟ ᚨ

The priest on the roof - not that he had been much of a priest in the end, Gunnar considered- was nearly unrecognizable. Inside, the house was a disaster. Vigi's wife lay by the hearth, looking unharmed but truly dead. The bodies of servants and retainers were in a pile in one corner. There was no sign of the animals. Gunnar did not wish to be there, but it was preferable to hearing Kveldulf outside, and he wished to give his friend privacy.

He approached the pallets, and saw one was still occupied. He bent down. It was Haraldr. The boy was alive! He carried his fragile form outside, ran to get some water. He did not spare a thought to who this boy was, only what he had been through. He would see no more death this day.

ᛡ ᛉᛚᛂ ᛋᛐ ᛍᛈ ᛉᛚᛂ ᛋᛐ ᛍᛈ ᛉᛚᛂ ᛋᛐ ᛍᛈ ᛉᛚᛂ ᛋᛐ ᛡ

She was there as the sun set, as shadows slowly grew, stretching out from each blade of grass, from the tiniest pebbles. Something called out to her from this place, some tone that rose above the shifting winds, the small things stirring in the earth, the water as it lapped the shore. She had heard it from the moment she set foot to ground.

And now she was at the source.

She stood over it, looking down at the crumpled and ruined body, bled out between the rafters of a home filled with death. It called to her still, and now she could feel it, like an ember. Something still resided in this flesh.

She drew it towards herself, drew it out of the broken body that had housed it. This form- human, decaying already- had housed something far more ancient than itself. Whatever else the dead man had been, he had become a vessel for something, something oddly familiar to her, which was now slipping from this world even as she watched. But she was Sinmara, and it was hers to recall, to renew.

As she considered this, another presence came, unbidden, to her attention. There was something else swirling about here, something else that still lingered, refusing to dissipate. It seemed connected to the bolus of the dead man's stolen power, sustained by it, yet distinct from it. And somehow, it, too, seemed familiar.

She had inspiration then. She sent forth a mote of pure intention, set it spinning. She watched as it drew both energies towards and around itself, like flax about a distaff.

Then she was alone no longer. Another presence had joined her; she could see its hazy form attempting to resolve in front of her.

"Who are you?" she asked.

A voice sounded, somewhere between her ears and her brain.

"I...I am..."

Sinmara grinned in success, then concentrated all her attention on the presence, concentrated on the parts of it she could sense, the tiny specks of matter and possibility that gathered here. Remember, she asked each of them. Remember.

The form in front of her became a little more solid, absorbed and reflected a little more light.

"Who are you?" she asked again.

"I am...I...am..."

She saw the sparks as connections were made, as events sorted themselves into effects and causes, as symmetries became memories.

And then before her stood another, fair of face, ruddy-cheeked, bright eyes blinking in the fading light. He patted at his chest, regarded his hands.

"Hello," she said.

He looked up at her, startled, as if he hadn't realized she was there.

"Who are you?" they both asked each other at the same time.

"I am Sinmara," she said, after a moment.

"I am...Tryggvi?"

He still seemed confused.

Sinmara looked down at the earth, where darkness forever gnawed at the roots of the world. She looked above the horizon, where ribbons of shifting color rose into the night sky. She cast her sight far across the whole of the land. Here and there, a gentle and welcoming light spilled out from the homes of the prayerful, from the homes of people who would never know that now they were her people, too. Hers to protect. She looked at Tryggvi.

"Greetings, brother. There is so much to do! Help me, and together we will learn more than you ever dreamed."

They made their camp for the night on one of the hills above Vigi's farm. Tomorrow they would have to go back to bury the bodies. There was no way to seek assistance, and Haraldr would be no help.

Neither man spoke of what had happened there, no more than he had to.

Kveldulf had calmed himself, but said little since that afternoon. There was nothing to say, for either of them. They lay on their bedrolls while the moon rose, awake but unspeaking, hearing nothing except the gentle wind and the occasional wheezing groan from the injured boy.

Then Kveldulf sat up suddenly, startling Gunnar. He cocked his ear, and stared into the darkening night.

Just as Gunnar was about to ask if everything was alright, Kveldulf's face was lit up by an amber glow. Gunnar turned to see the source.

Light shone from the hill below them. It was as if a tall door had opened in the grassy earth, and from it warmth spread out into the night air. Gunnar could feel it even from where he lay. And just before the door, shadows stretching away from its radiance, were two figures, walking side by side.

Gunnar was never quite certain why he looked away, but something made him avert his eyes. He looked at his friend instead. Kveldulf's cheeks were wet, but he stared ahead unblinking, until the ghost of a smile showed on his lips.

Gunnar turned back then, but by the time he had, the light was gone, and there was only a hill. He lay his head down, and closed his eyes. In the morning, he would remember it only as a dream.

Kveldulf sat up through the night, watching the moon travel across the sky, until the sun rose again.

For his part, Orri, lying on his side not far from the camp, saw nothing. He had been well fed on barley cakes and the best of Vigi's stores, and he slept now, getting some much deserved rest. The breeze passing through his long coat made him seem to shimmer in his slumber.

He dreamt, as all things do. What he dreamt of, none can say, for
the dreams of beasts cannot be captured in the words of men. But even in the depths of his slumber, still he heard the wild hymn. Still he heard the song that had led his kind across the steppes, led them over mountains and tundra, guided them through the forest primeval, back when they were small, and weak, and prey for dragons. Even then the call had been with them, singing out the joys of the day, the secrets of the night, the freedom of earth and rain and air, the exultation of being, of making and being unmade. That night, and all his nights, Orri heard the voiceless song, song of songs, a single note, all notes, the harmony of the void, perpetual, bookended by infinite rests. Always the same song, always lifting and carrying a new story: borne by aether, birthed in fire; born of water, born of stone.

Acknowledgments:

Like me, this book would not exist without the love and support of numerous people. I would like to thank my parents, family, and friends, and everyone who taught, sheltered, or fed me over the years. Several people read early drafts of this book and gave me excellent feedback, and I am forever in their debt. Special mention goes to Dr. Matthew Weissman, who encouraged me to complete Julia Cameron's *The Artist's Way*, from whence sprang this project. It was my great dream to write a novel; I hope all those who helped me along the way see their great dreams come true too.

Author Info:

Brendan Edward James Baker was born in Cleveland, OH, and grew up in Oak Park, IL and Brownsville, TX. He attended the Texas Academy of Mathematics and Science, Carleton College, and the University of Michigan Law School. As a Mellon Mays Undergraduate Fellow, he spent a year at Oxford University studying medieval history and languages, and he has published two papers on Old English poetry. *The Stone Doors* is his first novel. Baker lives in Denver, Colorado.

⌘

CPSIA information can be obtained
at www.ICGtesting.com
Printed in the USA
LVHW011920051020
667983LV00006B/1982